Impossible
To
Forget

ALSO BY IMOGEN CLARK

Impossible To Forget

IMOGEN CLARK

LAKE UNION
PUBLISHING

Text copyright © 2022 by Blue Lizard Books Ltd
All rights reserved.

Published by Lake Union Publishing, Seattle

www.apub.com

Amazon, the Amazon logo, and Lake Union Publishing are trademarks of Amazon.com, Inc., or its affiliates.

ISBN-13: 9781542021180
ISBN-10: 1542021189

Cover design by Sarah Whittaker

Printed in the United States of America

The unlikeliest people are hiding halos beneath their hats.

Anonymous

August 2018

My dear friends,

If you are reading this, then I must be dead. (I've always wanted to say that – so very Agatha Christie! And please don't cry, Leon. It's only a bit of fun. x)

Seriously though, I want to thank you all for being there for me over the last couple of months. It's been pretty tough, but having you lot in my corner has made it easier to cope. To be honest, I don't know what I'd have done without you. I couldn't have wished for a better bunch of mates.

But there's just one last thing I need to ask you to do for me.

Obviously, my biggest concern is my beautiful girl, Romany. I will never understand a universe that lets a parent die before they have finished preparing their child to live. It's all kinds of wrong. Yet we are where we are.

Without me, Romany will be left all alone. Even though she's about to turn eighteen, she's really still a child with so much to learn about the world, good and bad. She needs someone to be there for her, a guardian if you like, to guide her until she finds her feet. It won't be forever, just until she finishes her A levels and gets a place at university, but I can't bear to think of her struggling through school on her own. I had to do that, and I don't want history repeating itself.

That's where you come in. I charge you, my dearest and most trusted friends, with the vitally important task of steering her through the challenging months ahead.

I know it wouldn't be fair to suggest that just one of you shoulders this massive responsibility, so I've decided to ask you all to play to your individual strengths.

Maggie – as my most highly qualified and pragmatic friend, please would you help Romany with all things legal and formal, and anything else that she should read before signing. I was never any good at that stuff and I know you'll make a much better job of it.

Leon – to you I leave her cultural needs. Make sure that she listens to all kinds of music and not just whatever crap is in the charts. She should read loads, and write if the muse puts in an appearance, and I want her to be a regular at the theatre and the cinema. Art galleries too – basically all the things that will lift her day-to-day life above the mundane and make her wonder.

Tiger – I need you to keep her horizons wide. Make sure she travels whenever she can and absorbs different ways of life as easily as she absorbs sunlight. Help her to keep her eyes, and her heart, open.

And finally Hope. You may wonder what you're doing here. I know we've only known each other for a comparatively short amount of time, but I think I know you well enough to ask you to help, and something tells me that you would be the perfect candidate to keep an eye on Romany's relationships, friendships and affairs of the heart. Please show her how to judge people accurately and fairly, so that she can forgive the weaknesses of others.

So, even though my baby girl is setting forth on life's great adventure without her mum by her side, she will have you four, her guardian angels, to protect her. I know that she couldn't be in better hands.

All my love, forever,

Angie x

1

The solicitor removed her glasses, settled them artfully on top of her head and looked up at the collected ensemble. The four guardians sat slack-jawed, trying to process what they had just heard. Merely losing their friend Angie was not enough, it appeared. Now they had to step up and take responsibility for her child too, or at least parts of her. It was hardly surprising that they had turned a little pale.

The solicitor waited, giving them each a chance to absorb the letter's contents, and as they did she eyed them all with mild curiosity. Who were these characters to Angie, she wondered, and how had they ended up being cast in these unforeseen and rather challenging roles?

Directly opposite her sat the daughter, Romany. She was tiny, built as if a breath of wind could blow her away like a cobweb, but there was something in her not-quite-brown eyes that suggested that she was more robust than she might appear. She was barely eighteen and already she had had to deal with the terminal illness and death of her only parent. You didn't manage that without coming apart unless you had some inner resources to draw on. And she didn't look as if she was coming apart. There'd been no drama or histrionics. She had listened to the reading of the letter calmly and without reaction.

The solicitor knew that her client's wishes would have come as a surprise to all five of them. Angie had been very clear on the matter of secrecy, almost gleeful in fact, at their meeting several weeks before.

'I'm not going to tell them what I'm planning,' she had said. By then, her skin had taken on a yellowish pallor and was pulled tightly across her cheekbones, making them appear angular and sharp. 'I'm sure they'll all say yes if I ask them now, but I'd rather not give them the option. If they don't know what's coming, they're less likely to make excuses or refuse.'

The solicitor's training made her uncomfortable with such vagaries and she wanted to object, get Angie to put something more concrete in place for the girl; but then again, Romany had already turned eighteen and so technically, there was no need for the appointment of a single guardian, let alone four. Whether the chosen ones were prepared to step up to their allotted tasks was not a legal matter and therefore not one with which the solicitor need concern herself unduly. She had the sense that there was something else at play here, though, some greater purpose that she couldn't quite put her finger on.

But she wasn't paid to decipher clues from her clients. She had drafted the will and read the letter out as instructed and with that her responsibility for the matter ended.

Romany took a tissue out of a pocket now and held it in her hand, anticipating tears, but none fell. The same could not be said for Leon. Tears were streaming down his cheeks and he wiped them away noisily using a blue cotton handkerchief that had been ironed into a neat square. He was a plain man, his features unremark-able, his dark hair parted neatly and combed to one side as his mother might have done for him on the first day of school. Angie had mentioned that he was a chemical engineer, this information imparted with a degree of scorn as if it were a laughable career choice, although it seemed perfectly acceptable to the solicitor, who had firm and possibly old-fashioned ideas about what constituted a good job.

Maggie, the friend newly responsible for Romany's contractual well-being, opened her mouth to speak and the solicitor, anticipating a clashing of legal horns, cut across her.

'I also have Angie's will, a copy of which will be provided to each of you. She appoints you all as her executors . . .' She saw Maggie raise a neatly shaped eyebrow. 'I am aware that having so many executors is unusual, and I counselled Angie against it. However, she felt that it was important, in the circumstances, that you each had equal responsibility for her estate. That said, you can sign a Renunciation if you wish to resign from the role.'

The guardian named Tiger (a ridiculous nickname for a man in his fifties, she thought) seemed to shift uncomfortably in his seat and then cast a sidelong glance around the room at the others, but when he failed to catch anyone else's eye he turned back to look at her and did not speak.

The solicitor's eyes were drawn to the one called Hope. The woman was outstandingly attractive and consequently quite mesmerising. The solicitor was reminded of a tall tank of luminescent jellyfish that she'd once seen in an aquarium. Beautiful, but ever so slightly threatening. Now, though, the woman's brow was creased, and her mouth not quite closed as her eyes flicked around the others. Where Tiger looked irritated by the news, the word the solicitor would choose for Hope was baffled.

She continued.

'Now, on to more practical matters. Obviously, as Romany here is now of age, she could live alone. However, in light of her being in her final year of school, Angie was keen that someone should move into their flat to help support her.'

Now they looked anxious, mouths tightening and sidelong glances being cast as they played through the possible options in their heads. The solicitor could almost see their minds whirring as they thought up excuses as to why this might not be practicable for them. She was tempted to let them sweat a little longer. Her days in the office were very long and generally uneventful, and making people to whom she had no duty of care squirm a little might add a touch of spice. But then again, she did feel sorry for the poor girl. This was her life, after all. She pressed on.

'Angie has requested that Tiger should move into her flat for the next year whilst Romany finishes her education. She hoped that Romany will take up a place at university next September and then will no longer need anyone to live with her. The arrangement would be rent-free, as Angie left funds to cover the mortgage payments. There is also money to cover basic utilities, food and other household expenses for Romany and from which you, as a householder, would also benefit.'

Maggie's expression suggested that she thought Tiger had very much fallen on his feet with this proposal, but Tiger seemed to have other ideas.

'Hang on,' he said, sitting up in his seat, suddenly alert. 'Angie said what? That I'd move in? Well, that's a total non-starter. There's no way . . . I mean, what was she thinking? I can't do that. Of course I can't.'

His eyes flicked around the room, desperately looking for support from the others, but they sat in silence – no doubt, the solicitor thought, delighted that this particular imposition had not landed at their feet.

'I've got stuff to do, you know?' he continued to protest. 'Places to be. I'm supposed to go to Guatemala to meet some buddies next month and then I was planning on heading down to South Africa for Christmas. Does she really expect me just to drop all my plans to babysit her daughter? And for a YEAR! It's ridiculous.' He sat back in his chair, arms crossed, as if this was the final word on the subject.

Romany was sitting very still, clearly not wanting to draw attention to herself, the daughter in need of a babysitter. One by one the others seemed to remember that she was present, and glances passed between Maggie and Leon before Leon spoke.

'Come on, Tiger,' he said in a low voice. 'Think of where you are. This isn't the time.'

For a moment Tiger looked irritated, but then he softened. 'Look, I'm sorry, Romany. I know none of this is your fault, but you can see how it is. It's just not practical. I'm a free spirit, you know. I've never even had a place in England. I just come and go as the mood takes me. That's how it's always been. Your mum knew that. I thought she understood.'

Romany nodded but she didn't lift her eyes from her shoes. The solicitor was beginning to question the wisdom of having her present at this meeting at all, but her client had been insistent about that, too.

'It's okay,' the girl said, her voice barely above a whisper. 'I'll be fine on my own. Like the solicitor lady said, I am over eighteen and Mum has left me the money I'll need. Really. Please don't worry about me. You can call in when you're around to make sure I'm okay. And you can tell me about your travels. I'd love to hear where you've been.' She gave Tiger a valiant smile. Oh, she was one tough cookie, this one.

'Thanks, love,' he said, as if this was a decision made. Relief was radiating from him like the stench of stale sweat from a runner.

The solicitor pondered. Whilst she and her client had discussed the possibility of her friends rejecting her requests, Angie had been so adamant that it wouldn't happen that they had failed to make a contingency plan. Now a mild but growing sense of unease was taking root. This whole situation was so unusual that she really had no feel for how best to proceed. Romany was of age so there was no practical problem if Tiger refused to move in, but it did render Angie's statement of wishes somewhat superfluous.

She was about to comment when Leon spoke.

'That's just not good enough, Tiger,' he said, his harsh tone at odds with his rather mouse-like appearance. 'Angie wanted you to stay with Romany and the least you can do is try to make that happen. It's only for a year, whilst she finishes her A levels. It's hardly a life-long commitment.'

'Well, I don't see you offering to move in,' Tiger snapped back.

'I'd do it in a heartbeat,' Leon replied, 'but it's not as easy for me. I work away a lot, and long hours too. It just wouldn't be practical. You've got no job, no partner, no ties. It's like you've always said, you are free to go where the wind blows you.'

The solicitor saw Maggie roll her eyes.

'And for a while,' Leon continued, 'that needs to be here in York, in Angie's flat.'

'But that's the point!' said Tiger, frustration making him sound more like a child than a man in his fifties. 'I need to be free to roam, man. It's who I am.'

'For God's sake,' muttered Maggie.

'Look,' interrupted Hope. 'I know I'm the outsider in this merry little gang, but could I make a suggestion?'

They all turned to look at her as if they had forgotten she was there at all. The solicitor was unclear how Hope fitted in. From the confusion on her face, it was obvious that she didn't understand it either. She was younger than the other three, in her thirties to their fifties, and she was beautiful in a way that would make you turn and stare like you might if you saw a zebra clip-clopping down the high street. Everything about her looked as if it had been formed with purpose and great care, her eyes just the right size and shape, her nose just pointed enough but not too much so. Her hair shone with health and her skin actually glowed as if she had had a filter applied over her face.

She was seated a little apart from the others. Was that because she was an outsider, or had there been an argument, the solicitor wondered, some rift that had happened just off stage and away from her view? Perhaps it was her beauty that they found off-putting? The solicitor had read in a magazine that beautiful people sometimes found it hard to make friends – how her heart ached for them, the poor little darlings. But perhaps that was the case here. She had their attention now, though.

'You said . . . Tiger . . .' Hope seemed to hesitate over his name as if she, like the solicitor, found it mildly risible. 'You said that you were meeting friends abroad next month. So, why don't you move into Angie's flat just for the time being? Then, when you need to go on your trip we can look at how the land is lying and decide what to do next.'

'That's a good idea,' said Leon. 'Thanks, er . . .' He paused, searching for her name. 'Hope?'

So, they didn't know each other, the solicitor thought. This really was the most peculiar arrangement.

Tiger stuck his bottom lip out as he thought about Hope's proposal and then, finding nothing to object to it in, nodded his head. 'Okay,' he said. 'That could work. And I suppose it'd be good not to have to sofa-surf until then. All right. I'll do it.'

'It's not that big a deal,' muttered Maggie under her breath. Tiger didn't appear to hear her or if he did, he chose to ignore her comment.

She was sharp, that one, the solicitor thought, and from what she had seen, an unlikely friend for Angie who, from their meetings, had seemed much more easy-going. She wondered briefly how the pair had ended up being close enough for Angie to ask

11

this enormous favour of her. In fact, what was asked was more than a favour. Angie had given each of these four a chunk of the responsibility for the thing that was most precious to her in the world – Romany. It was a huge ask, whichever way you looked at it.

'Does anyone have any questions?' she asked them.

Leon looked as if he wanted to say something but then seemed to think better of it.

'When do I have to move in?' asked Tiger.

'That is a matter for you and Romany to agree,' the solicitor replied. 'As far as I am concerned it could happen today.'

Romany gave Tiger a weak smile and nodded as if this proposal was acceptable to her.

'Well, if that's everything, my secretary will give you your copies of the documents as you leave. If anything occurs to you later, please feel free to ring.'

The solicitor stood to indicate that the meeting was now over, and one by one the guardians followed suit and then trooped out into the reception area, each nodding their thanks as they passed her.

As Romany left, the solicitor placed a hand on her arm. 'Your mother was a lovely woman,' she said. It was unlike her to make such a personal statement and she was surprised that this one had slipped out, but then Angie Osborne had been a surprising person.

As she tidied the meeting room for its next occupants, the solicitor let her mind drift over the oddness of what had just happened. Then she looked at her watch and after that she didn't give the matter another thought.

2

'Shall we find a café?' asked Maggie as the five of them stepped out of the solicitor's office and into the street beyond. 'I don't know about you lot, but I wouldn't mind a little chat about what just happened.'

'Café be damned,' said Tiger. 'What we need is a pub and a stiff drink.'

Leon nodded and Maggie noticed that his bottom lip was trembling as he fought to control his emotions. He had always been prone to tears, right back from when they were teenagers. It could be irritating at times but now she found it endearing and she would have comforted him, except that Tiger was there. She herself felt strangely calm, her tears, for now at least, boxed away out of sight. It wouldn't help anyone if she got upset as well.

'Actually,' said Romany, 'I have to get back to school. I've already missed double chemistry.'

Tiger shook his head disbelievingly. 'What does that matter, Romey? They'll make allowances. Your mum just died.'

Maggie's head whipped round and she frowned at him. The last thing they needed was for Tiger to start passing his questionable values on to Romany, or the four of them would fail before they had even begun.

'What?!' Tiger said, palms and eyebrows raised. 'She did! And school shouldn't expect Romey to go in, not so soon.'

'But I want to go,' objected Romany. 'I've missed enough already. And the one thing Mum really wanted was for me to do well in my A levels. I'll be back at the flat later if anyone needs me.'

'I'll see you there, then, roomy,' replied Tiger, and held his hand up for a high five. Romany ignored it.

'For God's sake, Tiger,' muttered Maggie. 'Are you sure you're okay, Romey? You know we're here for you, don't you?' She gave Tiger a withering glance. 'You just need to ask us.'

Romany nodded. 'I'm fine, Auntie Maggie,' she said. 'I'll see you later.'

It felt incongruous that Romany still called her 'auntie'. Maggie wasn't an aunt, was no relation at all, and using the old-fashioned label had never seemed to fit with Angie's relaxed attitude to life. And yet she had insisted on it, as if by making Romany call her 'auntie' it would give her daughter something she lacked – an extended family. Maggie, herself an only child, had no children of her own, but Romany was like the niece she would never have.

They found a pub and went inside. It was more of a bar than a pub, with lots of light and space designed for standing rather than sitting, but it suited their purposes.

'What's everyone having?' asked Leon as they settled at one of the few tables. They glanced at one another before placing an order, each seeking permission from the others.

'I think I might need a brandy,' said Maggie, and as she did so she felt Tiger relax at her side.

'Me too,' he said quickly. 'Bit of a shock, all that.'

There was a pause. Maggie wasn't going to be the first to offer to go to the bar and consequently pay for the round. That was the thing with people you had known for most of your life. They always came up true to form. Tiger never had a bean to his name. How

14

he had made it through the last thirty years or so she had no idea. And here he was again, sitting on his hands. She counted off the seconds in her head. One, two, three . . .

'I'll go,' said Leon, just as she had known he would.

'No, I'll get this first one,' she replied. It wasn't fair for Leon to get caught up in the mind games she played with Tiger. 'What would you like, Leon? Hope?'

'I'll just have half a lager shandy,' said Leon. 'I need to be getting back to work.' He checked his watch as he spoke.

'Mineral water,' said Hope, and Maggie felt the small knot of resentment in her stomach tighten a little more. She needed to get over that now that Hope was going to be around for the foreseeable future, but would it hurt the woman to say 'please'?

Maggie bought the round, distributed the glasses and then resettled herself at the table. They all took a sip of their drinks, no one wanting to be the first to pass comment. Tiger took a second swig and then downed the rest of his brandy in one.

Maggie blew out her lips. 'Well,' she said, sitting back in her chair, 'I didn't see that coming, did you? God bless Angie but, bloody hell, she certainly knew how to put cats amongst pigeons.'

'She did indeed,' replied Leon, nodding slowly. 'And I'm not very clear on what she wants us to do, on a day-to-day basis, I mean. I'm supposed to help Romany with her reading and going to the pictures and so forth, but how do I actually go about that? Do I send her books, or a reading list maybe? It seems a bit prescriptive. She's a teenage girl. I'm not sure we'll have much crossover in our tastes. Or perhaps I should make sure she's read certain books, like as part of her general education? I wish Angie had given us a few more clues.'

'Well, that was Angie all over,' replied Maggie. 'Vague. Remember that time she took us all on a magical mystery tour and it turned out she had no idea where we were going either?'

A fond smile rippled around the table.

'And her cooking!' said Tiger. 'Some of the things we ended up eating just because that was what she had in. Do you remember when she put bananas in the pasta sauce because we didn't have any veg?'

He ran a hand through his sun-bleached hair. It was starting to turn grey, Maggie noticed, although the strands were well disguised by the blond. It was thinning on top, too. If he wasn't careful, he was going to look less bronzed beach bum and more ageing hippy. He still had that magical something, though, she thought. She batted the inconvenient thought away.

They sat for a moment, each lost in their own memories. Hope, perching on the front of her chair and ready to leap up at any second, kept looking up at the clock above the bar. Okay, Maggie thought, she couldn't join in with their reminiscing, not having been part of their group, but did she have to make her lack of interest so very obvious? Maggie could feel her resentment growing stronger. Soon it would have little legs and everything. Why had Angie got Hope involved anyway? Couldn't she just have stuck to her old friends when allocating the tasks? It would have made life so much simpler. Now, as well as trying to work out how to make things work for Romany, they were going to have to get a measure of Hope on top. It was an added layer of complication that they didn't need.

'I'm not sure what I'm meant to do either,' said Tiger. 'She gives me travel to mentor and then makes me stay in her flat! It makes no sense. I haven't lived in one place since I left home when I was Romany's age.'

This wasn't true, Maggie knew; of course he had. What he meant was that he had been unable to settle in any one place. He did have a point, though. It was ironic that he should be given travel and then asked to stay put.

'If you think about it,' said Leon quietly, 'it makes perfect sense. You can just move in there at the drop of a hat. All your stuff is in that blessed rucksack and you don't have to leave anywhere, or anyone, else to do it.'

'That's as may be,' replied Tiger, 'but I don't see the rest of you having to put your life on hold to carry out Angie's last wishes. You can just keep going like you were doing. I've got to change everything I've ever known. I mean, it's not that fair, guys, when you actually think about it.'

Hope spoke now. Her voice was clear but she didn't make eye contact with any of them. 'Yes, but you do get to live rent-free for a year. Sounds like a pretty cushy number to me,' she said.

Tiger opened his mouth to object and then closed it again. What could he say to that? She was completely right.

'What we need to remember,' said Maggie, 'is that Romany is an adult. She can make her own decisions. We are just there to help guide her until she finds her feet. There are going to be plenty of things that she'll want help with. She needs to know that she only has to ask.'

'Maggie's right,' said Leon. 'None of us knows exactly how this is going to work. So, I suppose we just need to be guided by Romany and take our lead from her.'

The four of them nodded enthusiastically at this, but Maggie couldn't help thinking that it was more to convince each other than anything else.

'So, I'll move in and cover the day-to-day stuff,' said Tiger. 'And the rest of you can just step in as and when required.'

'I suppose so,' said Leon.

'That's easy enough,' said Tiger with a resigned grin. 'I mean, what could possibly go wrong?'

3

THE EIGHTIES

1985

Maggie cast a discerning eye around her new home and gave a nod of satisfaction. Her law textbooks were lined up neatly on the bookshelf, their unbroken spines promisingly broad. Her new record player, bought with the proceeds of her summer work experience at a prestigious firm of solicitors, sat on the chest of drawers next to a selection of her favourite compilation tapes. On the desk sat a pristine A4 pad, her pencil case and the black angle-poise lamp that had come with the room. The enamel had chipped off the lamp in several places, which was disappointing, but perhaps she could paint over the larger bare patches with nail varnish so they weren't so glaring. There was also an umbrella plant in a plastic pot, which her mother had given her for good luck. It stood about a foot tall and was too big for the desk and too small for the floor but, like the lamp, it would do for now. The narrow bed, far narrower than her bed at home, she was sure, was made up with her blue and white checked duvet cover and matching pillowcase set, and her blue towels sat in a neat pile on the end. Look out, University of York: Maggie Summers had arrived.

Of course, exciting though it was to be there, the room was far from ideal. It was barely big enough to swing a cat in. The walls were white-washed breeze blocks that made it feel disconcertingly cell-like and the carpet was faintly tacky under her feet. But Maggie could overlook all that. She was here. She had arrived at university. She had made it happen for herself, and she was going to do everything in her power to ensure it was a success.

Now that she had her new room arranged just so, she was starting to feel curious about her neighbours. The door to her room, B27, led off a long corridor of similar doors. Maggie had requested a quiet area. She was here to work, and whilst she wasn't averse to letting her hair down from time to time, she was no party animal. So far all seemed well on that front, however. She had seen a boy with lank dark hair scuttling into the room opposite hers when she had gone to check out the bathroom, but he didn't look the wild party type either. He had offered her a tentative smile, which she had returned politely. She had no real need for friends, but manners cost nothing.

For a moment, she contemplated knocking on the doors to her left and right, but decided against it. She would meet the occupants in due course and there was no point initiating any kind of relationships with them in case they got the wrong idea about her. In any event, either the rooms were surprisingly soundproofed, which she doubted, or their occupants were yet to arrive.

Maggie selected an Everything but the Girl album from her collection of records, slid it out from its sleeve and put it on the turntable. Then she sat back on her bed with de Smith's *Constitutional and Administrative Law*. So far, she had got to chapter 7, 'The Privy Council', and she'd admit to finding it a bit of a struggle if pressed, but she imagined that the course wouldn't all be as dry as this. Once she got started, she was sure that there would be more interesting things to get her teeth into.

Outside her window she could hear people, other freshers she imagined, laughing and calling to one another in the warm September afternoon. She allowed herself a small smile. This was who she was now: a law student at the University of York. She was on her way to achieving her life's ambition – everything was going according to plan.

By half past five she was beginning to feel hungry. Dinner was to be served in the refectory from five until seven thirty, so she would wander down around six so as not to look too keen. She wasn't completely sure of the way, but she had the map that they had given her at registration and it couldn't be that far. Maybe she would go for a little pre-dinner stroll, just to get her bearings. She decided that this was a good idea and, slipping her room key and her purse into her shoulder bag, was about to step out into the corridor when, without warning, her door burst open.

There stood a girl, she assumed a fresher like herself. She was dressed in a pair of cheesecloth trousers and a tie-dyed T-shirt and had battered espadrilles on her feet. Her hair, the colour of a fox's brush, was held away from her face by a scarf and was all matted together in knotted rats' tails. She was tanned to a deep golden brown that looked like it had taken more than two weeks in the sun to achieve.

'There's no bog roll,' she said without introduction. 'In the loo. Have you got some?'

Maggie was completely thrown, partly by the appearance of the girl, which was like nothing she had ever seen before, but also by the abrupt conversation opener. Then, before she'd had chance to gather her thoughts, the girl pushed her gently to one side. She let out a low whistle as she took in Maggie's room.

'Who has a room as tidy as this?' she asked. 'Seriously, did you smuggle a slave in here with you?' Her eyes settled on the new sound system. 'That's a nice piece of kit,' she said appreciatively. 'Are these your records? What have you got? Can I have a look? Police, Squeeze, Kate Bush . . .' The stranger flicked her way through the records one by one. 'All a bit mainstream for me,' she concluded. 'But I've been travelling for a year. My tastes are more global, you know.'

Finally, Maggie found her tongue. 'Excuse me,' she said shirtily. 'But you can't just barge in here and start going through my things.'

'Oh, sorry,' said the girl, although she sounded anything but. 'No offence intended. I'm Angie.'

She waited for Maggie to reciprocate but Maggie was damned if she was going to share anything with this impertinent intruder, from her name to her loo roll.

'Well, I've got no toilet paper, so I'd like it if you left now, please?'

Maggie thought about the pack of sixteen rolls that she had neatly stacked in her wardrobe and hoped that a blush didn't give her away.

'No worries,' said Angie. 'I'll try next door.'

She breezed out with as little concern as she had breezed in, but as she turned to knock on the next door she looked back at Maggie.

'I really like the Cocteau Twins, though. *Treasure*'s a fantastic album.'

And then she was gone.

Maggie closed the door and sat down on her perfectly smoothed bed as she fought against the warm spread of pride that was rippling through her. She really didn't care that the weird-looking but quite cool girl had praised her musical taste. It couldn't be of less interest to her.

4

Five minutes later Maggie decided she could wait for food no longer, but she opened her door at exactly the same moment as the geeky-looking boy opposite opened his. She saw him flinch, his first reaction to close his door again and re-emerge when the coast was clearer, but then he seemed to reconsider, and smiled at her as he had done earlier. His smile was less tentative this time, and it transformed her opinion of him from the class stiff to someone who she might like to spend time with.

'Hi,' he said. 'Again. I'm Leon.'

'Maggie,' said Maggie. 'I was just going to see if I could find something to eat.'

'Great minds,' replied Leon. 'Or at least, I imagine your mind must be great or you wouldn't have wound up here.'

Oh, thought Maggie. Not the shrinking violet that she had assumed.

'How great my mind is remains to be seen,' said Maggie modestly. 'But I am starving. Shall we go on a food hunt together?'

They each turned and locked their rooms, Maggie mindful of the introductory talk about security that they had been given on arrival.

'I think it's this way,' offered Leon, and they set off towards the fire doors that punctuated the long corridor.

'So, what are you here to read?' he asked. Maggie noticed his use of the old-fashioned expression and appreciated it. She prided herself on the use of correct terminology. Every time anyone asked her what she was going to 'do' at York she shuddered inside.

'Law,' she said proudly. Would that ever fade, she wondered, the frisson that she felt when she uttered that word?

Leon raised an eyebrow, like most people did when she told them, as if studying law was something that merited particular deference.

'And you?' she asked. It would be something dull like maths, she thought, or economics.

'Chemical engineering,' he said, and now it was her turn to be impressed. She wasn't entirely sure what that even entailed – she had focused on the arts at school – but now wasn't the time to confess to her ignorance.

'Blimey,' she said, because what else was there to say?

They left the hall of residence and followed the signs to the refectory. The campus was dominated by a huge man-made lake at its heart which shimmered and sparkled in the late afternoon sunshine. Students sprawled on the grassy banks chatting and laughing. It was all so perfect.

'Do you know anyone else here?' Maggie asked Leon, prompted by the little groups of freshers.

'There's a mate of a mate in the second year but he's in a different college, and a couple of girls from school are here too, but I doubt they'd acknowledge me if they saw me.' He gave her a wry little smile. 'Our ideas of what constitutes cool don't really tally.'

Maggie could understand that. She had never been particularly 'cool' herself, not that it bothered her. She had more important things to focus on.

'I don't know anyone either,' she said. 'Most of the people from my school have gone to places in London.'

'I thought you sounded a bit southern,' Leon said. He made it sound like an insult, but he was grinning, so Maggie decided he didn't mean anything by it.

'Worcester,' she replied. 'You?'

· 'Leeds.' He rolled his eyes as he added, 'I know, just down the road. But my mum worries about me and the course is just what I wanted.'

'I don't think it matters,' said Maggie. 'The main thing is that we're here.'

'True enough,' replied Leon.

Following the increasing hubbub and the slightly sickening smell of canteen cooking, they arrived at the refectory. There was already a queue snaking out of the doors and into the corridor.

'Looks like they've all had the same idea,' said Leon.

Maggie nodded. The food smelt unappetizing, overcooked and stodgy.

'I think I'm just going to get a salad,' she said. 'It's so hot in those rooms, isn't it? Shall we sit together at a table over there, or would you rather split up and take pot luck somewhere else? I won't be offended.'

For a second Leon looked horrified at the idea of having to find another person to talk to. 'No, I'm happy to sit with you. Unless you'd rather . . .'

'That's fine by me,' said Maggie. He was a nice enough guy and the expedient option. It was to be hoped, however, that she didn't come to regret her current friendliness and spend the rest of the year trying to shake him off. She had once read that observation in a novel but now she couldn't remember for the life of her which one.

Soon the two of them were sitting side by side looking out at the collected mass of new students. They seemed to fall into two camps: those who had found a gang to cling to and moved about in unison so tightly that you could barely slide a piece of paper between them, and those who were resolutely alone. Maggie had thought that she wouldn't care who she met in the early days, but now that she was here and saw just how alone the singletons looked, she felt very grateful for having stumbled across Leon. And he seemed like a reasonable bloke, once you got past the Marks and Spencer jeans and the accountant haircut. He was even quite witty, in an understated kind of way.

The salad was passable. Leon had opted for a pasta dish that looked flabby and as if it had sat under hot lamps for too long, but it didn't seem to put him off and he worked his way through the plateful as they plucked conversational starters out of the air. He lived in Leeds, as he'd said, with his parents and a younger brother who liked football and wanted to play for Leeds United. It was clear from the way he told the story that this wasn't an ambition that Leon shared but he seemed proud of him, nonetheless.

Then there was some commotion by the servery that caught Maggie's attention. It was that girl again, the one who had barged into her room demanding toilet paper. She was standing with her hands on her hips and shouting at the blue-rinsed woman who was serving at the counter.

'No, "love",' she said with measured sarcasm. 'Fish is not veg-etarian. Fish is fish. Vegetarian means it's made of veg-e-ta-bles. Oh, never mind. I'll have the tomato soup. Or has that got some chicken hiding in it?'

Leon raised an eyebrow.

'How to win friends and influence people,' he said with a grin.

'Did she knock on your door looking for loo roll?' Maggie asked. 'Earlier, I mean.'

Leon shook his head.

'Her name is Angie. She's very . . .' Maggie searched for the word. 'Very . . . direct.'

25

'So I see!' replied Leon. 'I bet she takes no prisoners. What's she studying? Did she say?'

Maggie couldn't swear to it, but she suspected that the expression on his face was one of admiration. Maybe he wasn't that interesting after all, not if he found something to admire in Angie.

'I didn't ask,' she said tightly.

'I bet it isn't law or chemical engineering,' he said wistfully. 'More's the pity. She'd really up the ante in the lecture theatre.'

'I'm not sure I need that kind of interesting in my lectures,' said Maggie.

But Leon wasn't really listening to her. His entire focus was on Angie.

5

Term was a few weeks old and a routine of sorts had begun to establish itself. Maggie now felt confident of where she was as she made her way around the university campus and no longer faced the ignominy of having to consult the huge maps that were scattered along the walkways for clues. The Law Department was fairly central and therefore easy to find, and she knew where the students' union and her college bar were, not that she had frequented either much thus far.

Maggie had decided before she had even arrived in York that the typical student lifestyle was not for her. She wasn't averse to the odd night out, she had thought, but rolling in in the wee small hours on a regular basis wasn't something that she had intended to do.

Now that she was here, it seemed that her prediction had come true. Her big nights out were commendably few and far apart; however, this was not for the reasons that she might have thought before she arrived. The truth was that Maggie was not fully engaging in student life because she had no one to engage in it with.

It wasn't as if she was shy. She had no difficulty in introducing herself to strangers or suggesting an arrangement of some sort to them. The problem lay in finding the kind of people for whom she would happily use up a precious evening, an evening when she might otherwise have been studying.

Maggie had been unimpressed with the people on her course, who all seemed to be terminally dull or a bit cliquey. This left her with the people in her college or, more specifically, her corridor, but the pickings for new friends seemed a little sparse there, too. She liked Leon well enough and they had been out for a drink a few times, but he would insist on inviting the girl from the room next to hers, Angie.

With Angie came crowds of people. They seemed to flock around her as if she were a prophet. Maggie wasn't sure whether they all wanted to be her friend or were merely curious about her. A few weeks into term and Angie still looked as if she had just stepped off the beach. Maggie was beginning to conclude that this was just her style and it certainly distinguished her from everyone else.

However, Angie had not grown on Maggie. She was just as brash and direct and, well, rude, as Maggie had found her to be on her very first day of term, and so far she had done nothing to alter Maggie's opinion of her. Their second encounter had been equally unpromising. Each corridor had a small kitchen at one end with a fridge, a hob and a microwave where students could make snacks for themselves if they got peckish or had missed the meal service in the refectory. Maggie, struggling with the food on offer there, had stocked her clearly labelled shelf of the fridge with the wherewithal for various meals. She had written on each packet with a perma-nent marker as well, so that there could be no confusion over what belonged to whom.

She had gone to prepare herself some beans on toast, but when she arrived Angie was already sitting at the tiny Formica table. She too had chosen beans for lunch and had a tall glass of milk at her elbow. It wasn't until Maggie noticed the distinctive blue pattern on the plate that she was using that she became concerned. It wasn't that she was mean, but this was her plate, and cutlery too for that matter, and she would rather not have to share, particularly when others' standard of washing up did not always match her own.

'I'd really rather you didn't use my stuff,' she said to Angie, trying to hit a note of friendly authority.

Angie looked at her blankly.

'That plate. And that pan,' Maggie clarified. 'They're both mine.'

'Oh,' replied Angie. 'I thought they were for everyone to use. You know, communal.'

'No,' said Maggie. 'They're mine. I brought them from home.'

'Sorry. Didn't realise,' Angie said.

Well, that was easy enough, thought Maggie. Hopefully she had made her point and there would be no repetition.

'It's just a plate, though,' continued Angie. 'I can't see how it matters much.'

Maggie bridled a little. 'Well, it's just that when people use other people's stuff, it means it's not there when they want to use it themselves,' she said. She was using her most balanced tone of voice, and what she was saying was so reasonable and obvious that she couldn't quite understand how Angie could object.

'Can't you just use one of the others?' Angie asked. 'There are plenty in the cupboard.'

'But then I'll annoy someone else by taking their things. It just works best if everyone sticks to their own.'

'Well, I don't have any so that doesn't work very well for me,' Angie replied.

'That's hardly my fault,' said Maggie under her breath.

It was all right though. Maggie wasn't petty-minded. On this one occasion, she would use somebody else's things herself and then, when there was nobody looking, she would gather up all her items and take them out of harm's way.

She opened her cupboard to get her last tin of beans, but it wasn't there. In fact, her tuna, pasta and a tin of rice pudding that she had been saving for a special occasion all seemed to have disappeared too. Maggie opened the fridge. Her loaf of bread was down to the crusts and someone had put her milk bottle back in even though there was nothing but the last dregs left in the bottom.

'Are you eating my food?' she asked, outraged.

'Dunno,' said Angie. 'It was in that cupboard. I'll get you some more when I get a minute.'

'And what am I supposed to do now?'

'The shop's open until five. You could get something there.'

The cheek of her. Maggie could hardly believe what she was hearing. The idea of taking someone else's food without permission was so alien to her that she couldn't quite get her head around it. And did Angie really expect her to replace her own stuff?

'I can't believe you!' she said. 'You eat my food and then, instead of offering to replace it, you suggest that I go out and get it myself!'

Angie put the last forkful of food in her mouth and then sat back and stared at Maggie, as if it was her who was being unreasonable. 'I don't know why you're getting your knickers in such a twist. It's only a tin of beans.'

'And bread. And half a pint of milk! You can't just take what you want, you know. It doesn't work like that.'

Angie shrugged. Then she stood up, dropped her dirty plate into the sink on top of the pan and left the kitchen. Maggie just stood there open-mouthed, for a moment too flabbergasted to speak.

Then her full fury filled her. She stormed after Angie and shouted up the corridor at her retreating back. 'You can't just leave it like that. Get back here and wash my stuff up!'

But Angie had reached her room, opened her door and let it close behind her without even turning round.

'And I want my food all replaced by the end of tomorrow,' Maggie continued, although there was no point at all. Angie wasn't listening.

Indignation fanned the flames of her anger as she took all the dishes out of the sink and ran hot water into it. She accidentally squirted in more washing-up liquid than was necessary as her fingers squeezed tightly around the bottle. The waste also made her curse Angie under her breath. How dare she? And to be so blatant. And with absolutely no hint of an apology. It beggared belief. Maggie fumed away under her breath as she washed all her things and dried them on her neatly pressed tea towel. She was still muttering to herself as she carried all her possessions from the communal kitchen back to the safety of her room.

6

It was during the Easter term in her first year when Maggie met Tiger. She ran into him, quite literally, as he headed into Angie's room and she headed out of hers. She was racing to her afternoon lecture, uncharacteristically late, having become absorbed in an episode of *Neighbours*. She'd opened her door and launched herself at speed at exactly the moment a tall, tanned Adonis of a young man, dressed only in a barely adequate hand towel, had stepped across the corridor to open Angie's door. Maggie's momentum meant that she ricocheted off him, dropping her bag and very nearly ending up on the floor herself. A lever arch file full of notes sprang open as it hit the ground and disgorged its contents in a disorderly muddle on the carpet.

'I'm so sorry,' she began, bending to retrieve her notes whilst making sure that her gaze didn't settle on the skimpy towel.

'Hey. Someone's in a hurry,' said the man. 'It's not good for you, you know. Stress.'

He bent down to help her with her things, holding the towel in place around his waist with one hand, and their heads almost touched, his blond and tousled, hers dark and tightly pinned back. She could smell peppermint toothpaste on his breath and his skin was still damp from a recent shower, but she was so flustered that she barely allowed herself to make eye contact with him.

'Sorry,' she said. 'Sorry. I'm late for my lecture. Or nearly late.'

'I'm sure they won't start without a beautiful creature like you,' he said.

It was the corniest line Maggie had heard in quite some time, but somehow when it came out of his mouth it sounded entirely reasonable. She could feel her cheeks flame.

The papers regathered, they stood up and he raised a hand – the one not protecting his dignity – in a wave of sorts.

'I'm Tiger,' he said. 'Mate of Angie's. And you are . . . ?'

'Maggie,' she managed. 'I live next door,' she added, and then could have kicked herself, as that much was probably obvious. 'And I need to go. Nice to meet you . . .' She wanted to repeat his name, to attach some significance to the delivery of it, but was stymied. Surely, he wasn't really called Tiger. Who would do that to their child? Instead, her sentence seemed to float in the air unfinished.

Then she set off up the corridor, her heart still beating faster than usual.

'I'll be staying for a few weeks,' he called after her. 'So, no doubt I'll catch you again.'

She heard Angie's door open and then bang closed as she reached the fire doors.

Staying for a few weeks? Had he really said that? Obviously, people had guests for the weekend sometimes, and there was an occasional visitor to their corridor mid-week, but for 'weeks', plural? Maggie wondered if that was even allowed. She doubted very much that it was. It was just like Angie to flaunt the rules. Maybe she had sublet her room to him and gone to sleep somewhere else. Maggie wouldn't have put it past her.

Then again, what did she care if it meant that that gorgeous bloke was sleeping just the other side of the breeze-block wall?

She failed to concentrate as hard in her tort lecture as she perhaps should have done, and then hurried back home afterwards to see how the land lay, but there was no sign of the visitor. Her curiosity about him trumped her embarrassment at appearing nosey, and she knocked on Leon's door. She and Leon were good friends now. She liked his unassuming nature and his dry wit, and she could just about overlook how he seemed to be as obsessed with Angie as everyone else.

'Come in,' shouted Leon, and she opened the door and let it close behind her.

Leon's bed was still unmade and most of his clothes seemed to be on the floor, but Maggie forced herself to ignore the mess. Her eye was caught by a single black sock dangling from the keys of the alto saxophone that lived on a stand in the corner, but she looked beyond it to where Leon was sitting.

'Oh, hi Mags,' he said when he saw her. No one had ever called her Mags, but she allowed it because it suggested a degree of intimacy between the two of them that she liked.

'Have you met Tiger?' she asked him outright without bothering with any explanation.

Leon looked confused and shook his head. 'Tiger? Is that a person or a soft toy?'

'A person. A bloke. He's staying in Angie's room.'

'Oh, him,' said Leon with a trace of disgust. 'The blond one who thinks he's God's gift to women? I've not met him, but I saw him earlier. Is he a mate of Angie's, then? From a different college?'

Maggie thought about this possibility but rejected it. 'I don't think so. He said he was staying with Angie for a few weeks. He wouldn't say that if he had his own room on campus.'

'Maybe he's shagging her and it's easier to do if he's on the spot.'

'Don't be so crude, Lee,' Maggie replied prudishly, but actually, she found the thought that Tiger might be in a relationship with Angie wildly unsettling, even though it was the obvious solution to the puzzle of what he was doing in her room.

'If he's really going to be here for weeks then no doubt we'll find out more,' Leon said.

'It must be against the rules though,' Maggie pressed on. 'Having a guest for such a long time. Do you think I should report it?'

'No!' exclaimed Leon. 'Definitely not. Honestly, Mags. You can be such a goody-two-shoes sometimes.'

He smiled at her affectionately as he said this, which took the sting out of his words. Also, it was true – she was a goody-two-shoes. She was happy to claim the title. Doing as she was instructed was so much a part of who she was that the thought of being in contravention of something made her heart beat a little faster. Rules were rules and made to be followed, and her inclination to report any infringement felt almost as natural as breathing.

But then again, if she reported Tiger he would have to leave and that, she suddenly realised, would not be good. There was no denying he was attractive, but on top of that (and she certainly wouldn't say this to anyone else) she had felt a definite spark between them. Their encounter had been over so quickly that it had barely had a chance to ignite into anything more obvious, but it had definitely been there.

'Hmmm,' she said to Leon. 'Maybe you're right, and I don't suppose he's doing any harm. It must be horribly cramped in there, though.'

'I doubt they'll have noticed,' replied Leon.

He winked at her and she felt herself bristle. She did not want to think about whatever Angie and Tiger might be doing together in the tiny, untidy space.

Later, as she tried in vain to concentrate on her contract law essay, Maggie caught herself straining to pick up any noises coming from the next-door room that might give her more clues as to what was going on in there, but there was nothing. Either they were both very quiet in their lovemaking or there was not very much happening on that score. She really hoped it was the latter.

7

Over the next couple of days, Maggie found herself having to leave her room at the exact second she heard Angie's bedroom door opening, but generally it was someone going into the room and not coming out and they disappeared without giving her a chance to strike up a casual conversation. Finally, though, the timing worked, and she emerged at precisely the right moment to speak to whoever it was. Her heart plummeted, though, when she saw that it was Angie and not Tiger.

Despite what Maggie felt was a tangible antipathy demonstrated towards Angie on her own part, Angie didn't seem to have noticed, but then Angie appeared to breeze through her life without being troubled by whether she was upsetting anyone else. She continued to 'borrow' Maggie's food from the fridge without ever replacing it and when Maggie's crockery was no longer available to her, she had just moved on to using someone else's. It was as if other people's lives made no impact on hers whatsoever, and Maggie had decided that her own life would work best if she was friendly, but not friends, with Angie.

But now, as she had orchestrated a bumping into her in the corridor, she couldn't waste the opportunity to get more information out of her about the mysterious man in her room.

'Hi, Angie,' she opened. 'How are you?'

'Sound,' replied Angie. If she was surprised at the uncharacteristic attempt at conversation, she didn't show it. 'You?'

Maggie nodded. 'Good, thanks. My course seems to be going well at least.'

Angie turned to head up the corridor, already bored by what Maggie had to say so Maggie spoke more quickly.

'I bumped into your friend, Tiger, the other day. Literally walked right into him.'

'Oh yeah. He said. Said he nearly showed you his crown jewels by accident!'

Angie grinned at her. She was pretty when she smiled, Maggie thought, less 'too cool for school', and she felt an absurd wave of pleasure that Tiger had mentioned their encounter. He must have noticed that spark, as well.

'He seems nice,' Maggie continued.

'Yeah, he's great. I met him when I was travelling in my year out.'

Well, that made sense, thought Maggie. He too had that worldliness about him that Angie had and that the rest of them, there fresh from school, seemed to lack.

'And is he studying here too?' Maggie asked, hoping that her questioning sounded more natural than it felt.

'God, no! He's just passing through on his way to Thailand.'

'Ah,' replied Maggie.

A sense of disappointment settled heavily over her. He had only come to visit Angie and wasn't staying. Whatever that little frisson between them had been, it was clearly going to amount to nothing. Angie set off again, but after a few steps she stopped and turned back to face Maggie. Her eyes ran up and down her as she weighed something up, and Maggie tried not to feel judged.

'Actually,' Angie said after a moment, 'we were thinking of having a bit of a gathering here tonight. Come if you're free. Bring a bottle.'

And then she was gone, breezing up the corridor, trailing a silk scarf and the unmistakable smell of patchouli in her wake.

A gathering. What was that? A party? Something else? Maggie hadn't been invited to either gatherings or parties thus far. She wasn't really sure what the form was, but she was definitely interested. As soon as she was certain that Angie had gone, she crossed the corridor and knocked lightly on Leon's door, but there was no answer. She tried again a little louder, but he clearly wasn't inside. He probably wouldn't know what Angie meant by a gathering either. His social life wasn't much better than hers.

As she let herself back into her own room, she decided that she would go whether Leon was invited or not. She'd be able to hear what was going on through her wall in any event, so there would be little chance of getting any work done. And even if Tiger was spoken for, at least she could gaze at him for a bit. There was nothing wrong with that.

She had better buy herself a bottle.

◆ ◆ ◆

As Maggie had thought, there was no danger of not hearing the gathering once it got underway, and she was ready to join the fun. She had put clean jeans on and a newish top and taken more care than usual over her make-up. The result wasn't at all bad, she decided as she looked at herself in the mirror.

Now, though, she had to decide how to arrive. By the sound of it, things had spread out from Angie's room and into the corridor right outside her door. There was music playing and she could hear talking and laughter. It sounded like they were having fun, whoever they were.

However, it was one thing knowing that there was a party to which she was invited happening right outside her room, but it was quite another just opening her door and joining in. She doubted she would know anyone there. The people she had seen from Angie's sociology course, whilst not looking as bohemian as Angie, were still quite intimidating in their coolness. Maggie refused to be daunted by them, but all the same . . . She really hoped that Leon was out there. It would be okay if she could just go and sit with him. But how could she tell until she opened her door? And once she had done that she could hardly just close it again and slink back into her room, not without provoking some comment or other, when they were literally right outside.

Oh, this was ridiculous. She was an adult. She should just open the door and join in and if she decided it wasn't for her, then she could wander off to the college bar instead and pretend that that had been her plan all along. She took a deep breath, ran her hands though her hair and pulled her shoulders back. Then she picked up the bottle and opened the door.

There weren't as many people as she had imagined there would be, based on the volume. A little group of four or five sat on the floor between her room and Leon's, and Angie was lying on her stomach, her head supported on her hands and her body half-in, half-out of her room. There was no sign of Tiger.

'Room for a little one?' Maggie asked, and she dropped to her bottom and sat cross-legged on the floor outside her door. Immediately she twisted the cap on her bottle of Thunderbird and took a swig. Normally she would have brought a glass with her, but she hadn't wanted to appear prissy. The cheap wine tasted sharp on her tongue, but she could feel the alcohol starting to work almost at once.

'Absolutely,' said a boy she hadn't seen before, and he opened up the little circle so that Maggie wasn't sitting on top of him.

'Everyone, this is Maggie,' said Angie. 'She's doing law, though God only knows why anyone would want to.'

'You do know that the law is a social construct designed to . . .' began another who was wearing a heavy donkey jacket with a Coal not Dole badge on the lapel. The halls of residence were notoriously warm and he must have been roasting hot dressed up like that, Maggie thought.

'Oh, shut up, Dave,' said Angie. 'Leave her alone. And anyway, it's far too early for that kind of talk.'

She gave Maggie a wink and Maggie felt a rush of gratitude. She could more than hold her own in a debate, but she would rather get the lie of the land before she marched into battle.

'We were just discussing whether I should stand for something in the Student Union elections,' continued Angie. 'If you want to be president in the third year then you have to have had a couple of other jobs under your belt before then, to get a bit of a track record so that people will vote for you.'

'And do you want to be president?' Maggie asked incredulously. The idea of standing for office wasn't something that had ever crossed her mind, but even as she spoke her brain was considering whether it might be a useful thing to have on her CV.

Angie tipped her head to one side whilst she considered. 'I haven't really decided,' she said, as if the taking of the position was entirely in her own gift and not the outcome of a highly competitive election, 'but I just think there are issues that need to be addressed that aren't being. Getting kids from non-privileged backgrounds to uni for a start. Making sure that everyone gets a bite at the cherry no matter who they are and where they're from. I mean, most people made it here because their parents supported them, gave them aspirations and encouragement.' She pulled a face that

Maggie couldn't quite interpret – anger, maybe, or bitterness, and then continued. 'But there are loads of others who are perfectly smart enough to get the grades, but no one backs them. It probably never occurs to them to even try to get into uni, and they just end up doing the same as everyone they know, so nothing ever changes. Unless someone shakes things up, of course.'

Maggie listened intently. This was the first time she had heard Angie talking like this. Yes, there was plenty of political chat around campus – the plight of the miners, what people would do to Margaret Thatcher if they ran into her on a dark night – but this was the first time Maggie had heard anyone talking from the heart about something that really mattered to them. And this was important to Angie; that much was clear from the conviction in her voice.

But then, as if she had let more of herself show than she'd intended, Angie changed the subject. 'Get out here, Tiger,' she called behind her into her room, 'and bring that bloody guitar. You must have found it by now. It's not like there are many places it could be hiding!'

At the mention of his name, Maggie felt her heart lurch and she took another swig of her wine, more to disguise the lurch than anything else.

And then Tiger appeared.

It was the first time Maggie had seen him since the towel incident and she had forgotten just how very sexy he was. This time he was wearing battered 501s and a plain white T-shirt that showed off his out-of-season tan to perfection. Maggie almost gasped at the sight of him. He was holding a guitar that was almost entirely covered with stickers of all shapes and sizes and he looped the strap around his neck and strummed a couple of chords as he lowered himself to the ground.

'When did you last play this baby, Angie? She sounds bloody awful.'

Angie shrugged and Tiger began to tune the guitar, working his way down each string in turn until he was satisfied.

'Any requests?' he asked the group, but when no one spoke he began to pick out the first few arpeggios of 'The House of the Rising Sun'. He was surprisingly good, and his fingers moved confidently across the frets. Then he began to sing. He sang less well than he played, but it was still good to listen to and Maggie was transfixed. There was something magical about a person who could play an instrument whilst their peers watched. It wasn't so much the skill itself – she had piano to Grade 8 – but the unflustered self-confidence that it took to display their abilities to others. In Maggie's experience that part was rare and, she discovered now, extremely attractive. Then someone else began to join in, but their contribution was more of a wail than an actual tune and the moment was spoiled. Tiger kept playing the melody but he stopped singing to allow the others their comedy moments.

After that they worked their way through a repertoire of Doors and Beatles classics, although it was rare that anyone knew the words to an entire song. Tiger would play the opening chords of something to great enthusiasm, but then moved on when it fell flat due to a lack of lyrics.

'Where did you learn to play?' Maggie asked him when he finally stopped to take a drink.

Tiger shrugged. 'Just picked it up, I suppose. I spend a lot of time in hostels and there's not much to do in the evenings. It just kind of rubbed off.' He looked at her as he spoke, his eyes meeting hers and Maggie felt it again – that indefinable something.

'You're really good,' she said, with a smile that she hoped expressed her thoughts. She was going to have to create an opportunity for them to be by themselves, and she thought wistfully of her beautifully tidy bedroom just the other side of the door. Maybe when the party started to break up a little, or if the others went off in search of more fun elsewhere . . . He winked at her and her insides wobbled a little.

'Oh look. A party in my corridor,' said a familiar voice to her left, cutting across her thoughts.

She hadn't noticed Leon arrive – when did you notice Leon at all, really? – but here he was, and if she didn't play the situation carefully, he would attach himself to her and spoil whatever chance she might have with Tiger.

'Hi,' she said, a little brusquely.

'Hi!' said Tiger with far more enthusiasm. 'I'm Tiger. Mate of Angie's. And you are?'

'Leon,' said Leon. 'That's my room there.' He nodded at his door, now totally inaccessible for the mess of sprawling students that lay in front of it.

'Have a drink, Leon,' said Tiger, pulling one of his cans free from its plastic ring and passing it to him.

'Cheers,' said Leon. 'I'll just . . .' He leaned over the throng, unlocked his door and chucked his rucksack on to his unmade bed.

'Is that a sax?' asked Tiger, peering inside the room.

The saxophone sat, as it had done since the beginning of the year, on its stand in the corner. Maggie had never seen Leon play it. It had even crossed her mind that he had only brought it as an accessory to decorate his room, a kind of pointer to the sort of person that he aspired to be, like a record collection or bookshelf. She had asked him about it once, but he had just brushed her off. He hadn't offered to show her or even seemed prepared to talk about it. If he could actually play, then the contrast between him and the confident and relaxed way that Tiger handled Angie's guitar couldn't have been more marked.

Today, at least, the instrument was free of underwear adornments. Maggie waited to see how Leon would reply.

Simply, it appeared.

'Yes,' he said.

'I assume you play,' Tiger pressed.

'I do,' said Leon.

It was like the two of them were stalking one another with their words.

'Go on then,' challenged Tiger.

Maggie watched with interest. She assumed that Leon would respond in that shy, modest way that most people did when asked to play in public. That would certainly accord with what she knew about him. And Tiger was so chilled and cool that that alone would surely put Leon off.

So, when Leon said, 'Okay,' and stood up, she couldn't have been more surprised. Her feelings changed then to something more protective. She liked Leon. She didn't want these people to laugh at him, to snigger behind his back. He had missed Tiger's turn and so didn't know how well he had played, that the musical bar had already been set quite high. Part of her wanted to cause a distraction so that he didn't have to put himself through the embarrassment.

But Leon wasn't a child, and she wasn't his mother.

She watched as he attached the strap to the saxophone and looped it over his head. He took the cap off the mouthpiece and licked the reed, making sure it was suitably damp. Then he put the instrument to his lips and blew.

8

He played Gershwin's 'Rhapsody in Blue'.

The opening trill caught the assembled crowd. Hands holding drinks hovered in the space between waist and mouth as surprise and then astonishment circulated. The music was lilting. The notes hung in the air, suspended on invisible threads and then faded and disappeared only to be replaced by others so entirely perfect that it was hard to believe that they hadn't been there all the time. They twisted and turned, were bent in and out of shape, grew and were then dismissed as Leon's fingers moved across the valves. It was as if the music had taken hold of them, hold of the air even, and kept them motionless, like a charm.

Maggie felt her jaw drop.

How was this unassuming boy, who she'd thought she was getting to know quite well, capable of producing such a beautiful sound and yet she hadn't known, had had no idea whatsoever? How had he kept it hidden? Why didn't his talent just shine out of him from the moment he woke up in the morning, in his sleep even! There was absolutely nothing about Leon, no clue whatsoever, that might give away this part of him.

Angie was the first to break the spell.

'Bloody hell, Leon!' she said. 'You kept that quiet. You play like a pro. A real pro.' She cast her gaze around the collected group for confirmation of her thoughts.

'Respect, man!' said Tiger. 'Wow! I mean, just WOW.'

Leon, who seemed to have been transported to some other plane whilst playing, lowered the sax and looked at his feet and suddenly the Leon that Maggie knew, self-effacing, a bit nerdy and bland, reappeared. He shrugged one shoulder but didn't seem to know what to say.

'Leon, you're incredible,' said Maggie. 'Where did you learn to play like that? And how come I've never heard you?'

Leon shrugged again. 'I don't play that often here. There never seems to be time. Sometimes, late at night . . .'

Maggie had heard haunting jazz sax playing when she'd been writing essays in the small hours, but it had never occurred to her that the music was actually live.

'I've heard you,' she said. 'Or at least, I think I have, but I didn't realise it was you. I thought it was just someone playing a record. It never crossed my mind. I mean, I'm sorry, I just had no idea.'

'It's okay,' said Leon, turning to put the sax back on the stand.

'Well, that's it,' said Angie definitely. 'You're dropping chemical engineering right now! What a waste! You should be in London playing Ronnie Scott's. Or somewhere in New Orleans.'

Leon came back to the corridor and sat on the floor. He picked up his half-drunk can and dropped his gaze to the floor, shaking his head. 'No,' he said. 'That life's not for me. I need a proper job. One that will actually pay the mortgage that I'm hoping to get.'

'But you can't do that,' Angie insisted. 'Not now. You owe it to yourself to be a musician. Hell, with a talent like that you owe it to the world.'

Leon's cheeks blazed and he squirmed slightly, clearly uncomfortable at being in the spotlight for so long.

He nodded at the guitar that was still in Tiger's hands. 'Your turn,' he said.

'I am never playing again after that!' replied Tiger with a grin. 'What am I but some totally untalented hack?'

But he did lift the guitar again and started to pick out 'Hotel California'.

'Don't you know anything from this decade?' asked one of the others in a mocking tone, and Tiger immediately stopped playing mid-line.

'There's nothing from this decade worth playing,' he replied.

'Touché,' said Maggie, and then wished she hadn't in case it made her sound over-intellectual. She felt warmth creeping up her throat, although the wine wasn't helping in that regard either.

'Fair point,' muttered the heckler.

Angie was still staring at Leon as if no one else was present.

'Seriously, Leon,' she said. 'You have to do something with that talent. I mean. Seriously.'

Leon still looked decidedly uncomfortable. His ears and neck had gone red as well, pimples standing out angrily, and he stared resolutely at the carpet as if hoping that this would make Angie stop chiding him.

After a few moments, she seemed to give up and started talking to the others. She was right, though, Maggie thought. Leon really should make more of his talent, but she understood his thought processes. It was far more sensible to get a degree and a real job, and then play his music as a hobby; a wonderful one, but still a hobby.

They stayed in the corridor chatting and drinking for a while longer until they started to get complaints from some of the other residents about the noise levels.

'I think we've outstayed our welcome,' said one of Angie's gang, as another door opened and then banged shut, the occupant expressing their displeasure. 'Shall we head over to the Union?'

Maggie wasn't keen on that idea. She was already up later than she'd intended to be. But then again, there was the draw of Tiger. If he was going to the Union, then perhaps she should go, too.

'I think I'll call it a night,' said Leon ruefully. 'I've got a nine o'clock lecture. I really should . . .'

'Don't be so boring,' laughed Angie. 'You've got the rest of your life to go to bed early. Come to the Union with us!'

Leon was obviously wavering. He looked at Maggie as if she could answer his quandary for him, but she just shrugged.

'Oh, what the hell!' he said. 'I'm in.'

This was so unlike Leon, Maggie thought, wondering whether she had got him all wrong after all. She was glad, though. He was such a lovely person, and it would do him good to be out. This thought made Maggie feel like his mother, so she dismissed it and turned her attention back to Tiger. He too seemed a little reluctant to go to the Students' Union. Maggie felt that he was holding back. Was he waiting to see what she was going to do before he committed? She hardly dared even think that.

Angie's friends stood up, making complaining noises about pins and needles in legs and feet, and soon they were ambling noisily down the corridor with Leon in tow. Angie herself had disappeared back into her room to replace the guitar, leaving Maggie and Tiger alone in the corridor.

'So, Mags,' he said. 'You coming?'

Her dilemma was almost palpable. She also had early lectures and a tutorial that she needed to be sharp for. She had had enough to drink for one night, too. Any more would risk a hangover, which she could ill afford. And the Students' Union wasn't the ideal place for the intimate tête-a-tête that she had in mind. It could be so loud in there that it was almost impossible to have a decent conversation.

'Or we could just go for a walk around the lake,' he suggested, leaning in towards her so that his thigh brushed hers. His voice was softer now that there were just the two of them. 'I promise not to push you in,' he added with a smile. He seemed different, less brash, the performance that his life seemed to be paused for a moment.

Maggie raised an eyebrow as if to say that if he even tried to push her in she wouldn't hesitate in taking her revenge, but before she had time to reply Angie reappeared wearing the moth-eaten Afghan coat that made Maggie's skin crawl.

'Right!' Angie said. 'Let's go,' and set off after the others.

Maggie dithered for a second, but it was too long.

'Definitely not coming?' asked Tiger, taking a step away from her. The electricity escaped immediately.

Maggie's heart sank and then her irritation rose. What was going on here? It felt like he was two people – the gentle romantic who had suggested a quiet moonlit walk, and the life-and-soul party animal that he was with Angie. Her mind flicked to John Travolta's character in *Grease*.

Well, that wasn't good enough for Maggie. He was either interested in her or he wasn't. There were no half measures.

'No,' she said decisively. 'I don't fancy it.'

This was a lie, but she looked Tiger straight in the eye as she delivered it. She saw the tiniest twist of his mouth, the raise of an eyebrow, but then he set off up the corridor, catching up with Angie in three steps.

'Sleep tight then, Maggie,' he called out over his shoulder without turning round. 'Don't let the bed bugs bite.'

Angie slipped her arm through his as they walked, relaxed, unselfconscious. 'God, do you remember those bed bugs in Goa . . .' she began, and then they pushed through the double doors and were gone.

Maggie let herself back into her room, fighting her feelings of disappointment. She'd made the right decision, she told herself. In fact, she had probably just had a narrow escape, not allowing herself to be seduced by a bloke who was basically a dick. Tiger would definitely turn out to be a player. He certainly looked like one. It was a wise move on her part not to get involved. She would save herself some heartache later on.

But as she tucked herself up into her narrow bed and flicked off the light, she thought about his expression when she had turned him down. She was sure she'd seen a trace of regret in his eyes.

9

Maggie hadn't given much thought to who she might move in with for the second year, but when she overheard some other first years discussing it in the refectory, she realised that she needed to. The idea had popped into her head earlier in the term but then she had got so caught up with her course and thoughts of the coming exams that it had drifted out again. Actually, if she was being completely honest, this wasn't true. She had pushed the idea out of her mind because it was a problem that she wasn't entirely sure how to solve.

As the year had worn on, not much had changed with her social life. Whilst Maggie had got to know people on her course a little better, there was no one amongst them that she would feel comfortable approaching about accommodation for the following year. In fact, she thought that she might have missed the boat in any event. Going by the overheard conversation, it appeared that people had already split into groups and were searching for houses accordingly. She would have to live with someone, though. That much was obvious, as she couldn't afford to rent a place on her own.

Then her mother had raised the subject.

They generally spoke on a Sunday morning after 'The Archers' omnibus, her mother ringing the public pay phone in the corridor. Maggie would sit on the floor beneath the handset waiting for it to ring and hoping that no other call came in in the interim.

'Have you had a productive week?' was always her mother's predictable opening gambit, and Maggie would confirm that she had indeed, whether it was true or not. In her carefully curated weekly reports to her mother, she made sure that she never gave any cause for concern. Her mother was likely to panic if she thought anything was not the best it could possibly be, and it was preferable to let her think that. And actually, there was no cause for concern. Maggie's life at university was progressing as she felt it should. She was getting good marks, and all was on track for her eventual step up to the next stage of her plan.

'I was talking to Jenny,' her mother said next.

Maggie's heart sank. Whenever her mother spoke to the mothers of Maggie's friends, she always came back with some life detail or other that Maggie was either lacking or failing in.

'She said that Louise has found a house for next year already. You haven't told me where you'll be living in September,' she said, her voice slightly petulant. 'It was terribly awkward, Jenny knowing all the details about Louise and me knowing nothing. I just had to bluster and make things up. I think I got away with it. You have got somewhere to live, I assume. And with some nice people.'

She pressed the word 'nice' and Maggie understood exactly what her mother meant. 'Nice' meant suitable, from good, solid middle-class homes, preferably where the parents still occupied the same house, and who were studying 'proper' subjects like her. Maggie could count on the fingers of one hand the people that she knew in York who would fit her mother's definition and she didn't like most of them.

'Oh yes,' replied Maggie instantly. 'It's all organised.'

'So, tell me,' her mother insisted. 'I don't want to have to be caught on the hop again.'

Well, if you stopped gossiping about me and trying to show off how well I'm doing at every turn, then you wouldn't get into awkward situations, thought Maggie.

'There are just one or two details still to iron out,' she replied vaguely, 'but as soon as I know everything, I'll let you know. I have to go now, Mum,' she lied. 'There's a huge queue for the phone. I'll tell you more next time. Thanks for ringing.'

Maggie put the phone down and looked up and down the empty corridor. This house business needed addressing. And soon.

She retrieved her ten pence pieces from the top of the phone and went to knock on Leon's door.

'Come in,' came Leon's familiar voice.

Maggie opened the door, bracing herself for the customary chaos. Leon was at his desk, poring over textbooks that were almost as thick as her law ones. His bedding was strewn in a heap that draped across the end of the bed and on to the floor. Maggie suppressed a shudder.

'Morning,' she said brightly.

When he saw who it was, Leon's face lit up, or at least that was how Maggie interpreted his expression.

'Have you got a minute?' she asked, suddenly feeling a little shy about what she was about to ask him.

'Of course!' he replied enthusiastically. 'Come in. Sit down.' He waved his hand around the room as if indicating that she could pick her spot, but there was something far too intimate about sitting on his unmade bed, and no other option. She stayed standing.

Maggie hadn't really given any thought to what she was going to say, coming as she had, directly from the conversation with her mother. She didn't want to look desperate, but he might know of somewhere that would suit her. In the moment, she decided that it would be best to just come out with it.

'I was just wondering where you're going to live next year. We haven't really talked about it, have we? It's going to feel really strange, us not living opposite one another any more, but we'll keep in touch, I hope.' She tried not to sound too doubtful about this.

She did really want to stay friends, although it might be hard if they ended up in different parts of York.

Leon slumped into his seat and blew his lips out. 'It's a bit of a nightmare,' he said. 'I think I missed the boat when everyone else was sorting theirs out. It all happened so early in the year and I couldn't get my head round it. But then the people I know got themselves into little gangs and found places and I was left out. I reckon I'm just going to have to go back home and come in by train every day. The journey will be hell, but I'm not sure what else I can do now. It's too late.'

Maggie nodded as she contemplated the larger hell that would be having to live at home with her parents again, although Leon didn't seem to share her aversion to families. Perhaps his was reasonable and easy to live alongside.

But then a more relevant thought started to take shape in her head. Maybe she could live with Leon? She liked him well enough. In fact, there was very little to dislike about him. He was generally cheerful, didn't seem to smell, closed his mouth when he chewed and didn't do any of the other things that she considered to be deal-breakers. He was a boy, of course, which was a mark against him. It wasn't that there was anything between them – Maggie would never think of him in those terms – but she knew the fact that they really were 'just good friends' would make no difference to her sceptical and mistrusting mother. It might be better if there were a gang of them living together, a couple of each sex. That would feel less odd. Still, beggars couldn't be choosers.

The thoughts were all racing so hard around her head that she didn't realise that Leon had spoken to her until she saw that he was staring at her expectantly.

'Sorry, what?' she said.

'I said, what about you? Where are you going to live?'

'I haven't got anywhere either,' she confessed. 'I just, well, I'm not sure what happened actually, but somehow I haven't sorted it. I thought I might ask them whether we can stay in halls in the second year. There may be some places somewhere.'

As she said this, it crossed her mind that it might be the perfect solution. It would certainly be the easiest.

But Leon was shaking his head. 'Third years only, apparently,' he said, 'I already asked,' and Maggie's little bubble burst.

She sighed. How had she let this happen? It was so unlike her, but maybe in the back of her head she had been hoping for this solution all along, but just hadn't wanted to be the one who brought it up in case Leon got the wrong idea.

'And of course, Angie's not fixed anything up either. She's not even looking for a place. She says she's just going to crash on people's floors and sofa-surf her way through the year.'

Maggie tutted. 'That's so like her. She's so impractical.' As she said this, she tried to cast from her mind the thought that, in this matter at least, she and Angie appeared to be exactly the same.

'Actually,' said Leon, 'if she can make it work, I'd say it was a pretty good idea. She won't have to pay any rent, for a start.'

Maggie rolled her eyes. 'She's such a freeloader. Does she have no shame?!'

The solution to their collective problems was obvious now, but Maggie hesitated, unwilling to take the plunge. The conversation stalled for a moment as they each seemed to be considering their next moves.

Leon bit his lip for a moment and then he said, 'Shoot me down if it's a crap idea, but what if we looked for somewhere together – the two of us? Or even the three of us. There are bound to be some houses left, especially smaller ones. Might be fun?' he added doubtfully.

'Maybe,' Maggie replied, keen not to reveal her hand, but also aware that she was all out of options. If Leon did go back to Leeds, then she really would be up the creek without a paddle. 'I'm not sure about Angie, though. Me and her . . . well, it's a bit hit and miss.'

'Oh, she's all right,' said Leon. 'I mean, I know she's scatty as hell and has some odd ideas about the concept of personal possessions, but fundamentally she's a nice person. And I don't think the sofa-surfing thing is her plan by choice. She was with another group, but they had a massive row about something or other and it all fell apart. I think she might be up for a house-share. Shall I ask her?'

Maggie thought about it for a second or two but really, what choice did she have? If she wanted to live with Leon, then it looked like Angie would have to come too.

'Okay,' she heard herself say. 'Thanks.'

10

There was something exciting about going back to York to start the second year of university. Of course, it had been exciting the previous year too, but back then the buzz that Maggie felt had been accompanied by a certain apprehension about setting out on this totally new path. This time, most of that path was clearly in view. Maggie knew what university life entailed, she could find her way around the campus and York itself without difficulty, and felt positively grown up when compared to the anxious-looking huddles of first years. It was hard to believe that just a year ago that had been her – but surely, she hadn't looked quite so nervous.

The one new thing this year was their student house and Maggie was genuinely thrilled about it. Having a room in halls was one thing, but you still felt a lot like a fresher. A whole house to live in was much more like being a real adult, even if she was having to share it with Leon, Angie and a girl called Fiona whom she hadn't yet met.

'How can you live with someone that you don't know, Margaret? Isn't that taking unnecessary risks?' her mother had said when Maggie had made the schoolgirl error of confessing the fact to her.

'It's no different to last year, Mum. I didn't know anyone then, either,' she replied, not unreasonably.

'But that was different,' her mother had said. 'You had your own room. With a lock on the door. Now you'll be sharing with a total stranger. Who knows what she might be like or who her friends are?'

Maggie had sighed inwardly. 'I'm sure she's very nice, Mum, and perfectly normal. She's a friend of Angie's from her course, so it's not like she's a stranger. It's just that I haven't met her yet. And she's a last-minute step-in for someone who dropped out over the summer. We're lucky to get her at such short notice.'

The girl that they had been going to share with, also from Angie's course, had failed her exams, and her re-sits, and so wouldn't be returning to York. Maggie had kept this information to herself. Her mother was sniffy enough about sociology undergraduates without giving her any more ammunition.

'And I can't say I'm that happy about you living with a boy, either,' her mother had continued along a similar vein of disgruntlement. 'What if he sees your underwear in the laundry? And you'll have to make sure you wear your dressing gown at all times. Boys can't be trusted, you know. They're only after one thing.'

Maggie could have explained that she had rarely met a man less likely to pursue her sexually than Leon, but she would never convince her mother so she had just promised that she would be careful and left it at that.

As they turned the corner into her new road, Maggie held her breath. She had wandered over to visit the house several times at the end of the previous term, standing in the street and staring up at the windows, wondering what it was going to be like to live there. She had even chosen her bedroom (first floor, overlooking the garden) although she hadn't mentioned this to the others. No doubt they would allocate the rooms by some sort of lottery.

Maggie watched her mother's eyes narrow and her lips squeeze themselves into a tight knot as she took in the kind of place that

Blake Street was. Bins blocked the pavements, grimy net curtains hung at badly maintained windows and peeling stickers rather than shiny brass numbers adorned the doors. As she saw the place through her mother's eyes, Maggie knew that she had been making serious allowances for its shabbiness.

'It's that one,' she said as the car slowed. 'Number 23.'

Number 23 did at least look reasonably smart, its front door relatively newly painted in a cheerful red. Her mother drew the car to a halt outside. Her silence spoke volumes, but Maggie refused to be put off by it. She opened the door and hopped out, the house key ready in her hand. Her mother got out as well, reluctantly, making a huge show of locking and then double-checking all the car doors.

Well, Maggie wasn't going to let her mother spoil her excitement. Ignoring her tuts, she slid the key into the lock and the front door swung open. The carpet, she noticed at once, was a little more threadbare than she had remembered, but it looked clean enough. The hallway led through to a dark sitting room that was lit by borrowed light from the tiny kitchen at the back, the front room having been given over to a bedroom. There were two old-fashioned sofas in there and a rickety coffee table. All of them might have come direct from a skip if you judged by appearances only. Maggie pushed on through to the kitchen. That too seemed shabbier than she had remembered it, the lino curling away from the floor and a couple of the laminate cupboard doors badly chipped. It was perfectly serviceable, though, and it looked clean.

Maggie didn't want to look at her mother, knowing all too well the expression that would be on her face. Why couldn't she be pleased for her, just this once? Of course, the house was a little down at heel – it was a student house – but the only thing dampening Maggie's spirits was her mother's palpable disapproval.

'Right,' she said, making sure by her tone that her mother would understand that she was not to criticise. 'I'll start to bring the stuff in from the car, shall I?'

The corners of her mother's mouth continued to turn resolutely downwards.

'Which room is yours?' she asked.

'I'm not sure yet,' replied Maggie. 'I think we'll sort that out when everyone is here, but I can put my stuff in the sitting room for now. Keys, please.'

Maggie held her hand out for the car keys and then sidestepped her mother to get back out into the street. A ginger tomcat had jumped up on the car and was preening itself on the warm bonnet. Her mother mistrusted cats, but Maggie let it stay where it was.

'We're going to be neighbours,' she said to it quietly. The cat eyed her languorously but didn't reply.

She began the task of decanting her life from car to house yet again. She was getting better at packing now, and was more discerning about what was essential for her life in York and what merely desirable. When she got back into the sitting room, her arms filled with bags and boxes, she found her mother talking to Angie. A dull foreboding flooded through Maggie, but Angie seemed to be doing a good job of appearing perfectly normal, if you looked past her wild hair and jumble-sale-chic attire. Even though her own feelings about Angie were still ambivalent at best, she was happy to give a good show of being friends to keep her mother off the scent.

'Hi Ange,' she said as breezily as she could manage, and dropped the boxes on to the sofa. 'Good summer?'

'Not bad,' replied Angie.

'Angela was just telling me that she has been travelling in Europe over the summer. Italy, did you say? And Greece.'

'Yeah. I had an Interrail ticket. You can go pretty much wherever you want.'

'We went to Cornwall, didn't we, Margaret?'

Maggie was sure she saw Angie smirk at this, but the greater evil here was her mother's displeasure so she said, 'Yes. But I'd rather have been in Greece. Was it hot?'

'Roasting,' replied Angie.

'Are the others here yet?' Maggie asked then, casting her eyes around for signs of anyone. 'I suppose we need a full house so that we can pick rooms. We'll draw straws, shall we?'

'You can if you like,' replied Angie, 'but I've bagsed one upstairs, the one that looks out over the garden.'

Maggie's jaw tightened. How did Angie always get exactly what she wanted? There were rules about these things. You couldn't just do as you pleased and ignore the wishes of everyone else. It wasn't fair. But this wasn't the time or place to have it out with her. Any hint of dissent amongst the ranks and her mother would sniff it out, and that was to be avoided at all costs. Quickly, Maggie reversed her thinking. If this was how it was to be, then she would pick her second-choice room at least and leave Leon and this Fiona girl to fight it out between them. It was astonishing how quickly one could slip into Angie's 'out for yourself' view of life. In fact, it felt quite liberating to be doing something purely for herself rather than worrying about the sensibilities of others.

'Okay,' she said. 'I'll have another quick whizz round and look at the other rooms,' and before her mother could mention short straws, she was off up the stairs.

There were two further rooms up there, now that the one that she had earmarked as hers was taken – a double room that looked out over the road, and a tiny box room that could barely fit more than the bed. She ignored that one, but stepped into the front room to see if she could feel herself living in it. It was a reasonable size, and quite light with a big window under which sat a teak desk and a wooden ladder-backed chair that looked like it had come from a school. She crossed the floor to look out of the window. The cat was still asleep on her mother's car, she saw, and there were two little boys playing football with a yellow tennis ball a little further down the street. It was a nice enough room, she thought; not the one she wanted, but nice enough.

Then she remembered that there was another room downstairs, in what must have been the sitting room of the house when it was a family home. She turned on her heel and clattered back down the narrow stairs. Her mother and Angie were still chatting in the sitting room and she ignored them and went straight into the front room. It was huge by comparison to the others, having the bay window that the room upstairs lacked but also an extra area to the side that must have been taken up by the staircase.

Maggie began to reframe her thoughts. Was the extra floor-space worth the inconvenience of being on the ground floor? There was a tiny shower room off the kitchen she remembered from her tour of the house, which might surely end up being mainly hers if all the others were upstairs. Plus, the room had a kind of cut-off feeling that she quite liked. Yes, this one would do very well.

'I'm going to take this one,' she shouted through to the others, and then headed back to the sitting room to collect some of her boxes.

Her mother spoke before she had even seen the space. 'Oh, I don't think that's a good idea, Margaret. You'll be terribly vulnerable living on the ground floor. All those strangers wandering about at night with nothing more than a pane of glass to protect you.'

This thought hadn't occurred to Maggie, and as the possible ramifications revealed themselves to her, she felt her nerves tighten a little, flight-or-fight hormones making her scalp tingle. Her mother was, as ever, right. It would make much more sense to give Leon this room and then the three girls could all live in the relative safety of upstairs.

And yet she didn't want to do the sensible thing. The room had other advantages, and when did you ever hear of someone breaking a huge plate glass window to get into a house? Intruders sneaked in and out through small spaces, surely.

Mainly, though, and with all thoughts of personal safety pushed far from her mind, if Maggie took this room it would be one in the eye for her mother, who quite clearly had other ideas. Also, it would show the world that Maggie Summers was a force to be reckoned with, fearless and brave enough to sleep downstairs. And it had the added bonus of sending a message to Angie Osborne. Maggie wasn't entirely clear on what that message might be, but she felt sure that it needed to be sent.

'Well, I think it's perfect,' she said to her mother. 'Now, could you help me shift this stuff?'

11

'Do you remember my mate Tiger?' Angie asked them one night near the end of the autumn term.

Maggie felt a jolt in her stomach. Did she remember Tiger? Oh yes. She had never quite been able to dispel the image of him in the corridor dressed in nothing but a towel. And she had tried, she really had. After he had abandoned her that night at the corridor party, she had wanted nothing more than to dismiss him as being unworthy of her thoughts, but her imagination had had other ideas and so there he still was, clearly preserved in her memory.

Before she had time to speak, though, Leon did. 'Yeah,' he said. 'Nice bloke.'

Angie nodded in agreement at this judgement of her friend. 'He's been in the south of France since the summer, picking grapes or some such,' she said. 'But the season's come to an end, so he'll be back in the UK for a bit while he decides what to do next.'

'What does he actually do?' asked Maggie. The idea of someone just floating about from one place to another was so far from her own world view that she found it almost impossible to comprehend. 'I mean, where does he live? And what's his plan for when he's finished travelling? He won't have any qualifications.'

Angie threw her a pitying look that made Maggie feel small. 'Why does he have to DO anything?' she asked. 'He's a nomad.

That's what he does. He's travelling the world, taking it all in, earning enough to keep himself going and not being a bother to anyone. Not everyone needs a plan for every minute of their lives.' She threw Maggie a look that invited challenge, but Maggie remained tight-lipped. There was no point getting into spats with Angie. They were never going to agree, their approaches to life being as different as chalk and cheese. Maggie liked to plan. Angie and Tiger, or so it appeared, didn't. That was fine.

'Anyway,' Angie continued, 'I was wondering if he could stay here for a bit. He could have Fiona's room.'

House-sharing with Fiona hadn't worked out well. She had turned up in September but only lasted a few weeks before she decided that sociology wasn't for her after all, and had dropped out of university altogether. Maggie had come home from her lectures one day to find a brief but explanatory note on the kitchen table and Fiona's things all gone. The rent was paid until Christmas, so they had just left the room empty and continued as they were, the three of them.

'Won't he be sleeping in your room?' Maggie asked, the question slipping out of her mouth before she had time to think. The effect on her cheeks was instantaneous and she feared the blush might be flooding down her neck as well. The question had been whether Tiger was welcome to stay in their house, not whether he and Angie would be sleeping together. That really was none of her business. And yet, she really, really wanted to know.

Angie eyed her curiously. Maggie saw her take in her flaming cheeks and then the merest hint of a smile shivered across her lips. Maggie braced herself for the teasing that was about to land, but then Angie turned her attention to packing her bag ready for her lectures.

'God, no!' she said. 'I've no idea where he's been. He'll definitely be in Fiona's room. Most of the time, at least.' Her eyes met

Maggie's for a fraction of a second. The smile was gone but Maggie couldn't read the look that had replaced it.

'Don't see why not,' said Leon, apparently oblivious to the covert conversation that was taking place under his nose. 'The room's just sitting there. Might as well have someone in it. I assume he can chip in for bills and food and stuff.'

Angie nodded, although Maggie thought the gesture lacked conviction. Grape-picking probably wasn't the most lucrative of occupations. Angie turned to Maggie, awaiting her approval. Maggie willed her face to stop letting out her secrets and aimed for an expression that said I don't really care one way or the other.

'Yes,' she said breezily. 'Fine by me.'

'Great,' said Angie. 'His train gets in at three thirty so he should be here around four.'

Maggie rolled her eyes. So, Angie had already made the plan and implemented it. It didn't matter what she and Leon thought. Tiger was coming anyway. Earlier in the year, she would have been irritated by having been played like that, but she was getting used to it. A similar thought had clearly just crossed Leon's mind as well, and he threw her a lopsided grin as he raised an eyebrow.

Her mind turned to practicalities.

'There's no bedding in that room,' she said. 'Fiona took everything with her.'

'He'll have his sleeping bag,' Angie replied, as if the comment was so pointless it hardly merited a response.

'Well, I wouldn't want to spend every night in a sleeping bag,' Maggie managed, 'but if he's all right with it . . .'

'Shall I cook?' asked Leon, figuratively stepping between them. 'I can do a big pot of chilli for us all.'

Leon's culinary skills were limited, but his narrow range of dishes were all wholesome and tasty.

'Great,' said Angie. 'Thanks, Leon.'

She gave him a sparking smile. It was no wonder that she had him under her spell, Maggie thought. It worked less well on her, of course.

Maggie had a tutorial to prepare for, so she retreated to her room where she stayed, emerging only to replenish her coffee and make herself a sandwich at lunchtime. When the doorbell rang just after four, she had pretty much forgotten they were to have a houseguest.

And then she remembered. Tiger! Her heart drummed against her ribs, and she tried to tell herself to calm down. There really was no reason to get this excited. It had been one moment in a corridor nine months earlier and she'd probably misinterpreted it anyway. But she couldn't help herself, and there was nothing wrong with having a bit of a crush, was there?

What should she do? She couldn't answer the door when she looked so awful. Her plan had been to tidy herself up before he arrived – brush her hair and put a little bit of make-up on, maybe change her top. But then she had become caught up in her tutorial preparation and had lost track of time. And now it was too late. He was here.

As she sat, frozen at her desk trying to decide, the doorbell rang again. Was she the only one in? She hadn't heard the others go out, but then she had been so engrossed in her work that perhaps she wouldn't have done. How dreadful did she actually look? Maybe she should just . . .

The doorbell rang for a third time and was accompanied by a rhythmical knocking. She couldn't leave him just standing on the doorstep.

Then she heard footsteps thundering down the stairs, the door being flung open and squealing from Angie. 'Hi! How are you? So great to see you! You look amazing. How was France? Did you find the house okay? Oh, it's so good to see you.'

Maggie could hear the lower rumble of Tiger's voice, something about getting in the house and a laugh and suddenly she didn't really care what she looked like any more; she just wanted to say hello. She stood up from her desk, crossed to the door and stuck her head out. Tiger was standing on the doorstep, his rucksack on the pavement next to him. He was tanned to a rich almond and his hair was even blonder than it had been before. Maggie's whole body shivered. Angie was hanging from his neck, her legs wrapped tightly around his waist like a little monkey. It appeared to be an intimate moment and suddenly Maggie felt as if she were intruding.

Then Tiger caught sight of her over the top of Angie's head and his smile broadened.

'Maggie! Hi!' he mouthed, and something about the way he looked at her told her that she hadn't misinterpreted anything the last time they'd met.

'Hi,' she replied quietly. She needed to remember to breathe.

'God, I've missed you,' Angie said, sinking her face into his neck, apparently oblivious to the undercurrent that was passing between Maggie and Tiger. 'Come and have a cup of tea and tell me everything. And no missing anything out. I want to hear all of it!'

She hopped down and then took his hand and pulled him past Maggie's door and into the heart of the house, leaving her standing there. She thought about following them, but this was so clearly Angie's moment that she decided against it. There would be plenty of time to catch up later.

She went back to her desk and settled down, but she knew she would struggle to refocus her attention on her books. That smile, that private moment that they had just shared. Whatever there was between the two of them, it was clearly unfinished business.

12

Angie and Tiger chatted continuously until dinnertime. Maggie could hear the low rumble of voices punctuated by peals of laughter coming through the wall into her room. She would have loved to saunter into the sitting room and join in, but she didn't. It wasn't that she felt totally excluded, although that was part of it; it was more that this was clearly a precious time for Angie, and somehow, despite the tension that there still was between the two of them, Maggie didn't wish Angie any ill. She wanted her to enjoy the reunion without anyone getting in the way.

It was clear that Tiger was special to her, that there was a deep bond between them. The separate rooms thing had been a surprise to start with, but actually, the way the pair of them interacted with one another put Maggie more in mind of siblings than lovers. Nothing she had seen had ever led her to a different conclusion, although this might have been wishful thinking on her part.

Then again, she would swear that whatever she had felt between herself and Tiger before was still there. He'd only spoken two words to her, but she knew. More could develop there, if she wanted it to.

But did she? That was the question. Tiger was only passing through. He was like a cowboy in one of those black and white films that her father enjoyed so much, blowing into town and then blowing back out again. And she still couldn't dismiss the way he had left her standing there in the corridor that time. She had decided then that he was a player, and nothing had happened to change her mind about that. Tiger was definitely a girl-in-every-port kind of bloke, and heartache no doubt followed him around like a shadow. Was there really any point getting herself in a lather about him when he had all this going against him?

On the other hand, what was the point of life if you didn't get yourself into the occasional lather?

Maggie changed her top, freshening her deodorant as she did so, pulled a comb through her hair and added a flick of dark mascara to her eyelashes. Casual insouciance, that was what she was shooting for and, she thought as she looked at herself in the cracked mirror, she had hit her target.

In the sitting room, Angie and Tiger were sprawled on the sofas, taking up one apiece. Leon was in the tiny kitchen chopping veg for his chilli and joining in with their conversation, asking questions where appropriate. Maggie was suddenly sorry that she had spent so long in her room. If she had known that Leon was here as well, she would have emerged sooner. Despite her confused feelings about Tiger, she was genuinely interested in what he had been up to since they had last seen him.

But it appeared she had missed all that. The three of them were now talking about who was the prettiest of Charlie's Angels. The boys seemed to be plumping for Farrah Fawcett's character, Jill, which was so disappointingly predictable. Boys always seemed to fall for that blonde hair/blue eyes thing.

'Kelly was definitely the best-looking,' Angie said. 'With those cheekbones, and all that shiny dark hair. In fact,' she said, turning to look at Maggie, 'you have a look of her, Mags.'

They all turned to look at her as if to confirm or deny Angie's statement.

Maggie pushed her hair away from her face self-consciously. 'Oh, I don't know about that,' she said modestly.

'Actually, you do look quite like her,' said Leon. 'From what I can remember, anyway. It's been a while.'

'Imprinted on a teenage boy's memory forever, that show,' said Tiger, his eyes shining mischievously. 'That and *The Six Million Dollar Man*. When I wasn't having impure thoughts about Farrah, I was trying to run really fast and see round corners.'

They all laughed, and Tiger took his legs down from the sofa so that Maggie had somewhere to sit. She lowered herself on to the cushions carefully, making sure that no part of her touched him, but then as soon as she was seated, he swung his legs back up and flopped them down in her lap. She tensed and then relaxed into their new proximity. No one else seemed to have noticed.

They chatted easily, the four of them. The housemates did get on all right when they were just three, but the addition of Tiger to their number seemed to release something that was generally lacking between them, a kind of ease with one another that wasn't usually there.

When the chilli was ready, Angie cracked open a bottle of cheap red wine and they sat with plates on their knees to enjoy it.

'How's it going with the sax?' Tiger asked Leon as he wiped his plate clean with a slice of white bread.

'Oh God, Tiger,' interrupted Angie. 'You have to tell him. He barely touches the thing outside the house. All that talent and it's just going to waste. He has to go to America and make his fortune. You have to go, Lee,' she added, turning to Leon.

Leon shrugged. 'Yeah, maybe one day. But I've got this degree to do first.'

This was an old argument and Angie seemed to realise that he was stuck on this course of action. 'Yes. But after that . . .' she tried.

'She's right,' said Tiger. 'You should do it.'

Leon looked down at his plate. 'It's all right for you two,' he said. 'You do as you please and make it look so easy. But I'm . . . Well, I'm not really like that. I want to get a job, a mortgage, you know, all that boring stuff our parents did.'

'Not so much my parents,' said Angie wryly.

Angie never talked about her home life and Maggie wondered if now, with Tiger here and the second bottle of wine open, might be the moment. It seemed it was just a passing comment, though, and Angie continued along the path she had been on.

'But why, Leon?' she asked, as if he had suggested that he wanted to spend his life standing in a bucket of cold water. 'There's time for all that. In the future.' She waved a hand at some mythical time to come. 'What about NOW? You need to grab life with both hands and hold on to it tight.'

Leon was looking increasingly uncomfortable and Maggie felt the need to leap in to defend him.

'Actually, I know what Leon means,' she said. 'I'm the same. I just want to get through this and then get on with my career. I'm dying to start work as a solicitor.'

'But that means you don't get the most out of this part of your life,' said Angie. 'You're so busy looking forward to what is to come that you're missing what you have in the here and now.'

Maggie thought about her words and then dismissed them. It was something that she had considered and rejected before. For her, university was a means to an end. If she managed to have a good time on top then so much the better, but it really wasn't the main reason for being there.

'I'm fine,' she said. 'I'm perfectly happy in the here and now. I just have my eyes on the prize, that's all.' She turned to look at Angie. This apparent honesty between them all was new, and she didn't want it to slip between her fingers. 'And what about you, Ange?' she asked. 'What does the future look like for you?'

Angie considered for a moment, picking up her glass but then putting it down again without taking a drink. 'Bright,' she said. 'My future looks bright.'

Maggie wasn't sure how she could reach that conclusion based on the available evidence, but now wasn't the time to question her reasoning.

'And what do you see there?' she pressed.

'In my crystal ball, you mean?' Angie said. She mimicked mist floating before her with her hands and rolled her eyes up into her head. 'I have no idea. Which of us can see into the future? I just know that whatever I end up doing, it will be exactly the right thing for the time.'

Tiger nodded his head appreciatively at these words of wisdom, but Maggie was less convinced. She could see nothing on which to base a statement like that in Angie's life so far. Everything was so haphazard, so accidental. The randomness of it made her shudder. But her own life? Now that was a different story. Structured, ordered, planned and going exactly as she wanted it to.

Having finished eating, Tiger swung his legs back up on to Maggie's lap. They were even closer to one another now. She longed to put a hand on his thigh as it rested on hers, but knew that she couldn't do it and make it look natural. She left her hands where they were at her sides, but then, as if he had read her mind, Tiger found her fingers with his. Maggie started at the unexpected contact, but then, relaxing a little, she allowed his thumb to explore her palm as she cast a sly glance at Leon and Angie to make sure that they hadn't noticed the altered status quo. However, they were still laughing and seemed oblivious.

'Why don't you get your sax out now, Lee?' suggested Angie. 'Let's have a bit of soul to match our mood.'

Leon's face made a feeble stab at objection and then he went to fetch the instrument from his room. As he set it up, Maggie, who had been sitting upright on the sofa with Tiger's legs draped across her, allowed herself to tip sideways so that her head was on his chest. At once he put an arm across her, his fingers finding the bare skin on her back where her top had ridden up. Maggie let her eyelids close as she enjoyed his touch, gentle and with no agenda, but more intimate than she had known for some time.

Leon played 'Smooth Operator', which was perfect for the mood, and then 'Careless Whisper', and as the haunting melodies filled the room, Maggie began to feel that maybe Angie had a point. Perhaps there was more to university life than just a law degree.

13

The following day Maggie came back from her tutorial and let herself into the house. She had been hoping that Tiger might be in on his own, but as she opened the door the place had a still, silent quality that suggested that it was empty, and Maggie's disappointment rose. She wasn't sure what was going on between her and Tiger, if anything at all. The previous evening, after Leon had chilled them all into a state of extreme relaxation, they had just drifted to their beds. Maggie had been grateful. She hadn't even kissed Tiger yet, and didn't want to run before she could walk, but she had been left with the unsatisfactory feeling of not really knowing quite where she stood, a state she wasn't used to.

She went straight into her room and dumped her bag on her desk. Then she went out to make herself a cup of coffee before she settled down to some work. There were dirty dishes in the sink from breakfast, but Maggie barely flinched. Was she becoming more forgiving? It seemed unlikely, but perhaps it was true. She hadn't got as far as washing up for someone else yet, but she was happy just to leave the dishes there rather than going on the warpath after the culprit.

The kettle boiled and as she poured the hot water into her mug, she thought she heard someone moving around upstairs. Maybe she had been wrong; perhaps there was someone in after all. She took her coffee and headed back to her room, but as she crossed the hall-way, she distinctly heard someone sobbing. It was such an intimate sound that she felt guilty for overhearing it. Perhaps whoever it was hadn't heard her come in and thought they were alone? It had to be Angie. Leon was a sensitive soul and not beyond a few tears, but there was genuine pain in the sound that Maggie was listening to.

Maggie hovered on the threshold of her bedroom as she tried to decide what to do. She didn't want to intrude, but at the same time Angie might welcome someone to talk to. She should at least offer, even though she was certain she would get short shrift.

She turned and began to pad quietly up the stairs until she was standing outside Angie's door. The sobbing seemed to have abated a little and now the sounds were more gulps and sniffs. Maybe whatever it was that was wrong had passed. Then again, she was there now, so she might as well see if there was anything she could do to help.

She lifted her hand and rapped lightly. 'Angie? It's me, Maggie. Are you okay? Can I get you anything?'

The room fell silent as if Angie was holding her breath, but then Maggie heard a sniff. She took it as an invitation to open the door.

Angie was sitting on the floor, surrounded by balls of the toilet paper that she had clearly been using as tissues. When she looked up, her face was pink and blotchy, and her eyes swollen to slits. It felt to Maggie like this was a private moment that she shouldn't be witnessing, and yet this diminished and forlorn Angie was such a different spectacle to the Angie that she usually saw that she felt herself drawn to it, almost as if to an actress on a stage.

'Oh, Angie,' she said as she stepped into the room and immedi-ately dropped down to Angie's level. 'What on earth is the matter?'

Angie just shook her head and tore another strip of toilet paper from the roll at her side. She blew her nose noisily. 'It's nothing,' she said.

Why did women always say that when it was patently untrue?

Maggie tried again. 'Come on, now. There's obviously something. It's not like you to be down.'

'I'll be fine in a minute,' Angie said.

Maggie wasn't sure whether she was being dismissed. They had never been close, the two of them. Perhaps it wasn't her place to interfere now? But Angie's customary confident breeziness was gone. Her shoulders drooped and her head hung low, and Maggie divined that her concern wasn't entirely unwelcome.

'Just talk to me,' she said as she settled herself down next to Angie, signalling her intention not to leave. 'It'll feel better if you let it go, and I might even be able to help.'

As she said the words, Maggie thought about how ludicrous they sounded. What did she have to offer Angie? Angie was supercool, and she was, well, she had to admit it, a bit of a square by comparison. She stiffened a little as she waited for Angie's rebuff but instead, Angie moved across and launched herself at her, wrapping her arms around her shoulders. Maggie's automatic reaction was to tense at this unexpected contact, but then she relaxed into it, put her arms around Angie and squeezed her back gently. She could feel Angie beginning to sob again, and she found herself leaning into their embrace still further.

'It's all so shit,' said Angie, her voice muffled by Maggie's shoulder.

'What is?' asked Maggie.

'Everything.'

Maggie wasn't sure where to go from there, so she just held her, waiting until Angie had regained her composure, and then released her.

Angie sat back. 'Sorry,' she said, without looking up.

'There's no need to apologise,' said Maggie. 'I'm just worried about you, that's all. What's so shit?'

Angie sniffed and wiped her nose with the heel of her hand. 'Everything.'

They were going round in circles and Maggie tried not to become irritated with the illogicality of it all, but then Angie seemed to realise the same.

'I mean, I'm here. University is supposed to be the best time of your life, but I feel like it's all happening somewhere else to someone else, do you know what I mean?'

Maggie nodded. She did know. In fact, she knew precisely how that felt.

'And I have no idea what I want to do when I've finished my degree. Tiger says I should travel like him, but that's not for me. I don't want to spend my whole life running away. I like England. I want a base. I want to get a job and a flat and settle down. He says that that's selling out and that I'm just buying into the corporate dream, but I don't think it is. I don't want a corporate job, but I do want a job. I just have no idea what kind.'

And with that the tears started to fall again.

Maggie was at a loss to know what to say. This wasn't something that had ever worried her. She had been steadily working towards her plan to be a solicitor for as long as she could remember and at no point had she ever doubted that she would pull it off, or that it wouldn't be exactly what she hoped for when she finally got there. She could see, though, that not having such a clear path to follow might be unsettling.

Then again, this was Angie! Angie, who seemed to float through life with no plan, borrowing or taking what she needed and without giving a damn about any of the things that felt important to Maggie. That was hard to get her head around.

'I really don't think you should worry, Angie,' she said now, in a tone that she hoped didn't sound dismissive or superior. 'We're only halfway through uni, there's plenty of time for deciding what you want to do next. Just ignore Tiger. What does he know, anyway? His lifestyle is totally unsustainable. Sooner or later, he's going to want to stop travelling and settle down and he'll have no education and next to no prospects. You're smart and articulate and pretty and you'll be able to get whatever job you decide you want to do, I'm certain of it. If I were you, I'd stop fretting about the future and just concentrate on getting the best degree that you can.'

This was a lie. If Maggie really were Angie, she would be worried to death. But then again, Maggie would never have come so far without a plan.

Angie blew her nose messily and threw the snotty loo roll on the carpet. Maggie tried not to flinch.

'You're probably right,' she said.

There was a pause, and Maggie wondered whether she should leave Angie to it, duty discharged, but then Angie spoke again.

'You have no idea how much I envy you,' she said, staring directly into Maggie's eyes in a way that made Maggie want to drop her gaze. 'You know exactly who you are and where you want to go. It's impressive. And rare. I think you're the only person I know who's that certain about things.'

Maggie knew how rare it was, but she tried to look modest rather than proud.

'And I'm not trying to do the whole "woe is me" thing,' Angie continued, 'but when you get a start like I had, it's hard enough to plan what you're going to have for lunch, let alone the rest of your life.'

Maggie had no idea what kind of start Angie had had. It hadn't been like hers; she knew that much, but because she hadn't wanted to pry, Maggie was sketchy on the details of Angie's childhood.

'I'm sure it was hard,' she replied vaguely.

'It was pretty grim. Did you know that my mum got rid of me when I was only ten? Just handed me over to Social Services like I was nothing to do with her any more. And you don't get much careers advice in children's homes. They just want to get you through and out the other side without becoming an addict or getting picked up by a pimp, or worse. School was quite helpful. My form teacher went through all the paperwork and that with me. And by some miracle I got the grades and a place here. Then I got a job stacking shelves for a couple of months which meant that I could go travelling, but there's no grand plan, not like you have. In fact, there's no plan at all.'

Maggie shook her head silently. She suddenly felt very humble. 'You've achieved so much already,' she said. 'I basically had uni handed to me on a plate. All I had to do was keep doing as I was told. But you. To get over all those hurdles. It's a miracle. It really is.'

The pride that Maggie had felt moments before evaporated. What had she actually achieved when you stood it next to what Angie had done so far? And seen in this context, Angie's more irritating habits made more sense – the borrowing of things, the food-taking, all of it. Maggie felt ashamed. Who was she to be so precious about a few tins of beans in the light of all that?

Angie shrugged. 'I don't know about any miracles,' she said with an eye roll. 'I'm not Jesus Christ. But I have had to decide stuff for myself. And it's hard. And sometimes, like today, it's scary too.'

'Well, I'd suggest you stop listening to Tiger,' Maggie said. 'His counsel's not that wise.'

The ghost of a smile crossed Angie's face. 'Yeah,' she said. 'Tiger's talents lie in other directions. As I think you've noticed.' She raised an eyebrow at Maggie.

'Tiger's a nice bloke,' Maggie replied weakly. She still wasn't clear what there was between Angie and Tiger and she didn't want to overstep any marks.

'He is,' said Angie. 'Heart of gold, really.'

She grinned properly and it was as if the old Angie had re-entered the room, the only sign that there had been anything wrong being the pile of snotty loo roll on the floor.

'Are you sure you're okay?' Maggie asked, reeling slightly at the sudden change of direction.

'God, yes,' said Angie dismissively. 'And I need to get a shift on or I'm going to be late for my lecture.'

She swept all the balls of tissue paper into her hands, stood up and deposited them in the wicker bin by the desk. It felt to Maggie as if Angie was scrubbing the last few minutes out of existence and she wondered whether she would regret her candour later. Well, that was okay. They weren't close and were never likely to be. This had probably just been Angie in a rare moment of weakness and she had simply happened to witness it. She hoped she might have helped a little bit, though. And she would try to be more forgiving from now on, now that she had a better idea of where Angie was coming from.

She stood up too and crossed the room to the door, stepping over Angie's discarded clothes and books as she went.

'Right,' she said, 'I'd better get on, too. Have a good day. I'll see you later.'

'Sure will,' said Angie without looking over. 'And Maggie . . .' she added.

Maggie assumed that she was about to receive a word of thanks, but instead Angie said, 'Me and Tiger.' She shook her head.

Maggie had no idea what she meant. Was Angie saying that there was nothing between the two of them, or was she warning her off? Either way, it seemed that Maggie had been kidding herself to assume that no one else had noticed the spark in the air between her and Tiger.

She let herself out and closed the door behind her, heading to the kitchen. Her coffee was now half-cold, so she tipped it down

81

the sink and began again. It was a shame, she thought as the kettle reboiled, that she and Angie weren't closer. Maggie's conscience was pricking her. She had misjudged her housemate, made assumptions based on what she had seen rather than taking the time to actually get to know her, but maybe it wasn't too late to change that. And didn't they both feel that university wasn't quite turning out to be the highlight that they'd expected? Perhaps they did have something in common, after all.

Her coffee made, she went back to her room and settled herself at her desk. She was just finding the thread of Lord Denning's argument in the case that she was reading when Angie appeared at the door. She had washed her face and there was no trace of her upset apart from maybe a little puffiness around her eyes. Maggie assumed she was going to tell her something about not being home for dinner or some other domestic banality but instead she met her gaze and said,

'About before. Thanks, Mags.'

There was something in her tone and the simplicity of what she said that made Maggie feel that something had shifted, some door had been unlocked between them. It was as if they now shared a secret that drew them to one another in a way that they hadn't been before. The idea made her feel surprisingly warm inside.

'You're welcome,' she replied with a smile.

14

They were enjoying a lazy Saturday morning, Maggie sorting out her notes from the previous week at the kitchen table and Leon reading a magazine. A pot of lukewarm coffee sat between them with an empty bottle of milk and a half-eaten bowl of cornflakes, none of which Maggie had felt the need to clear away.

Tiger sauntered into the kitchen, fully dressed, which was unusual for that time of day. He moved about the room collecting his things with a surprising sense of purpose as Maggie watched, curious about what had prompted the tidy-up but also enjoying having an excuse to focus her attention on him without feeling awkward.

'I'll be getting out of your hair tomorrow,' he said as he unhooked his denim jacket from the back of a chair.

Maggie's heart jolted. The duration of Tiger's visit had been characteristically vague, with none of them, including Tiger himself, being quite sure how long he intended to stay. Having overcome her initial wobble at his arrival, she had got used to having him around and felt sure that they were still building up to something, slowly but steadily.

But now, he was leaving, and so soon. Panic flooded through her. She wasn't sure what she'd been hoping for, but she had expected that there'd be more time for the situation to play itself out.

'I've got a coach booked down to Dover tomorrow,' Tiger continued, 'and then I'm heading to St Petersburg.'

'St Petersburg, as in the Soviet Union?' clarified Leon, looking up from his copy of *New Musical Express* and staring at Tiger open-mouthed. 'I thought we couldn't get beyond the Iron Curtain. Won't they just chuck you in a gulag and leave you to rot?'

'Only in spy novels, mate,' said Tiger. 'It's pretty safe to travel there as long as you don't do anything stupid. They watch you like a hawk, and you can't really wander about on your own, but you can go and see. So, I'm catching a train from Paris on Monday night.'

'What's this?' asked Angie, wandering in in an oversized Choose Life T-shirt that had gone a bit grey in the wash and a pair of baggy leggings, her auburn hair tied back with one of Leon's socks. She had clearly only just got up.

'Tiger's leaving us,' said Leon. 'Tomorrow.'

Angie crossed the room and threw her arms around Tiger. 'Oh mate, that's a bugger. I'll miss you,' she said. 'Where are you going?'

'St Petersburg,' replied Tiger.

'Cool,' said Angie. 'Well, we'd better have a send-off party tonight then. Give you something to think about when you're freezing your bits off in Siberia.'

'St Petersburg is nowhere near Siberia,' said Leon. 'God, Angie, didn't they teach you anything at school?'

Angie swallowed and Maggie thought of their conversation about her childhood. She wondered how often she got caught out like this, holes in her education exposed. Then again, the geography of the Soviet Union wasn't Maggie's specialist subject either.

Angie recovered quickly enough. 'Absolutely nothing, Leon mate. I know *nada, rien, nichts, niets*,' she said wryly.

Maggie noticed that as usual, Angie seemed to have decided to throw a party without any consultation with the rest of them, but for once she didn't mind. It might be exactly what she and Tiger needed to finally decide where they stood.

'A party, great idea,' she said enthusiastically.

Leon gave her a sideways glance, as if he didn't quite believe what he'd just heard.

'Just us, or shall we invite a few people over?' asked Angie.

Maggie, who didn't have a few people to invite over, would rather that it was just the four of them, but she could see the advantage of a houseful. It would give her and Tiger more opportunity to make themselves scarce without drawing any attention.

'Let's see who's free?' she said. 'Make a proper night of it.'

'Okay. I'll go and do a ring round. Anyone got a phonecard?'

Maggie rolled her eyes, got the newly purchased phonecard out of her purse and handed it to Angie. 'Try not to use it all up,' she said. 'It's still got £2.40 on it.'

'Thanks,' said Angie, slipping the card into her hair and heading for the door.

'Aren't you going to get dressed first?' asked Maggie, but Angie just shrugged.

By the end of the day, they had mustered about ten guests who had all promised to bring their own drinks. Leon offered to make a chilli, his signature dish, and Maggie bought some plastic plates, forks and cups from Woolworths. Angie made a bowl of her world-famous punch, and they moved Leon's sound system downstairs so that they could have some music. Maggie knew that it would have made more sense to use hers as her room was on the ground floor, and was immensely grateful to Leon for not suggesting it. Finally, Angie threw scarves over all the lights to create more of an intimate mood and they were ready to party.

The four of them gathered in the lounge and Angie filled plastic cups with punch, handing them round proudly.

'Best punch you'll ever drink,' she said.

Maggie took a sip and recoiled involuntarily. It had quite a kick.

'What did you put in it?' she asked through her coughing.

'Oh, you know,' replied Angie vaguely. 'Bit of this, bit of that.'

'A lot of that,' laughed Maggie, 'going by how it tastes.' But she took another mouthful.

By nine o'clock, no one had arrived.

'What time did you tell everyone to come?' asked Leon.

'I didn't really. Just said we were having a house party.'

'So, they might not show up until after the pubs shut, then?' asked Maggie.

She tried not to let her irritation show, but this was so typically Angie. Maggie didn't want loads of people she didn't know arriving at the house at midnight. That wasn't what she wanted at all, but as the evening wore on and the guests were still conspicuous by their absence, it looked as if she would get her way. No one came.

'We don't need anyone else, anyway,' said Angie, her voice slurring a little as the clock ticked past ten. 'We're a party all by ourselves.'

She turned up the volume and 'Don't Leave Me This Way' filled the room.

'The perfect tune,' she said, sashaying over to where Tiger was sitting on the sagging sofa. 'I can't believe you're abandoning me again,' she added as she grabbed his hand and pulled him to his feet, almost losing her balance in the process.

'You could always come with me,' replied Tiger, immediately finding the beat and moving smoothly into a bouncing movement. He looked as if dancing came as naturally to him as walking. Maggie's dance style was more step than dance, with a bit of jumping up and down if she'd had too much to drink. She'd like to dance with Tiger, she thought, but having seen him move, her confidence deserted her. She reached for her plastic cup instead and took a deep slug of the eye-watering punch.

'I can't,' shouted Angie, having turned the music up to its maximum. 'I like it here and I've got a degree to get.'

Tiger took her hand and spun her in and out whilst Maggie watched. Part of her longed for it to be her that Tiger was dancing with like that and part of her was relieved that it wasn't. She had another drink.

'I've got an idea,' said Leon, disappearing into the kitchen and emerging seconds later with the cornflakes box. He set it on the floor. 'So, you have to pick the box up in your teeth, but you're only allowed to have your feet on the floor.'

Maggie wasn't keen on drinking games as a rule, but this one sounded innocuous enough.

'Okay,' said Angie, still dancing with Tiger. 'Show us how it's done.'

Leon bent over and easily took the box between his teeth and stood up. He grinned like the cat that had got the cream.

'I'm not being funny, mate,' said Tiger, 'but that's the crappest game I've ever seen.'

Leon raised an eyebrow, unfazed by the criticism. 'Go on then, Tiger. Be my guest.' He gestured at the box.

Tiger took a step towards it, looked at it and then began to bend down. It quickly became apparent that he didn't have the flexibility that Leon had. He straightened up and tried again, this time bending one knee rather than both, and managed to get his face closer to the box but not close enough to pick it up.

'God, Tiger, you're rubbish at this,' laughed Angie. 'Let me have a go.'

Angie picked the box up but didn't make it look as easy as Leon had done. 'Ta dah!' she said through gritted teeth, the box wavering in the air.

Maggie knew that she was going to have to take her turn, but she had absolutely no idea whether this was something that she could do or not. She didn't want to look like an idiot if she couldn't, but she knew she'd look worse if she didn't try at all.

Angie put the box down. 'Your turn, Mags,' she said.

Maggie had rarely felt quite so self-conscious as she folded her body in two and reached for the box, but then was delighted to discover that picking it up was easy. A wave of relief rushed through her.

'Let me have another go,' said Tiger and, by copying the one-legged approach that Angie had adopted, he managed to pick the box up without falling over.

'Okay,' said Leon, plucking the box from Tiger's teeth. 'Now we tear this off' – he tore a strip of cardboard from the top of the box – 'and have another go.'

'I'm going to need another drink if I'm going to get all the way down there,' laughed Tiger.

They kept going round and round. Tiger dropped out on round three and Angie toppled over on round five and declared herself out. That just left Maggie and Leon. As each bent lower over the remains of the cereal box, Angie and Tiger cheered and whooped as if it were an Olympic sport.

Maggie hadn't thought herself to be particularly competitive, but with the punch racing round her bloodstream and Tiger watching her, she found that she really wanted to win. As the box got lower and lower the feeling grew. Leon was stiff competition, though, and they matched each other until there were only a couple of inches left of the box.

Leon went first. He was still making it look easy, his hips and torso allowing him to bend low enough. It looked as if he could have licked the carpet if he'd needed to.

It was less easy for Maggie. There was a real danger that she would topple over and land on her nose. She repositioned herself, planting her feet further apart, but then she lost her balance and fell. Rolling on to her back, she grinned up at the three faces looking down at her.

'I give up!' she said. 'You win, Leon.'

Leon began a celebratory circuit of the room, arms raised and cheering, and Angie tucked in behind him. Tiger dropped and straddled Maggie, pinning her arms down with his knees.

'Got you,' he said. 'There's no escape.'

He leant over so that she could feel the warmth of his breath on her face. She gave a half-hearted struggle to try to get free, but he sat firm, grinning at her. This was the moment, she thought. He was going to kiss her, and she didn't care that Angie and Leon were there to witness it. She just wanted it to happen. She looked into his face, trying to signal this with her eyes. He must know, surely. They couldn't get this close to one another and it not lead to a kiss.

But then she heard Leon shout, 'Maggie's down. All pile on!'

And then he was on her legs behind Tiger and the moment was gone. She could feel Angie come in and sit behind the two boys, and soon they were all lying on top of her, her breath being forced out of her lungs as their collective weight bore down. She could tell that Tiger was doing his best to take the bulk of their weight with his body, and moments later he tipped to one side and they all fell in a heap on to the carpet, gasping for breath.

'Are you trying to kill me?' she laughed, and they all denied it.

One by one they got to their feet, Leon offering Maggie a hand and hauling her up.

'Well done, Mags,' he said. 'A worthy opponent in the cereal box challenge, but, as it turned out, not quite up to the mark!'

'How did you do that, Lee? You must have been secretly practising for years,' said Angie. 'It's like the bloody saxophone all over again.'

Leon shrugged. 'I am a man of many hidden talents,' he said, grinning at her.

'Hmmm,' she replied. 'What time is it anyhow?'

'It's nearly twelve thirty,' said Leon. 'I don't think anyone's coming to our party.'

'Good job,' said Tiger. 'Someone drank all the punch! Well, there's a bit left. Who wants a bit more?'

They all passed him their cups and he scooped out the remainder.

'A toast!' said Angie. 'I don't care that no one showed up. I've had the best time with all my favourite people. Who needs anyone else? Please raise your glasses.' She held her cup aloft. 'I mean, your plastics. To us! Mates forever!'

A slurred echo of her words reverberated round the room.

15

THE NINETIES

1993

There was to be a gathering of the clans. Well, not actual clans, but Angie and Maggie had been invited round to Leon's place for dinner. Since university none of them had moved very far. Maggie and Angie were both still in York and Leon had gone back to live in Leeds so they were all within forty-five minutes of one another. Obviously, it wasn't the same as when they all lived in the same house, but they kept in touch and tried to meet up when they could.

Usually when they got together, food was just something that happened because they had to eat. It had never been the focus of the arrangement and so, when the formal invitation had arrived through the post and Angie had opened the crisp white envelope, she had nearly fallen off her beanbag. Who invited someone for dinner by letter? What was wrong with just ringing them up and asking them round? And this was from Leon, which made the whole thing even more extraordinary.

She and Maggie made the trip to Leeds together, Maggie driving whilst they speculated wildly about what on earth was going on.

'Maybe he's finally taken that contract at Ronnie Scott's,' said Maggie, 'and wants to celebrate in style with his oldest friends.'

'Sadly, I think it's more likely that I've taken up with Brad Pitt,' replied Angie. 'And believe me, I haven't.'

They pulled up outside Leon's flat, the ground floor of an old Victorian pile in Headingly which was surrounded on all sides by students and so was, as Leon had told them, 'reassuringly cheap'.

'Shit!' said Angie. 'We haven't brought a bottle. Shall we nip over to that offie and get something?'

'No. I've brought one of each,' said Maggie. 'They're in the boot. Right. Let's go and see what this is all about, shall we?'

It was obvious that something had changed in Leon's world within seconds of him opening the door. He was wearing a gingham shirt and a pair of beige chinos in place of his usual jeans and T-shirt. Angie was about to comment, but something about his expression made her hold fire. He was giving her the distinct impression that he would rather have been dressed differently and that she was not expected to tease him about it.

Instead, she threw her arms around him and squeezed him tightly. 'You're looking very dapper,' she said, but couldn't resist adding, 'Is this an interview or something?'

Leon didn't reply, opening the door wide instead and taking the proffered bottles from Maggie. 'Come in,' he said. 'Come in.'

The flat had been transformed. Usually, it was barely a step up from their student houses with books, sheet music and old coffee cups scattered across every surface. Now, though, everything was put neatly away, and the stark overhead lights had been eschewed in favour of more intimate table lamps. There was only one reason that Angie could envisage for these changes: Leon had a girlfriend.

Following her gut instinct, Angie glanced around the room and, sure enough, there was a woman sitting on the sofa behind them. She was smiling, but she made no effort to come forward to greet them.

'So, you two,' Leon said as the three of them stood rather awkwardly in the tidy space, 'I'd like you to meet Becky. Becky, this is Angie and Maggie, two of my oldest friends.' As he spoke, he rubbed at the palm of one hand with the thumb of the other and Angie realised, with a rush of affection, that he was nervous. But were the nerves about them meeting Becky or Becky meeting them?

Finally, Becky stood up, but she stayed where she was as if Angie and Maggie were contagious.

'Hi,' she said, managing a small, brief smile. 'Lovely to meet you. Leon has told me so much about you both.'

Angie took her in. She was small-boned and pointy-featured. Her fair hair was very straight and hung around her face, sitting on her shoulders. She was pretty enough, but in a precise kind of way, nothing about her standing out as being unusual or particularly interesting. She wasn't at all the kind of woman that she would have chosen for Leon, but precisely the kind that Leon would choose for himself.

'Hi, Becky,' said Maggie, and walked across to shake her hand. Who did that, thought Angie, apart from Maggie, of course? But Becky seemed perfectly at ease with the gesture.

Leon fussed around getting them drinks, but almost at once Becky excused herself to go and see to the food, leaving the three of them together.

'Leon, you dark horse!' said Angie. 'You didn't tell us you have a love interest. What happened to the Three Musketeers? One for all and all that?'

Angie was joking, but Leon frowned and shuffled in his seat.

'Sorry. I was going to tell you, but I wasn't sure where I stood with her and it felt too soon to make a big deal about it, but then

Becky suggested that we invite you over so you could meet. And so, here we all are.'

Ah, thought Angie. That formal invitation made sense now. It had been Becky's doing. She should have known that Leon wouldn't come up with something like that on his own.

'And she's living here?' asked Angie. This much appeared clear both from the flat's transformation and the fact that Becky was now in the kitchen on her own doing things to the food.

But Leon shook his head. 'No, not yet,' he said. 'We're taking things steady.'

Angie caught Maggie's eye, trying hard to keep her facial expressions under control. Becky had changed almost everything, and yet she hadn't even moved in. Poor Leon.

But who was she to judge? The important thing was that he was happy, and he did appear to be that, at least.

The three of them chatted easily, catching up on news until Becky called them through to eat.

The table that stood in the corner of the kitchen and on which they had eaten many a pizza and takeaway curry had also undergone an upgrade of sorts. There was a tablecloth and real napkins, and Leon's mix-and-match wine glasses all twinkled in the light coming from five tall candles that were dotted around. Angie had to hand it to Becky, who was obviously responsible. It looked amazing.

'Please sit,' Becky said. Her smile was a little bigger now. It must just be nerves, Angie concluded, that prompted the slightly aloof aura that she gave off. Angie could forgive her that. It was often a bit awkward, meeting new people, especially people who knew each other as well as they did. It wouldn't be surprising if she felt a little bit intimidated.

Angie pulled out the chair nearest to her to sit, but Becky shot out a hand to stop her.

'Not there, please, Angie,' she said. 'You're over there next to Maggie and then Leon is on this side with me.'

Angie had never been told where to sit before and it grated against her rebellious streak, but she didn't want to cause an atmosphere for Leon's sake.

'Okay,' she said sharply. She moved to the other side of the table. 'Here?' she asked, pulling out a chair.

'That one is for Maggie,' said Becky.

Angie eyed her coolly, pulled out the final chair and sat down.

'Glad we've got that sorted,' she said under her breath, and then felt Maggie slap her gently on her thigh.

'So, it's watercress soup and melba toast to start with,' said Becky, handing out bowls carefully. The soup was a rich green with a swirl of white cream across the top. It wouldn't have looked out of place in a restaurant and Angie had to admit when she dipped her spoon in and tasted it that it was excellent.

'So, what do you do, Becky?' asked Maggie.

'I'm a PA,' she said. 'To the managing director of Lutterworths, the furniture shop. You might have heard of them.'

Angie hadn't, but Maggie nodded enthusiastically.

'That must be interesting,' she said.

'And challenging,' Becky agreed. 'There's far more to being a PA than people realise. It's a highly responsible position.'

Was she competing with Maggie, Angie wondered? If she was, then she was on a hiding to nothing. Maggie had just been made partner at her law firm, the youngest that there had ever been. There was no way that a glorified secretary had more responsibility than that.

'And you're a solicitor?' Becky said to Maggie.

'In commercial property,' replied Maggie. 'I buy and sell those huge out-of-town developments, for pension funds mainly.'

Becky nodded, but she clearly didn't want any more detail. 'And you're a masseuse?' she said to Angie, pronouncing it as if she might catch something simply by having the word on her lips.

'I'm an alternative therapist,' corrected Angie. 'I give holistic treatments. Not massages.'

'How's it going?' asked Maggie.

'It's early days, but who knows. It might be a goer. In a few years' time I'd love to get some premises and maybe hire someone else too, but it's not always that easy to find the right fit.'

'I suppose that might be a bit tricky,' said Becky, and Angie wasn't sure if that was a comment about the nature of her business or her personally. She decided to give Becky the benefit of the doubt.

'Yes. I need to find someone whose ethos matches mine. I'm really interested in . . .'

But Becky stood up, scraping her chair across the floor, and started to collect the bowls. 'It's boeuf à l'orange and dauphinoise potatoes with string beans next,' she said.

'The soup was delicious,' said Maggie to Becky's back.

Angie raised an eyebrow, but was careful to make sure that Leon didn't see. She didn't want to upset him, even if his girlfriend was rude – and, Angie was beginning to suspect, not that bright.

As the evening progressed and the wine flowed, the conversation drifted back to their York days. Angie watched as Becky twitched in her seat with nothing to add, and desperate to turn the subject back to something she knew about.

'Have you heard from Tiger recently, Ange?' asked Leon.

'Yeah. He's in Australia living in the outback and working on a sheep farm. He's loving the space, but I think he's missing company. He's planning to move to Sydney soon and then go on to New Zealand or maybe over to Bali.'

'A nice concrete plan then?' smiled Leon. 'How very Tiger!'

'Yeah,' laughed Angie. 'You know him.'

'Actually, my boss, Mr Lutterworth Junior, has been to Australia,' said Becky. 'He said it wasn't up to much. There's nothing there, apparently. No culture or anything.'

Angie looked at her to see if she was joking, but nothing about her expression suggested that she was. 'The Aboriginal Australians are one of the oldest civilisations on earth,' she said. 'Maybe Mr Lutterworth Junior didn't really take much notice of what was all around him.'

'Oh, I'm sure he did,' said Becky quickly. 'He's very observant. But he said there was nothing. No old buildings or anything.'

Angie looked across at Leon, assuming that he would help her out, but Leon seemed to have had all his attention absorbed by the pattern on the tablecloth.

'I suspect your boss went with preconceived ideas,' she said icily. 'And only saw what he wanted to see.'

But Becky ignored her. 'It's tiramisu for dessert,' she said, and began to clear the plates.

They left not long after that. Maggie spun some line about having work to do the following day and Leon, who would usually have encouraged them to stay a bit longer, looked relieved that the evening was coming to a prompt conclusion.

'So, great to see you both,' he said as they stood at the door. 'We must do it again soon.'

The kisses that they exchanged were unconvincing.

◆　◆　◆

'Well, that'll be the last we see of him until he kicks her into touch,' said Angie as they drove away. 'She hates us.'

'Speak for yourself,' said Maggie indignantly. 'I got on perfectly well with her! But I take your point. She is a bit of a cold fish and

I'm not sure what Leon sees in her. He doesn't normally go for controlling women, does he?'

'Have there been any other women?' asked Angie. 'Controlling or otherwise? I can't think of any girlfriends that lasted more than a week or two. Maybe she is exactly what he's always wanted but couldn't find until now.'

'Perhaps she was nervous,' said Maggie. 'It must be daunting, meeting us when we're all so close. Maybe she's usually a little less, I don't know, abrasive?'

'Maybe,' said Angie. 'But my spidey-sense tells me that what we saw tonight is the real Becky.'

'Well, if that's true then we'll just have to put up a massive charm offensive and win her round,' said Maggie. 'Although I say "we", I really mean you, seeing as you were such a massive hit with her.' Even though it was dark in the car, Angie could hear the smile in Maggie's voice.

'Hmmm,' she replied. 'You mean, we need to save Leon from himself. Again.'

16

1997

Angie's client lay on the treatment bed. Even though she was motionless with her eyes closed, Angie could feel the nervous energy radiating off her. Every muscle was pulled taut. She could even see the tension in her flickering eyelids.

She was used to this. Her clients were often incredibly nervy before their first treatment and she had learned not to take this personally. It was nothing to do with her. She was just the facilitator. Sometimes it was the fear of the unknown that made them anxious, the fact that they were here for a treatment that they didn't yet quite trust and weren't really sure what was going to happen. Sometimes it was more to do with the client themselves and the underlying reason that they had come for treatment in the first place.

Either way, Angie had learned that the best way to deal with it was to be calm and gentle and hope that as the client relaxed, their anxieties would float away.

But not, it appeared, in this case. The client, Mandy, who had been recommended by a friend of a friend and about whom Angie knew next to nothing, suddenly opened her eyes and sat bolt upright. If Angie had been any closer to her there would have been a clashing of skulls, maybe even putting a tooth or two in jeopardy.

As it was, Angie had been turning up the volume on her CD player to cover the hum of the traffic outside and had been well out of harm's way when Mandy had risen from her bed like something out of *Beetlejuice*.

'I'm not sure this is for me,' said Mandy, her words crisply cropped. 'I think I'd better just call it a day.'

She swung her legs off the side of the treatment bed and started reaching for the ground with her toes. Angie leapt into action. Bookings were pretty thin just at the moment and she couldn't afford to miss any and still pay the rent. She had already had to steal from the groceries pot to pay the gas bill. She could have lived with a less-than-warm flat – she had survived far worse, after all – but a chill in the air did not create the right ambience for the clients and so her gas bill was always high.

'Please don't worry, Mandy,' Angie said now in her gentlest voice, pressing the client's name in an attempt to create an intimacy of sorts that their relationship didn't merit. 'Everyone gets a little anxious before their first treatment. I see it all the time. It's perfectly understandable, but honestly, you have absolutely nothing to worry about. Reiki is a totally natural process. As I explained, I won't even have to touch you if you'd rather I didn't. It's more a case of the transfer of energy. And that's the beauty of it. When I use the energy that runs through my body to realign the blocked energy in yours, then you will feel the benefit straight away.'

Of course, this wasn't always true. More than once, Angie had been accused of being a charlatan, a fake and a fraudster by clients who, despite her best endeavours, seemed unable to take any benefit from her treatment. Angie didn't mind – she knew that you can't please all of the people all of the time – but she hoped that the dissatisfied few kept their opinions to themselves and didn't do anything to undermine her business. At this stage, she had no idea which kind of client Mandy would turn out to be. So, all she could do was try and reassure her and then hope for the best.

'All I ask,' she continued, her voice as calm as she could make it, 'is that for the next few moments you place your trust in me and if, after we've started, you feel in any way uncomfortable, then you can just let me know and I will bring the treatment to an end. Now, what is there to worry about in that?'

Mandy's face suggested that she could see a very large amount to worry about, but she bit her lip, nodding with a minute gesture and lowered herself back on to the bed. She looked even less relaxed than she had done before, and a muscle had now begun to twitch in her neck as well. Angie would start work there and release that first, she decided, and she lowered her breathing and began to prepare.

She took the kantha quilt that she had brought back with her from India and laid it gently across the woman's body. Mandy flinched at the first touch and opened her eyes again, but this time she let them flutter closed almost straight away. Then Angie struck her Tibetan singing bowl with its felted wooden mallet and the clear ringing chime filled the room. The sound never failed to calm Angie. It reminded her of the ashram in Goa that she had discovered during her year out and that she still hoped to get back to one day. When the bowl's pleasing tone reverberated around her head, she felt safe and warm. She could almost imagine the Arabian Sea lapping at her toes, hear the bright-feathered parakeets calling to one another in the swaying trees. What she needed to do now was to transfer the sensation of well-being that it instilled in her to Mandy, who was currently a bag of nerves on the bed before her.

As she hovered her hands over Mandy, her eyes closed and her head clearing, she focused her attention on shifting the negativity that was blocking her client's chakras. It wasn't hard. Even with sceptical clients Angie found that if she could only get them to submit to her, she could reach a place somewhere deep inside them.

101

Whether they chose to acknowledge this was a different matter entirely. Sometimes a client would deny feeling anything at all, but Angie knew that that was only because they were not allowing themselves to accept the treatment. They would get down from the bed, shaking their head and complaining that they weren't in any way transformed, but it was amazing how many of them rang to make a second and third appointment.

She was relieved to feel, however, that Mandy was different. The relaxation of her body beneath Angie's hands was palpable. Despite her initial reluctance, it quickly became apparent that Mandy was going to submit herself entirely. Angie loved this part of her job, knowing that she had spoken to a part of someone that had, until then, been locked away; that she had released something inside them that even they didn't know was there.

She worked steadily, keeping up a commentary on what she was doing so that Mandy could relax still further into the treatment. By the time Angie had finished she knew both that some good had been done and that Mandy would be booking another appointment. By the time she struck the singing bowl again to signal the end of the treatment, Mandy was almost purring.

'Now,' whispered Angie, 'you just stay there for a few moments whilst you recentre yourself. I'll just be over there.'

Ideally, she would have a separate treatment room where she could leave the client to recover, but this was a one-bedroom flat and she wasn't about to give up her own inner sanctum to her clients. As it was, the treatment bed was set up in the middle of the lounge and she tried to disguise this by keeping her personal detritus to a minimum (no mean feat for Angie), and with the strategic use of throws.

Mandy came back to herself relatively quickly, and then sat up and wrapped her arms tightly around her torso as if defending herself from whatever power had just taken hold of her.

'How was the treatment?' asked Angie. 'Were you aware of anything that you don't normally feel, not that that's necessary, but sometimes clients do say . . .' She stopped talking. She needed to catch herself before she did this – lead her clients down a path that would allow them to criticise her – but this time there was nothing to worry about. Mandy was gushing.

'That was amazing,' she said breathlessly, her eyes shining. 'I don't know how to describe it. It was like I felt really warm, right here.' She pointed enthusiastically at her core. 'And then really cold. And my legs kept tingling. Is that normal, tingling legs? I practically melted into the table. I'm sorry I was so jumpy beforehand. I just had no idea what to expect but that . . . that was wonderful.'

Angie beamed, but she wasn't about to get lost in the praise. This was a business. She had to keep her focus. 'And so, shall we book you in for next week? Maybe we can move forward to me placing my hands on you, through your clothes I mean,' she added cautiously, but there was no need. Mandy was nodding vigorously as if she would be happy to be treated stark naked if that was what Angie suggested.

Money changed hands, an appointment fixed for the following week and Mandy appeared to float down the stairs and out into the street beyond, closing the door gently behind her. Another satisfied customer.

Angie began to redress the treatment bed for her next client. There were just the two today, but Mrs Meehan had been coming for a while and always booked a double session. The three appointments were enough to just about keep the wolf from the door. She was going to have to find something else, though. Living hand to mouth like this was manageable, but she had no savings and no way of improving her lot. She had been one step away from the street before, but she wasn't risking that happening again – not if she could help it.

17

Jax was coming to visit and there was a lightness in Angie's chest that threatened to bubble out into gleeful giggles and whoops, which wasn't that convenient in a holistic treatment room. It had been more than three months since she had last seen him, and six months the time before that. Theirs wasn't what you might call a conventional relationship. Living at opposite ends of the country and in an impecunious state for much of the time meant that days spent together were rare and precious. But they did what they could and so far, it seemed to be working out okay.

Angie had never been in love, and she was reluctant to label her feelings for Jax in these terms. Her life had shown her that love was for the weak, for those who lacked imagination, for misguided seekers of the 'happy ever after'. None of these terms could be applied to her. Being dependent on another person had never worked out that well for her. The last time it had happened she had been ten and the person had been her mother, but she had quickly discovered that she was much better off fending for herself. If she didn't rely on anyone else then no one could let her down. And no one could hurt her, either. She'd been hurt enough. She wasn't open for any more heartache.

But Jax was great. He made her laugh, and she fancied the bones of him. Like her, he wasn't interested in commitment. They had talked it through at various points in their relationship and concluded that they were both singing from the same hymn sheet as far as that was concerned. Commitment was bourgeois and unnecessary, but they were happy to carry on as they were for the time being in an uncommitted but monogamous relationship.

She busied herself cleaning the flat, which felt mildly ironic, given the squalid conditions where they had first met and spent time together. It was different now, though, and if she had a flat, she might as well do what she could to make it welcoming.

She ran a cloth around the basin and heard herself humming 'Things Can Only Get Better'. The wretched tune had been stuck in her head forever, and even though the election had taken place over a week ago with Labour romping home to victory, not least, no doubt, because the theme tune was stuck in heads across the nation, she couldn't seem to shift it. It was driving her nuts.

She looked around the flat and nodded to herself in satisfaction. Everything was ready. She had no client bookings for the next twenty-four hours, the fridge was full and the bed was clean. There was nothing to do but spend time enjoying each other's company. It was going to be a perfect weekend.

Jax was hitching up to Yorkshire and so his ETA was a little vague, but he had rung her from a phone box on the A61 just outside Leeds and so, assuming he could pick up a lift for the last stretch without too much bother, she wouldn't have much longer to wait. She was struggling to settle to anything, though. If she'd had a television, she could have turned it on for some mindless tea-time drivel, but the third-hand set she had borrowed from a friend had finally given up the ghost. It now sat in the corner of her lounge, hidden beneath a tie-dyed scarf, and was currently serving as a plant stand.

Her fluttery brain turned an unexpected cartwheel towards Leon. He once told her that he'd pick up his saxophone in moments of nervous tension and lose himself in his music. Angie had always envied him that escape. She wondered idly if he still did that or whether Becky had put paid to it.

She hadn't seen him for ages. Their lives had headed off in opposite directions after he'd met Becky. He was married now. Married! She and Maggie had been invited to the wedding and they had gone as each other's plus one. It had all felt very grown up and middle class to her and she couldn't quite believe it was happening, or that her friend had chosen to marry Becky. Leon had seemed radiantly happy and so Angie had had to conclude that she was missing something about his bride. There had been precious few meetings since that first dinner party – Becky's doing, she imagined – and so Angie hadn't had a chance to review her initial opinion of her; but Becky clearly made Leon happy and that would have to be enough. In the Christmas card that had as usual arrived promptly at the beginning of December, written in the neat girlish script Angie had come to recognise, it said that they had had a baby – a boy. Leon had a son! This had been such a surprise that Angie had shouted out loud when she read the news. It made her sad, though, that Leon hadn't thought to tell them that Becky was even pregnant. There had been a time when she and Maggie would have been top of the list, but days turn into weeks, months and finally years and you can lose the habit of keeping in touch.

She wasn't surprised by Leon's tumble into conventional life. If any of them was going to do the two-point-four children thing, then she supposed it was going to be Leon, although she had never quite given up on the hope that he would eventually drop it all for the smoky Blues clubs of New Orleans. Never say never.

But Leon and his sax were of no use to her now. She needed to find something to do to pass the time whilst she waited for Jax to arrive. Perhaps she could do some meditation. That might help calm her down. But just as she settled herself cross-legged on the sofa, there was a knock at the door. He was here, and faster than she had thought. He must have picked up the last lift easily.

She bounced up, heart drumming, and raced down the stairs to answer the front door, ready to hurl herself into Jax's arms, but as the door swung open she saw that it wasn't him but Tiger standing on the doorstep. Every fibre of her being sagged in disappointment.

'Surprise!' he beamed, but then his smile slipped as he took in her expression. 'Well, that's a great welcome, I must say,' he added.

Angie managed a small smile. 'Hi, Tiger,' she said.

'Well, you could look the tiniest bit pleased to see me,' he said. 'Can I come in?'

Angie desperately wanted to say no. Jax would be here any time now and everything was ready for him. The very last thing she needed was Tiger playing gooseberry.

'It's not that convenient right now,' she managed. 'I mean, if I'd known you were coming . . .'

Tiger looked a little taken aback, but ploughed on regardless. 'Oh, you know me,' he said. 'There's never a plan. I just go where the wind blows me.'

Well, the wind could blow him right back to where he'd come from, Angie thought. 'Yes, but I've got someone coming to stay. They'll be arriving any minute now. In fact, I thought you were them.'

'Even better,' said Tiger as he pushed her gently to one side and began to climb the stairs. 'The more the merrier. We can have a little party. I've got some great weed. Hid it in . . . Well, you don't need to know where I hid it, but Customs didn't find it.'

Angie sighed, took a long look down the street to see if Jax was anywhere on the horizon – he wasn't – and then set off up the stairs after Tiger.

'And there's no need to worry about me. I don't need much. I can kip on the sofa. I won't get in your way and I promise not to be too dazzling for your friend.'

This would be the moment to tell Tiger that rather than the girlfriend he seemed to assume was coming to stay, Jax was very much all man and Tiger would not be welcome whether he was on the sofa or not, but somehow the words stayed locked in her throat. What would be the point? She knew from past experience that there would be no shifting Tiger, not tonight at any rate. And he was one of her oldest friends. She couldn't just kick him out on the street, not when he had only just arrived.

Tiger dumped his rucksack on the floor in the middle of the room and flopped down on the sofa so that the length of him took up every inch. He was grubby and in serious need of a close encounter with plenty of hot water and soap, but other than that he looked well. According to a hastily scribbled postcard, he had turned thirty in a yurt somewhere in the Atlas Mountains, but to look at him Angie thought you would probably still place him in his mid-twenties. His body was tanned and athletic-looking and his face glowed with health. That must be what a life with no worries did for you.

'Beer?' he asked expectantly. 'As in, any chance of a . . . ?'

Angie sighed and took a bottle from the fridge. She passed it to him, and he flicked off the top with his thumbnail and took an appreciative swig.

'Ahhh. That's better,' he said. 'I've been looking forward to that.'

Angie was tempted to comment that there were plenty of other places to buy beer between wherever he had come from and her flat, but Tiger was Tiger. He was just acting true to form and she had never objected to his behaviour before, so it hardly seemed fair to start now.

'So, how've you been?' he asked her. 'Still here, I see. It's a nice little place.'

Angie shrugged. 'It suits me,' she said. 'But listen, Tiger. I really do have someone coming tonight and so if you could, you know, kind of make yourself scarce for a bit that would be great. The pub down the road is all right.'

If she could get him out until closing time at eleven o'clock then at least she and Jax would get a bit of time to themselves.

A smirk spread across Tiger's face. 'Like that, is it? You haven't gone and got yourself a bloke whilst I've been gone?'

Angie rolled her eyes as if she couldn't have cared less, but inside her she could feel a tell-tale heat building. She hoped she didn't blush. Tiger would never let her live it down. They had always been as one on the subject of relationships, neither of them feeling the need to find a partner in the traditional way of things. Sex had been something that had just happened, like them watching a film together or sharing a sunset. Fun, but with no emotional engagement. But now she had Jax, which not only altered the dynamic between her and Tiger, but almost felt like a betrayal of their unspoken agreement to float through life without commitment.

'Life goes on,' she said. 'I don't just sit around the place waiting for you to get back, you know.'

'Does that mean sex is off the agenda?' he asked. 'That's a bit of a bugger. I was looking forward to that almost as much as the beer.'

'God, you're such a charmer. And just because we might have done that in the past doesn't mean it's on the cards now.' She meant her voice to be light, but actually she could hear an uncharacteristic barb in her words.

Tiger clearly heard it too, as he put his palms out to her. 'I know, I know. I'm sorry. I was joking. Of course, I don't expect. I wouldn't . . .'

Angie nodded reluctantly. 'I know. It's just . . . Well, I like this bloke, Jax, it feels different to the others, kind of special, you know?' It sounded so cheesy, even to her.

'Is he some form of demigod?' Tiger asked. 'Or has he put you under a spell? You going all soppy over a bloke! Who are you and what have you done with the real Angie Osborne?'

'Don't be such a dick, Tiger,' she said. 'He's nice, that's all. And the whole world doesn't revolve around you, you know. Stuff happens whilst you're busy floating about the planet without a care.'

Tiger's face fell and Angie wondered whether she might have gone too far, but then he rallied.

'Well. I'm chuffed for you,' he said. 'I really am. It's about time you found someone special.'

He wrinkled his nose in a way that reminded her of when he was eighteen, and the tension that had settled on them dissipated. Resigned to what would be, Angie helped herself to one of the beers from the fridge and sat down on top of him.

18

They were just into their third beer each when the doorbell rang again. By that time, Angie had almost forgotten that she had been waiting for Jax and her first response to the bell was a mild irritation that someone was disturbing them. And then she remembered.

She got up hastily, flattening her hair with her palms and rearranging her clothes.

'Do I look okay?' she asked Tiger.

'You look hot!' he replied. And then, 'I don't mean hot as in too warm. I mean hot as in . . .'

Angie nodded. 'I got it. Thanks. Could you, er . . . ?' She cocked her head at his prone position.

'Oh, yeah. Don't want to look as if I live here. Might give your man the wrong impression. What's his name, anyway?'

'I told you. Jax,' Angie said.

'Jax? Isn't that a girl's name?' said Tiger as he levered himself into a sitting position.

'It's short for Jackson,' replied Angie. 'And could you do something with those?' she added, nodding at the empty bottles as she flew towards the stairs.

'Yeah. Right,' said Tiger vaguely.

At the front door, Angie gave herself a second to compose herself. She sucked her lips in and took a deep breath, which she released slowly as her head cleared. Then she opened the door.

She had forgotten how sexy she found Jax. Well, not forgotten exactly, but he still made her head and her stomach spin a little when she first saw him. He was taller than her but not tall, and his nut-brown hair hung around his shoulders in soft spirals. He had those eyes that look like melted chocolate, too. It was his eyes that did for her every time. Come-to-bed eyes, he'd once told her they were, the cocky so-and-so.

'Oh God, it's so good to see you. I thought you'd never get here. It's been like torture waiting for you.'

He opened his arms and she fell into him, his arms closing around her and squeezing her tight. She could smell the cut-grass scent of outside on his jacket, and beneath that, his own earthy aroma.

'Hi, baby,' he said. 'You missed me then?'

Angie nodded into his shoulder and stood, enjoying his physical presence until he gently pushed her away from him.

'Aren't you going to invite me in?' he asked.

'Yes, sorry. Come in, come in. But an old mate from my travelling days has just turned up unannounced. He does this from time to time. His timing is awful. I'm really sorry but I'll get rid of him tomorrow.'

'Tomorrow?' said Jax, disappointment thick in his voice.

'I know. It's a bummer, but he's only just got back to the UK and he's got nowhere to go. I'll sort it, though. I promise.'

Jax sighed, a slightly impatient sound tinged with irritation, but he didn't complain as he followed her up the stairs to the flat.

Angie was pleased to see that Tiger had indeed moved the bottles, tucked his rucksack behind the sofa and was sitting cross-legged

112

on the floor when they walked in. He stood up at once, proffering a hand to Jax who took it and shook it.

'Hi. Sorry about this, mate,' he said. 'I had no idea Ange would be entertaining. But look, I can get out of your hair. Where's this pub that you mentioned, Ange?'

'Don't worry, mate,' replied Jax. 'No need to race out on my account.'

Angie felt aggrieved. Of course, Tiger should be going out. It was beyond question. 'It's the Masons Arms, Tiger,' she said. 'Just down the road, by the zebra crossing.'

'Oh, right,' said Tiger enthusiastically, but his body language suggested that she had told him to go and take a late-night dip in the River Ouse.

'Don't be stupid,' said Jax. 'There's really no need. You might as well just stay here.'

His body language also belied his words, but what could Angie do if Jax was determined to be noble? She could hardly manhandle Tiger out on to the street. She went to the fridge, removed three bottles of beer from her dwindling stash and handed them out.

'Now you're talking,' said Jax and fell into the sofa, which objected loudly as if it had had just about enough of people abusing its springs.

'So, how was the journey?' asked Angie, positioning herself in Jax's lap so that there was no question of Tiger sitting anywhere but on the floor, which was where Tiger promptly placed himself.

'Long,' said Jax. 'I blame TV. I'm sure that before we had all this wall-to-wall crime drama it was much easier to hitchhike.'

'Definitely,' said Tiger, nodding fiercely. 'You used to be able to get a lift pretty much as soon as you stuck your thumb out, but now you can be standing about for hours before anyone picks you up.'

'You don't think it's got anything to do with the fact that neither of you are handsome youngsters anymore?' Angie asked with a smile. 'I think people are more reluctant to pick up adult men, and who can blame them? You could be serial killers for all they know.'

'Who are you calling a serial killer?' laughed Jax.

'Yeah, who are you calling a serial killer?' echoed Tiger. It made him sound like a child aping the adult in the room and Angie felt a bit embarrassed for him, but if Tiger noticed the awkwardness, he didn't show it.

'So, where did you two meet?' he asked.

'Up a tree,' replied Jax, throwing a grin at Angie that made her stomach flip.

'Well, not quite,' she clarified. 'We were both at Newbury.'

Tiger looked at them blankly and shook his head as if this meant nothing to him.

'The bypass protest? God, Tiger. Do you not watch the news?'

Tiger shook his head again. Angie supposed he didn't. He was rarely in the country long enough to get much of a grip on what was happening, and it was feasible that he might have missed the entire thing.

'So, they wanted to build a bloody great bypass,' said Jax. 'It was going to cut through whole swathes of Berkshire green belt. One hundred and twenty acres of ancient woodland destroyed just like that. Sites of scientific interest, the works. The road just went straight through the middle. Ten thousand trees massacred.'

'Bad news,' replied Tiger.

Jax rolled his eyes. 'You could say,' he replied sarcastically.

'So, loads of people went to protest,' said Angie, taking up the story before Jax had time to. 'There were all kinds there, from vicars and the WI to women left over from Greenham Common, and some that had been at Twyford Down. You've heard about that, right?'

Tiger shook his head again and Jax tutted.

'Even Johnny Morris was there!' continued Angie. 'You know, from *Animal Magic*? You must remember *Animal Magic*?'

Tiger began humming the distinctive theme tune.

'Yeah, that's the one.'

'And so, you two just ran into each other?'

Angie looked at Jax and smiled. 'Jax had been on site since the summer. Him and the others built themselves this whole village in the trees. Twigloos, they were called, their little houses. Dead cute. And clever. A feat of engineering really, the way they all lived up there. They could move about from tree to tree without ever having to come down.'

Jax nodded. 'Yeah. We stayed up there for months. There was like this real solidarity, you know. Anyway, then one day Angie showed up in the tree next to mine and we got talking and . . .'

'Not that convenient,' said Tiger. 'Love up a tree! Did you . . . ? I mean, up a tree!'

'For God's sake, Tiger!'

Tiger shrugged as if the question was just begging to be asked. 'So, what happened?' he asked. 'You must have come down eventually. Did you win?'

'In the end they cut the trees down,' replied Jax. Angie could still hear the bitterness in his voice.

'With you in them?' said Tiger, his eyes wide. 'How did that work?'

'Well, as good as. The bastards cut all the branches so we couldn't get down and then used cherry-pickers to pull protesters off. We held fast for as long as we could.' Jax hung his head as if he was single-handedly responsible for the failure of the protests against the new road.

Angie put out a hand and stroked his back reassuringly.

'Blimey!' said Tiger, taking a swig of beer. 'High drama in the treetops.'

He was grinning to himself as if he found the whole episode deeply entertaining, and Angie threw him a warning look. She was beginning to regret the four beers and not getting rid of Tiger when she'd had the chance.

'It was bloody serious, mate,' said Jax. 'There were people there prepared to die for the cause. I mean, actually die.'

Angie thought that Tiger was going to laugh at that, but somehow he managed to swallow it.

'I'm sure, mate. Big roads. Bad news. Seriously bad news,' he said, shaking his head.

Angie could feel Jax's body tensing beneath her. The last thing she needed was for these two to have a full-blown row.

'Anyway,' she said. 'So, that's where we met. Right, I'm suddenly knackered. How about we retire to the bedroom, Jax?' She gave him a wink which under normal circumstances would have been signal enough, but Jax, it appeared, was still gunning for a fight with Tiger.

'What you don't seem to understand,' he said pointedly, 'is just how much damage the road is doing. We can't replace all that woodland, you know. You can't just plant a few trees and hey presto, it all grows back. It was a habitat for God knows how many different species. The mammals, of course. Everyone thinks about the badgers and the cute little rabbits. And the birds obviously lost their homes. But the insects and the plant life. And the microscopic organisms like lichen and fungi. They had been growing there forever, since the Big Bang for all we know. And then they were all gone. Just like that. Totally unforgivable.'

'Yeah,' said Tiger. 'I can see that. Poor little bunnies.'

Jax sat up so quickly that Angie had to hold on to the sofa so that she didn't get flung to the floor.

'Are you always this much of an arse?' he said to Tiger.

Tiger shrugged. 'I'm just saying, man, that when you've seen as much of the planet as I have it's hard to get too worked up about a tiny patch of woods in a tiny country like England. Destruction of the rainforests. Now there's a serious issue. Destroying the ozone layer. Shit. Yes! Let's get worked up about that. But a bunch of tree-huggers in leafy Berkshire – I'm sorry, but I just don't see it.'

'Boys, boys, let's take this down a notch or two, shall we?' said Angie. They weren't boys, of course, but fully grown men, although their behaviour might suggest otherwise. 'Let's just agree to disagree, shall we?'

She pulled a meaningful face at Tiger, widening her eyes in her effort to get him to back off. She knew from experience that once Jax got the bit between his teeth it would be harder to distract him, and she really didn't want her weekend spoiled by a stupid argument like this one.

'Yeah, sorry,' said Tiger. 'I guess we all have causes that are close to our hearts.'

Jax didn't reply, but that was good enough for her.

'Right,' she said. 'We'll see you tomorrow, Tiger. Sleep well.'

Tiger looked at the clock on the wall. 'It's eight forty-five,' he said, as if he were a primary school child objecting to his bedtime. Then he caught her drift. 'Ah, right. I'm a bit knackered myself as it goes. It'll do me good to have an early night. I'll see you two tomorrow.'

Angie mouthed 'sorry' at him and then took Jax's hand. 'Come on, you. Let's go and catch up on what we've missed.'

She grabbed the last two beers out of the fridge and pulled a still fuming Jax into her bedroom, banging the door shut behind them.

'That bloke is a total jerk,' spat Jax almost before the door shut.

'He's all right, really,' she replied, not wanting to irritate Jax any further but still feeling the need to defend Tiger. 'He's just not tuned into the stuff that we are. He travels so much that he finds it hard to focus on the micro. But his heart's in the right place.'

Jax harrumphed, pacing up and down like a leopard. It wasn't that big a space and he could only go a few steps before he had to turn round. Angie tried not to laugh at him. That really wouldn't have helped.

She lowered herself down on to the bed and arranged herself provocatively.

'Come and lie down, baby,' she said. 'Forget about Tiger.'

She patted the cover next to her but Jax was having none of it.

'What's the story, anyway, between you two?' he asked.

Angie knew what he was getting at, but it really wasn't going to make things any better if she gave him all the details.

'We met on my year out,' she said. 'In India. And then I came home to go to uni and he stayed where he was. He's been travelling ever since. He doesn't have a base in the UK any more so if he comes back he floats around begging favours until it's time to leave again.'

'Bloody scrounger,' said Jax. His mood seemed to be getting blacker by the minute and Angie could see her lovely precious time slipping away from her.

'Oh, let's not worry about him,' she said. 'Come here. Relax. Have another beer and let's just chill. I can give you a massage if you like, release those tangled chakras.'

He seemed to relax a little then and came to lie down next to her. A wave of excitement rippled through Angie's body at the proximity of his to hers. She swung her leg over his hips, sat astride him and began to rub at his shoulders and the top of his neck.

'You're so tense in there, baby,' she said as her thumbs worked at the knots. She hoped that this didn't set him off again, but he finally seemed happy to leave Tiger where he was on the other side of the door.

She wasn't really surprised that Jax didn't understand Tiger or their unusual relationship. Sometimes, she wasn't sure that she understood it herself. They had been friends for over a decade, although the time actually spent together over that period couldn't have amounted to more than a handful of weeks since she had been back in England. And Jax was right – Tiger was something of a scrounger. He'd show up out of the blue, just as he had done today, and expect shelter and food whilst making no effort to contribute to the cost. He did help around the flat; it wasn't as if he expected to be waited on hand and foot. And she supposed that he had to hang on to whatever cash he managed to earn to pay for his living expenses when he was abroad. But still, he definitely seemed to expect that she would be up for supporting him when he arrived.

Still, whilst she didn't have so much spare cash herself, she didn't begrudge him it. He had been there for her, in India, when she had most needed a friend. He had sat up with her late into the night as she had tried to make sense of what had happened to her in life thus far – her mother, the children's homes, the feelings of never belonging, never being secure or safe. It was Tiger who had listened without judgement, not tried to fix anything – what could he fix, anyway? – but had just let her work it all through in her own head. And for that she would be eternally grateful to him in a way that she would never be able to fully explain to someone else.

She would be the first to accept, though, that Tiger was far from perfect. His thirty-year-old self hadn't really changed that much from the eighteen-year-old she had first met. His outlook remained unsophisticated, despite all that he had seen in the world, and his needs were very simple. Angie had discovered a long time ago that there was very little point trying to get into any kind of political argument with him. He just had no interest, and anything that he did say was generally just a parroted version of what he had heard others say rather than a genuinely held belief.

But Tiger had something about him that none of her other friends shared. A kind of courage. It took balls to have no base, no stuff, to go where you wanted with neither aim nor plan. She didn't think she could do it – well, not for year after year. She liked to think that she kept her horizons wide but at the end of the day, her dreams were tethered, like a hot air balloon, so that they couldn't just float off whither they would. Tiger's were different. The only thing holding him back was gravity.

But she couldn't explain any of this to Jax. All he saw was an irritating ignoramus who was trespassing on his patch. That was fine. She didn't feel the need to share what she and Tiger had with Jax. If he was going to be in her life for any length of time, then he would get used to the random appearances of Tiger at inopportune moments. And she did hope that Jax would be in her life, for a while longer at least.

And with that in mind, she turned Jax over beneath her so that he was facing up and began to kiss him with everything that she had.

19

Princess Diana was dead and the entire country, as far as Angie could tell anyway, had gone completely mad. She had never heard so much weeping and wailing and gnashing of teeth. The carpets of flowers placed outside Kensington Palace also had to be seen to be believed. There were more flowers strewn on the ground than must have been grown in an entire summer, or so it appeared. It felt, Angie thought, as if everyone had channelled any bit of sadness or grief from their own lives into the mourning for this stranger. As a result, the atmosphere was weird, the energy somehow disjointed.

Angie did feel sorry for the little princes though, following behind their father to look at the floral tributes. They looked like miniature adults in their ridiculous grown-up costumes, keeping a stiff upper lip as they must have been taught to do. All this repression of grief would only store up problems for them in later life, Angie was sure. She wanted to shout at them to scream and cry and release those pent-up emotions in whatever way felt most natural to them, but who was she to tell them anything?

But despite all the oddness, normal life had to continue. Long before anyone had known what was coming down the track for the princess, Angie had received a bright orange envelope through the post. It contained a cheerful invitation, also orange but with jaunty blue elephants scattered across it, inviting her to attend Thomas's first birthday party. Initially Angie had been confused by it, not being immediately sure who Thomas was. She didn't know any children and certainly none well enough to be invited to their birthday party. The RSVP request cast light on the mystery, however – Leon and Becky. Was their child one already? Angie supposed he must be. It was hardly the kind of thing that you made up.

Angie had to swallow down her resentment when she saw Becky's name. Becky had stolen Leon from them, or Leon had allowed himself to be stolen. Angie wasn't sure which was worse. But at least she'd been invited to the birthday celebrations, even if she was a duty invite. Maybe Becky would feel less threatened by Leon's old friends from now on. Angie hoped so, because she and Maggie weren't a threat to her. Well, not really.

Then Maggie rang. At least Angie saw Maggie more frequently than she saw Leon, but even with Maggie it was hard to get together, so busy were they with their day-to-day lives. They spoke every week, though, keeping up with each other's news. Maggie seemed to be doing well at work and when they did meet, she was always beautifully and expensively dressed (though Angie's eye was not that tuned in to these things), and she drove a natty little convertible that Angie secretly coveted. But there didn't seem to be much in her life outside her job. Her social life was made up mainly of work-related dinners or dull parties with her colleagues, and there was no suggestion of any romance. Maybe being a lawyer was like being a policeman. You ended up being married to the job.

'Have you been invited to the birthday party?' Maggie asked now.

'What birthday party?' Angie had replied, just out of badness because she knew the suggestion that Maggie had put her foot in it would make her squirm.

It did.

'For Leon's boy's birthday, Thomas, you know.' And then, 'Oh my God! Have they not invited you? I'm so sorry. That's so insensitive of me. I had no idea. I just assumed because I'd got one that . . . oh God. How embarrassing.'

Angie, grinning down the phone, let her off the hook. 'You're so easy to wind up, Mags. I'm only kidding,' she said. 'Of course I got one. Are you going to go?'

'Oh, for God's sake,' tutted Maggie. 'You can be very irritating, you know, Angie Osborne. Anyway, I thought that if you were invited then we could go together and if it's totally awful, we can slope off and go and get a cup of tea somewhere. What do you think?'

Angie liked the idea a lot. She was determined to try a little harder with Becky from this point on, but it would be easier to do that with Maggie by her side. Leeds was less than an hour away and Maggie had the natty car. If she drove them there Angie wouldn't even have to fork out for the train fare.

'Why not?' she replied. 'Let's go and meet Leon's progeny!'

So, a plan was made. On the day of the party, Saturday 6 September, Maggie would pick her up from the flat and drive them both to Leon's house.

But that was before anyone knew that it would be the day of the biggest funeral since Winston Churchill's.

When Maggie picked Angie up there was not a soul out on the street. Everyone, it appeared, was inside watching the service on the television. Angie had no television and wouldn't have watched anyway, but Maggie seemed quite aggrieved.

'You would have thought that they'd push the party back a couple of hours,' she said as she set off down the deserted road. 'I'm taping the service, but I would much rather be watching it in real time.'

'Why?' asked Angie. For once she wasn't trying to be difficult. She really didn't understand. 'You didn't know her.'

Maggie turned and stared at Angie before snapping her head back to look at the road. 'No,' she said. 'Of course, I didn't *know* her, but it feels like I did.'

Angie shook her head. Wasn't this just rubbernecking of the worst possible kind?

'And those poor boys,' Maggie continued. 'They've lost their mother.'

Angie sniffed. 'Lots of people lose their mothers,' she said. 'That's just life. And she wasn't even royal any more. Not that that should make any difference. I can't see why one dead rich person merits all this fuss.'

Angie could feel the irritation rising up from Maggie, who had clenched her jaw so hard that Angie could see the outline of it through her cheek.

'Well,' said Maggie huffily. 'I'm just saying that I, for one, would have liked to have watched it. But we are where we are. Now, there's a map on the back seat. I've written the route down on that piece of paper. Can you navigate once we get into Leeds? I'm okay in the city centre, but I get a bit lost in the suburbs.'

Angie smiled to herself. Of course, Maggie had the route written down already.

'Yep,' she said, 'but don't blame me if I get us lost.'

'You can't get lost. All you have to do is just . . .' Maggie turned to face her and then realised that Angie was joking. She rolled her eyes. 'Oh, ha ha,' she said. 'Very droll.'

Leon's house turned out to be a neat little semi in a road of neat little semis, each nearly identical, with neat square gardens at the front and clean cars parked on neat driveways to the side. It was Angie's idea of hell.

'How has this happened?' she asked. 'Our lovely Leon living in this suburban horrorfest.'

'I think it's quite nice,' said Maggie.

'Nice. That's precisely the word.' Angie pronounced the word as if it meant the precise opposite. 'This isn't Leon, though. He's got so much more about him than this.'

'No,' disagreed Maggie. 'This *is* Leon. It's just that you've always wanted him to be someone else.'

Angie considered this for a moment.

'No,' she said. 'I want him to be true to himself. And this . . .' She waved her arm in the direction of the street. 'This is not it.'

Maggie got out of the car and popped open the boot from where she took out a small box exquisitely wrapped in blue paper with white curling ribbon. Angie looked at it curiously for a moment. Then it occurred to her what it was.

'Shit!' she said. 'Am I supposed to have brought a present?'

Maggie looked at her, eyebrow raised. 'Well, it is a birthday party,' she said sarcastically.

'Oops,' said Angie. 'It never even crossed my mind. I don't suppose . . .' She looked balefully at Maggie's box.

'No!' said Maggie indignantly. 'This is my gift.' Then she sighed and rolled her eyes. 'Oh, I suppose so. I haven't sealed the card, suspecting that something like this might happen . . .' She eyed Angie like a schoolteacher with a disappointing pupil. 'And . . .' She went back into the boot and brought out a second box identical to the first. 'I do have this one spare.'

She grinned at Angie.

'It's a train and there were some carriages too, so I bought both and got them to wrap them separately. You owe me fifteen quid. Pay me when you've got it,' she added.

Angie felt humbled. Not only did Maggie know her well enough to know that buying a gift would never have occurred to her, but she had fixed the problem for her too. That was why cool, organised, slightly anal Maggie was her friend. Why she was Maggie's friend she had absolutely no idea.

20

There were blue balloons with Happy First Birthday written on them tied on to the gatepost and attached to the knocker of Leon's neat front door.

'I love the way people do that with the balloons,' said Maggie. 'It makes the birthday into a real community affair. I always smile when I see them.'

Angie had never seen birthday balloons on houses before. She assumed that this was because having children was so far off her agenda that she had never noticed or maybe it wasn't something that they did in York, although that seemed unlikely. Then again, Maggie had no children either, so Angie wasn't sure why it was a practice that had registered with her. They had talked about children from time to time, most recently on the arrival of the birthday party invitation.

'Don't you think it's strange that of the four of us, only Leon has settled down and had a kid?' Angie had asked.

'Not really,' Maggie replied.

'But I'm thirty-one, and you're not far behind me,' Angie had continued, 'and yet we're both still single and childless.'

'Child-free,' corrected Maggie. 'Happily child-free in my case. And no, I don't think it's strange. Unusual maybe, but not when you look at who the four of us are. None of us has taken the traditional path, except Leon. I'm not saying that it won't happen. Thirty-one is no age and there's still plenty of time for you to have a baby if that's what you want.'

'But you don't want?' asked Angie. She had always assumed that Maggie wanted children, but now she came to think about it, she realised that it wasn't something she had ever actually said.

'No, I don't think so,' Maggie had replied thoughtfully. 'I love my work and I could only carry on with that and have a child if I employed a nanny. Why have a child if I never see it because I'm always at work?'

'Plenty of women use childcare,' objected Angie. 'It doesn't make them a bad parent.'

'Of course not,' said Maggie. 'I think it might even make them a better one. I just know that I wouldn't want to divide my attention like that. And it's all immaterial anyway because I don't have anyone to father a child.'

'Well, that's easy enough to fix,' said Angie.

'How? With carefully timed one-night stands? I'm not sure that's for me,' laughed Maggie. 'What about you? Do you still want kids?'

Angie had thought for a moment. She wasn't sure that Jax was the fathering kind, but then she didn't exactly have a lot of experience of fathers in general to know what the fathering kind might be. She did want a baby, though. Or, to put it another way, she couldn't imagine a future without children in it.

'Yes,' she'd said. 'I think I do.'

◆ ◆ ◆

Maggie knocked on the door of Leon and Becky's neat house. They could hear the ear-piercing screeching of small children coming from inside.

'It's not too late to change our minds,' said Angie with a smirk.

The door opened and there stood a harassed-looking Leon, a plastic toy lawnmower in one hand and a disposable nappy in the other.

'Oh, it's you two. Thank God. Please, come in and talk to me. If I get caught in another conversation about baby signing or swimming lessons for newborns, I shan't be responsible for my actions!' He opened the door wide and ushered them in. 'And on top of all that it's the bloody funeral and half the mothers are watching it and bawling their eyes out. I was expecting crying children but not crying parents. Hang on.'

He disappeared into what appeared to be the sitting room and returned a moment later sans nappy just as Maggie was depositing the gifts on the hall table, balancing them carefully on top of a huge pile of others.

Seeing the identical wrapping, Leon smirked at them both and winked at Maggie. 'Thanks, Mags.'

Angie rolled her eyes. 'And me,' she said, but she couldn't quite pull off the fake indignation and grinned back at him. 'You got me. Presents are always Maggie's department.'

'You should have pushed the start time back,' said Maggie pointedly, clearly still irritated about missing the funeral.

'Becky said that,' said Leon. 'But I was sure that it wouldn't make any difference. I mean, the woman's dead!' He shook his head in mock despair. 'How wrong can you be?'

Maggie raised an eyebrow at Angie but didn't say anything. 'Well, it will be over soon enough. Is there anything we can do to help?'

Leon grinned at her. 'You always were great in a crisis, Mags,' he said. 'But no, I think we have it under control. Becky tried to get the pass the parcel started but no one was interested so she's given up and gone to join the rest of them gathered around the TV. And the babies are with their mothers so it's all good. Drink?'

Maggie looked at her watch as if to question the earliness of the hour, but Angie ignored her.

'Yes, please. What have you got?'

'Red, white, beer and then some organic, non-sugary juice. And water.'

'Beer, please,' said Angie without missing a beat.

'Coming right up. Mags?' Leon asked her, but she shook her head.

'Driving,' she said. 'I might just go and . . .'

'It's through there,' said Leon, nodding in the direction of the television, and Maggie scuttled off.

Angie followed Leon through the house to the kitchen where a group of men, she assumed the dads, were standing around holding bottles of beer and chatting. Leon was still grasping the lawnmower as if his life depended on it. Suddenly noticing that it was there, he deposited it by the back door next to a little blue plastic truck that also appeared to have been a birthday present, judging by the ribbon adorning its steering wheel.

'This is Angie,' he said to the assembled crowd. 'Mate from uni. No kids. Lucky sod.'

Angie bestowed a grin on them all and then took the proffered beer.

A few pleasantries were swapped for a moment, but then the men drifted back to their own conversations leaving Angie and Leon to one another.

'This is a great set-up you've got here, Lee,' said Angie, gesturing vaguely. 'And a garden too. Shall we go outside for a bit? You can show me round your estate.'

Leon threw a glance towards the sitting room, but everything seemed to be calm in there for the moment, so he nodded. There was a stairgate blocking the way to the back door that he released with a deft flick of his wrist, then opened the door and stepped outside.

The sky was a pale elephant grey with darker rainclouds looming on the horizon and threatening to roll in.

Leon looked up appraisingly. 'It just needs to keep dry until one o'clock, when they all leave,' he said. 'Becky wanted to do the whole party outside, but that seems to have fallen by the wayside, what with the funeral. I don't suppose there'll be much time left by the time they've finished with that, but then we can go back to plan A. Maybe we'll just end up going on for longer.'

Angie wasn't sure exactly what kind of party a bunch of one-year-olds actually required. Could they even walk, let alone run around? She had no idea. Babies were a totally closed book to her. If she had remembered that a birthday gift was required, she would have had no idea what to buy. She wasn't interested enough to ask Leon about it, though.

The garden was, like the rest of the house, very ordered, with a green striped lawn in the middle and tidy beds around the edges. There were patches of colour everywhere, all clashing wildly with one another but at the same time creating an overall impression of cohesion.

'Does Becky garden as well as everything else?' she asked with a smirk. 'I suspect she is actually Wonder Woman in disguise.'

From what she had seen of the place so far, Becky seemed to be superhuman. Nothing was either out of place or less than beautiful, although from the little Angie knew about her, this wasn't surprising. Becky was definitely the kind of person who would make sure that her house radiated just the right vibe.

However, Leon shook his head. 'No,' he said. 'The garden is all my work.'

A fond smile crossed his face, as if he saw the garden as an additional child.

'Bloody hell! Really?' exclaimed Angie. 'You never fail to surprise me, Lee, but I didn't have you down as a budding Alan Titchmarsh.'

Something crossed Leon's face that might have been hurt at being underestimated, but it was so fleeting that Angie wasn't sure it had been there at all.

'I've always liked growing things,' he said. 'When I was a kid, my dad gave me a patch in his garden. I grew veg to start with. Nothing complicated. Carrots, radishes, that kind of thing. But after a couple of years, I switched to flowers. I love putting the colours together, keeping the interest there all year long. It's dead easy in summer, of course, but from now until spring it's more of a challenge. Like pitting your wits against Mother Nature.'

'Well, you seem to be winning,' said Angie appreciatively. 'It really is lovely, Lee. Really.'

The barest wash of colour flushed across his cheeks and then was gone.

'Thanks,' he said. 'It's a kind of escape. From . . .' He cocked his head in the direction of the house. 'Well, you know. Babies can be exhausting, and they don't respect anyone else's needs.'

Angie recalled that he had once said much the same to her about his music when they had been living on opposite sides of a corridor.

'And what about your sax?' she asked, certain that it couldn't be far from his mind, either.

He shrugged sadly. 'I don't play much these days. There never seems to be the time. And I used to play at night but that keeps Thomas awake. Apparently.'

This final word was added in a tone that suggested that he wasn't convinced it was true, and Angie had to agree. In her experience, there was little more soothing than listening to Leon play jazz.

'Sounds to me like you're under the thumb,' she laughed, but she was only half-joking. Leon had always been a bit stiff, not really wanting to step that far from the path, but this wasn't the life that she had envisaged for him, not even close.

'No, not really,' he replied. 'I know you had big dreams for me, Ange, but they were your dreams, not mine. I always wanted something much smaller, more in line with what my family expected of me. And we've worked hard to get what we have, Becky and me. I'm proud of it.'

Angie had no concept of doing what her family wanted her to do. In fact, she couldn't even imagine what that might be, but she could feel Leon slipping away so she changed direction. 'And so you should be,' she said quickly. 'It's lovely what you've made, the pair of you.'

He smiled at her, grateful, it seemed, that she was not going to criticise his choices, but Angie thought that she could see regret there, too. Surely a part of him must wonder, must have played through the 'what if' scenarios in his head. He had such a talent, of that there was absolutely no doubt. And now he wasn't even playing music at all. It was such a waste and he must know that in his heart, if he ever dared to look there. There was nothing, however, to be gained from pointing that out to him now.

'And what about you, Ange?' he said, turning the tables on her in a way that she hadn't seen coming. 'Do you have any regrets?'

Did she? Looking back wasn't an occupation that Angie had ever wasted any time on. What was the point? She couldn't change the past.

'No! Of course not!' she replied breezily. 'When you've got no plan then what is there to regret? Life is just one long adventure. I love what I do. My business is building up nicely and my clients are great. It'll be a little holistic empire soon.'

Leon put his arms around her and squeezed her tightly. 'It's so great to see you, Ange,' he said. 'Don't ever change.'

Angie was a little taken aback, but she squeezed him back.

'You remind me of . . .' he continued. 'Well, it's just great to see you. Let's make sure we don't let things slip too far.'

'Maybe we can meet up some time, just the three of us,' she suggested. 'It's been ages. We could go to a bar in Leeds, get some food. It'd be just like old times.'

Leon nodded, but something about his face told Angie that he didn't think it would happen.

'They're not small forever, Lee,' she added. 'Kids do grow up, and then maybe it'll be a bit easier for you to get away. And even you must get some time off for good behaviour.' She doubted that it was Thomas's age that was the stumbling block here, but she'd taken comfort from the fact that Leon did seem to want to see them more often, even if the logistics were tricky. 'I'll tell you what,' she continued. 'Next time Tiger shows his face, let's all go out. It'll be great. I know we're all busy but I'm sure we can manage one night off without the world coming to an end.'

Leon gave her a rueful smile. They both knew that she was really talking about him.

'Don't you worry,' she added. 'You'll have to run pretty fast to shake me off. I'm not going anywhere.'

They were still outside, happily chatting about life's inanities, when Maggie joined them. Her face was red and blotchy and her eyes had narrowed, but her make-up appeared to have remained perfectly in place. She had probably worn waterproof mascara especially, Angie thought.

'Hi, you two,' she said as she approached.

'Is it all over?' asked Leon.

'Not quite, but there's only so much emotional upheaval a girl can take, so I've bowed out early. What are you up to?'

'Just setting the world to rights,' said Angie.

'Is the world all that wrong?' asked Maggie. 'It all looks pretty good from where I'm standing.' She let her gaze wash over Leon's glorious garden.

And Angie decided that she was right. Life wasn't perfect, but it wasn't bad, either. Unless you were Princess Di, of course.

21

THE NEW MILLENNIUM

2000

Angie lifted the little plastic stick and peered at the tiny window. One line for not pregnant. Two for . . .

Was it there? Could she see the faintest shadow of a thin blue line in the second window? She wouldn't like to testify to its presence in court but, in her heart, she knew the answer with or without the line. She was closely enough in tune with her body's energy to know when something was different, and this was most definitely different. Her heart rate was higher than usual and her breasts were sore for no reason that she could see. But even putting the meagre physical symptoms aside, Angie just knew that she was carrying a tiny little embryo inside her. She couldn't explain why, but she was certain.

She examined the stick again. The second line was faint, there was no denying that, but it was most definitely there. She was pregnant.

Feeling slightly dazed, she began to wander around the flat, picking things up without purpose and then replacing them. Pregnant. With child. A bun in the oven. It didn't matter which way you put it. In approximately eight months from now, all being well, she would be a mother. A mother!

The fact that she found herself here wasn't a total surprise, however. She had stopped taking her pill a while ago. It had never sat well with her, pumping artificial hormones into her system. Taking it had begun as a matter of convenience around the time of the Newbury protests. Living up a tree was hard enough without having to worry about periods on top. Then she had met Jax and the pill had really come into its own. After that, continuing to take it had been more habit than anything else. But in recent years, as her interest in holistic healing had grown, she had become more uncomfortable with the idea of swallowing a chemical every day. And as she had sex so rarely, it hardly seemed necessary.

So, she had taken a chance, played fast and loose with Mother Nature; Russian roulette against the chances of everything being in alignment. And she had lost.

Or maybe she had won?

Angie would have been lying if she'd said that the chance of finding herself pregnant had not occurred to her. Of course, there was a risk that sex without contraception might lead her there. And yet she had proceeded exactly as before, making no attempt to reduce the risk, and this suggested to her that in her heart she thought a pregnancy would not be so disastrous. She was thirty-three years old and she had always fully intended to have a child at some point. It was just that that point had never arrived.

But it was here now, stomping down the street with a full ticker-tape parade and trumpets blaring. This was the moment when Angie Osborne was to meet her destiny and have her child.

She went to stand in front of the mirror and turned sideways, pulling her yoga pants down to her hips to reveal the place where the egg had lodged itself. There was nothing to see, no outward indication of the frantic multiplying and remultiplying of cells inside. She let her fingers trace across her skin with the lightest of touches, the wonder of it overwhelming her. It was like magic, an alchemy of sorts. From the least prepossessing components, her body had created a living thing. It was nothing short of miraculous.

A baby.

Jax. She would have to tell Jax and she knew that he would take a little longer to come round to the idea. Theirs was a very 'in the moment' kind of relationship, the future being something that rarely came up in conversation. They had floated happily from one encounter to the next as the years drifted on. From time to time, she had suggested that things might work better if they lived in the same county at least, even if not the same building. Her holistic health business was thriving and that tied her to York, but Jax moved from job to job as opportunities arose. He was, as he liked to tell her, location-independent, and yet there seemed to be a certain reluctance to head much further north than Birmingham.

'Being apart is what keeps us together, babe,' he had said the last time she suggested that he might want to look for something a little closer to her, and she had accepted that because she thought he probably had a point. There was a lot to be said for independence and Angie treasured hers. But if there was to be a baby? Well, that would change things, surely?

She wouldn't tell him just yet, she decided. After all, it was very early days and she might set the cat amongst the pigeons for nothing. And they weren't due to be seeing each other for a couple of months. He had only just been up to visit her – as her current state attested; this must be a Millennium Eve baby, or thereabouts, and January was barely two weeks in. There was no harm in keeping her news to herself for the time being, whilst she got her head around it.

Well, maybe not entirely to herself.

Later, after the last client of the day had gone home, Angie picked up the phone and dialled Maggie's number.

'Are you busy?' she asked. 'Do you fancy meeting up for a drink tonight? Or tomorrow?'

There was a slight hesitation before Maggie spoke that might have been interpreted as reluctance, but Angie knew was simply the sound of Maggie reconfiguring her plans for the evening.

'That would be great. Usual place? Eight?'

They tried to meet once a month or so, although sometimes that stretched a little. Whilst Maggie had the fuller diary, it was actually Angie who cancelled the arrangement most often, usually because she was too tired after a day on her feet to make the trip back into town. Of course, Maggie would only cancel if the four horsemen of the apocalypse trit-trotted through her office, but then that was Maggie all over.

The 'usual place' was a wine bar on Goodramgate, more Maggie's kind of place than Angie's to be honest. It had a smug, self-satisfied air about it to Angie's way of thinking, and seemed to be frequented by the type of people who wore a suit and tie to do their important job and then talked loudly about it in public. The stench of heady perfumes and aftershaves could sometimes be enough to floor a rhinoceros. Angie always made sure that she wore her brightest, least conventional outfits and then enjoyed the turned heads and elbow nudges as she made her way through the wall-to-wall Boss and Armani to join Maggie.

Maggie was there first – of course – and had already been to the bar. A crisp gin and tonic and a pint of snakebite sat on the table in front of her.

'I assume that's okay,' she said as Angie sat down, nodding in the direction of the pint glass.

Angie looked at the glass, then back at Maggie and twisted her face.

'I'm sorry,' said Maggie, getting quickly to her feet. 'I just assumed. I'll go back to the bar. What do you want?'

'A pint of orange juice?' replied Angie.

'Hungover?! On a Wednesday,' said Maggie, but then she must have seen that she was wrong. 'Oh my God! You're pregnant!'

The routes that Maggie's mind followed never failed to impress Angie. She would never have leapt so deftly to that conclusion. In fact, she doubted whether it would even have occurred to her. And yet Maggie had nailed her news in one shot. It was almost disappointing.

She nodded.

'And . . . ?' Maggie continued.

She was being asked whether this was a good thing or not, Angie understood. Here she was, not four hours since she had discovered the truth for herself and she was having to jump one way or the other.

But she found that this was not a difficult answer to give.

'It's good,' she said, nodding as she spoke as if confirming the fact to herself. 'Yes. Definitely good. A surprise – it's most definitely a surprise – but a good one.'

Maggie beamed; a big broad smile that held nothing but joy at the news.

'I'm delighted for you,' she said. 'Congratulations. Let me go and get you that orange juice and then you can tell me all about it.'

She returned a few minutes later with a pint glass full to the brim of orange juice, ice cubes clinking against the side as she put it down carefully on the table next to the abandoned snakebite. Angie thought that the snakebite actually looked far more appealing. She'd had a shock, after all. But she dismissed the thought. This could be the first of the very many sacrifices that would follow.

'So?' said Maggie. 'Tell me everything.'

'Not much to tell. I did a test this afternoon and that's pretty much it.'

'And what did Jax say? I assume it is Jax's?'

Maggie knew about Jax now, although she had never met him. He wasn't the kind of partner that you paraded at a dinner party, and their time together was so rare that Angie guarded it preciously.

She stretched her face into a look of mock horror. 'What *are* you saying?' she said.

'Okay.' Maggie smiled. 'But it's always best not to make any assumptions. So, what did he say? Is he pleased too?'

Angie scratched at her dreadlocks. 'He doesn't know yet. In fact, no one knows but you and me.'

The look of flattered delight that appeared on Maggie's face touched Angie's heart. But then Maggie returned to her pragmatic self.

'How come?' she asked. 'Are you worried he won't be as pleased as you are?'

'It doesn't really matter what he thinks,' replied Angie, a tinge of defiance in her voice. 'It's my body.'

'Yes, obviously,' said Maggie. 'But it's his baby. He has a right to be consulted.'

'And I'm not saying that I won't tell him. I'm just saying not yet. I'm barely four weeks pregnant. There's no harm in keeping it to myself, and you,' she added, 'for a couple more weeks whilst I think through all the implications.'

Maggie gave a little nod in recognition of the validity of the point.

'And how do you think he'll react?' she asked.

Without having met him, Maggie had no way of predicting this for herself, Angie realised. Then again, Angie wasn't entirely sure she could call it, either.

'I think he'll be shocked at first,' she replied. 'But then I think he'll like the idea.'

'And if he doesn't . . . ?'

Maggie always did this – asked the question that Angie would rather not know the answer to.

'If he doesn't then he can swivel,' she said with more vitriol than she had expected. 'But I think he'll be okay with it.'

Maggie nodded, accepting this. 'And what about you?' she asked more gently. 'How do you feel?'

'I'm excited,' Angie said. And as she said it, she realised that she really was.

'Well, I have news too,' said Maggie with a smile, 'although it's pretty paltry by comparison to yours.'

'Oh yes?' said Angie, taking a slurp of her drink and pulling a face as she tasted orange juice and not the alcohol that her brain had clearly been expecting.

'I've been asked out. On an actual date,' said Maggie, one eyebrow raised.

Maggie's love life was quiet, to say the least. In all the time they had been friends, Angie had never known her go out with anyone for more than a couple months.

'My life is my work,' Maggie had said more than once. 'When I'm busy there isn't time for a relationship and when I'm quiet I just want to sleep to get ready for when I'm busy again.'

'But don't you get lonely?' Angie had asked. She had stressed the last word, the question really being about the apparent lack of sex in Maggie's life, but Maggie had batted the question away.

'Not really. I have all I need.'

Angie wasn't sure how this could be true. Then again, didn't she survive for most of the time on her own, Jax only making the trip north every few months? She wasn't pining away from lack of human touch. But then she knew that it was there for her, however infrequently. Angie had difficulty believing that Maggie was quite the island that she made herself out to be, and yet Maggie just kept proving her wrong.

'Who's the lucky bloke?' Angie asked now.

Maggie's cheeks bloomed and Angie grinned at her. Here they were, thirty-three years old and Maggie still blushed when she talked about boys. It was sweet really.

'His name is Adam,' Maggie said, 'and he's a pension lawyer. He lives near Thirsk and he has a golden retriever called Charlie.'

'I hope he's more interesting than he sounds,' Angie said, laughing. 'Pensions! Christ. Is he sexy?'

Maggie contemplated the question for a moment.

'Define sexy,' she replied eventually.

'You know. Does your heart race when you see him? Does he make you want to pull him into the nearest stationery cupboard and bonk the arse off him?'

Maggie contemplated further.

'No,' she concluded. 'But he is perfectly pleasant, and he doesn't talk about pensions the whole time.'

'Oh, well he sounds practically perfect,' said Angie sarcastically.

Maggie gave her a stern look. 'It's just a dinner date, Ange. I'm not about to marry him.'

'Bloody good job,' said Angie. She let a beat go by and then she said, 'Tiger rang last week. He's in Andalucía, near Granada somewhere. He says the Alhambra is beautiful and that I need to get myself over there. Practical to the last, eh?'

Angie knew it was wicked of her to tag Tiger on to a conversation about sexy men, but she couldn't help herself. She watched Maggie carefully for the reaction that she knew would come.

Maggie set her face into an expression of feigned indifference and said, 'Oh? How is he?'

'Same as ever,' replied Angie. 'The happy wanderer.'

Maggie nodded, and Angie let a pause punctuate the conversation. Maggie would never be drawn on her feelings for Tiger. Angie had thought it was something to do with not wanting to step on her toes, and she had tried more than once to make it clear that her own friendship with Tiger was almost totally platonic, but still Maggie kept her counsel.

'Is Adam the Pensions Lawyer as sexy as Tiger the Nomad?' she teased.

Maggie gave her a withering stare. 'I'm sorry I mentioned Adam now,' she said. 'I shan't next time and you'll need to get your gossip fix from somewhere else.'

She was grinning.

22

Business was brisk at Angie's wellness centre. As well as the reiki, she was now offering energy psychology and well-being coaching. She had also taken on a reflexologist, Kate, who she had met on a training course, and the pair of them had moved into premises off Fossgate and rebranded the place as Live Well. It was a world away from working out of her lounge. The centre had a little reception area and two treatment rooms, and there was even a tiny shower room that had been craftily shoehorned into what had once been a storage cupboard. Her clientele was growing all the time, and mainly by word of mouth, which Angie found very gratifying.

Of course, things would have to change when the baby was born, but Angie was certain that she could take the baby to work with her. Babies were small and portable, weren't they? And they slept a lot. So, by reshuffling her hours a bit and maybe taking someone else on part-time, she could keep things ticking over until she was ready to go back full-time. She wasn't fazed by what lay ahead. Like everything in her life, she would just make it up as she went along.

What was currently taking her attention were the difficulties that came with working through her constant nausea. Whilst she had been mercifully spared full morning sickness, the waves of low-level queasiness could come upon her at any minute, which she found just as stressful. She had tried ginger in all its forms – raw, crystallised, tea, and even just as a plain ginger snap – but it did little to quell the fear of constantly being on the brink of disaster. Acupuncture was also supposed to help, so she had booked herself an appointment with a practitioner that she knew. The results, she had to admit, were mixed, despite her strong desire for this to be the panacea she sought, but it had given her something else to focus on for a while. She had just been on the verge of having to tell Kate what was happening to her body and why she had caught her devouring a packet of salt and chemical-laced prawn cocktail crisps at eight in the morning, when the sickness finally lifted, and she began to feel more like herself. It was such a relief to feel normal again, and she congratulated herself on having made it through the first three months relatively unscathed.

But Jax still didn't know.

Angie had told herself that this was because she wanted to tell him face to face and was waiting for his next visit before she broke the news. It was a perfectly reasonable stance to take, and so it had allowed her not to examine her motives too closely. The Easter holidays were almost upon them and Jax had managed to swing the bank holidays off, so he was planning to come north for a long weekend. Angie's excitement at seeing him was barely tainted by the apprehension of how he might react to their news. The longer she had to get used to the idea of the baby herself, the stronger her conviction that Jax would be fine with it. There was even the tiniest hint of a bump now for him to relate to. How could he not fall in love with the idea when he could rest his hand on his growing child?

And if he didn't? Well, that no longer mattered that much. Angie had moved beyond those concerns. She was happy. If he was too, then that was perfect, but if not, she would just manage without him. She was under no illusion that he would up sticks

145

and move to Yorkshire, and so whatever he said, she knew that she would be pretty much on her own anyway.

When he rang the doorbell on Good Friday and she bounded down to open it, it took him less than a minute to realise what had happened. Something about the look on her face, perhaps, her glowing skin, her serenity. Whatever it was, Jax could see it in her straight away.

He looked into her eyes, holding her gaze a moment longer than he might have otherwise, and then let his eyes drop to her stomach.

'How did that happen, then?' he asked.

She thought his tone suggested curiosity rather than anger, but she had been hoping for a more enthusiastic response to her revelation. Angie held her breath, ready to defend herself and her unborn child, but hoping that she wouldn't have to.

'I don't know,' she said, not entirely truthfully. 'But it did.'

'And, how are you?' Jax asked. His features softened a little, as if the shock was wearing off.

'I'm great,' she replied. 'I was a bit sick at the beginning, but now . . .' She paused, still not sure of how he would feel about her having kept their news to herself, secretly buried deep inside her with the embryo.

'Good,' he said, but he didn't ask how long she had known she was pregnant or when the baby would be born. He was clearly still processing. 'Are you going to let me in then?' he asked instead.

They were still standing on the doorstep, she realised now, but first she took a step closer to him and wrapped her arms around his neck.

'God, am I glad to see you,' she said into his collarbone as she breathed the familiar scent of his body deep into her lungs. He hugged her back, his wiry arms squeezing tightly around her so that she felt protected and safe. She had lived most of her life without any touch. Sometimes, she even wondered whether she had chosen her profession to make up for what was so lacking in the rest of her life – physical human contact. But he was here now, and things were going to be all right, or at least that was what the hug suggested.

They broke apart and he followed her up the stairs. She wanted to ask him about his trip, to try and keeps things normal, but the words wouldn't come. She resisted the urge to turn and climb the stairs backwards so that she could watch his face.

Once in the flat she could finally look at him properly and concluded that his expression was bemused more than anything else.

'A baby,' he said. 'Us. God. I mean . . . Well, God.'

Angie grinned back at him.

'And how far gone are you?'

'About fifteen weeks. It's due in September.'

His eyes dropped to her stomach again, and she lifted her top to show him the small but distinct rounding.

'I've never thought about being a dad,' he said. His voice was wistful, as if this thought was genuinely occurring to him for the very first time. 'It is mine, I assume,' he added, but she could tell that he was joking. She punched him lightly on the arm.

'And you're happy with the whole single parent thing?' he asked.

And there it was. His actual response to her news. Angie felt the security of his embrace, moments before, leaving her. It was a shock, but she wasn't surprised, not really. Jax didn't want security and a baby. She didn't doubt that he loved her, but that was all there was.

'Of course,' she said, raising her chin a little higher. 'I'm not expecting anything from you.'

'Good,' he continued, nodding. 'Because I can't give you more than we have now. You know the score, babe. It's just not practical.'

'I do know that,' replied Angie. She could feel the little peep-hole of hope that she had allowed to open up inside her closing like a touched sea anemone, its tiny tentacles being sucked safely back inside. She was fine with this. She had known that if she decided to have the baby then it would be down to her. Jax might lend moral support from afar, might even contribute financially, but the day-to-day survival of the child would be down to her and her alone.

And she had been through it in her head a hundred times – she was totally confident in her own ability to not only rise to the challenge, but to shine. What she lacked in a role model she more than made up for in sheer determination to make a better job of it than her own mother had done.

'But I want to be a part of its life,' continued Jax. 'I want it to know who its daddy is. Even though I'm not around much.'

Suddenly, all became clear to Angie. This was who she was in a relationship with. The level of commitment that he had been prepared to offer her was now being matched by what he would give to their child. And she had been prepared to put up with it. It had even suited her.

But no longer.

'Well, let's see how it goes, shall we?' she said.

23

Maggie heard the news when she got home from work. There was a message on the answerphone, the little light blinking like a welcome beacon as she stepped into her hallway.

Quickly she hit play.

'It's me. I can't talk for long. I've only got one 10p and the Nazi midwife won't give me any change. Anyway, the baby has landed. It's a girl. Seven pounds five. Cute as a button. Mother (that's me!) and baby both doing well. Can you ring Leon? And Tiger is staying in my flat for a bit. Can you ring him too? No name yet. Please come and see us. They are going to keep me in for a couple of days and I'll go out of my mind on my own. Bring decent food. The stuff in here is disgus . . .' BEEP BEEP BEEP. 'Got to go. Come tomorr . . .'

Then the line was cut.

Angie had had the baby and it was a girl! Maggie wrapped her arms tightly around her shoulders and gave herself a big squeeze, swaying from side to side as she thought about it. A tiny baby. Born and safe. It was perfect.

But how on earth was Angie going to cope? The practicalities threatened to dispel Maggie's joy almost at once. Angie's only income came from the business and she had no savings, as far as Maggie knew. If she couldn't work, then she would soon run out of cash. The flat was rented, so she might lose that if she didn't keep up the payments, and then there was the rent on Live Well, too. And just how patient would her clients be once they realised that they could actually get their treatments elsewhere from someone who hadn't just had a baby and was perhaps more focused as a result? On top of all that, what worried Maggie most was that Angie didn't appear to be worrying about any of it in the least.

And where was Jax in all this, she wondered – and not for the first time. Once they had established that he was definitely the father, there being no other potential candidates, he seemed to have fallen from their discussions, Angie refusing to be drawn on what his role would be. Maggie had assumed that he was going to come up to York and help, at least in the early days whilst Angie found her feet, but she realised now that Angie had never actually said this. There had been no falling out between the pair of them, though, not as far as she was aware anyway, so Maggie imagined that at least one ten pence piece had gone on telling him that his daughter had arrived. Maybe he would be at the hospital, too. She might finally get to meet him.

In the meantime, she would continue to worry for Angie, Maggie decided. Someone had to, as Angie seemed incapable of worrying about herself. Thus far, she had shown no doubts about her ability to bring a child up on her own, not a single one. But was this just plain naivety? Maggie had always admired Angie's relentless optimism. This time, however, she couldn't help but think that it might be slightly misplaced.

For now, though, she had been charged with a task and she needed to discharge it. She picked up the phone and dialled Leon's number. After just two rings, Becky answered.

'Hello,' she said, her voice tight and in a half-whisper. Maggie checked her watch. It was seven thirty – bedtime. A more sensitive friend might have waited until Thomas and his younger brother were clear of bath and bedtime routine before interrupting, but Maggie was not attuned to the movements of a house with small children within it. She cursed herself silently for her lack of thought.

'Hi Becky. It's Maggie,' she said quietly, as if the infants were actually in the room with her. 'Is Leon there?'

'He's putting Thomas to bed,' Becky replied shortly. 'Can I get him to ring you back?'

'Yes, please,' said Maggie. 'Tell him Angie's had a little girl. We're going to visit tomorrow at two if he wants to come.'

There was the briefest of pauses.

'A girl. How lovely,' said Becky, although her tone suggested that she wasn't pleased. Had she been hoping for a girl, Maggie wondered? Surely healthy children should be enough. 'I'll tell him,' Becky added.

'And get him to ring m . . .'

But Becky had put the phone down.

Next, she had to ring Tiger. Maggie hadn't known that he was back in York, not that it would have made any difference to anything, not really. Still, if there was a chance of bumping into him as she went about her daily business, she would rather know. The fact that they might have inadvertently shared an aisle in a supermarket somewhere gave her the briefest of thrills and she rolled her eyes at herself. She was thirty-four years old. Would she ever get over her adolescent infatuation with him? It wasn't as if they had ever got any further than a chemical spark and a bit of harmless flirting. Each time there had been hope of something more solid, the opportunity had been snatched away from them. She hadn't even seen him for – she added it up in her head – it must be at least five years, possibly more. In the early days after leaving university, she had tried to keep tabs on his comings and goings by gently probing Angie for information, but once Angie had become wise to what she was doing, she had stopped. She could endure many things, but relentless mocking from Angie wasn't one of them. She had some pride to maintain, even now.

She dialled Angie's number, her hand trembling as she punched out the digits. It rang three, four, five times. He wasn't there. He must be out somewhere doing something that had nothing to do with her. Maggie let a little fantasy that he was actually on his way over with a celebratory bottle of wine play out in her imagination. So, when the ringing finally stopped and a male voice answered, she had almost forgotten what she had been doing.

'Hello,' he said, his voice thick as if he had only just woken up.

'Tiger? It's Maggie.'

'Oh hi. Sorry, I was asleep. Jet lag. Body clock's all over the shop. You okay?'

Maggie smiled to herself. No change there then. Would there ever come a time when having no base and being constantly on the move lost its appeal for him? She had to assume that he would reach that square eventually, but they weren't there yet, it appeared.

'Yes, I'm fine. I'm ringing because Angie asked me to. She's had the baby. It's a girl.'

The whoop that came down the line was so loud that Maggie had to hold the phone away from her ear until he had finished. She smiled as she waited for him to return to her. That natural exuberance of his was contagious, even now.

'So,' she continued once he had stopped shouting, 'she asked if you, me and Leon will go and see them tomorrow. I'm not sure when visiting is but it's usually around two o'clock. I can swing by and pick you up if you like,' she added.

'That would be great. I could walk, but I've got no idea where the hospital is.'

'It's no trouble. You're on my way,' Maggie said. 'I'll be with you around one thirty. That should give us plenty of time to get there and park.'

'Fantastic. Thanks Mags. See you then.'

He had put the phone down leaving Maggie feeling as if an opportunity had somehow been squandered. Should she ring him back and ask if he was busy that evening? She was pretty sure he wouldn't be, and she certainly didn't have anything on. Her hand hovered over the redial button, her finger outstretched, but she didn't press it.

24

Maggie's stomach was like jelly as she drove up Angie's street the following day searching for a parking space. It was ridiculous, she told herself, that she should be so nervous, and yet . . .

She found a spot a couple of doors down from Angie's flat and turned off the engine. She felt compelled to check her appearance in the vanity mirror, but she resisted. She had looked fine when she had left her house not fifteen minutes before. Why would anything have changed since then? She needed to get a grip. This was not a date. She was picking up Tiger to take him to see Angie and the new baby. That was all.

She rang the doorbell to Angie's flat and moments later she could hear Tiger locking the door and then pounding down the stairs towards her. She saw his shape through the opaque glass of the internal door and then there he was.

Tiger.

He hadn't changed. His hair was still bleached blond by the sun and spiking up around his face like a corona. His skin was tanned to a rich mahogany, which made his eyes appear even more blue and his teeth white. He was a little heavier than he had been, his rounded stomach pushing gently against the buttons of his cambric shirt, but in essence he was just the same. She wondered what he saw when he looked at her, but she felt confident that she wasn't ageing too badly. She certainly wasn't in danger of bursting out of her clothing.

'Well, look at you,' he said. His face was lit up with what certainly looked like genuine pleasure and Maggie felt herself relax a little.

'Hi. You look well. Just in from . . . ?'

'Vietnam,' he said. 'The killing fields and all that. Landed a week ago and got here on Wednesday.'

'Didn't you want to go with Angie into hospital, be her birthing partner?'

He pulled a face. 'God, no. All that blood and . . .' He blanched before her eyes, the healthy tan fading instantaneously. 'I don't do well with . . . Never been that good with medical stuff.'

Even describing what he didn't like was too much of a challenge for him, it seemed. Maggie shook her head like she might if he were a boy who didn't like carrots.

'It's not really medical though, is it,' she said, 'having a baby? I would love to have been there. It must be incredible to see a baby born.'

And as she said this, she realised that it was true. Why hadn't she thought of that before? She could have asked to be Angie's birth partner. She was never going to experience childbirth for herself so that might have been the perfect alternative. Too late now, though.

'So, why weren't you there?' he asked, a little defensively.

'Wasn't asked,' Maggie replied simply, and immediately realised the flaw in her embryonic and now unfulfilled plan.

Tiger grinned again, the chilliness leaving him as quickly as it had arrived. 'That's Ange all over. Independent to the last.'

They reached Maggie's car and Tiger patted the roof appreciatively.

'Nice wheels, Mags,' he said, and then got in. 'And no sign of Jax either, I assume,' he said as he fastened his seatbelt.

'No,' replied Maggie. 'I'm not sure whether it was in the plan for him to come up, but he doesn't seem to have done if he's not at the flat.'

'He's not there,' said Tiger. 'Thank God. He's a bit intense for me, you know what I mean. Everything's a bit serious.'

'I've never actually met him,' said Maggie, feeling slightly put out that Tiger had done.

'I've only met him the once, but believe me, you're not missing much,' he said. 'I know Angie likes him and all that, but I didn't warm to him. You wouldn't either.'

Maggie thought that she would have preferred to have been given the chance to make her own mind up on that, but decided that she had no option but to take Tiger's word for it, at least for the time being. Now that the baby was here perhaps there would be more opportunities to be introduced.

They drove to the hospital, Tiger talking all the way, telling her about Vietnam, what he'd seen, where he had stayed and who he had met. He made it sound magical and exciting and for a few minutes Maggie was caught up in the romance of it all, until she thought about how Tiger had nothing and no one. Her life wasn't entirely enviable, but at least she had a home and a job and stability.

Once at the hospital, they followed the signs to the maternity ward and were ringing the buzzer to be let in almost bang on two o' clock.

They found Angie in a bay at the far end of the corridor. She was sitting up in bed, dressed in a baggy paint-spattered shirt with the baby at her breast. Her auburn dreadlocks were tied away from her face in a cotton scarf. She looked tired but radiant.

'Hi, you two. Come see what I made!' she said in a stage whisper.

With delicate movements as if she were touching a butterfly wing, she pushed the hospital-issue blanket away from the tiny infant so that the side of her face, the top of her shoulder and a wrinkled little hand were visible.

'Here she is. Romany Rose Osborne.'

Maggie took a step closer and bent over to look at the baby. 'Oh, Ange. She's so beautiful.'

In truth, it was hard to see much of the baby from that angle but actually, it was the fact of her that was beautiful. Angie had created this tiny, perfect little person and her facial features, whatever those turned out to be, were of no importance next to the miracle of her birth.

'She's got my nose,' said Angie proudly, and Maggie was more than happy to take that on Angie's say-so.

'And how was it, the actual birth?' she asked. She had listened to enough birth stories over the years to have a fairly clear handle on what amounted to a good one and what didn't, even if her own personal experience was lacking.

'All over pretty quickly,' said Angie. 'No pain relief, of course. I used my pranayama breathing exercises. The midwife said she had never seen anyone so calm for a first birth.'

Tiger was looking a little queasy again, but this seemed to be all the detail they were going to get.

'And have you got everything you need?' asked Maggie.

Angie shrugged. 'They've got nappies in here, although they said I should probably get some myself. I'm going to use washable ones, so I'll buy them when I get home. Jax sent a pack of three babygros so that should do her for now. I'm feeding her myself so what else do I need?'

The question was sincerely asked. Maggie thought of the baby shower parties she had been invited to through work, the mountains of tiny clothes and mysterious equipment that one baby seemed to require. But actually, perhaps Angie was right. Clothing, nappies and food – these had to be the basic needs of any newborn.

'Well, maybe I can get you some nappies to be going on with,' she offered, 'and a couple of extra outfits so you don't have to wash every day.'

Her eyes scanned the room for Angie's birthing bag and rested on a tiny beaded tote that was hardly big enough to carry her own day-to-day necessities, let alone what was needed for a stay in hospital for two people, even if one of them was very small. She was reminded of their first day at university, to which Angie had also turned up woefully unprepared. This time it was different, though. She couldn't just wing her way through this. Now she had a child, there were responsibilities that she had to step up to.

Angie must have sensed something of her thought pattern. She spoke, her voice so quiet that Maggie had to strain to hear her. 'Thanks, Maggie. I can do it, you know. And I will. This baby is going to have the best I can possibly give her. She is going to grow up happy and safe and secure and loved.'

'Of course she is,' said Maggie. 'Of course she is.' And despite her doubts over the practicalities, she knew it was true.

25

It was only when Maggie got home that she realised that Leon had not shown up at the hospital. She and Tiger had stayed for the whole of visiting time, each taking turns holding Romany and rocking her gently to sleep. Tiger had regaled them with more stories from his travels and when Angie had napped, her head drooping forwards as her eyes closed, the two of them had sat in silent wonder, awed by what they saw.

Of course, Angie wasn't the first of them to have a baby – Leon had two already – but somehow, the fact that Angie was a mother held more sway so soon after the birth. Fathers faded into the background, unable to hold a candle to the mother. Yes, Leon had two sons, but he hadn't pushed them forth into the world and so somehow, as far as their group was concerned at least, Angie's achievement was so much more astonishing.

No one had mentioned whether Jax was coming or how Angie was going to cope, or what she would do with her business whilst she took some time away with Romany, but none of that seemed to matter next to the birth of a healthy child. They were all practicalities, details to be worked out at a later stage.

Maggie made herself a cup of tea whilst she processed all this. And then she picked up the phone and dialled Leon's number once more. This time he picked up.

'We missed you at the hospital,' she said, once the obligatory questions about his family were out of the way.

There was a pause.

'What?' he said. 'Why were you at the hospital? Are you okay?'

'Yes. We went to see Angie – she's had the baby. It's a girl, Romany Rose. I rang last night to tell you, but you were putting Thomas to bed so I asked Becky to pass the message on. Did she not say?'

'No,' replied Leon. He sounded confused as to why this might have happened, although if pushed, Maggie might have suggested that Becky had failed to tell him on purpose. 'She didn't say. She must have forgotten. I'm sorry. How was Angie? How are they both?' Maggie could hear the genuine delight in his voice and felt irritated with Becky for denying him the chance to see Angie and Romany for himself.

'They are amazing,' she replied. 'Romany is so gorgeous. She's totally perfect. A little gem. And Angie is positively buzzing although she's exhausted. Tiger was there too. He's staying at Angie's for a couple of weeks before he goes away again. It's such a shame you weren't there. But maybe the four of us can get together when Angie gets home. I think they're going to discharge her tomorrow or Monday.'

'Yes,' said Leon, 'that would be great,' but something about the way he said it told Maggie that it wouldn't happen.

◆ ◆ ◆

Angie and Romany were discharged the following Monday and Maggie drove across York to the hospital to pick them up. Angie had said that there was no need to bother and that she would get a taxi, but Maggie wouldn't have put it past her to save the fare and try to walk with the baby on her shoulder.

Of course, Angie had no car seat, and no need for one as she had no car, and so Maggie, assuming that this might be the first of many such trips, took a detour to Mothercare. After a thorough examination of the very many types of car seat that were available, she decided to buy one that came with a carry cot and pushchair. These items, however, turned out to be extraordinarily complicated and Maggie had to concentrate hard as the shop assistant explained the many working parts and how they all slotted together.

'It's a gift,' Maggie explained when the assistant was clearly confused by the lack of either a bump or a baby. 'For a friend,' she added unnecessarily.

'Lucky friend,' said the assistant, her eyes flicking to the price tag.

Maggie also bought washable nappies and liners, a bucket to store them in, a bumper box of disposable nappies in case Angie had a change of heart, a changing mat, some tiny vests and baby-gros, a set of bedding for the carrycot and a little green elephant in plush velvet that was so soft that she had to fight the urge to tickle her lips with it. The total bill was eye-watering, but Maggie didn't mind. She had enough money, and Angie would have bought nothing in readiness. It would be a pleasure to give her the items and make a useful contribution to the new household.

When she arrived at the hospital to pick Angie up, she found her dressed and ready to leave, although she had brought so little with her that it was hard to tell if she had packed up or not. She was just staring at the sleeping Romany, confounded, as if she couldn't really believe that she was real, and when she looked up, Maggie could see her eyes glistening.

Maggie lifted the car seat up high, as if it were a flag seized in battle.

'All set?' she asked.

'What's that?' asked Angie, looking at the seat in confusion.

'My new car seat,' said Maggie, 'which I am going to use to transport your baby back to your flat. Or were you going to let her roll around on the back seat?'

'I was just going to hold her,' said Angie, but the midwife who was stripping the bed shook her head.

'You can't do that, Angie. It's against the law,' she said. 'And anyway, we wouldn't let you leave if you didn't have a suitable car seat for Baby.'

Angie shook her head as if she was astounded at the bureaucracy of it all, but she smiled gratefully at Maggie.

'Is there ever anything that you don't think of?' she asked her.

'Nope,' replied Maggie. 'Right, do you want to get her in it?'

Angie picked the sleeping Romany up out of the bassinet. The baby flailed her arms about and threw her tiny head from side to side in protest, but she didn't open her eyes. Angie settled her into the seat and Maggie showed her how the straps fastened, and then the little group of three left the maternity wing.

'I bet they think you're my girlfriend,' said Angie, and Maggie rolled her eyes.

Maggie's convertible car had almost no boot space and so her purchases were crammed into the back seat, leaving very little room for Angie to sit, but somehow, they managed to squeeze in, Angie lowering herself into the seat gingerly.

'What is all this crap?' Angie asked, flapping a hand at the plastic bags and boxes. 'Your car's never a mess.'

'All this crap, as you so delightfully put it,' replied Maggie in a mock arched tone, 'is my gift to Romany to celebrate the occasion of her birth.'

Angie looked more carefully then, peering into each bag in turn and then finally looking at the huge cardboard box containing the 'travel system'.

'Oh my God, Mags. This lot must have cost a fortune.'

'Well, Romany must be worth it,' replied Maggie.

There would be no gushing expressions of gratitude, she knew that, and that wasn't why she had been so generous. The single, 'Thanks, Mags,' that she heard coming from the back of the car was all she needed.

'You're welcome,' was her simple reply.

They arrived back at Angie's flat, a raggle-taggle bunch with Angie carrying the lighter of the plastic bags of booty and Maggie bearing Romany in the car seat before her like a crown on a velvet cushion. As soon as the key was in the door, Tiger appeared, eager as a puppy to be involved in some as-yet-unknown way.

Maggie chucked him the car keys. 'Go and bring the rest of the stuff in, would you please?' she asked him. 'And don't forget to lock it afterwards,' she was compelled to add, but then wished she hadn't.

He disappeared down the stairs and they went inside. Mercifully, the flat was tidy. Maggie had worried that Tiger might have turned it into even more of a squalid mess than it usually was, but it appeared that he was more domesticated than she had given him credit for. On top of the tidying, he had also made a pink paper banner on which he had written 'Welcome Home Romany' in a surprisingly beautiful font. Hidden talents, Maggie thought.

Angie laughed out loud when she saw it.

'Look at that, Romany,' she said to the sleeping baby. 'Uncle Tiger's been busy.' She sounded completely delighted by his efforts.

Tiger reappeared carrying bags just in time to catch her appreciation. Maggie saw the expression that passed between the pair of them and felt a twinge of something that might have been jealousy, which she dismissed at once.

'Cup of tea?' asked Maggie, resting the car seat containing the sleeping baby gently on the carpet in the centre of the room, where it would be obvious and not get tripped over.

'I'll make it,' said Angie, but Maggie silenced her with a particularly hard stare.

'There's a reason it used to be called a confinement, you know,' she said. 'You sit down, and I'll make it.'

Angie looked like she was going to object to being ordered about, but then her shoulders dropped and she sank to the sofa.

'Thanks, Mags. Do you know, in India ancient traditions said that the mother should stay inside for forty days after giving birth to let her recover and bond with her baby.'

'Well, there you go then,' replied Maggie. 'Although I'll have to go back to work. Tiger can step up.'

'Step up to what?' asked Tiger, reappearing and tossing the car keys back to Maggie.

'I was just saying that maybe you can stick around for a few weeks whilst Angie finds her feet,' Maggie said.

Tiger's horror flashed across his face. 'I wasn't planning on being around that long,' he said cautiously. 'I've been here two weeks already and I have a ferry booked at the end of next week to head over to the Cyclades to catch the last of the heat.'

Maggie opened her mouth to object, but Angie spoke first. 'That's fine. I'll be sick of the sight of you by then anyway.'

Tiger grinned at her, happy to be let off the hook, and started to investigate the travel system boxes, but Maggie caught Angie's expression. It was a mixture of worry and sadness: she wasn't sure which was the more dominant.

So, the task of keeping an eye on Angie over the coming weeks and months seemed to have fallen to her, Maggie thought. Tiger was only any good if your plan didn't impinge on his, Leon was in Leeds and had his own family to contend with and there was neither hide nor hair of Jax. Angie would be fine, given time – she was far too resilient to be otherwise – but in the meantime Maggie would be there if she needed her.

26

Romany was four weeks old and there was still no sign of Jax. Angie wasn't surprised, not really, but she was disappointed. She had hoped for more from him than he had demonstrated himself capable of, and she couldn't help but feel let down. To be fair to him, he had made no promises about his involvement and so none had actually been broken. But still, Romany was his daughter. You would have thought that he would be just a little bit curious.

Yet it appeared not. He had rung a couple of times to make sure she was okay and to hear news of Romany, but that was all. He hadn't offered any financial support or given any idea of when he might come to visit them. Angie teetered between cutting him some slack and cutting him out of Romany's life entirely, depending on the day. Or sometimes, the hour. But in the meantime, he appeared to have fallen into a black hole.

And into a black hole was where Angie could feel herself slipping, too. The flat, never tidy at the best of times, was bordering on being a health hazard. Discarded plates scattered with the remains of snatched meals sat on every surface together with old coffee cups, the rancid milk forming greenish skins over their contents. She had given up with the washable nappies, although she told herself that this was only a temporary measure, but was almost at the bottom of the box of disposable ones that Maggie had bought. Nappies in little plastic sacks were overflowing from the bin, and whilst Romany's breast-milk poos were still pale and smelled inoffensive, the sickly-sweet smell of whatever they sprayed the nappy bags with was cloying in her nostrils. She longed to throw the windows open, but she worried that the fresh air would render the flat too cold for Romany. Autumn had arrived with a vengeance, dispelling all hope of a languid Indian summer.

The main problem, as Angie saw it, was the sheer bone-tired exhaustion that she felt all the time. It left her with neither the energy nor the resolve to do anything. In her post-birth plan, carefully and optimistically made before Romany had arrived, she had been intending to go back to work on the Monday of the week to come, believing that a month at home with a newborn was more than enough time to recover from the birth and adjust to a new way of living. She had imagined taking Romany with her to Live Well and leaving her somewhere safe and quiet to sleep whilst Angie treated her clients. She would feed her in between appointments, she had thought, and build some time into the day for cuddles, too.

She could see now how ludicrously naïve this plan had been. She was barely ready to leave the flat, let alone offer healing to her clients. Kate was doing a sterling job holding the fort, but she couldn't offer the same treatments as Angie and so they were constantly losing business as clients drifted away to their competitors. The current situation was unsustainable. Angie had to get back to work soon, or there would be no business left to get back to.

But she was just so tired. The mere thought of getting showered and dressed was more than she could manage some days, let alone actually doing it. For the first time in her life, she realised that she almost felt some sympathy for her fallible mother, bringing her up alone for her first decade at least, before she relinquished Angie into the arms of the state, defeated. Never before had she considered the struggles that her addicted mother must have endured. She had been so busy focusing on how spectacularly she had failed instead. Now that she had had a taste of them, was she perhaps a little more inclined to understand?

But the thought was quickly dismissed. She and her mother were not alike at all. Romany was a tiny baby and whilst Angie looked as if she had barely survived Armageddon, her daughter was totally loved and nurtured. Her mother had let her down consistently, from the moment she was born. Even though Angie hadn't seen her since her teens, she was constantly reminded of how her woeful legacy still left its mark on her life, like the shadow of an ink stain that would never quite wash out.

No, there were no points of comparison between her and her mother, Angie told herself sternly and often. What she was going through was just the baby blues, according to the visiting midwife. All perfectly normal apparently, and in no way suggesting that she was, or would become, an unfit parent. The midwife had helped her tidy up and suggested that she might want to be a little more diligent with the washing up, and Angie had joked about how the flat had looked before the addition of a newborn baby and promised to make a bigger effort. But no sooner had the midwife left than things seemed to slip out of her control again. Where did anyone find time to do anything when they had a baby to care for?

Despite what the midwife had said, Angie certainly didn't feel like a fit mother just then. She smelled, for a start – a musty, earthy tang that came from too long spent in the same clothes. She lifted an arm, took a tentative sniff at her armpit and recoiled. That was definitely more than just a musty smell. That was some serious body odour. Her dreadlocks smelled, too – she knew it even before she grabbed a handful of matted hair and thrust it under her nose.

There had been children who smelled in the children's homes. Despite the attempts of staff to comply with basic hygiene standards, there were always some kids who slipped the net and escaped the shower. It hadn't been so bad when she had first arrived, pre-pubescent and with no body hair to speak of. But as they all grew and their hormones began to kick in, the ones who had been a little ripe as pre-teens began to positively hum.

There was no smell that Angie associated with her dysfunctional childhood as much as human body odour. Even now, the merest whiff of an unwashed body was enough to send her back into the darkness of those times. If a client arrived at Live Well who even looked as if they might not have had a recent encounter with soap and hot water, Angie would find herself feigning a full appointments diary. She would rather turn people away than have to take that smell back into her nostrils. And yet here she was, smelling just like they did.

She needed to snap out of it.

She would start today.

Right now.

She unlatched Romany from her breast, where she had been comforting herself rather than feeding, and laid her down gently in the carrycot. Then she went into the kitchen to find the scissors. Obviously, they weren't where they should have been, and it took her a while to locate them under a bag of defrosted peas that she had taken out of the freezer, slit open and then failed to replace.

With scissors in hand, she went into the bathroom, stood in front of the mirror and took a long look at herself. Her face was sallow, plum-coloured circles rimming her hollow eyes. She even looked like her mother, she thought, although her current poor complexion was a result of a lack of fresh air and exercise rather than addiction. She gave herself a tentative smile and was pleased to see how much difference it made. That was more like it. Angie Osborne had re-entered the building.

She lifted the scissors and let them hover by her ear for a moment and then, in one decisive snip, she cut through a dreadlock.

It fell into the basin and lay there looking for all the world like a dead rodent. Without giving herself a chance to stop, she snipped at the others and they fell one by one, limp and lifeless, into the porcelain until there were none left. Then she stopped and stared. Her hair was now a couple of inches long and sticking up from her head like a hedgehog, but freed from the dreadlocks, she could see the auburn colour once more and what was left felt silky between her fingers. She was transformed. Gone was the Angie of the last decade and here was someone new. A new Angie to begin this new part of her life.

27

Angie was astonished at how sore her scalp still was days after the dreadlocks had gone. She had washed her hair over and over until all the loose hairs had disappeared down the plughole, but what was left insisted on standing up on end and any attempt to flatten it made her sore scalp cry out in protest. It would just take time, she decided.

The rest of the transformation was easier to achieve. She had thrown every item of clothing into the washing machine whether she had worn it recently or not. She had taken three black bags of rubbish out to the bins and removed anything that was beyond its sell-by date from the fridge. From now on, she decided, she was going to be far more careful about what she put inside her body. Not only did she owe it to Romany to stay as healthy as she could, but also a more natural approach to life felt right. For years, she had been talking about healthy diets and lifestyles to her clients without entirely practising what she preached, but the time had come to make a change. She would miss cheese, and the rare bacon sandwiches that she sometimes made for herself when she was drunk, and beer – she would really miss beer – but it felt right, like this was something that she should have done a long time ago.

On top of the changes in the kitchen, she had even set up a corner of her bedroom as a baby-station of sorts, with the changing mat and nappies and all Romany's little outfits. She couldn't guarantee that they would stay put, but at least her intentions were good. Her home hadn't looked so tidy for ages, and definitely not since she had moved her business out of her lounge and into Live Well. And that felt good, too. A welcome element of control was creeping back into her life.

By the end of Sunday, the flat was, if not exactly show-house tidy, then certainly transformed beyond recognition, and Angie felt far more positive about her future as a result. What kind of an excuse was the fact that she had just had a baby? Pretty poor, she thought. Thousands of women gave birth every day, many in far more challenging situations than she found herself in, and they didn't have the luxury of wallowing in self-pity. They got up and got on with their lives without complaint or thoughts of giving up. And Angie Osborne was just as good as they were. She was no quitter.

On Monday morning, with Romany dressed in the largest of her babygros, all the others now being a little too tight, Angie wheeled the pram round to Live Well and parked it in the little yard at the back. Then she scooped her baby up in one arm and headed inside and up the stairs. The familiar scent of lemongrass wafted into her nostrils as she opened the door, and the tinkle of the bells over the door brought Kate out from her room. When she saw who it was, she broke into a huge smile, but then her mouth fell open as she took in Angie's new look.

'Oh my God! Your hair looks fantastic! Wow! Turn round – let me see the back.'

Angie obliged, turning full circle on the spot. Her hair was now sitting a little flatter to her head but was, as yet, without a style.

'Can I touch it? Is that too weird?' asked Kate, putting out a tentative hand and rubbing it across Angie's newly shorn head. Angie flinched a little, her scalp still not fully recovered from the shock. 'It's so soft.' Kate laughed. 'It feels gorgeous. What made you chop them all off?'

Angie shrugged. 'New beginnings, I suppose,' she replied simply.

Kate made a fuss of Romany next, who, whilst not yet smiling, did not object to the attention. Then, with mugs of steaming green tea in front of them, they sat down to discuss how best to proceed. By lunchtime, they had agreed on a new part-time working day for Angie and had rung the nursery down the road to get a place for Romany.

'Why did I think I could bring a baby to work?' Angie said, the mere idea now entirely ludicrous to her.

Kate gave her an indulgent smile 'Well, you didn't know,' she replied diplomatically.

And nobody dared correct me, Angie thought but didn't say.

But she was on it now. By the end of the week, the appointments diary, whilst not yet full, was looking much healthier, and life was beginning to return to some sort of reality.

◆ ◆ ◆

How could Romany be two months old already? Angie couldn't understand how the days had whizzed by so quickly, and at the same time it was almost impossible to remember life without her daughter in it. The workings of time were one of life's great mysteries. The chaos of the first few challenging weeks was only too fresh in her mind, but at the same time, she could barely remember how low she had felt back then. Now, though, the fear and despair had cleared and, whilst she still had the odd day when things seemed bleak, she no longer felt frightened by what lay ahead.

The two of them now had a routine, of sorts, and Angie sensed that they were learning to understand and trust one another. When she put her daughter to her breast, Romany's clear eyes searching for hers, she knew that she had discovered the all-consuming maternal love that you read about. This was how it felt to love another person totally and unconditionally. The feeling was new to Angie, but already she knew she would never lose it, that it had become a part of who she was.

It was a Saturday teatime in the flat and she and Romany were enjoying a cuddle on the sofa when the doorbell rang. Angie wasn't expecting anyone. Maggie called by sometimes but, being Maggie, she always rang beforehand to check that it was convenient. She would never just turn up unannounced.

Settling Romany into the crook of her arm, Angie went downstairs. The clocks had changed and the street was already dark, the sodium orange of the streetlights turning the night sky a chocolatey brown.

At first, she didn't recognise who was standing on her doorstep. And then she did.

Jax. He was here. After all this time. Just standing there on her doorstep in the dark.

The shock made Angie feel woozy and she put one hand out to grab at the doorframe as the other tightened its grip around Romany.

How was she supposed to feel? She searched for the appropriate response to his unexpected arrival, letting her heart rather than her intellect guide her. Shock at his sudden appearance slipped quickly into delight at seeing him after so long, before she remembered how abandoned she had felt, and then anger finally prevailed. She concentrated on making sure that her face reflected the last of these emotions and stared at him impassively. He chewed on his lower lip and kicked at an invisible mark on the paving stone with his foot. At least he had the good grace to look ashamed.

He looked different. Like her, he had cropped his hair short and his face was clean shaven. Angie had never seen him with anything less than a five-day shadow of bristles and it didn't sit right. He almost looked ordinary, like any man you might pass on the street rather than the eco-warrior that she had first met. But then again, she supposed, she now looked pretty much like any woman. Perhaps they were growing up.

And then he smiled, a restrained, slightly sheepish expression, and she finally saw him in this stranger: her Jax. She could sense her resolve to punish him melting away, but she was determined to try, at least for a while. He deserved to be given a hard time, given his lack of communication. She redoubled her efforts to look cross.

'Hi,' he said, his voice tentative, almost questioning, as if he were unsure what kind of reception he was about to get.

Everything inside Angie was crying out to welcome him, but she kept it all in check.

'Hi,' she replied coolly.

'Sorry to just show up like this. I hope it's okay. I would have rung, but . . .' His sentence careered to a halt under the weight of the lie it contained, but she wasn't going to make this easy for him. She let him plough on unchecked.

'And you look great, Ange,' he continued. 'Really good. I love the hair. It suits you short.'

She shrugged. His new look suited him too, but she wasn't about to give him the satisfaction of telling him so.

'And this must be Romany,' he said. Angie was grateful that he had used her name and not 'my daughter'. Somehow that felt easier to deal with.

She nodded.

Romany eyed him curiously with her wide eyes, no longer the pure blue they had been at birth but not yet settled into a specific colour of their own. He put out his hand to touch her and Angie had to fight the impulse to pull her child away. His hand looked so huge next to Romany's face that it was almost like a threat, even though Angie knew that Jax would never hurt either of them, not physically at least. He ran the side of a finger delicately down her cheek as if he could hardly believe that she was real flesh and blood.

Angie pressed her lips tight together. It felt important that he spoke first even though she had no end of things that she wanted to say to him, not least to ask what on earth he was doing descending on them unannounced and so late in the day.

'I'm sorry,' he said, simply. 'I let you down and I am really sorry. I know it's not good enough, but it's the truth. I was scared. I didn't know what to do or think. So, I did the easiest thing and did nothing. But it was really crappy of me. I can see that now.'

Angie met his eyes with hers and stared into them, without letting any hint of understanding escape. He was going to have to beg if he wanted to be back in her life. Just turning up out of the blue when it suited him might have worked when there were just the two of them to consider, but it wouldn't wash now. They both deserved more than that.

'Can I come in?' he asked. 'Please.'

Angie was tempted to send him away just to make a point, but if she did he might disappear and never come back and she couldn't risk that, no matter what he had done.

'Okay,' she said.

She turned and led him up the stairs. She could feel Romany become still in her arms as she watched him over Angie's shoulder. The two of them would be at eye level with one another, Angie thought, father and daughter sizing each other up for the very first time. She resisted turning round to see what they made of one another.

Once in the flat, she and Romany sat on the sofa. but she didn't invite him to join her and so he was left standing awkwardly, looking down on the pair of them.

'So, how have you been?' he asked. 'You look great,' he repeated.

'It's been hard,' Angie replied simply. 'But we're getting there now.'

She knew how to play this now. She wasn't going to ask him for anything, she determined. If he wanted to offer to help then she would hear what he had to say, but she wasn't going to beg. However, it seemed that he had no such intentions.

'Good,' he said. 'That's good. And she's been well?'

Angie nodded.

He put a hand to his chin to rub at the stubble that was no longer there and instead ran his palm over his hair and round the back of his neck.

'God, it's good to see you, Ange,' he said. 'I've missed you. I really have.'

'Not so much that you'd actually do something about it though,' she replied tartly. 'We've been here the whole time, you know. You could have come before now.'

He dropped his gaze to the floor. 'I know, but I didn't know how it would be,' he said. 'Whether you'd want to see me.'

'You could have asked. Our baby is almost two months old and you've rung twice. Twice!' Her voice was louder than she intended, and she checked herself. Shouting at him would achieve nothing and might upset Romany.

'Yes, I'm sorry. I truly am. It's just that . . .' He took a deep breath, his eyes now rolling up to look at the ceiling. Anywhere but at her, Angie thought. 'The thing is,' he continued, 'the thing is, I met someone else. There's someone else.'

The pain was instantaneous and real, as if someone had taken aim and fired a bullet straight into her chest. For a second she couldn't take in any oxygen; all her airways seemed blocked and panic shot through her as she struggled to breathe. In all those times when she had thought about him and why he hadn't been in touch, knowing she was caring for their child on her own, the possibility that he might be in a new relationship had never occurred to her. She had assumed that the silence was because he was trying to get his head around the fact of Romany, and that when he had, he would come back and they would rebuild something going forward, an understanding between them that reflected their new status as parents. She had even hoped that they might get back to something of the way they had been before, given time. She still loved him, in her own, slightly dysfunctional way. She had thought that she might love him even more, now that he was the father of her baby.

But he loved someone else.

The whole time she had been suffering, wallowing in his silence and trying to interpret it, he had been happily tucked up with another. He had not been struggling to get his feelings in order or wondering how best to approach this new part of their life together, or any of the many other options that she had played out in her head. No, he was just in love, plain and simple. There had been barely any word from him because he was too busy screwing another woman.

Angie wouldn't cry. Not only would she not give him the satisfaction of it, but there were no tears to be had within her. She had learned that years ago – if you cried, or showed any kind of weakness, then someone else would step in and take advantage whilst your mind was elsewhere.

'Right,' she said instead. She wouldn't ask him for details, wouldn't give him the chance to absolve his guilt by trying to explain himself, but it seemed that she couldn't stop him telling her.

'I went back to college,' he said. 'To get some skills, so I can get a job. I met Sam there and we just kind of clicked.'

Angie couldn't care less about how they had 'clicked'. She didn't care about his college course and she didn't care about Sam. All that mattered now was her and Romany.

'That's that then,' she said. 'Well, you'd better go.' She stood up to indicate that the conversation had come to an end.

Jax looked surprised. 'What? Just like that? But I've come all this way.'

'Not my problem,' replied Angie.

'Can't I even hold her?'

Angie tightened her hold around her daughter. All her instincts were screaming at her to protect her child. But then she remembered her own parents, how her mother had driven her father away before she had had the chance to form any memories of him, and then driven her away too. She thought of her freshly minted promise to Romany that she would not let history repeat itself, that she would always be the best mother that she could be. Jax had let her down. He had let her down in ways that she couldn't even begin to get her head round just yet. But that was between her and Jax. It was nothing to do with Romany. Jax would always be her father, no matter what happened between the two of them.

Using every ounce of strength that she had, she straightened her arms and passed a wriggling Romany over to him. He took her, holding her under her arms, her legs kicking beneath her. Then he pulled her into his chest and held her tightly. His face twisted and tears began to trickle down his cheeks as he stroked her fair, wispy hair. Angie watched dispassionately, shielding her heart from any emotional response, just as she had learned to do as a child.

Romany began to grizzle and Jax threw Angie an anxious look, seeking guidance on what he should do.

'She's hungry,' Angie said flatly.

She took the baby back and immediately Romany began to root against her T-shirt, banging her little head on Angie's collarbone in frustration.

'Maybe I should go,' said Jax uncertainly.

'Yes. Probably,' Angie replied.

He looked lost and forlorn and filled with regret, but he only had himself to blame for her response. She sat down on the sofa and began to prepare to feed Romany. She didn't look at him.

'Is that it, then?' he asked, making one last stab at getting her to engage, feeble though it was. Four words to save four years.

Angie had to make a choice. He seemed to want to keep in touch on some level, although there had been no suggestion of any financial contribution which would have been the most help. If it were up to her, she would let him leave and drop all contact. But this wasn't about her. It was about Romany. She needed to leave the door open for her child.

'Let's see, shall we?' she said.

It was the best she could offer.

28

2006

Having a party for her fortieth birthday had seemed like such a great idea to Maggie back in January when she and Angie had first mooted it. Angie had also turned forty earlier that year but, as she had pointed out, Maggie's house was far more suitable for a grown-up party than her little flat. And so Maggie, wooed by the idea of a social occasion that was too far away to worry about, had agreed. But now that the event was upon her, she was far less convinced.

It was never going to be a big do. Maggie had invited her team from the office plus their partners, which amounted to around thirty people. She could have told herself it had been a conscious decision to stick to just this social group so that everyone got along, which would make for a better party, but in truth Maggie knew that her colleagues were her social group. She had neither the time not the inclination to nurture any other friendships.

And anyway, she had her 'uni bunch', which was how she described them to anyone who asked. Angie and Romany were coming, as were Leon and Becky with their sons Thomas and James. And possibly Tiger. Maggie knew it was doubtful that Tiger would show up. She wasn't even convinced that he would have got the invitation. Angie said that he did pop into internet cafés from time to time so he might have seen her email, but if he had then he hadn't bothered to reply. So, whenever the butterflies had started up in her stomach at the possibility of seeing him, Maggie had wafted them away. She needed to grow out of Tiger.

The weather forecast was appalling so, of course, they were having a barbecue, with carefully selected meat alternatives for the vegetarians. In the planning stage, she had pictured her guests milling happily on the lawn in the late afternoon sunshine and only drifting inside when the autumn chill sent them in search of warmth. And even then, she'd secretly hoped that they would stay outside and not traipse dirt into her house. But there was no hope of that now. All her guests, adults and children alike, would have to be entertained indoors.

She had bought a gazebo so she could still cook outside at least, but as for the rest of it, they would definitely be in the house. Maggie looked at her pale cream carpets and the French-polished coffee table and sighed. *C'est la vie.*

Angie and Romany arrived first, by arrangement, in order to provide moral support. Angie was carrying an enormous birthday cake. Every available inch of its chocolate coating was adorned with a sweet of some kind and it was dotted all over with candles, many sticking out from the sides at ninety degrees so that the wax would drip directly on to whatever it sat on instead of dribbling neatly down to the candle holders. Maggie's face burst into a smile the moment she saw it.

'Happy birthday, Auntie Maggie,' said Romany, grinning and bouncing on her toes at Angie's side. 'Do you like your cake? I decorated it, didn't I, Mummy?'

So much was obvious, and Maggie felt her heart swell at the effort that Romany had clearly made for her and for Angie, who had made it happen.

'I LOVE my cake,' said Maggie, bending down and sweeping Romany up into a hug. At almost six, she was getting a little bit big to be lifted like this, but she wrapped her legs around Maggie's hips and did her best to help bear the load. 'Thank you, Romany!' She showered Romany with little kisses on the top of her head.

'What can we do to help?' asked Angie, carrying the cake through to the kitchen and then coming to an abrupt halt in the doorway. 'Oh, not much, I see,' she said. 'Blimey, Mags. Do you never just go with the flow?'

'Preparation is key to success,' Maggie replied, gently setting a wriggling Romany back down. 'You remember that, Romey,' she added as they followed Angie into the kitchen, where nibbles, drinks, plates, cutlery, sauces, glasses, salads, breads and pretty much anything that you might need for a successful barbecue were all laid out in poker-straight rows along the granite surfaces.

'That's right, Romes. You listen to your Auntie Maggie,' said Angie. She turned and gave Maggie a squeeze. 'Happy birthday, Mags,' she said. 'I got you something, but I left it at the flat.'

Her eyes stayed focused on the preparations and Maggie saw her cheeks flare. There would be no gift, but Maggie couldn't have cared less. The cake said everything that needed to be said.

'I don't suppose you've heard from Tiger,' she said, not wanting to bring the subject up but not being able to resist asking.

Angie smirked and Maggie braced herself for the ribbing that was coming her way, but Angie just shook her head.

'Nah. Not even sure where he is. No doubt he'll be spending his fortieth on a beach somewhere. Lucky sod.' Angie's eyes dropped to Romany to see if she had heard. Maggie had noticed how she tried to moderate her language when her daughter was around and, whilst being surprised that it mattered to her, appreciated the effort that she made. Romany was counting the glasses, walking up and down the rows pointing at each one in turn as she mouthed the numbers, and hadn't heard.

◆ ◆ ◆

The guests started to arrive and congregated in the kitchen. Maggie flew around them in turn, accepting gifts and offering drinks. As they all knew each other, there was no need for any introductions other than Angie and Romany, and Angie had that covered. She had lost none of her confidence over the years, Maggie thought as she watched her friend walk straight up to a group of strangers and cut across the conversation, but now Maggie found that she was more in awe of it than irritated.

Time was ticking on and still there was no sign of Leon and Becky. Maggie had half-expected them to cancel – things were still pretty chilly between them and Becky, who had never really warmed to their charms – but she had heard nothing and so had to assume that they were on their way. It would be nice for Romany, if nothing else. She seemed to enjoy the company of Leon's boys, who played with her as indulgently as if she were a little cousin. The boys were chips off Leon's block, not Becky's.

Richard, her fellow partner and well-known bon viveur, had offered to run the barbecue for her and soon the delicious smells of charring beef were wafting through the house, and gradually guests drifted from the kitchen and into the conservatory which adjoined the impromptu tented kitchen outside. There was no carpet in there; Maggie noted this and then berated herself for caring. She allowed herself a small moment of congratulation. It was a lovely party so far and everyone seemed to be relaxed and having a nice time.

When Becky and Leon finally arrived, however, they changed the atmosphere for Maggie all by themselves. She was just coming out from checking the towels in the downstairs cloakroom when she heard them bickering on the doorstep before they knocked.

'So you say, Leon, but it's not all about you. I'll stay for thirty minutes and then we'll make our excuses.'

'You're being ridiculous. Maggie is one of my oldest friends. Is it too much to ask to come to her birthday party?'

There was no reply to this. Apparently, it was.

Maggie loitered in the hallway waiting for the doorbell to ring, and after a moment or two it did. She waited a moment longer, set her face into a smile and then opened the door. Leon was standing on the doorstep. He looked grey and tired, like someone recovering from a long and arduous illness, but he returned her smile when he saw her. Becky's face was set like granite and the boys were investigating the stone sundial that stood in the middle of the front garden, far from their bickering parents.

'Happy birthday, Maggie. So sorry we're late.' He shrugged as if to say, 'you know how it is,' but gave no excuse for their tardiness. There was no need. Maggie had heard all she needed to. He pressed a tasteful bouquet of white calla lilies and roses into her hands. There was no card.

'Come in, come in,' she said enthusiastically. 'Good trip over, I hope. Let me take your jackets. Boys, if you want to go to the kitchen you can help yourself to a drink. Romany is here. She's dying to see you. And wait until you see the cake she made.'

Thomas and James pushed past their parents, each giving Maggie a sheepish grin as they went.

'Happy birthday,' said James quietly as he passed her, and Maggie whispered a thank you.

The atmosphere between Leon and Becky was so strained that Maggie kept talking, desperately trying to paper over the cracks.

'Drinks are in the kitchen. The food is pretty much ready, I think. Shame about the weather but there's no guarantee of anything, is there? Angie is here somewhere. You'll hear her.'

'I'm afraid we can't stay long,' said Becky almost before she was in the house. 'My mother's not been well, and I don't like to leave her too long.'

'Oh, I'm sorry to hear that,' Maggie said. 'Nothing too serious, I hope.'

Leon looked at his shoes and Becky ignored the question.

At least the party was in enough swing for their frostiness not to show to other guests, but Maggie noticed Becky pour herself a large glass of white wine and then stand by the window, looking out over the garden with her back to the room.

'Have you got anything soft?' Leon asked.

'Of course,' replied Maggie, and reeled off the multitude of alternatives. 'Is everything okay, Lee?'

Leon nodded and seemed unwilling to get drawn into details.

Maggie changed direction. 'I can't believe how much the boys have grown,' she said.

Leon beamed. 'I know! We can barely keep them in school uniform, and you should see the size of their feet!'

'And it'll be secondary school before you know it,' added Maggie. 'Is Thomas still enjoying his football?'

'Oh yes. He lives and breathes Leeds United. He's just like my brother, in fact. And he's still training with the academy. I don't suppose it will come to anything, but you have to let them try.'

'Try what?' asked Angie, who had just appeared at Leon's side.

'I was just talking about Thomas and his football,' Leon said. 'He wants to be a professional and even though it's so tough to get into, I feel that it's up to us to support him to at least try.'

'To encourage him to follow his dreams and not settle for what he thinks he ought to do?' said Angie, eyebrow raised. 'Yes. I definitely think that's what you should be doing.'

Leon's eyes rolled heavenward as if to tell her, I know what you're saying, but let's not say it today. 'And James is enjoying his drama group,' he continued. 'He was in a little show in the spring. I know I'm biased, but he was definitely the best on the stage.'

'I bet he was,' said Maggie. 'They're a credit to you, Leon. To both of you,' she added quickly, shooting a quick glance at Becky who was still staring out of the window.

They chatted on, exchanging news, interrupted only by occasional warnings to the three children who raced around the adults stealing food and giggling, but after what felt like no time at all, Becky began looking at her watch. She came across to where they were chatting and threw meaningful and not that subtle glances at Leon, who took the hint almost at once.

'Well, I'm sorry Mags, but we're going to have to love you and leave you. I'm sorry it's been so short-lived.'

'But you haven't even had any food yet,' objected Maggie, but she could see that she was on a hiding to nothing. Leon shrugged and pulled a face.

'Let's get together again soon,' said Angie. 'Just the three of us,' she added, staring so pointedly at Becky that Maggie felt her own cheeks warm.

'Great idea,' replied Leon.

It took a few minutes to round up the boys and prise Romany off them but then they were ready to go.

'Thank you so much, Maggie,' said Becky, poised as if on starter's blocks at the door. 'It's been lovely.'

Maggie didn't even smile. What was the point? They both knew the score. Becky went to the car, taking the complaining boys with her, leaving Maggie and Leon on the doorstep.

'Are you really okay, Lee?' she pressed quietly.

'She means well,' he replied. 'She just prefers to socialise with her own friends.'

Maggie nodded and pulled him into a hug. 'Well, we're here for you,' she said into his ear. 'If you need us. Never forget that.'

They stood there in the embrace for a moment longer until Maggie heard a sharp blast on a car horn.

'Better go,' said Leon, unwrapping his arms from around her. Then he took her hand in his. Maggie couldn't remember them ever holding hands before and it felt peculiar, but not awkward.

'Thanks, Maggie,' he said. As he spoke, he looked directly into her eyes. For a moment, Maggie thought she saw something there that she had never seen before, but then it was gone. She must have been mistaken.

Later, after the guests had all gone, declaring the party a success as they went, and Maggie was finishing off the tidying up, she tried to recapture his expression in her mind, but it eluded her. She wasn't really sure that it had been there in the first place.

Tiger never appeared.

29

THE TWENTY-TENS

2013

Hope took a deep breath and pushed open the classroom door. It was a good ten years since she had last set foot in an educational establishment, but it still had that same smell – hot bodies, stale food and bleach. Did all places of learning smell like that, she wondered? She imagined that they must do. This wasn't her old school, but if she closed her eyes then it might have been.

There was a low-level hum of chatter in the room, again, just as she remembered there being at school. Lots of people not concentrating on the job in hand. That had been her, back in the day – sitting as far from the teacher as she could get away with and firing spitballs of paper across heads with her ruler.

Still, that was another time, a different Hope.

The desks were arranged in pairs, each facing the whiteboard at the front. That was a blessing, at least. She hated it when the room was arranged into a horseshoe so that the discussions were forced to be more participatory. She had no wish to get to know anything at all about her fellow students, to discuss topics with them or hear their views. The only important person in this room would be the tutor, although there was no sign of him as yet. She hoped he wasn't going to be one of those scatty types who was too easily led off topic and filled the allotted time with anecdotes that were of little interest to anyone else. Teachers like that were a dream when she'd been at school, but she wasn't a child any more. She was here to learn.

The room was almost full, and Hope cursed silently to herself. She had intended to be here first so that she could get her pick of the places, but the phone had rung just as she was leaving: an international call that she needed to take to make sure that the rest of the day continued to run smoothly in her absence. By the time she had sorted the problem, she was twenty minutes behind where she had wanted to be. There were still a few spare places scattered about, though, and she spotted, with relief, a double desk in the back row. She made for that one, keeping her head dipped and her cap pulled down low, and laid claim to it.

She sat on one of the chairs and put her bag on the other one. There were plenty of other free places. No one would come and sit next to her if it looked like she was saving the seat for someone else. She might even be the last to arrive. She took her pencil case and new notebook out of her Mulberry briefcase, a gift from a shoot in London a few years ago but still pristine, and placed them neatly in front of her. She was ready.

Moments later the door opened, and a boy came in and headed straight for the desk at the front. He wasn't really a boy, Hope knew, but he could barely be out of university. She batted down a mild pang of irritation. She was here to learn, so she expected the tutor to be at least older than her own twenty-eight years, and preferably in the balding and middle-aged camp so she could be sure that they knew more about their subject than she did. The tutor took a slim-looking laptop out of his messenger bag and opened it up on the desk in front of him. Hope's paper and pen felt instantaneously outmoded. It hadn't occurred to her to bring her own laptop, but she would next time. She took a sly glance at her fellow students but some of them didn't even appear to have paper and pen.

A few moments passed as the tutor – Carl Watts, according to the course details in the Further Education Prospectus that had landed on her doormat the previous month – hooked his laptop up to the system and opened up PowerPoint and then, when he was sure that all was ready, clicked on to the first slide and cleared his throat. The murmuring diminished.

'Good evening, everybody,' he began. 'My name is Carl Watts, and I will be your tutor on this course, which I've snappily titled "Building your Business from Scratch One Step at a Time".'

He looked about the room proudly, as if he really believed that this was a snappy title, and Hope's heart sank a little. If the tutor turned out to be an idiot, then she might have to have a rethink. She hoped this was his stab at a little ironic humour, although she feared that he really was as pleased with himself as he looked.

'So, over the next thirty weeks, I shall be taking you through every element that you'll need to master in order to make your business a success. And when we get to the end you should have a pretty cool business plan that you can take to the banks, or even venture capitalists, to get that all-important loan.'

Oh God. Maybe this was too basic a course, Hope thought. She knew next to nothing, her business only recently having got off the ground, but she wasn't sure that she could stand being patronised by someone who had clearly only ever talked the talk.

'Now, some of you may be wondering what qualifications I have to be teaching you about this stuff.'

Someone in front of her sniffed, and Hope wondered if they were also less than convinced about his credentials.

'Well,' Carl continued with the air of someone who had the winning hand in a game of poker, 'I have an honours degree in economics and an MBA from University College London.'

Not quite the same as actually running your own business, though, is it? Hope thought. She supposed that if he did have any practical experience then he would be out there making money rather than teaching, although maybe his business had crashed in the recession and this was a stopgap. Either way, she wasn't filled with confidence.

Still, she thought, he had to know more about it than she did. She pushed her doubts to the further reaches of her mind and prepared to concentrate.

There was a noise to her left, the classroom door opening and closing. Somebody was late. Hope didn't bother turning to look, hoping that whoever it was would settle themselves quickly and with a minimum of fuss, but then someone spoke to her.

'Sorry. Can you shift your stuff so I can sit down?'

There were plenty of other places free and not encumbered with obvious defence mechanisms such as her bag, so why had this person picked her to disturb? She turned to look at the woman and got as close to a snarl as she dared in a full room of people, hoping that that would be enough to put her off and send her scuttling to another desk. It was likely that wherever they sat tonight would end up being their places for the entire course, given what creatures of habit people were. She didn't want to get stuck with someone for the entire thirty weeks.

But her less-than-welcoming expression made not a jot of difference. The woman just stood there, waiting for her to remove her things from the other chair and seeming oblivious to the vibes that she was radiating. If Hope had not been so irritated, she would have been impressed by her sheer front. People were turning in their seats to see why the newcomer wasn't sitting down and so, reluctantly, Hope removed her bag and slotted it in at her feet. The woman threw her a grateful smile and sat down, but made no effort to get anything out to help with her studies. She just leant back in her chair and turned her attention to the front of the room.

'Can I borrow some paper? And a pen, maybe?' she whispered.

Hope rolled her eyes, but tore a couple of sheets out of the back of her A4 pad and took a biro out of her pencil case. She passed them across without making eye contact with the woman.

Carl pressed on with a brief overview of the various modules of the course, and at eight thirty he proposed that they stop for a comfort break, pointing out where the coffee machines were in the building.

'Back in fifteen please, people,' he called over the sound of chairs being scraped on the lino.

Hope cringed.

'Did he just call us "people"?' asked her neighbour, and for the first time Hope turned to look at her.

She was older than Hope. She wasn't that great at ages, but she would place the woman closer to fifty than forty, although she had great skin and her hair was a rich auburn with no greys and looked entirely natural. She was wearing clothing that Hope would describe as either eccentric or hippy depending on her mood, with lots of unusual chunky jewellery in bright colours.

'I fear he did,' she said, giving the woman a mock grimace.

'God,' said the woman. 'What an idiot. I hope he knows his stuff or I'm out of here. The last thing I need is to be patronised by some bloke who has chosen to teach adult education courses for a living.'

Having said out loud what Hope would only ever have thought, the woman now had Hope's full attention.

'I thought the same,' replied Hope. 'I'm Hope, by the way.'

She lifted her baseball cap a little so she could make eye contact with the woman. She generally wore a cap. It stopped people staring. She braced herself for the woman's response to her. It always happened when she first met people, and sometimes for many meetings beyond then, and she didn't consider herself to be arrogant to expect it. It was just something that had to be got out of the way.

'I'm Angie,' said the woman. And then, 'Oh my God, you're so beautiful. I don't think I've ever met such a gorgeous-looking person.'

For once it was Hope who was wrong-footed. Her looks prompted a number of responses but ones quite as direct as this were rare.

She lowered her eyes modestly. 'Thanks,' she said.

'I bet it's a pain in the arse, being so bloody jaw-dropping,' Angie said. 'It must get in the way a lot, like being really rich. I suppose it makes it hard to work out who likes you for you and who just wants to be near you for other reasons.'

Hope just stared at her, open-mouthed. This woman's perception was startling.

'Precisely!' she said. 'That's spot on, actually. Do you know, no one has ever articulated it quite like that before?'

'And you won't be able to say it because if you did, you'd come across as all "Poor me. No one understands how I suffer for being so stunning."' Angie pulled a 'woe is me' face that made Hope smile. 'I have the same problem,' Angie continued, sucking her cheeks in and pouting so that she looked more like a goldfish than a supermodel.

They both laughed.

'Do you want to get some coffee from that vending machine he mentioned?' Hope asked, but Angie shook her head.

'I don't do caffeine,' she said.

'What? Not at night or not ever?' Hope asked, aghast.

'Not ever,' replied Angie. 'I aim for as pure a diet as I can get, so no chemicals or stimulants, artificial or otherwise.'

'Blimey,' said Hope. 'That's impressive. No alcohol either, then?'

Angie shook her head. 'Nope. I had a baby twelve years ago and I just decided that I needed to make some changes. Nothing like that has passed my lips since.'

'I won't tell you about my daily coffee consumption then.' Hope laughed. 'It would make your eyes water. So, I assume you're here because you're setting up a business?'

Angie pulled at one of the silver hoops in her earlobe and flicked at it with her nail. 'Actually, I'm expanding the one I already have,' she said proudly. 'So, I thought it might be better if I learned a bit of stuff first. It's a treatment centre for holistic health. It's been going for years and business is good, so I'm looking at opening at a second site. Trouble is, I've been basically making it up as I went along until now. I feel like I need to get a better handle on how things should be done. You know what it's like when you don't know what you don't know?'

Hope nodded. She understood that completely.

'And so here I am. How about you?'

Hope hadn't really told anyone about her business idea. She had bounced the concept off her boyfriend, Daniel, but only in a vague way so as not to give him the chance to knock it down before she'd really worked at it. Now she felt suddenly shy at having to say it out loud. But what was the point of being here if she couldn't even tell anyone what she was planning?

'I'm going to start a business importing Italian swimwear,' she said.

Angie nodded. She looked impressed, at least. 'I don't really follow fashion, as must be obvious,' she said, gesturing to her clothing. 'But from what I can tell, we don't seem to have that much stylish swimwear here. The last costume I bought came from Marks and Sparks.'

Hope shuddered.

'Well, that's what I thought.' Angie laughed. 'But I wasn't sure where else to go. And I'm assuming that you know a fair bit about the market,' she continued. 'You're a model, right?'

Again, Hope was surprised, but this was so refreshing. This woman had just assumed that she was a model and stated it as if it were any other job. Most people got sucked into the glamour of it, asking her endless questions about where she'd worked and who she knew. Angie seemed to see her beauty as a commodity that she would obviously be exploiting – it was as simple as that.

'Well, I was,' Hope said. 'Work started to slow down a bit and I decided I needed to diversify before it dried up completely. Your thirties are a bit of a dead zone for modelling and I'm nearly there. So, I thought about importing. I have the connections and I know what will look good on women and how to show it to its best advantage. And it's definitely a gap in the market. But I know nothing about business. I don't even have any GCSEs.'

'Well, why would you when you look like you do?' asked Angie. 'I assume you didn't need any qualifications to get work.'

Hope shrugged. 'Well, no. But it's not like I'm stupid or anything,' she added, suddenly wanting to explain herself.

'That much is obvious from what you've just said. I'd call it pretty astute actually,' Angie said.

Hope could feel her cheeks blush in spite of herself. 'Thanks,' she said.

It felt great to have someone acknowledge her idea as at least having potential, and she already had the impression that Angie wasn't in the habit of saying what she thought people wanted to hear.

The other students were starting to shuffle back into the classroom, brown plastic cups in hands, and take their seats. Hope turned back to face the front, signalling that the time for chatting was over, but, she thought, maybe it wouldn't be too terrible to sit next to Angie for the next thirty weeks.

30

By week three of the course, Hope had concluded that Carl, the tutor, was irritating in the extreme but that he did actually know his stuff. Having decided that it wasn't very satisfactory making notes on her laptop, she had invested in a lever arch file together with a set of coloured dividers, and the sections were filling up nicely. The pleasure that she felt at seeing the neat pages of notes was something new for her. This must have been what it felt like to be a swot at school.

She was still getting on well with Angie, too, although she had yet to turn up for class with her own equipment. Hope didn't mind; she had bought enough supplies for both of them and doled them out at the start of each session, having worked out that if she gave paper and pens to Angie to look after then they wouldn't make it back for the next class.

She had learned more about Angie in the fifteen-minute comfort breaks that Carl gave them mid-session. It appeared that she was a single mum to a twelve-year-old who, from the stories that Angie recounted, was wise beyond her years. There was no man on the scene, as far as Hope could tell. She had asked her about the child's father, in a roundabout way to start with, and then more directly. Angie had sighed and looked a little wistful at the thought of him.

'I think Romany's dad was probably the love of my life,' she said, 'but I didn't realise it at the time. If I had, I would probably have made a bigger effort to hold on to him.'

'Did he not want to be involved with his daughter?' Hope asked.

'I think it was more that he didn't really know what to do,' Angie replied. 'Even though we weren't kids, the idea of commitment was all very new for both of us and we didn't really think things through very well. Plus, Jax lived down south so I barely saw him as it was. And then when Romany was born it took us both by surprise. Not the fact of her. I mean, we knew I was pregnant. It was more the consequences. I should have worked out what I was expecting from him and told him straight away, but I didn't and so he just kind of wandered off. It was more of an accidental thing really.'

It seemed bizarre to Hope, but then she had never done anything by accident. 'Do you ever hear from him?' she asked.

'Not any more,' said Angie. 'We did to start with, but then we moved house and I didn't let him know. So now he wouldn't know how to get hold of us even if he wanted to.'

She fell silent for a moment. Hope thought that not giving someone important your new address wasn't something that you did by accident, but it wasn't for her to comment.

'It's no bad thing, I suppose,' Angie added. 'We're doing just fine on our own.'

Was it ever in the best interests of a child to have no contact with a parent if that parent had done no wrong? Hope wasn't sure, but then she didn't have any children herself. She couldn't quite let it drop, though.

'And what about Romany?' she asked. 'What does she think?'

Angie shrugged. 'It's not been an issue so far. When she was little and first worked out that other kids had two parents she asked where he was, and I told her that he lived a long way away. Now it rarely comes up. I suppose with Facebook and things it wouldn't be that hard for her to track him down when she's older, but at the moment she seems happy enough as we are. She's got enough on looking after one parent as it is!'

Angie grinned, but something told Hope that Angie would be making a pretty good job of parenting on her own.

'And how about you?' Angie asked her.

'No kids. A boyfriend but it's pretty new. Seems to be going all right so far.'

Angie raised an eyebrow, but Hope wasn't up for sharing much more. She had met Daniel at a reception that she had been invited to in York for a breast cancer charity that she was involved with. She had noticed him, buzzing about the place looking purposeful and possibly a little stressed, and she had concluded that he must be something to do with the organisation of the event, rather than a guest.

It turned out that his restaurant had provided the canapés, which were actually a cut above the cardboard offerings she was usually served. Their paths had crossed when he caught her shoulder with the edge of a tray of goat's cheese tarts and sent them sliding down the front of her flame orange Carolina Herrera dress. The dress was borrowed and insured, but the look on his face had been priceless.

'Oh my God! I'm so sorry. Here, let me . . .' But he was at a loss to know what to do. He could hardly start fishing the tarts out of her cleavage.

She'd enjoyed watching him panic for a moment or two and then she began to laugh. 'It doesn't matter,' she said. 'These things happen, and I was just thinking that I might head off home anyway.'

'Oh God,' he said. 'Well, you must give me your contact details so that I can pay for the cleaning of the dress.'

Hope looked down at the grease-stained silk. A blob of goat's cheese was sliding majestically down her hips.

'I think the dress is beyond saving,' she replied wryly.

'Shit,' he said, and for a moment she'd thought he might actually cry. 'This is the first one of these events that we've been asked to do, and I really need it to go well.'

'The food was delicious,' Hope had said, putting a finger down her dress to retrieve a tiny square of sun-dried red pepper and popping it into her mouth provocatively.

For a moment, he seemed to forget about the crisis as he watched her, but then the full enormity of the disaster he had created returned to him. He ran his hands through his hair. He was quite good-looking, Hope thought.

'Oh shit,' he said again. People had started to notice what had befallen her and were beginning to point.

'Look, I'll go to the ladies' and clear up the worst of it. You go and retrieve my coat from the cloakroom, and I'll meet you in reception.' She opened her purse and fished out the cloakroom token. 'My name is Hope Maxwell, in case they wonder why you're retrieving my stuff. You can tell them that I sent you. They know who I am.'

He hadn't questioned this but scampered off in the direction of the door. Hope thrust her shoulders back and used her best catwalk strut to carry her to the ladies'. The whole incident struck her as funny, really, and it would get her out of having to chat to any more dignitaries, which was almost a blessing.

The next day, the most enormous bouquet of flowers had turned up at her agent's offices. Carrie rang her in great excitement.

'Who is Daniel the Clumsy? Whoever he is, he appears to be very sorry!'

There was a phone number on the card and so Hope had rung him, more to reassure him once again that no harm had been done, and from that there had been dinner and now a relationship of sorts. But she kept all this to herself. Angie was lovely, but Hope wasn't the kind of person who overshared.

Angie, however, was. She kept Hope entertained with endless stories about the things that her daughter did and said. Usually that kind of detail annoyed Hope – was there anything more boring than listening to other people talking about their children? – but Angie managed to make her tales self-effacing and highly amusing. It got so that Hope almost felt as if she knew Romany, even though she had never met the girl. And Hope was nearly tempted to go and try one of Angie's outlandish treatments, having heard so much about them over the weeks. Nearly . . . but not quite.

31

2016

Maggie could hardly believe it. It was thirty years since she, Angie and Leon had started at university. Well, thirty years and about six months to be precise, but with everything that had been happening she had missed the actual anniversary. Where had the time gone? It was such a cliché, but it really did feel like it had just been yesterday when she turned up in York, full of hope and ambition. The world had been her oyster back then, and she had believed that she could do whatever she set her mind to.

And until that point, it had been true. Whatever Maggie Summers had decided should happen, happened. It was as if she had a hotline to whoever was in control of the universe. Maggie Summers wants to go to university to read law. Tick. Maggie Summers wants to be a solicitor with a prestigious firm of solicitors. Tick. Maggie Summers wants to be made a partner. Tick. The list had gone on and on. Until everything changed.

Thirty years!

Well, this was definitely something that needed celebrating. She grabbed her mobile and created a WhatsApp group. She called it 'Thirty Year Reunion!' and chose a picture of the lake that dominated the York university campus from Google for the image. Then she typed her message.

Hi both. I've just realised that it's thirty years since we first met in York. Sounds like an excuse for a get-together to me! What do you think? Up for it?

Would they be up for it, she wondered? Her finger hovered over the send button. Angie certainly would, Maggie felt sure, although they might have to stay in York for their night out. Romany was fifteen now and certainly old enough to be left for an evening whilst her mother went out of town, but Angie had always been hugely protective of her in a way that she had never been about anything else in her life. If the reunion happened, it might be best to suggest that they stick to York rather than head over to Leon's neck of the woods.

Maggie was slightly less sure of how Leon would react. He'd had a rocky time recently and might not feel like celebrating. She had first wondered if something was awry in his world when there had been no Christmas card from his family the Christmas before. Becky was generally very organised, her cards arriving promptly in the second week of December. Maggie's own cards always went out in the first week and so she doubted she could have been accidentally overlooked. Of course, she might have been cut from the list on purpose, although Becky had put up with her for all these years so it would have been odd if she had suddenly changed her mind. Curious, Maggie had rung Angie to see if she had received a card.

'Hang on!' Angie had said. 'Just putting you on speaker while I check.'

It clearly wasn't a big job to look through her Christmas greetings, as she was back on the line moments later. Either she had received very few or, more likely, she hadn't bothered to open the ones she got. Maggie visualised her own card – carefully chosen and with an individual and thoughtful message handwritten inside – sitting amongst a pile of circulars and bills, unopened and unloved.

'Nope,' she said. 'Nothing here either.'

'That's unusual,' said Maggie. 'Becky is generally so fastidious about these things.'

'Anal, you mean,' replied Angie. 'No offence,' she added quickly.

Maggie didn't take offence any more. Angie had always struggled to grasp that a life ordered beyond what she saw as reasonable was the very kind of life that Maggie prided herself on having. What Angie saw as anal, Maggie considered to be just good planning.

So, Maggie had then texted Leon, not mentioning the lack of a Christmas card per se, but asking after him and the family in a more general way.

A few moments later her phone had rung. It had been him.

'Hi, Lee,' she'd said. 'And a merry Christmas to you. How's it going?'

'Oh, you know,' he said. 'It's going. And how about you?'

'I'm fine. No news.' She could feel her cheeks burning but she wasn't ready to tell him about what had happened. She wasn't ready to tell anybody.

'Life just ticks on really,' she'd continued. 'Well, races by at breakneck speed actually. How are we nearly fifty, for a start? I think I'm in denial. Doing anything nice for Christmas?'

There was a pause at the other end of the line and Maggie felt the atmosphere shift.

'Actually, I'll be on my own this year,' he said. His voice had sounded thick all of a sudden, as if his throat had closed and was only allowing part of the sound out. 'Becky and I, well, we split up in the summer.'

Maggie had been momentarily lost for words. What kind of a friend was she to have let this happen and not to have been there for Leon? She racked her brains, trying to think of the last time they had been in touch. Easter, maybe? Surely not that long ago, but then life had a habit of racing by. It could well have been six whole months since they last spoke. And in that time his marriage had collapsed.

It was sad, but it wasn't really a surprise. Becky had never been quite right for Leon, in Maggie's opinion at least, and she had seen tensions in their relationship over the years, but she had always assumed that they arose because Becky had never really taken to Leon's university friends rather than it being indicative of wider problems in the marriage. But, putting her own views aside, she felt awful at having let Leon go through the marriage break-up on his own, even if she had had no clue that it was happening.

'Oh, I'm so sorry, Lee,' she managed. 'Are you okay? Are the boys okay?'

Leon sniffed. 'Thomas is away at uni now and doesn't seem to be bothered. It's hit James a bit harder, but then he always was the more sensitive one.'

More like his dad than his mum, thought Maggie.

'So where are you living?' she asked. 'You're still in Leeds, I assume.'

'Yep. Becky's stayed in the house and I've got myself a little bachelor pad down by the river in the centre of town. It's handy for work and there's room for James to come and stay whenever he wants.'

Maggie couldn't quite take it in. It seemed so unlikely. But then, unlikely things happened all the time. Just look at her own situation.

'And are you okay?' she repeated, her voice tender.

Again, there was a little pause. Maggie wondered if he might be crying, but then when he spoke again there was no indication of it in his voice.

'Yes, I'm fine. It had been on the cards for a while, if I'm being honest. When the axe actually fell it was almost a relief.'

Maggie was dying to ask which of them had initiated the break-up, but that wasn't the kind of question you asked over the phone.

'And how are you?' he asked her.

How was she? Well, for the purposes of this conversation, she was fine.

'I'm fine,' she said.

They finished up with a swapping of the news that she had about Angie and Tiger, wished each other a merry Christmas and then ended the call. That had been four months ago. Surely, he would be up for a night out now to celebrate the thirty years thing.

Without letting herself overthink it any further, Maggie pressed send.

It didn't take long for her phone to ping with replies – Angie's consisting mainly of shocked-looking emojis and redacted expletives, Leon's more measured but still expressing surprise that it had indeed been thirty years. A plan was forged for food and wine in York the following Saturday night, Angie picking a restaurant that she knew would have enough vegan options for her to choose from.

Maggie was looking forward to seeing them both. She would do a little quiz, she decided, about things that had happened when they lived together. It would be funny, and it was nice to look back. She might even dig out some old photographs, too, although seeing the passage of time displayed quite so graphically might be a bit painful. Maggie had always thought that she was ageing well. She had hung on to her figure and kept her grey hairs at bay with regular and expensive visits to Vidal Sassoon in Leeds. Recently, though, the marks of time had become etched into her face, more deep wrinkles than fine lines. And fewer visits to the salon meant that her previously sharp cut had morphed into something more 'mumsy' and middle-aged.

Maybe she wouldn't bother with the photos after all. The quiz would be enough.

32

Angie was determined to get to the restaurant first, if nothing else to prove that she could do it, but somehow time had got away from her.

'You look nice,' Romany commented as Angie appeared from her bedroom in her going-out dress, a pale blue tunic printed with peacocks that she wore over mustard yellow leggings. 'Where are you going again?'

Romany was sitting at the table, surrounded by schoolbooks and printed sheets. Whatever happened to textbooks? Angie wondered. Too expensive these days, no doubt, but all those printed sheets year after year would surely add up to the cost of a textbook eventually. It didn't strike her as very green.

Romany had her chestnut hair tied up in a messy bun from which protruded two biros and a pencil, and seeing them there gave Angie such a rush of love for her studious child that she had to give her a squeeze.

'Oi!' objected Romany, but she allowed herself to break off for a moment for a hug. Romany was focused in a way that Angie had never been. So often her daughter reminded her of Maggie, which she could now see, with the benefit of hindsight garnered from almost fifty years' life experience, was perhaps no bad thing.

'I'm meeting Maggie and Leon, remember,' Angie said. 'Because apparently it's thirty years since we first met.'

'OMG! That's, like, a total lifetime,' said Romany, and Angie sighed.

'It's actually twice your lifetime,' she said. 'I thought you were supposed to be good at maths. And don't say "like".'

Romany rolled her eyes good-humouredly. 'It's pretty cool though, Mum. That you're still friends after all that time.'

Angie nodded thoughtfully. 'Yes,' she said. 'I suppose it is. It's funny. We should never have been friends in the first place. Not really. We're all too different, but we just sort of got thrown in together and stuck to each other.'

'That's probably why you're still friends now,' said Romany. 'If you're all so different then you're less likely to fall out.'

Angie planted a kiss on her daughter's forehead. 'You, my darling child, are very wise.'

'I know,' she said, mock-preening herself. 'It's one of the huge number of talents that I possess. So, where are you meeting?'

'No. 24. At seven thirty.' Angie looked at the time on her phone. 'And I'm late. Shit! Right, I'm out of here. Bed by ten. No wild parties or orgies. I'll lock the door behind me. Don't let anyone in!'

Romany raised an eyebrow and shook her head. 'I'm not six years old,' she said. 'Have a great time. Say hello to Auntie Maggie from me. And what's his name, Leon.'

'Will do.' Angie gave her another quick kiss and a squeeze of her shoulder and then left the flat.

It was cold outside and her dress wasn't thick enough. She should have brought a coat, but if she went back now she would be even later, and Romany would laugh at her for being disorganised. So, she set off at speed up the street, hoping that the exercise would warm her up sufficiently to not miss the coat.

When she arrived at the restaurant, the other two were already there and a bottle of something red had been opened and poured into two large glasses.

'Why am I always the last?' Angie asked breathlessly, dropping herself down into the remaining chair and pushing her hair away from her sweaty brow.

'Because you have a special talent for it,' replied Leon with a fond smile. 'Do you want some of this?'

He picked up the bottle and went to pour some into her glass, but she put her hand over the top.

'Why can't you remember that I don't drink any more? It's been fifteen years!'

Leon shook his head. 'I suppose because I always picture you with a beer in your hand,' he said, and she punched his arm. 'What can I get you instead?'

'Water is fine,' she said, and he shook his head.

'Don't you miss having a drink?' he asked.

Angie was about to give her stock answer about no longer needing alcohol, but then she remembered who she was talking to.

'Hell, yes! Sometimes I dream about beer, lots of little bottles all marching towards me like the brooms in *The Sorcerer's Apprentice*. But then I remember that this was my decision and no one forced me into it. And I do feel so much better without all that shit in my system.'

'Personally, I like a bit of shit.' Leon laughed.

Angie turned her attention to Maggie then. So far she hadn't spoken, but was sitting and quietly observing the other two.

'So, Mags,' Angie began before she had switched her gaze from one friend to the other. When she did, the rest of the sentence stuck in her throat. 'God, Maggie. What's the matter? You look bloody awful.'

Maggie tried to laugh. 'Gee, thanks for that, Ange,' she said.

'I'm sorry. But honestly, what's the matter? Are you ill? Is it serious?'

Thoughts of cancer or some other life-threatening illness raced through Angie's mind. She had never seen anyone age so quickly in such a short period of time. She tried to think when she had last seen Maggie, and concluded that it must have been when she had dropped round just before Christmas with gifts for her and Romany. That was only four months ago. How could a person change so much so quickly?

Maggie seemed to retreat a little, wrapping her arms around herself as if in protection from the glare of Angie's focus.

'I'm not ill,' she said. 'I'm fine.'

Angie didn't believe it and she said so. 'No, you're not. Something's definitely up. What is it? Come on. You can tell us.'

Maggie studied the table hard, as if the answer to the question was somehow caught in the striped grain of the wood. Her bony fingers pulled at the skin on her chin repetitively and with some force so that Angie wanted to put a hand out to stop her.

Then she took a deep breath.

'I lost my job,' she said.

She pulled her gaze up to meet their eyes. Then she straightened her shoulders and lifted her chin, as if she had decided to own this information. She reached for her glass and took a long drink.

Angie was stunned. Part of her thought that she couldn't have heard properly, although she knew that she had.

It was Leon who gathered himself first.

'But you're a partner,' he said. 'The boss. They can't do that, surely?'

'They can,' replied Maggie. 'And they have.'

'But why?' asked Angie.

Maggie must surely have been the best lawyer in the place. Angie knew nothing about the law, but she had never once had any doubt that Maggie would be brilliant at what she did. She was just that kind of person. Her skills brushed off her all the time, like lily pollen. They were just there, obvious.

Maggie shrugged. 'My face didn't fit any more,' she said. 'Too old, too traditional, too change-averse. Too risk-averse, more like it,' she added with a sardonic raise of an eyebrow. 'Anyway, whatever it was, I'm out. I am unemployed. And now, no doubt, unemployable on top.'

Angie wished that she had a beer. Taking a sip of water really didn't cut it when there had been a shock. And this was a shock. It had never once occurred to her that a disaster of any type, let alone one of this magnitude, would ever befall Maggie. Her life was bolted together with titanium: blast-proof, bomb-proof, everything-proof. It always had been, and Angie had assumed that it always would be.

'God, Maggie, that's crap,' said Leon. 'When did it happen?'

'Three weeks ago,' replied Maggie. 'Technically I'm still on notice, but they made it clear that they didn't need any help picking up my files. So they've put me on garden leave until the end of June. And then that's it. On the scrapheap just before my fiftieth birthday. Could it get any shittier?'

Angie could think of various things that would actually be worse, but this clearly wasn't the time to start pointing out how much Maggie had to be grateful for. Instead, she threw an arm around Maggie's shoulder. She felt her tense at the unaccustomed touch, but then she leant into the gesture and Angie squeezed harder.

'So, have you given any thought as to what you're going to do?' asked Leon.

Maggie threw him a look that suggested that she had thought about little else, but then she shrugged. 'Not really. Obviously, I'm being paid until the end of June. And I have plenty of savings, so money won't be an issue. Not for a while, at least. But after that? I have no idea. Get another job, I suppose, although who would want me is a bit of a moot point.'

'Of course they'll want you,' Angie said indignantly.

But she was talking about the other Maggie, she realised, the Maggie with a rock-solid plan who always got exactly what she shot for. She wasn't sure who this new version of her friend was. And neither, it appeared, was Maggie.

'Do you know what the hardest part is?' Maggie asked, without looking at either Angie or Leon but focusing instead on the bustle around the bar. 'If I'm not a solicitor then I have no idea who I'm supposed to be. For my entire life I have either been working towards becoming a solicitor or actually being one. I can't remember a time when it wasn't part of how I saw myself. And now that it's gone, I'm not sure what else there is. Not much, basically.'

Her bottom lip began to tremble, revealing the effort that she was having to put into not crying.

'But you're still a solicitor,' said Leon. 'You'll always be one.'

It wasn't a helpful thing to say and Angie wanted to kick him under the table, but Maggie seemed to take it in the spirit that it had been offered. She gave him a wan smile.

'Yes. But you take my point. No husband, no family, no social life to speak of, present company excepted. My work has pretty much been my life and my raison d'être. Now, if someone asks me who I am and what I do, I have absolutely nothing to say.'

Angie could see that she was really struggling to hold herself together.

'I know it must feel like that now, Mags, but we all know that's not true. We wouldn't be friends with a loser like that, would we, Leon?'

Leon grinned. 'No, we would not. Only the mega-successful can join our band,' he said. He gave Maggie a look that Angie had never seen pass between them before, caring and almost intimate despite his jokey comment, and she wondered if there had been conversations between them that she hadn't been privy to. She decided not. Leon was clearly as surprised by Maggie's news as she was. But maybe there was something else that she'd missed.

'Well, I'm glad it's not just me whose life has turned to shit,' Leon said, draining his glass and reaching for the bottle.

'Oh Leon,' Maggie said, 'hark at me making it all about my problems, and I didn't even ask how you were getting on. How are you?'

'I'm okay,' he said. 'I've had longer to get used to my new status than you. And it's all right really. I hadn't been what Becky wanted me to be for a while. Well, forever really, but it took her the best part of twenty years to work out that she couldn't mould me into her version of a perfect husband. So, when she suggested that our marriage had run its course, it was pretty easy just to agree with her. And living alone has a lot to commend it, I'm discovering. I can eat takeaway from the carton in my boxers and there's no one there to object.'

'Ew!' squealed Angie. 'Save us that particular mental image!'

Leon looked affronted. 'There's nothing there that you haven't both experienced before,' he said.

'Well, I'm not sure that I want to experience it again!' Angie said, and they all laughed more loudly than the comment deserved, a welcome relief from the tension.

The waitress arrived to take their order, but as no one had even opened their menu, Angie sent her away.

'So, does that mean I'm the only one that has their shit together right now?' she asked in delight. 'Praise be! It's a miracle! I've waited a bloody long time for my turn to come round.'

'And talking of getting your shit together,' said Leon, 'have you heard from Tiger recently?'

Angie saw Maggie start at the mention of his name. It's still there then, she thought idly, after all this time. There was something else as well. She thought she saw Leon's jaw tighten slightly. Had he and Tiger had words last time he'd been home? That seemed unlikely, but she couldn't think why else there might be any bad feeling between the two of them.

'Not seen him for about a year,' she said. 'No, wait, it'll be closer to two. God, is it really that long?'

'Well, time is flying,' Maggie said. 'Evidence – one thirty-year reunion dinner.'

'I suppose so,' said Angie. 'Last time I heard anything he was working at a diving school in the Caribbean. The Cayman Islands, I think, wherever they are.'

'As a dive instructor?' asked Leon. 'That's cool.'

'No!' replied Angie. 'Tiger?! Do you think he'd ever get himself organised enough to do a PADI qualification? No, he was taking bookings, driving the boats, cleaning the equipment. That kind of thing. Anyway, he's been there a while, so he must like it.'

'It's not like him to stay in one place for that long,' said Maggie. 'It must be going well.'

'Either that or he just can't save the money to move on,' replied Angie.

'Aren't the Cayman Islands a tax haven?' asked Leon thoughtfully. 'I imagine it's pretty expensive to live there.'

Angie shrugged. 'No doubt he'll be back when he gets bored. Right, I'm starving. Let's get some food ordered,' she said.

'And then I can test your memories with this little quiz I've devised,' said Maggie.

Angie groaned, but she didn't mean it. A little bit of gentle reminiscing to a time when life was simpler was probably exactly what they all needed.

33

By the end of the evening Maggie and Leon were really quite drunk and very sweet with it. Angie had feared that there might be tears, given everything that had been disclosed, but actually their drunkenness had slanted in favour of an enhanced perception of just how fond they all were of one another. Maggie's quiz had been the start.

'Who accidentally dropped their contact lens on the floor in the college bar during the Friday night disco and made the DJ turn the lights on so that everyone could look for it?' asked Maggie.

'Oh, I remember that,' said Leon. 'Wasn't it that girl whose room was directly above yours, Ange? The one with fabulous tits.'

'Leon!!' said Maggie so loudly that the people at the surrounding tables all looked round, causing Maggie to stare back defiantly in a most un-Maggie kind of way.

'What?' asked Leon indignantly. 'She did have great tits! What was her name? It's on the tip of my tongue. Guinevere or something.'

'Genevieve!' said Angie. 'Was that her with the contact lens? She was such a princess. I remember us all stopping dancing and crawling around on our hands and knees looking for it.'

'Completely ridiculous when you think about it,' said Leon, 'but if she'd asked us to walk backwards into the middle of next week we'd have done it for her. She was bloody gorgeous.'

Angie tutted loudly.

'Next. Who was caught in the act red-footed?' Maggie asked, moving neatly away from Genevieve's figure.

'Oh, that's easy!' said Leon. 'That lad who painted anti-Apartheid slogans on the Barclays Bank cashpoint in red paint and then left footprints for the police to follow leading all the way back to his flat. Idiot!'

'Wasn't he on your course, Maggie?' asked Angie. 'Not the greatest start to a career in the law.'

'He was. Wonder what happened to him,' Maggie said vaguely and then, with more conviction, 'Who could turn anything into a decent chilli?'

Angie and Leon both spoke at once. 'Me!' 'Lee!'

'They kept us going, those chillis of yours. You should come round one night, Lee, and make us another. For old times' sake,' Maggie suggested.

'I can do that,' he said and for a moment, Angie thought he was going to mention his newly single status, but he didn't. Instead, the three of them stayed safely cocooned in the past, in a time before any of them knew how things were going to turn out.

Around midnight the restaurant staff started putting chairs on the tables and mopping the floor and so, taking the hint, they left. The wine seemed to hit Maggie as she stood up and she swayed on the spot for a moment, giggling like a schoolgirl.

'I haven't been this drunk for . . .' she began, looking up at the ceiling and tapping her index finger against her lips. 'Forever,' she concluded.

Leon grabbed hold of her arm. 'Steady!' he said.

Even in this drunken state, Angie would have expected Maggie to shun the help, but she didn't seem to notice. Together they stumbled out of the restaurant and into the brightly lit street. There were a few people around, but they all seemed to be walking with purpose to a destination unknown. The evening appeared to be over.

No one suggested going on anywhere else, and Angie felt relieved. There was only so much reminiscing she could take, and she feared that if they let the conversation stray closer to their present situations, the evening would take a very different turn.

'Right,' said Leon decisively. 'Point me in the direction of a taxi rank.'

'Noooo,' said Maggie. 'Come and stay at my place. I've got a spare room with an en suite and I can definitely rustle you up a shiny new toothbrush.'

Leon's eyes flicked between the pair of them as if Angie could help him make a decision.

'Don't look at me,' said Angie. 'You're very welcome to come back with me but you'll be on the sofa, it'll be a scrum for the bathroom and you'll have to share my toothbrush!'

Leon looked back at Maggie. 'Are you sure you don't mind?' he asked.

'The more the merrier,' replied Maggie in a very un-Maggie-like way.

She slipped her arm through Leon's and, after saying their goodbyes, the pair of them strolled off in the direction of the taxi rank leaving Angie to make her own way home.

◆ ◆ ◆

It had been a lovely evening, Angie thought, letting herself back into her quiet flat and sneaking up the stairs for fear of waking Romany. There was something about old friends, she thought, a special depth of understanding that you never quite managed to reach with friends made later in life. The people who knew you when you were learning to know yourself had a more honest picture. They'd seen you when you were not yet entirely formed, when your outer shell hadn't quite sealed around you. As a result, there was less pretending. Friends like that would never let you get away with the stories that you could spin around yourself with newer people. And even though that could be scarily exposing, it was also good to be around them. You could skip past all that small talk and pleasantries stuff and cut straight to the heart of whichever matter needed to be discussed.

That said, once she and Leon had learned that Maggie had been sacked – sacked! Maggie!!! – they had managed to steer the conversational boat a long way from that particular reef, old friends or not. There would be time enough to unpick that in the coming weeks.

Leon seemed to be faring better with his new situation, but then he had had longer to get his head around the changes. Also, he had always had such low expectations in the first place, so he had less far to fall than Maggie. There was a kind of logic to his approach to life, Angie could see now. If you never aim too high, then you never have too far to fall. It was fundamentally self-limiting though, accepting that your life was never going to be more than you allowed it to be, and Angie didn't believe that that was what Leon really wanted. Fear of success, that was what was holding him back. His life would be much easier if it just trundled along the same path as his parents' had done. It was safe and secure and in many ways that was commendable. But it was such a waste! A waste of his musical ability and a waste of life in general. You got one spin on the merry-go-round. Surely it was a person's responsibility to make their ride as exciting as they possibly could?

Was it arrogance, Angie wondered, that she thought she knew better than Leon? Possibly; probably, in fact, but she was obviously right.

It wasn't too late, though. Now that he was free from the clutches of that controlling wife of his, would he be brave enough to do something with his talent? But even as Angie was thinking that, she knew it would never happen. Leon just didn't have it in him to push himself beyond where he had always been. Not without help, anyway.

She tiptoed through the flat, dropping her bag on the floor and kicking her shoes off so that one landed by the coffee table and the other half-under the sofa. There was a light coming from under Romany's bedroom door, so she pushed the handle down gently and peeped inside. Romany was asleep, *Lord of the Flies* open across her face where it had fallen. Angie padded across the room and lifted the book, folding the corner of the page to mark the place. Then she bent down to kiss her daughter on the head and to turn off her bedside light. As she did so, Romany stirred and opened her eyes.

'Nice night?' she asked.

Angie smiled and nodded.

'I must have fallen asleep,' Romany said, reaching a hand out from under the duvet to retrieve the book from her mother. And then, 'Mum!! Did you fold the corner?!'

'I didn't want you to lose your place,' replied Angie indignantly. She had been pleased that she'd thought not to just shut the book.

'Ever heard of a bookmark?' Romany said, but she was too sleepy to be actually cross and she let her eyes droop and then close again.

'Night, night, baby,' said Angie, and then retreated out of the room.

She was too awake to go to bed, so she made herself a cup of chamomile tea to try and help her nod off. Sitting on the sofa, curled into a ball with her fingers wrapped tightly around the mug, it occurred to her again that for the first time in thirty years, she was the only one whose life was flowing along nicely. She had her thriving business and her flat, which was at least half-paid for. And she had Romany, the most precious thing in the world. For all her lack of a plan, she had made something good out of her life. It might have been more down to luck than judgement, but all was spectacularly well in her world.

Of course, she took no pleasure in the difficulties that the others were facing. That wasn't how things worked. Life wasn't like a see-saw where you could only be at the top if someone else was at the bottom. But at the same time, it did feel fair that she should have a bit of good fortune. It was her turn. If anyone understood the universe's energy, it was her. Right now, it was her sun that was in the ascendant and for that she was very grateful.

Her mind cast back to that day in their second year at York when Maggie had caught her crying in her room. That day had been the start of their friendship. Until then they were just two people who had ended up living together through a series of random circumstances. But after she had accidentally revealed her vulnerability, a kind of reluctant trust had been garnered between the two of them that had been growing, little by little, ever since. At twenty, Angie had thought that she didn't need anyone, that she was strong enough to get through life on her own. But gradually she had come to realise that sometimes you really do need someone rooting for you. Over the years, that person had become Maggie.

And now, here they were with the roles well and truly reversed, Angie with her life on track and Maggie adrift and without a clue what to do about it.

Angie had no magic bullets for her friend. She didn't even know what her options might be. But she knew that she was going to be there when Maggie needed her.

34

A month after the reunion and Angie was still no wiser about Maggie's situation. She seemed to have gone to ground. Angie's calls went to voicemail and her texts were replied with cheerful but very brief responses from which no information could be readily discerned. Angie didn't want to pry, but at the same time she didn't want to leave Maggie stewing in her own juices. Brooding was no good for anyone. She had even offered her a number of therapeutic treatments, either from her or other members of her team, in case Maggie would rather not be treated by a friend, but they had all been politely but firmly declined.

She had to do something, though. Maggie was strong, but no woman was an island. Everyone needed some help sometimes, even Maggie; maybe especially Maggie. When things went up in smoke around Angie, she already had a whole armoury of defences built up over a lifetime of difficulties to help herself get back on her feet. This was, as far as Angie knew at least, the first time Maggie had ever encountered anything going other than entirely according to plan. She must surely need all the help she could get. And Angie was determined to be the one to provide it.

Then, as she walked to Live Well one clear blue morning, the perfect idea presented itself. She checked the weather app on her phone. Things were set fair for the entire weekend. It would be just what they needed.

She rang Maggie.

'I've had an idea. You have to say yes. No is not an option.'

'Good morning to you too,' replied Maggie.

Angie could hear that there was a lightness in her voice, and she felt relieved. Maybe things weren't quite as bad as she had feared.

'Tomorrow we're going to the seaside. You, me and Romany. We can do paddling and ice cream and eat chips out of the newspaper—'

'They don't serve chips in newspaper any more. It's unhygienic, apparently, although it did no harm for generations,' Maggie interrupted.

'Don't interrupt,' replied Angie. 'We'll go to Whitby and then we can take Romany to the Abbey and tell her all about Dracula, so it'll be educational too. What do you think, bearing in mind my previous statement that yes is the only option?'

'Er, yes,' said Maggie.

'Excellent. Right answer. You'll have to drive, though. You've still got a car, right?'

'Your tact is as solid as ever,' replied Maggie. 'But yes, I do still have a car.'

'Great. You can pick us up at nine. Bring a flask.'

'Anything else?' Maggie laughed.

'No. That's it. No. Wait. A towel. Right, we'll see you at nine.'

Angie rang off before Maggie had a chance to change her mind. Then she texted Romany telling her to cancel any plans she had for the following day.

Saturday dawned just as bright and blue as forecast, and Romany appeared at eight thirty dressed as if she was going to spend the day on Ibiza in August and not the east coast of England in May.

'You're going to need more clothes than that,' said Angie when she saw her in her skimpy shorts and tiny crop top. 'I know the planet is heating up a little more each day, but it's still not quite tropical in Whitby. And I don't want you getting cold and spoiling things.'

Romany sighed and rolled her eyes but retreated to her room to gather more layers.

When the doorbell rang bang on nine o'clock, Angie was feeling positively excited. A day out was just what they all needed. She pulled a tote bag out of the 'messy cupboard' and stuffed two towels into it. Then she filled a bottle with water, found her purse and raced down the stairs, leaving Romany to lock the flat.

Maggie was on the pavement dressed in a pair of navy trousers and a Breton-style jumper with a red scarf twisted round her neck. She also had a jacket. No concession had been made for the potential warmth of the day. Maggie had obviously been to the east coast before. She still looked very gaunt, Angie thought, but there was at least some colour in her cheeks and her smile was wide and genuine.

'Your carriage awaits,' she said, flourishing her arm in the direction of the car. 'Roof up or down?'

'Down!' chorused Angie and Romany.

'It'll be chilly,' warned Maggie. 'But I have blankets,' she added.

Of course she did, thought Angie.

It took a couple of minutes to drop the roof on the little car and then they were off, following the coast road out of York. It seemed that plenty of others had had a similar thought and the traffic was pretty much nose to tail until they reached the turn-off for Scarborough, where most of the traffic peeled away.

Once in Whitby, they left the car down by the harbour and set off towards the town.

'I'm ashamed to say that I've never been to Whitby,' confessed Maggie as they crossed a bridge and followed the crowds towards the Abbey. 'I know it's only just down the road, but somehow I never made the time to visit. The downside of a busy life, I suppose,' she mused, and Angie braced herself for the mood to slide, but Maggie seemed cheerful. 'These days, I have no excuse not to get out and about more. Starting right now!' She nodded decisively as if reinforcing the idea.

'We went to Scarborough on the train once,' Angie recalled. 'In the third year?' Maggie looked at her blankly. 'Or maybe that was me and someone else,' she added vaguely. 'Pretty sure I've never been here, either.'

Romany gave her a disdainful look. 'Call yourself a mother!' she scoffed. 'Isn't making sure that I'm well rounded and know my local environment part of your job description?'

Angie doffed an imaginary cap. 'Sorry, Miss. Will do better, Miss,' she said in a fake Cockney accent, although why she associated servants with Cockneys Angie had no idea.

'She's got a point,' said Maggie.

'Don't gang up on me! I'm doing my best here!'

Romany leant into her and gave her a little squeeze. 'Only teasing,' she said.

Was it good enough, though, her best stab at single parenting? It was a question that Angie asked herself regularly, measuring herself up against her view of a perfect mother (and father for that matter). She invariably found herself lacking, but that had to be normal, didn't it? Not many people considered themselves flawless in that regard, she was sure. Having no role model made things a little bit trickier, but at least she had, from experience, a pretty clear idea of what a parent was not supposed to do.

They made their way over a bridge and up an increasingly narrow street. The shop windows seemed to be mainly filled with cheap jet jewellery and skulls. Halfway up, they came across an odd photographer's shop. The window displayed sepia prints of families in Victorian costume. Angie thought they were antiques for sale at first but when, her curiosity piqued, she looked a little closer, she realised that they were actually modern-day photographs.

'Romey, look at these,' she called out.

Romany, who was walking a couple of paces ahead with Maggie, turned round and looked across.

'You can get dressed up in costumes and have your photo done,' Angie said, inexplicably taken with the idea. 'Look!'

'You can,' replied Romany. 'But why would you? Who wants a photo of themselves dressed like that?'

Angie looked again. She thought the pictures of people looking solemnly at the camera in fake crinolines and top hats were funny, but maybe not. Then she realised all the images had a man in them, domineering and commanding in a soldier's costume or dressed as the stern father figure. It seemed to round the shot off somehow, even though that did not align with her own views of what a family should be. It was only social conditioning that made her think that, she knew, or perhaps it was because the photographs reflected a distant past that she recognised from Sunday night period TV in which every family had a husband.

Romany was probably right, as usual. Having their photo taken in those costumes was a terrible idea, like buying a sombrero or a sarong on holiday – perfect in its home environment but less well suited to yours. And anyway, the three of them would make for a very sorry little family grouping. Maggie wasn't even family.

Angie left the shop behind and followed the others, moving slightly more quickly to catch them up.

Around the next bend they found the foot of crooked stone steps that led up to the Abbey. There was a stream of people climbing up one side and descending the other. Angie wasn't sure which group looked more exhausted.

Maggie and Romany were standing at the bottom and staring upwards, as if it were a mountaineering challenge.

'Are we going up?' Angie asked them.

'Oh, I think we must,' said Maggie. 'Can't come to Whitby and not see the graveyard.'

'Race you to the top!' said Romany and then she set off at speed, weaving in and out of other people as if she had a train to catch. A look passed between Angie and Maggie that suggested that a more sedate pace of ascent would be in order.

They began steadily, side by side, Angie congratulating herself as they climbed on what a nice day she had chosen for their trip, and considering where they might get some lunch, but by the time they were halfway up, her conversation fell away as she focused on just putting one foot in front of another. She had thought she was quite fit but clearly, she had been deluded. This was seriously hard work and as she puffed her way up, she resolved to do something about her general cardiovascular health.

Eventually, the top of the steps appeared and with it St Mary's church, and beyond that the remains of the Abbey, looming darkly across the skyline despite the sunshine. Romany was waiting for them, reclining on a wall like a fashion model, her long legs spread out in front of her.

'You took your time,' she said. 'I've been here for ages. Did you count the steps?'

'I had all on just getting up them,' replied Angie wheezily. 'I really must go back to that Zumba class.'

'I did. There are one hundred and ninety-nine,' Romany said with an air of triumph.

'That's what I got too,' said Maggie.

Angie looked at the pair of them and shook her head. 'I sometimes wonder if you're actually Maggie's kid, not mine,' she said to her daughter. 'I mean, who counts steps?'

'Who doesn't?' replied Maggie, and she and Romany exchanged a look.

'Well, I think you're both mad,' replied Angie, but secretly a warm rush of pride ran through her. 'Right, let's go and see what this is all about.'

They wandered along the path, past the church and the graveyard towards the visitor centre, only to discover that there was an entrance fee to get in. Angie eyed Maggie.

'How much do we want to go inside?' Angie asked.

Maggie shrugged. 'I'm happy to go in if you want to,' she said. 'Or not . . . Whatever you think.'

An indecisive Maggie was a new and unfamiliar beast, and Angie couldn't tell whether it was being fed by a lack of confidence or a lack of funds. She was prepared to pay the entrance fee, for all three of them if necessary, but she was also happy enough not to.

'Let's not bother,' she said and watched Maggie nod quickly, apparently relieved that the decision had been made for her.

So, they wandered back the way they'd come. At the steps, rather than heading back down to the town, they turned left towards the grassy bank and admired the view out across Whitby and to the open sea. The sun was climbing high and the air felt warm for May, the breeze playful rather than spiteful. The turquoise water in the harbour lay as flat as a millpond with barely a ripple.

Romany flopped down on to the grass, stripped her jacket off and rolled it up to make a pillow for her head. Then she lay back and stared up at the heavens, blue in the main but with slabs of heavy sooty cloud here and there, just to remind you that you were still in Yorkshire. Angie, seeing the benefit of staying put, at least for a while, sat down too. She pulled the towels out of her bag and offered one to Maggie, but Maggie had what must have been the neatest towel known to man in a little pouch in her handbag. She flicked it out and sat down.

'This was a lovely idea, Ange,' she said. 'Thank you for asking me. It's just what I needed, a trip out of York and some sea air.'

Angie took a deep breath, filling her lungs to the very bottom, held it for a count of five and then let it out slowly. She repeated the exercise several more times, feeling her heartbeat slow and her body release some of its stress. Her mind, though, felt strangely unsettled. She couldn't quite put her finger on what it was, but something was making her feel out of kilter. It felt as if there was something that needed to be spoken, to be released so that it could stop troubling her. She just wasn't sure what it was. Something to do with Maggie's future, probably. There were so many unanswered questions there and she hadn't delved, waiting instead for Maggie to want to talk to her. Something was definitely nagging at Angie, though, blocking her chakras and leading to this disconcerting feeling of imbalance.

And then she realised what was wrong. The unsettled feeling wasn't anything to do with Maggie, although that issue would need to be resolved in due course. No, the cause of her disquietude was the photographer's shop window: all those pictures of family groups.

Things like that didn't generally bother her. She had been without a family since she'd first been taken into care and so didn't think in terms of neat little nuclei. There was her and there was Romany, and that was that.

But what if that wasn't really that? Could it be that what worked well for her was failing to work for her daughter? It wasn't a discussion that they had had, not recently anyway, and suddenly, it felt vitally important to discuss it. Right there, right now.

'Romany?' she began.

Romany was chewing on a stalk of grass, pulling it between her teeth to extract the sweet innards.

'Mmm,' she replied lazily.

'Do you mind that you don't know who your father is? I mean, does it bother you?'

There. It was out. She had said it. She saw Maggie's expression change, grey eyes roaming across Angie's face curiously, trying to establish where this question had come from and whether she should be there to hear the reply, but Romany didn't move. She continued to stare up at the clouds as they scudded across the blue.

Nobody spoke. The birds sang, children shouted to each other as they ran up the 199 steps, in the distance you could just make out the chimes of an ice cream van, but not one of them said a word. Angie began to wonder whether she had failed to say the words out loud. Maybe the sentence, so clearly spoken, had only been in her head. She looked over at Romany to check for some outward indication that she had heard her. Romany was still lying on her back and staring at the sky, her legs crossed, the upper one swinging idly back and forth.

Angie turned to look at Maggie and raised an eyebrow. Maggie looked mystified too, so Angie supposed that her question had been audible.

'No,' said Romany eventually, and Angie switched her attention back to her daughter. 'I don't mind, it doesn't bother me, and I'm not interested,' she added.

Angie felt her heart soar, vindicated by those few words, not that she had ever thought, until that moment, that Romany had reason to blame her for anything. She and Jax had never made any particular decision about it. There had been no deeply held conviction that he should, or indeed, should not, be involved in his daughter's life.

It just hadn't happened.

Angie knew that Romany would have been well within her rights to be angry with her, to hold her mother responsible for her father's lack of contact. It had been Angie, after all, who had let the connection drop by not sending a forwarding address when they moved to the current flat.

However, Romany was unconcerned; or so it appeared, at least. Angie had been confident that Romany was not angry, but it was nice to have it confirmed.

'In fact,' Romany continued, speaking slowly with large gaps forming between her words, as if she were thinking through what she was saying just moments before the words came out, 'I would go as far as to say that if I were given a choice – to meet him or not to meet him – then I'd choose not.'

Angie's relief was palpable, but she tried not to let it show.

'Okay,' she said. 'That's good.'

Then Romany sat up, a sudden movement that made Angie jump, and started looking around her at the people buzzing backwards and forwards. 'Why? He's not here, is he? That's not why we've come here, to meet him?' Her head spun one way and then another, her face such a picture of anxiety that Angie reached out and hugged her.

'No, no,' she said soothingly. 'He's not here.'

Romany disengaged herself and continued to survey the surroundings, albeit in a less frenzied manner.

'No. I don't have any contact details for him,' Angie said. 'I mean, I'm sure I could track him down if you wanted me to . . .'

'I don't,' said Romany firmly. 'I'm fine. We're fine as we are. We don't need anyone, do we?' Her voice wavered a little towards the end and she looked at Angie as though seeking some confirmation.

'No. You're completely right. But I just thought I'd check.'

Romany settled herself back down on the grass, drama seemingly all passed.

'Romey,' said Maggie. 'Would you be an angel and go and buy me an ice cream from that kiosk over there? Get one for yourself and your mum, too, of course. I'd like a cone, please, just plain. Ange? Do you want one?'

Angie shook her head. 'No thanks,' she said.

Maggie got a ten-pound note out of her purse and handed it to Romany.

'Thanks, Auntie Maggie,' she said, and then strolled off in the direction of the kiosk.

Maggie looked straight at Angie. 'What on earth was that all about?' she asked.

'I don't know,' replied Angie. 'I saw those photos, all with dads in them, and suddenly it felt like I had to ask. I'm sorry. I probably should have waited until we got home.'

'Don't worry about me,' Maggie said. 'Romey seems pretty clear on what she wants.'

Angie laughed. 'She does, doesn't she?'

'She's definitely your daughter! But he's not here, is he?' Maggie's eyes narrowed as she searched Angie's face for any sign of a lie.

'No. No, he isn't. I haven't heard from him for years.'

'Good. Because that would be really bad, if you suddenly brought him back into her life when she's just said that she doesn't want him.'

Angie nodded. Maggie was right. And yet . . .

'I hope she changes her mind, though,' Angie said. 'When she's older, I mean. He wouldn't win any prizes for Partner of the Year, but he's not a bad bloke. Not deep down. It would be good for them to get to know each other eventually.'

'Possibly. But she's only fifteen. There will be plenty of time for all that when she's worked out who she is. And, as we know,' Maggie added, 'that can take quite a long time.'

Romany was coming back across the grass with a cone in one hand and a long bright orange lollipop in the other.

'Thanks, Maggie,' said Angie.

'What for? I haven't done anything.'

'You've done plenty,' replied Angie. 'You'll never know how much.'

35

Maggie let herself out of Leon's flat and set off in the direction of the train station. The first few times she had made the trip across to Leeds she had driven, but actually, she found the half-hour's train journey quite restorative, and now that she had time on her hands, she didn't mind the forty-five-minute walk from York station to her house. Also, she had started leaving a few bits and pieces at Leon's, toiletries mainly, so she didn't have to take a bag each time she went, and it was working well.

It had taken them both by surprise, this . . . she wasn't sure what to call it. Relationship sounded so grown up, but she supposed that that was what it was.

The first time they had had sex had been the night of the thirty years' reunion. It hadn't been on the cards, or definitely not Maggie's cards, when she had suggested that he stay the night with her. But somehow, when they got home, their bodies had had other ideas.

It had begun with one of those corny moments that you see in a film. Maggie stumbled a little as she stepped into the house, and Leon put out a hand to steady her, their faces close, closer than Maggie had ever been to him before. She could feel the warmth of his breath on her cheek and watched the look in his eyes change from surprise at their proximity to desire. Then they had kissed, tentatively at first, each not sure what the other wanted, and then with a passion that Maggie had rarely experienced.

The resulting sex had been frenzied and urgent. They were in her kitchen, her back against the cupboards. They didn't bother to get undressed, simply removing the articles of clothing that impeded them. This too might have been shot in a studio, except that they were both so drunk that they found everything funny rather than smouldering.

Afterwards, sitting rather awkwardly opposite each other at her kitchen table and drinking hastily brewed coffee, they had been more shell-shocked than anything. Maggie had never thought of Leon in those terms before. He was just Leon, her friend. Now, though, she wondered if there had been the odd signal over the years to suggest that the idea had crossed his mind before, signals that she had chosen to ignore. She was probably wrong, though. Reading men wasn't something that Maggie had had much practice with.

'Well,' said Leon, his eyes not meeting hers. 'That was fun and not quite what I was expecting. Are you okay? I mean, is this okay?' He looked at her then, a gentle questioning look that told her that the Leon she knew was with her.

Maggie, despite her age and the fact that she had just shared an extremely intimate moment with a man that she had known for more than half her lifetime, was suddenly as shy as a teenager. She could feel her cheeks burning and she lifted her coffee cup up in front of her face to hide them. She wasn't sure what to say, although she did feel suddenly sober, which was a blessing at least.

'Yes, I'm fine,' she managed. And then, 'I'm not sure what happened.'

Leon's grin was downright lascivious and threw her even further off-kilter.

'I know exactly what happened,' he said. 'And I'd like to do it again in a bit. If that's all right with you.'

◆ ◆ ◆

That had been three months ago, or at least it would be on Saturday. That made her feel like a teenager, counting anniversaries month by month, but was there anything so very wrong with that? There hadn't been time to behave like a teenager when she had been one. She had been too intent on where she was going and how quickly she could get there to be bothered with such trivialities. Now, though, with the surge of hormones flooding her brain, she wondered whether her younger self might not have got her priorities a little bit out of whack. This being in lust thing was so much fun.

Still, better late than never. Maggie was positively delighting in the buzz that she got each time her phone screen lit up. Even the surge of disappointment when it was someone other than Leon was kind of appealing. It made her feel more alive than she had in years. Leon was the first thing that she thought about when she woke up and, on the nights when she wasn't actually with him, the last, delicious thought to scamper across her mind before she drifted off to sleep. And she was enjoying every moment.

Leon, it seemed, was as bad as she was and he could be quite romantic when he put his mind to it, his text messages all sprinkled with little hearts and kisses. Maggie had thought that he was teasing her to start with, but no, this appeared to be a whole new side to him that had previously been hidden under his down-to-earth manner. When they had been together a month, she had found a little note in her purse, handwritten on a tiny scrap of parchment paper. It was a simple heart with an arrow scored through its centre and their initials carefully added, just like you might see in any schoolgirl's exercise books, but on the back he had written 'One perfect month'. It was so corny, and at almost fifty years old she felt that she ought to be impervious to its charms, but actually she had been unfeasibly touched by it and had placed it carefully between two store cards so that it didn't get bent or damaged. If she could have framed it and not looked like a love-sick fool, then she would have done.

There had been other little things since then. She had mentioned in passing that she was partial to Lady Grey tea, and the next time she went to his flat she had found a packet next to his habitual builder's variety. He also had cleared a drawer for her in his bedroom, and then been so apologetic about his level of presumption that she had had to kiss him to stop him worrying that he had done the wrong thing.

They had spoken about it one night, in bed after sex.

'Can I ask you something?' Maggie asked, her head resting on his chest as his hand caressed her back. 'It's a bit embarrassing,' she added.

'Oh God,' replied Leon. 'Do I need to brace myself?'

'No.' Maggie laughed. 'It's just, I'd never really thought about us like this' – she gestured at their naked bodies with an open hand – 'until that first night. Had you?'

'Have I always fancied you, you mean?' he asked bluntly.

Maggie's insides squirmed at the direct question. 'Well, yes. I suppose so.'

There was a pause whilst he thought about it, which spoke volumes in itself. She should never have asked the question, she supposed, if she didn't want to hear the answer.

'Of course I fancied you,' he said after a moment or two, 'but I didn't think there was much point. Between your studies and Tiger, I never seemed to get a look in.'

Had it really been that obvious, about Tiger? Maggie pushed herself up so that she could look into Leon's face.

'Nothing ever happened between me and Tiger,' she said.

'But you always wanted it to. Tell me I'm wrong.'

Maggie shrugged.

'So, to answer your question, yes. I've always fancied you. Happy now?'

Maggie smiled and lay back down, grateful that he hadn't asked her the same.

◆ ◆ ◆

She made her way up Call Lane, so vibrant and teeming with life after dark, but always slightly edgy when the sun came up and you could see all the dark corners. She felt her phone vibrate in her pocket and plucked it out to read the message. It was from Angie.

> *Am invited to 30th birthday party on Saturday. A 30th!!!*
> *Get me – down with the kids! Know no one except the*
> *birthday girl. Fancy being my plus one?*

Maggie's first thought was it would be time that she would rather spend with Leon. Then again, they had no particular plans for Saturday night. She imagined that the evening would consist of food and a bottle of wine on either her sofa or his, followed by sex, languid and luxurious or urgent and frenzied, depending on their mood.

But Angie didn't know this yet. Maggie wasn't sure why they had kept the relationship secret and she felt bad. Since the reunion, Angie had sent her a relentless stream of texts and phone messages, and she had been unusually elusive, either dodging Angie's questions or answering them with one of her own. The problem was just that Angie could be so very perceptive. She would see that there was something different about Maggie and have the details teased out of her in five minutes flat, and Maggie didn't want that. She loved having a secret. Nobody in the whole world knew, or even suspected, what she and Leon had done.

But it wasn't just that, Maggie knew. If Angie found out about her and Leon then she would mention Tiger, and Maggie didn't want to think about Tiger, not just now. And worse than that, Angie would know what Maggie knew in her heart but was ignoring: that Leon was her second choice.

She looked again at Angie's text message. Of course she should go to the party with Angie. Leon would still be there when she got back. And maybe she would tell Angie then, when they were in a crowded room.

That sounds fun, she typed. *I'd love to come. Where and when?*

36

'So, what do I need to know before we get there?' asked Maggie as she sat in Angie's flat waiting for her to finish getting ready.

'Her name is Hope,' Angie called through from the bedroom. 'I met her on that business course I did a couple of years back and we kept in touch. I don't see much of her now, but we just clicked on the course. Similar ideas about stuff. Same sense of humour, that kind of thing.'

'It's nice when you meet people who are on your wavelength,' replied Maggie, thinking how rarely that had happened to her.

'Yeah. It's good,' agreed Angie as she wandered into the lounge in just her knickers, her bra looped over one arm. Maggie's first reaction was to avert her eyes to protect Angie's modesty, but then again, Angie had no modesty, so Maggie steeled herself to just pretend that her friend wasn't walking around virtually naked.

'So, how to describe Hope,' Angie continued thoughtfully. 'She's quite direct. Very, actually. I mean, she takes no prisoners. In fact, I'd say she borders on the rude.'

Maggie opened her eyes wide in comedic shock. 'She must be really direct if you think she's rude,' she said with the merest shadow of a fear that Angie would take offence.

'Yeah, she makes me look like a shrinking violet,' said Angie without even a pause. 'Oh, and she's beautiful. I mean, beautiful like you've never seen a real person to be, beautiful.'

'Wow!' said Maggie. 'I don't think I know any beautiful people,' she added with a smirk.

'Thanks a bunch,' replied Angie. 'But seriously, she is. She was a model, and now she's set up this business importing swimwear. That's why she was doing the course, to learn the basics of business. And that's about all I know about her. She's got a house somewhere in town. She's got a boyfriend who's a chef. And that's it. I'm not sure why she's invited me to her do, to be honest.'

'Maybe she's so beautiful that she's got no friends.' Maggie laughed. 'Bet it turns out to be you, me, the chef boyfriend and a couple of maiden aunts all sitting round and playing gin rummy.'

◆　◆　◆

It wasn't like that at all. The party was possibly the most lavish and definitely the most stylish that Maggie had ever been to. It was held in the Hospitium in the Museum Gardens, a fabulous four-teenth-century, half-timbered building that backed on to the river and just oozed history. The stone walls glowed honey gold in the warm evening light and glass lanterns were dotted along the path from the gardens to the entrance to show the way.

A group of women, all considerably younger than Maggie and Angie, were milling around outside, champagne flutes in hands. They were elegantly dressed in expensive cocktail dresses of varying lengths and colours, and Maggie was glad that she had thought to wear one from her own meagre collection even if it was several seasons behind the times. It didn't matter what she was wearing, however. No one would be looking at her when there was so much that was more appealing on display. She had become resigned to the invisibility cloak that middle age wrapped around her, but she couldn't help but feel a little bit old and ugly, despite telling herself that these things were all relative.

Angie, of course, was totally undaunted by the sea of glamour before them. She cut her way through the group and into the hall itself. The room matched its occupants for style and elegance. The pale stone pillars that held up the timbered ceilings were festooned with garlands of eucalyptus, interwoven with tiny twinkling fairy lights. Light also flickered from dozens of wrought-iron candelabras that stood like sentinels, each holding nine tapered ivory candles and twisted round with dark green ivy. Tables and chairs, wrapped in crisp white damask, lined the edges of the room, with a space left in the centre of the room for milling and possibly dancing later. It looked like the sort of party where there would be dancing.

A handsome young man, no doubt a student, in a black waistcoat and trousers that clung in all the right places sashayed past them with a tray of glasses. Angie swiped a champagne and an orange juice and passed the fizz to Maggie, raising an eyebrow as she did so and cocking her head in the direction of the young man's bottom. Maggie suppressed an appreciative giggle. Since the thing with Leon had started up, she was suddenly seeing men in a way that she hadn't done for years. And it was wonderful. It made her feel alive, feminine and downright sexy.

'Bloody hell,' said Angie quietly once she had taken a sip of her orange juice. 'How the other half live, eh?'

'It's pretty impressive,' replied Maggie. 'Which one is Hope?'

Angie had a look around, but it wasn't hard for Maggie to spot the birthday girl. She was holding court in the centre of the room and wearing a floor-length gown in midnight blue lace, the skirt falling away into a fan of tulle. The bodice skimmed her flawless figure and her arms and shoulders, tanned and toned, were bare. The dress gave the illusion of nakedness beneath the tulle but was

241

actually lined in a near-invisible nude fabric. It was stunning. A group of well-wishers surrounded her, but somehow she was keeping them from standing in her personal space, as if she had a force field protecting her. She was, as Angie had suggested, the most beautiful woman Maggie had ever seen in the flesh.

'Oh my God,' she whispered. 'She's like a goddess. How is a creature who looks like that a friend of yours?!'

Angie gave her a gentle thump on her arm.

'Joking aside, though,' Angie said, turning to the wall so that she wouldn't be overheard. 'I think she was quite relieved to find someone to talk to who wasn't that interested in all this.' She swept her arm round the room dismissively.

'You have to admit, though, Ange, this world is kind of intriguing,' replied Maggie. 'I could be consumed by it, for a while at least.'

Another waiter was hovering nearby, and Maggie switched her empty glass for a full one.

'I think I prefer my people a bit closer to real,' said Angie.

'Do you recognise anyone else?' asked Maggie. She was half-thinking that there might be some minor celebrities amongst the guests, but she was unlikely to spot them. Angie lived with a teenager, which might keep her more in touch with that kind of thing, but Angie was shaking her head.

'Not a soul,' she replied. 'We'll say hello to Hope, stay for a couple of free drinks but then I vote we make a discreet exit. I doubt we'll be missed and it's not really my kind of do.'

'Nice to be invited, though,' said Maggie, and Angie nodded in agreement.

'Suppose so,' she said.

Hope turned her attention from her admirers then, and she must have caught sight of Angie because she raised an arm and smiled, mouthing 'Hi' in their direction. Maggie thought that this would be their lot. It seemed unlikely that the hostess would leave her friends to talk to them, but Hope broke away from her group and headed their way. She walked as if she were on a catwalk, her hips swaying gently. It was hard not to stare. Maggie saw the group that she had left nodding towards her and Angie with questioning expressions, but no one was that interested in who they might be and soon the glare of their attention was turned on someone else.

'Angie! Hi,' said Hope when she got close enough to them to be heard. 'I'm so glad you could make it.'

'Happy birthday,' said Angie. 'You don't do things by halves, do you?'

'Is it too much?' asked Hope anxiously. 'I never know how to pitch these things.'

It was a disingenuous comment, Maggie thought. Nobody put on a do like this without knowing exactly the impact that it would have. She felt a mild dislike for the woman begin to creep over her and she tried to bat it back down. It was far too soon to judge, but Hope had barely spoken ten words and already Maggie was unsure about her.

'God, it's perfect.' Angie laughed. 'Posh – but perfect. Are you having a great time, though? That's the main thing.'

Hope pursed her lips into a little knot and Maggie felt her dislike grow. She had all this and still she wasn't happy. It felt so entitled, so shallow, just like the party. Were these even her real friends, or just a gaggle of the right kind of people to have at a do like this, a deluxe rent-a-crowd? The whole thing lacked integrity to Maggie's mind, and she wondered why Angie had been taken in by it, by her. It was so unlike Ange to fall for anything fake.

'I'll be better when Dan gets here,' said Hope. 'He had to start evening service at the restaurant, but he promised me that he'd sneak away before it got busy and be here early. No sign yet, though. I'll have his balls on a platter when he finally shows his face.'

Angie pulled a sympathetic face and again, Maggie was surprised. She really must have a soft spot for this girl, otherwise she wouldn't tolerate this nonsense. Maggie decided that she needed to cut Hope some slack. Maybe this wasn't really what she was like, just part of some grand pretence.

'Forget him,' said Angie. 'It's his loss. You focus on having a lovely time.'

'Thanks,' said Hope. 'I'd better get back to circulating. Thanks for coming, Angie.' She turned to leave and then turned back. 'Oh, I'm sorry. You must be Angie's friend,' she said to Maggie. 'Nice to meet you.'

'Yes, this is Ma . . .' began Angie, but Hope had gone.

'You weren't kidding about the rude thing,' Maggie hissed.

'I think she's under pressure,' said Angie.

It was clear that she felt the need to defend her friend, and that irritated Maggie as well. Just who was the lifelong friend here and who the new pretender?

'It can be stressful, hosting, especially something like this,' Angie continued.

Maggie thought that this was no excuse for not even bothering to listen to her name, but she bit her tongue. The girl was nothing to her and she was unlikely to ever meet her again. Her shoulders were broad enough to bear a snub from such a self-obsessed little brat. And, she supposed, Angie liked her, so she must have something going for her, even if whatever it was wasn't immediately apparent.

As the evening progressed and the air temperature outside began to fall, more of the guests came inside and the room began to fill. The sound of chatting and laughter grew louder and eventually she and Angie gave up trying to talk and simply watched. For all the stench of entitlement that came off them, the guests were a fascinating bunch to observe. They were all good-looking and groomed to a level that Maggie could never achieve, but she noticed how they never focused on the people that they were talking to and always had one eye on the rest of the room. Many of them spent all their time taking photos of themselves, often without anyone else in the shot. It was a level of narcissism that was alien to Maggie, but which these Millennials seemed completely at ease with. In a way, Maggie was envious of their self-assured confidence, but surely life wasn't just a series of Instagram opportunities? At some point, even those as privileged as this lot appeared to be would have to face some of life's hard edges. She checked herself. She was starting to think like an old person; like her mother, in fact. What was wrong with celebrating the here and now and recording it to share with others? Just because she couldn't imagine doing it herself didn't make it reprehensible.

Maggie's mind turned to Leon, sitting, as he would be, on his sofa watching whatever was on the television, and her heart gave a fond little flutter. She had thought she might tell Angie about the two of them this evening, in a quieter moment, but the room was too loud and the moment all wrong. She had waited this long to say something. She could wait a little longer.

'Shall we go in a few minutes?' asked Angie, blowing her lips out and shaking her head at the parade of beauties before them. 'I'm not sure I can take much more of this spectacle!'

Maggie nodded and lifted her half-empty glass. 'When I've finished this one?' she asked, and Angie nodded.

They continued to watch. Someone new had arrived, a man dressed more casually than the majority in well-worn jeans and a T-shirt, with dark hair, greying slightly at the temples. He wasn't as picture-perfect as most of the others and had at least ten years on them. He made a beeline for Hope, approaching her with open palms, all apologies. Hope rolled her eyes but then she leant in and embraced him. This would be the boyfriend, Maggie thought. He really was late. It must have been approaching ten thirty. Still, Maggie couldn't help but have a sneaking admiration for him and his failure to get sucked into whatever this was.

She turned to pass her thoughts on to Angie, but Angie was also looking at him, staring in fact, her jaw slack.

'That must be the errant boyfriend.' Maggie laughed. 'Looks like he's forgiven, though.'

'Shall we go?' said Angie, turning on the spot to face the exit.

Maggie, slightly thrown, looked at her half-filled glass, then at Angie and then back to the glass. 'Yes,' she said. 'Just let me . . .'

But Angie was gone, pushing through the crowds and out into the cool evening beyond.

37

Angie did not sleep at all that night. When she got back to the flat, having said a rather perfunctory goodnight to Maggie (she would need to apologise for that, claim that she hadn't been feeling well or something), Romany was still awake and watching some reality TV programme that seemed to be populated by the kinds of people that Angie had just left behind at Hope's party.

'You're back early,' Romany said, without looking up from the screen. 'Was it any good?'

'Yeah, it was nice,' replied Angie. 'But I'm tired. I'm going to bed. Don't stay up too late.'

She walked over to the sofa and stood between her daughter and the television and then, cupping Romany's face in her hands, she bent down and kissed her forehead.

'Mum! I can't see!' Romany objected, squirming free and twisting to look around her and back at the screen.

Angie smiled weakly. 'You shouldn't watch this crap. It'll fry your brain,' she said, but she didn't do anything to prevent it. 'I'll see you in the morning.'

Once in her room, the door closed behind her, she flopped on to the bed and curled herself up in a tiny ball.

Jax.

It had been Jax. Even from a distance there was absolutely no doubt in her mind. Jax, Daniel Jackson, was Hope's boyfriend. Older, more conventional-looking, but most definitely him. His hair was longer than when she had last seen it and he had filled out over the years, but it suited him. Where he had been sharp-edged and pointy in the past, he was softer now, less angry-looking. Angie had always found him handsome, but objectively he perhaps hadn't been before. Now, though, fifteen years on, he seemed to have grown into his looks and was attractive in a scruffy, slightly chaotic way.

Angie held a hand to her chest and felt her heart pounding beneath her ribs. It hadn't stopped racing since she had fled the party, every part of her prickling with the adrenaline that her body had produced in response to the shock. She had barely heard a word that Maggie had spoken as they made their way back, Maggie to a taxi rank and she to her flat. She had just wanted to get back to the sanctity of her space so she could start to process what had just happened, although right now she wasn't sure where to start.

She began with deep breathing exercises, in through her nose and out through her mouth, to try and calm herself into a state where she could at least think straight, and gradually her heart rate slowed.

Jax was in York. How long had he been here, with the potential to bump into her around every single corner she had turned? It must be at least three years. Angie tried to remember how new Hope's relationship had been when they had first met, but the facts, such as they were, danced in her head and were impossible to catch. Angie hadn't listened that hard, not really having any interest in Hope's boyfriend.

Now she tried to delve deep into her memory for any snippets of information. He was a chef, she knew that. They had met at some do when he was doing the food and had spilled something down an expensive dress that Hope had been wearing. Angie remembered Hope telling the story, her eyes dancing with the sheer delight of it all, relishing how uncomfortable he had been about his mistake and how she had strung him along, knowing all the time that there would be other dresses.

What else? Angie squeezed her eyes shut as she tried to concentrate, but when she did that all she could see was Jax, open-palmed in abject apology to Hope, and then their embrace. Her Jax, in love with someone else.

She checked herself. She was being ridiculous. He wasn't 'her Jax'. He hadn't been for years. Hadn't he left her for someone else when Romany was a baby? That relationship hadn't lasted either, it seemed. He obviously didn't do commitment, full stop.

And she couldn't complain that he had someone new when she hadn't wanted him anyway. It had been her decision not to keep in touch. She had been the one who had let the tenuous links between them fall away. That surely told her something. Whatever the two of them had had, it had broken when she became pregnant. Their relationship just hadn't been strong enough to withstand the storm that an unplanned baby brought with it.

So, he had been in York all this time, she thought, yet she had never seen him. It wasn't that surprising. York was a city and she'd hardly been keeping an eye open for him. Also, she was vegan now, so she wasn't likely to be frequenting the kind of fine dining establishment that Jax ran, or even mix in the same circles as him. Hope's circles. She had seen who they were at the party tonight and if it needed confirming, then that had done it – she and Hope were like chalk and cheese socially.

They were quite alike in other ways, though, Angie thought, she and Hope. Was that what had attracted Jax to her in the first place? Had he seen something of Angie in her and been drawn to it, maybe without even realising that it was happening?

She was being ridiculous now. Apart from anything else, Hope was beautiful and bound to attract men, regardless of her personality. But there was, Angie supposed, a possibility that she was the reason that Jax was in York. Well, not her exactly, but Romany, his daughter. Maybe he had moved to York to be near his child and had hoped that he would bump into her one day.

But how would he even recognise her? The thought of Jax walking the streets of York and staring at every girl of approximately the right age struck her as unbearably sad. Poor Jax, deprived of the chance to contact his own flesh and blood simply because Angie had decided that she did not want to send a forwarding address.

Angie uncurled herself and sat up. The low murmur of the television had stopped and there was no longer a line of light underneath her bedroom door. Romany must have gone to bed. Her baby, untroubled by the fact that her parents had been in the same room together that very night.

So, what should she do now? It would be easy enough to get hold of him. All she had to do was ask Hope. But what would she say? Hi Hope. Would it be okay if I arranged to have coffee with Daniel because, guess what! He's the father of my teenage daughter! How weird is that!

No. She couldn't do that. She could track him down herself. A chef named Daniel Jackson with a part-share in a restaurant in York couldn't be that difficult to find.

But why would she? She didn't want him. She didn't want to do anything to spoil what Hope had with him. And, most importantly of all, Romany had made it very clear that she did not want to see him either.

No. Angie should leave things as they were. But at least now, if anything were to happen, she would know how to get hold of him. Suddenly she felt slightly less alone.

38

2017

It was bitterly cold and Angie pulled her coat round her and worked on the zip. Her fingers were icy-stiff, and the coat was a snugger fit than it had been the previous winter. She really was going to have to lose some weight. It hardly seemed fair when she ate like a bird anyway and led an active lifestyle, but it was, she supposed, one of the very many calling cards of the menopause. She wasn't very impressed with any of them so far. She was suddenly more tired than she had ever been and her back ached despite her lifelong yoga practice. If she let herself, she could become ground down by the injustice of it all. But she wasn't going to. Going through the menopause was a perfectly natural process that happened to every woman lucky enough to reach their middle age. Her downbeat response to it was all about mindset, and hers just needed a little bit of work. She made a mental note to write her feelings on the subject in her journal when she got home.

Today, however, was not a day for getting down in the dumps. Today she was going to see Tiger for the first time in over three years and she was insanely excited. This was the longest that they had ever gone without seeing one another, she calculated as she crossed the bridge and made her way along the city wall to the railway station to meet him. It had been far too long.

There were bright yellow daffodils all over, exploding from every grassy bank and trumpeting the arrival of a change in the season. Not that it felt like anything was changing just yet. There was definitely snow in the air, she could smell it, and the cruel wind whipping up off the river bit through to her marrow.

Once in the station, she settled herself on the circular bench in the forecourt to wait. She enjoyed watching the tourists mixing in with the locals, each easy to spot by the way they behaved as they left the station. The locals set forth confidently, clear on where they were going, the tourists emerging through the ticket barriers and then stopping, agog, as they found their bearings, phones and guidebooks at the ready to take them on a whistle-stop tour of York's top spots before coming back here to be whisked away by the train again.

Another twinge in her lower back forced her to shift on the uncomfortable wooden seat. Maybe she should go and see an osteopath or get Kate to give her some acupuncture. That might help. And she could have another look at her diet books. As well as helping her lose her newly rounded tummy, they might have something to say about what to eat to help with painful joints. Ginger was good, she knew, and broccoli.

And then there he was, strolling towards her, rucksack on his back. His rich mahogany tan made him stand out a mile from the pale, insipid people surrounding him. He seemed to glow, his shaggy blond hair forming a halo around his head.

Angie didn't quite leap up, mindful of her painful back, but she stood as quickly as was wise and pushed her way through the crowd towards him, ignoring the protestations of those who were in her way. When she reached him, she threw her arms around his shoulders and pulled him tightly into her, inhaling the familiar scent of him, unchanged after all these years. He rested his cheek on the top of her head, and she could feel his arms encircling her. For the first time in forever, she felt safe and cherished. She hadn't realised that the feeling had been missing from her life until this moment, and the thought brought tears springing to her eyes. She blinked them away, knowing that Tiger would only tease her for such a display of emotion and not wanting to give him the ammunition, not yet at least. There would be plenty of time for teasing later.

He was the first to break away.

'Okay, okay,' he said, his voice light and full of humour. 'Put me down, woman. You don't know where I've been!'

This was true.

'Let's go and get some food and you can tell me everything,' she said, giving him one final squeeze before loosening her arms and letting him free.

He grasped her hand in his as they set off towards the exit. His skin felt dry, from hours in planes and trains, she thought, and she could feel his rough skin, his calloused fingers scratching against her smooth, strong ones. They both had working hands, but their work had left very different marks.

They had a brief discussion about what kind of establishment they wanted to go to. Tiger thought it would be funny to settle his scruffy, unwashed self in the lounge of the smart hotel next to the station, just to irritate the management. He really hadn't grown up at all. Back in the day, this would have amused Angie too, but now she just wanted uninterrupted time with him without drawing any unwelcome attention. Also, she couldn't help but think that his unkempt traveller's appearance wouldn't cause the consternation now that it might have done back in the eighties. The sensibilities of the world had moved on in the previous three decades, although not, it appeared, for Tiger.

They found an ordinary café instead and settled down in a corner. Tiger leaned his precious rucksack against the wall next to him, stepping his foot through the strap so that no one could take it without alerting him. Angie thought that this kind of precaution was probably unnecessary here, especially given the size of the rucksack, but Tiger had done it as second nature without even seeming to be aware of the movement. An ingrained sense of precaution came as a result of years of carrying your life on your back, she assumed.

'So, where have you been?' she asked. 'Did you stay on in the Cayman Islands? That's where you were the last time I heard from you.'

Tiger ran his hands through his hair. It was beginning to thin a little now, Angie noticed, his forehead more prominent than it had once been and etched with long horizontal lines.

'God, no,' he said. 'Had to leave there in a hurry a year or so ago. Some local difficulty with the dive school owner's wife . . .'

He pulled the 'oops' face that she had known for decades and she shook her head.

'You're fifty years old. Have you not learned to leave well alone yet?'

'Christ, fifty,' he said, shaking his head. 'How the hell did that happen? But no, to answer your question, it appears not! Anyway, I hopped over to Jamaica for a season, but I didn't like the vibe there and someone told me about a new eco-village in Costa Rica, so I've been there. You have to go to Costa Rica, Ange. It's amazing. The people are so friendly and they've got the tourist/eco balance thing spot on. They haven't even got an army.'

He chattered on, telling her about the village, built from sustainable sources deep in the rainforest, and about the wildlife.

'And the bloody howler monkeys,' he said. 'When I first got there, I thought I'd never sleep again. They make such a racket. But it's like anything else really. Eventually you get used to them and then after a bit you don't even hear them any more.'

Angie listened to him, transported for half an hour or so to a place that she might never get to see, but just happy to be in his company. Then, when he'd finished telling his immediate news, he focused his attention on her.

'And how are you?' he asked. 'How's Romey, and the business?' Then his eyes met hers, his expression questioning. 'No. Forget them for now,' he said. 'How are you?' he asked again. The second time there was concern in his voice. 'You look tired, Ange,' he said.

'I look old, you mean,' Angie said, wrinkling her nose.

Tiger shook his head. 'No. It's not that. You don't look anywhere near your age. But you do look like you could sleep for a month.'

'Oh, it's just the bloody menopause,' she said.

Tiger put his hands up, palms facing her, and dropped his head. 'Okay! Too much information. Us blokes can't be doing with all that gynaecological stuff. It sets our teeth on edge.'

Angie laughed at him. That was Tiger all over – emotionally intelligent enough to ask the question, but never prepared to hear the answer.

'And to answer your other questions, Romany is amazing. Wait until you see her! She's gorgeous and intelligent and wise. And gorgeous. Did I mention that bit?!'

Tiger grinned at her. 'Of course she is,' he said. 'She's your kid. Remind me. How old?'

'Sixteen,' Angie said proudly.

'Christ! Already?'

'And you'll never guess who is back in town.' Angie paused for a heartbeat, even though there was no likelihood of Tiger coming up with a name. 'Romany's dad, Jax. Remember him?'

'The tree-hugger? Yes. Well, vaguely. Don't think he was that impressed by me. So, have you seen much of him? Are you two . . . ?' He winked and made a lewd hand gesture.

Angie raised her eyebrows in disbelief. 'You're never going to grow up, are you? No. We're not together. In fact, he doesn't know that I know he's here.'

Tiger looked confused. 'So, how . . . ?'

'Saw him at a party and then ran for the hills before he saw me.'

'Does Romey know?' he asked.

Angie shook her head, scrutinising his face for a hint of what he was thinking. 'She's made it very clear that she doesn't want anything to do with him, so I'm respecting her wishes.'

'But you don't agree?' he asked astutely.

Angie cocked her head to one side. 'It's up to her, I suppose. She's old enough to make her own decisions. But I can't see what harm it would do to at least say hello. I wondered if that was why he moved up here, so that he could be close to her. I have no idea, of course, but the thought crossed my mind.'

'Perhaps you should talk to her again,' Tiger said, pouring the last of his tea into his cup. 'If she knows her dad is so close then maybe she'll think differently.'

'Maybe,' said Angie, but she was doubtful.

'Or you could meet him without telling her,' Tiger suggested.

Angie went to take a sip of her peppermint tea to buy herself some time, but her cup was already empty.

'I thought of that too,' she said. 'And it would make sense to check in with him, so he knows that I know he's here. But . . .' She paused, hoping that Tiger would fill in the gaps for himself.

He did.

'But you don't want to stir the ghosts of the past,' he said.

'Precisely. I'd rather leave my memories of him safe where they are. And his of me.'

She blushed a little as she said this, ashamed of the vanity that she knew was, in part at least, keeping her from meeting the father of her child. She didn't want Jax to see her as she was now, over fifty, a bit fat, her skin lined and not quite clinging to her frame as once it had.

'Romey's a bit young to be making such a big decision for herself, though,' said Tiger then, with that quality he had for seeing straight to the heart of the issue. 'Plus, she might just be saying that because it's what she thinks you want to hear.'

Angie's insides screwed into a tight little ball. He was right. She knew he was. But she didn't want to address it. Not now.

'Maybe,' she replied, to close him down. 'I'll think about it. But I know where he is now, so at least we have options.'

'Options are good,' replied Tiger, seeming to understand that this part of the conversation was over.

They sat in silence for a moment, the hustle and bustle of the café continuing around them. China chinked, the coffee machine hissed, people chatted. The sounds of the world just doing its thing. It felt good, Angie thought, to pause. She should do it more often. Mindfulness was something that she talked about endlessly to her clients and she tried to approach each day being grateful for what she had at that moment, but sometimes even she got lost in the business of living.

'And how about you, Tiger?' she asked him after a while. 'What are your options?'

He gave her a quick grin. The expression was a familiar one, but was there something new in it now? Doubt, maybe, a disquietude that she hadn't seen in him before, or at least not recognised as such.

'I'll just keep doing what I do,' he said. His smile was broad now, with no hint of whatever it was she thought she'd seen in it a moment ago.

'You can't keep travelling forever,' she said.

'Why not?'

She thought that his tone bordered on the defensive, fleetingly, but that too was gone in an instant.

'As long as I have strength in my bones, I intend to keep seeing the world.'

'But don't you ever want to stop, to pick a place and just settle there?' she asked him.

Tiger shook his head. 'Not so far. And I can't see it happening, either. There's still so much to see.'

'There can't be that much.' Angie laughed, and Tiger shrugged.

'There's enough to keep me going for a while yet,' he said.

Angie couldn't let it drop, though. 'You could find a base somewhere, just so that you had a place to go home to, and then keep travelling from there,' she suggested.

'And how would I pay for it?' he asked simply.

This was a good point and not one that Angie had really considered. She nodded, accepting that he was right.

'Fair enough,' she said. 'How long are you here for? You're welcome to stay with us for as long as you like,' she added.

Tiger reached across the table and took her hand. 'You are the kindest person I know,' he said. 'But I can't do more than a night on that sofa. I'm on my way up to Newcastle. I met a bloke in Costa Rica who lives up there, so I'm going to stay with him for a month or so. I'll get some work cash in hand before I head off again. I'm fancying the Highlands and Islands of Scotland, do some bird-spotting, but I have to wait for the weather to warm up a bit.'

Angie had an idea, and suddenly it felt like the best one she'd had in a long while. 'Why don't you stay at least for tonight and I'll ring Mags and Leon. We can have a little party just like we used to. What do you reckon? Good idea?'

Tiger's face lit up. 'How is Maggie?' he asked fondly. 'Got herself hitched yet?'

'No. Not married. Never has been,' replied Angie. 'She lost her job, though. That was a hard blow. She's working again now but in some little office job. I'm not even sure what it is, but it doesn't involve the law at all.'

Tiger rubbed at the stubble on his chin. 'That's surprising,' he said. 'I thought she lived and breathed that stuff.'

'Yeah, me too. But being pushed out seems to have knocked the confidence out of her. She'll go back to it, though, I'm sure. She just needs time.'

'It'd be nice to see her,' mused Tiger. 'And Leon, as well,' he added as an afterthought.

'So, stay,' said Angie. 'Just one night if that's all you can spare, although you can always bunk up with me if the sofa is more than you can manage. You can ring your mate from my place and tell him you've been waylaid by your favourite person in all the world.'

'Who? Maggie?!' He winked at her and she stabbed a threatening finger at him.

'No, you moron. Me!'

Angie had missed this so much, had missed Tiger and the easy way they had of just being in one another's space. That hadn't changed in all the years that she had known him. In fact, Tiger didn't appear to have changed at all, either. She had, she knew that; but Tiger? He was the same person she had met on that beach all those years ago. Maybe that was what having no responsibilities did for a person? Perhaps it allowed you to stay as carefree as you had been at eighteen for your entire life? Angie wasn't convinced that he was entirely carefree, though. Were the obvious flaws in his nomadic lifestyle finally starting to occur to him? She suspected that he would never admit it, not even to her, but he must surely think about how the future was going to pan out for him. It was a rare person who didn't reach fifty and start to wonder what the second half of their life was going to look like. The problem for Tiger was that he would never be able to admit it. Through all the time she had known him, his mantra had been to live in the moment and to go where the wind blew him, but at some point he was going to have to work out that he was too old to be blown around any more.

But not yet, it appeared. His decision about her suggestion of a party was made in characteristic style – quickly and without much thought for what might happen next.

'That'd be great,' he said. 'It'll be cool to see the others. Newcastle can wait until tomorrow. Or the next day,' he added with a wink.

Briefly Angie considered whether she should tell him about Maggie and Leon. She hadn't lied when she'd said that Maggie wasn't married, but she'd not been entirely truthful either. Tiger was apparently still carrying a torch for her, even though, to Angie's certain knowledge, there had never been anything more than sexual tension between them. A lot of water had passed under the bridge since those student days, though, and whatever it was that hadn't quite happened was surely in the past now. That said, she didn't want to spoil her moment with Tiger. She would let Maggie and Leon tell him their news themselves.

A woman came into the café in a red coat that was covered in white freckles of snow. She brushed herself down, with lots of huffing and puffing to no one in particular, and Angie and Tiger both turned to look out of the window. The world had gone white whilst they had been talking. Large fluffy flakes were falling fast enough to cover the pavement in a thin sheen, and the light had taken on the flat quality that heavy snow-filled cloud brings with it.

Tiger's face lit up. 'Snow! I haven't seen snow for years! Let's go out and kick about it in!'

'Idiot!' She laughed, but she was happy to go outside and indulge him. Would he ever grow up? Angie hoped not.

He stood up quickly, heaving his rucksack on to his back with perhaps a little more effort than it used to take, and then set off towards the door, leaving Angie, as ever, to pick up the bill.

39

'Are we supposed to be dressing up?' asked Leon when Maggie appeared in the lounge wearing a black jumpsuit and a pair of spike heels. He was wearing the same jeans that he had worn all day but had at least changed his shirt. 'I thought it was just us and Angie and Tiger.'

Maggie could feel a blush starting on her exposed décolletage.

'No. Not particularly,' she said, trying to sound as casual as she could. 'I just thought it would be nice to make a bit of an effort, that's all. And I have a wardrobe full of nice clothes. I might as well get some wear out of them.' She wanted to ask him how she looked but it felt a little disingenuous, asking Leon if he thought she looked nice when she had dressed with an entirely different man in mind.

'Do I need to get changed as well, then?' Leon asked.

'Not if you don't want to,' replied Maggie. 'I doubt Ange or Tiger will notice what we're wearing anyway. Are you ready? Shall we go?'

Leon nodded. 'Do you want me to drive?'

'I don't mind. We can go in my car and leave it there. I'll walk over and pick it up tomorrow,' said Maggie.

'Okay, if you're sure,' said Leon.

It might be nice if they walked over together, Maggie thought. They would have done that at the start of the relationship, would have relished the opportunity to spend the time together with nothing to do but just talk. Things moved on, though, she supposed, and it did make more sense for just one of them to waste time collecting the car.

'I'll tell you what. Why don't I give you a lift over in the morning before I head back to Leeds?' Leon said.

Problem solved with an entirely practical solution. Maggie sighed internally. The gilt on their romance was definitely tarnishing a little. She might not have much relationship experience, but even she knew that the heady dopamine-laced days at the beginning of a love affair were generally short-lived. The lust that they had felt at the outset seemed to have been replaced by something less exciting, and they had slipped quickly into a comfortable companionable pairing, rather like she imagined marriage to be. It wasn't a bad place, but Maggie couldn't help thinking that somehow they had bypassed ten years or so. She supposed that was what happened when you started dating one of your closest friends. So much about your new partner was unsurprising, so little left to be discovered.

None of this had occurred to Maggie, however, until Angie had proposed the party with Tiger. Suddenly, all she wanted was to spend time with Tiger, and Leon, lovely, safe Leon for whom she had only affection really, was in the way.

But she had to be sensible. Tiger blew in and out like the clouds and Leon was here for her day after day. Maggie knew which side her bread was buttered, although the thought of Tiger was enough to make her insides clench. She needed to behave better, even if her misdemeanours were only in her head.

'It's a shame we didn't have a bit more notice of tonight,' said Maggie as she slipped her coat on and twisted a scarf around her neck. 'You could have taken your sax over and played for us.'

'Yes, I could have done,' replied Leon, as if this were actually something he might have done had the circumstances allowed. 'Typical Angie plan, eh? All last minute.'

'I imagine Tiger has only just drifted in from wherever he was. You know what he's like.'

The saxophone suggestion hadn't been entirely outlandish. Leon had been playing more now that he lived on his own, or so he told Maggie. Sometimes he even played for her, although it was a little bit loud in his tiny flat and you couldn't turn his volume down, which made it hard to relax and listen. Taking her cue from Angie, Maggie was keen to encourage him with his music. His first set of life choices hadn't worked out that well, so maybe it was time to try something new. With this in mind, she had suggested that they find a studio in Leeds somewhere.

'Why don't I buy you a recording session for your birthday?' she had suggested. 'You could cover some jazz stuff, the classics, you know,' she had said vaguely, not really being sure exactly what he might want to play. 'Maybe you could mix in a backing track or even pay for some session musicians to play with you. Then I'd have a CD and listen to you whenever I liked.' Maggie had been quite pleased with her idea by the time she got to the end of it, impressed that she'd managed to dredge some appropriate terminology from somewhere.

'Who listens to CDs anymore?' had been his only comment, leaving her feeling antiquated and stupid.

At Angie's place it seemed as if the party had already started. Music was pumping out through the walls and into the street; they could hear it as they parked the car in a space a few doors down, the dull thud of the bass drum reverberating into the dark night.

'Her neighbours must love her,' said Leon, laughing, and Maggie rolled her eyes.

The front door was open, and they let themselves in, Maggie clicking the latch behind them. Now they were inside she could identify the tune as 'The Only Way Is Up', a song that had been in the charts the year they graduated and which they had danced round their grotty student digs to, singing the words as if they had been written specifically for them. Maggie had been so sure then that the only way truly was up. Now she knew better.

They opened the door into the lounge and the wall of sound hit them, along with the smell of patchouli oil and beer. The room was in darkness, the only light coming from dozens of tea lights in jam jars dotted on every surface. All the furniture had been pushed back to make place for dancing and in the centre of the room Tiger and Angie were twirling, arms raised high above their heads, shouting the words of the song. Romany was curled on the sofa, watching them with an amused expression on her face. When she saw Maggie and Leon she shook her head in despair.

'Auntie Maggie! Thank God. Save me. They appear to have been possessed by a demon channelling the 1980s.'

'The eighties are in right now,' said Leon. 'Or so my kids tell me.'

'Not this bit of the eighties,' said Romany. 'They were playing Tiffany before. I mean, Tiffany!'

'There's nothing wrong with a bit of Tiffany,' shouted Angie over the noise. 'Help yourselves to a drink,' she added as she continued to spin.

Leon peeled off and went into the kitchen, returning a moment later with a beer for himself and a glass of white wine for Maggie. He handed it to her and then sat on the sofa next to Romany. Maggie took a large drink, almost downing half the glass in one. She felt the alcohol hit her system at once, the lightness flooding into her head like ink in a glass of water. Then she drank the rest.

'Hey, steady,' said Leon, raising what might have been a disap-
proving eyebrow, but she ignored him. She put the empty glass on
the windowsill and raised her arms, a little self-consciously, to start
dancing with Angie and Tiger, at exactly the moment that the track
came to an end. Maggie dropped her arms awkwardly, but no one
seemed to notice. Next on the playlist was Tom Jones's shockingly
bad cover of Prince's 'Kiss' and Maggie threw a questioning look at
Angie. Surely they would skip over this one? But it appeared not.
Tonight was, it seemed, all about full-on cheese.

Maggie began to swing her hips, conscious of Tiger to her left
and Leon on the sofa. She needed another drink to really do justice
to the track, but she would have to wait for a respectable amount
of time to pass before she refilled her glass. Angie seemed to be
managing just fine without any alcohol, but then Angie had always
been able to dance as if no one was watching. It was a skill that
Maggie envied, Angie's disregard for the views of others. She was,
Maggie thought, more comfortable in her own skin than anyone
else she had ever met. And was she perhaps the least? Well, maybe
not quite, but she still wished that she could let go as completely
as Angie was able to do.

Maggie decided to make a conscious effort to be in this
moment at least. What did it matter what she looked like? These
three middle-aged people were her oldest friends. They didn't care
how she danced, and neither should she. She kicked off her heels
and began to spin on the spot, swinging her hips. It did feel good to
just abandon everything. She should do it more often, she realised.
She closed her eyes and let the music, now 'Ride on Time', pulse
through her.

Then she felt hands around her waist, and she was being spun
round. When she opened her eyes she was face to face with Tiger,
their noses just inches apart. She felt his hands slip down the silky
fabric of the jumpsuit to her bottom whilst her heart rate soared.

Her first reaction was to pull away, but he held her firm as he continued to move in time to the music. There was a respectable distance between them, and he was just playing and not flirting, but Maggie yearned to close the gap so that their bodies touched all the way down.

'Hey! Put her down or you'll have Leon to answer to,' Angie said, grinning cheekily as she danced past them.

Tiger didn't let her go at once, but something about the quality of his hold changed. He looked over to Leon for confirmation.

'Hey, is this right, Leon? Did you stake a claim to the lovely Maggie when my back was turned?' he shouted over the noise.

Maggie didn't look to see how Leon responded. She didn't care. She just wanted Tiger to keep holding her and never let her go. But Leon had obviously confirmed Angie's words and suddenly Tiger's hands were no longer on her and he was standing palms-up in apology to Leon.

'Sorry, mate,' he laughed. 'Didn't mean to trespass.'

The euphoria of a moment ago dissipated in an instant and was replaced by a mixture of disappointment and irritation. What was she, a possession? Maggie stalked off the makeshift dance floor, picked up her wine glass and went to refill it whilst she worked out what she was feeling, what she was supposed to be feeling.

As she tipped as much of the wine into her glass as it would hold, the music in the lounge beyond changed again and Angie appeared in the doorway.

'Okay?' she asked gently.

Maggie took a deep breath and nodded, her bottom lip caught between her teeth.

'I'm sorry,' Angie said. 'I should have warned him. I assumed . . . well, I'm sorry if I made it awkward.'

Maggie shook her head. 'It's fine,' she said. 'No harm done. It's ridiculous, anyway; teenage crush that was never going anywhere.

I'm fifty years old and I have Leon. I need to get over it and move on.'

'Unrequited love,' said Angie wistfully. 'I don't think you're properly human if you don't have at least one. Actually, when you think about it, there's only Leon out of the four of us who got what he actually wanted.'

And then, before Maggie had time to quiz her on what she meant, Angie had danced back out of the kitchen. There was so much in that sentence that needed to be unpicked, but this was not the moment. Maggie took a gulp of wine, topped the glass up yet again and followed Angie back into the lounge. Tiger, not wanting to dance on his own, had plonked himself between Romany and Leon on the sofa and all three were just sitting there, like three wise monkeys, because the music was too loud to allow conversation.

'Shall I turn it down a bit?' Angie suggested, and then did so without waiting for a reply.

'So, what else have I missed?' asked Tiger, now that they could communicate without shouting. 'How long have you two been an item?'

'Just less than a year,' replied Maggie. She and Leon caught each other's eye, and his expression was a mixture of pride and adoration that immediately brought her back to reality. What was she doing mooning about Tiger when Leon was so much better for her? She responded to Leon's obvious affections with what she hoped was an unequivocal smile. 'It just felt right, didn't it, Lee?' she said. 'Like coming home.'

It wasn't quite the truth, but as she said it Maggie could feel something closing down in her. Enough. It was time to leave the Tiger fantasy where it belonged. In her past. She felt her shoulders relaxing immediately, the tension that she had been unaware she was holding on to seeping away, and she knew that that chapter was over. She was released.

'I missed my chance there, then,' Tiger replied and winked at Romany, who wrinkled her nose in teenage disdain.

That was all it was for Tiger, Maggie told herself. A chance. And suddenly she wasn't quite sure how she had let her infatuation with him run for so many years. Tiger had never been what she needed. And never would be.

'And Ange tells me you're not soliciting any more,' he continued, oblivious to the seismic shift that had just happened in her head.

Maggie rolled her eyes. This was the real Tiger – always light-hearted, up for the cheap gag. If he had made the 'soliciting' joke once over the years, he must have made it a thousand times.

'No,' she said. 'I gave it up about a year ago.'

Admitting this was also hard, and didn't seem to be getting any easier with time. Would she ever get used to it, the change in her status? It still hurt to admit that she had lost her prized career, and the reframing of the facts to something that sounded as if it had been her decision just made it worse, but she still couldn't bring herself to be honest and tell enquirers that she had been let go.

'What happened a year ago, then,' he asked, 'to bring about all this change?'

Maggie shrugged. 'The gods must have been bored that week,' she said with a laugh.

'Gods my arse,' said Angie. 'It was the universe telling you that you needed to change direction. You just haven't quite worked out which way up the map goes yet, have you, Mags?'

'No. Not quite yet,' replied Maggie.

How did Angie do that? How did she seem to know the things that Maggie hadn't yet fathomed for herself? It was very discombobulating.

'What are you doing instead?' asked Tiger.

'Oh, I've got a little job working front of house in an architect's practice in town.'

Tiger pulled a face. 'All those brains and qualifications and you're working as a receptionist? Something doesn't add up there.'

'It's not so bad,' replied Maggie, trying hard not to sound defensive. 'Obviously, it doesn't pay as well as what I was doing, but my needs are very simple, and it is nice to go home at the end of the day and not have to think about work until you turn up again the next morning.' This was her pat answer, the one she had trotted out to everyone who had asked the question. It almost sounded true.

'And I'm earning plenty,' added Leon. 'So she's not going to starve.'

Maggie knew that he meant this to be supportive and wasn't in any way boastful, but she felt her jaw tighten all the same. Not only did it make it sound as if she couldn't look after herself, but it might also have been taken as a bit of a sideswipe at Tiger, who only ever seemed to have enough money to last him to the end of the week. Deep down, she knew that Leon didn't mean it like that, and Tiger wouldn't have taken it that way either. The only person with an issue here was her. Belatedly, she gave Leon a weak smile and hoped that he hadn't noticed her delayed response.

'And what about you?' she asked Tiger, anxious to divert the attention from her. 'What's next?'

Tiger gave a sigh, as if his plans were equivalent to a job. 'Newcastle tomorrow for a while and then up north. I fancy seeing the Orkneys.'

'It's beautiful up there,' Leon said. 'Quiet, unspoilt.'

'I should fit right in then.' Tiger laughed, and they all laughed with him.

'Can I change the music?' asked Romany. 'Something a bit more up to date? It's like The Place Music Goes to Die in here.'

Angie leant over the back of the sofa and put her arms around her daughter, resting her chin on her shiny hair. She kissed her lightly on the top of her head.

'If you must,' she said, 'but then we need to go back to the eighties stuff later.'

Romany rolled her eyes at the prospect and then changed the music from her phone. Maggie didn't recognise the song but it was a female vocalist with an acoustic guitar and it reflected nicely the new, thoughtful mood that had taken over the room. Romany, it seemed, was blessed with her mother's levels of perception.

Maggie lowered herself carefully to the floor, conscious that her knees weren't quite as robust as they once were, and sat crossed-legged on the rug. Angie came round to join her. She might be carrying a little more weight than Maggie was around the middle, but Angie could still knock her into a cocked hat on flexibility. She sank to the rug in one fluid movement without even using her hands and tucked her legs up under her in a way that Maggie could now only dream of.

'Look at us,' Angie said affectionately. 'We've known each other for more than thirty years, we're all completely different. And I mean, *completely*.' She pressed the word for emphasis. 'And yet, here we all are. Still enjoying each other's company, still looking out for one another. Who'd have thought it, eh?'

Maggie smiled. 'Who'd have guessed that when you walked into my student room, unannounced I might add, and uninvited, demanding toilet paper . . .'

'I didn't demand!' objected Angie.

'I bet you did,' said Romany, and Maggie raised one eyebrow and nodded at her as if to say you bet your life she did.

'. . . demanding toilet paper,' she continued, 'little did I think that we would be sitting here tonight, still friends after all this time.'

'To be fair, neither did I,' replied Angie. 'I thought you were uptight and angsty.'

Maggie shrugged to acknowledge that that was a pretty fair assessment of her. 'Yet here we are. And I think it's fantastic. Let's have a toast! To unlikely friendships.'

They all raised their drinks and clinked, echoing the toast to each other.

Maggie leant over and rested her hand on Angie's leg, applying a little pressure, the equivalent of a hug. It was all down to Angie, the fact that they were still in contact, that she had Leon as part of her life, and Tiger too for that matter. And now there was Romany as well, the closest thing Maggie had to a child of her own. And somehow, Angie was the key to it all, Angie, who she had once thought to be the most selfish person she had ever met.

'To unlikely friendships,' Maggie said again.

40

2018

'If my mum wasn't dead, I'd kill her,' said Romany. 'What the hell was she thinking with this ridiculous plan? Like I need all these crappy mates of hers to look after me. I'm eighteen years old, for God's sake. An adult! And I do not need babysitting by an ageing hippy with a ridiculous name. I'm more than capable of looking after myself.' She puffed her lips out, folded her arms and leant back in her chair, making it balance on two legs.

'It does sound kind of shit,' replied Laura. 'It's a pity the hippy bloke had to move in. We could have had some cool parties at your place.'

Romany sighed. 'Actually, he wouldn't mind parties. He's pretty chill about that kind of thing. More than Mum was anyway. But what if I want to take someone back to mine? Can you imagine us in my room with him sitting on the sofa listening?'

'Well, that's no different to how it is at my house,' said Laura. 'I swear my mum can hear if me and Matt go within a metre of each other, and as soon as we do, she pops in to see if we want a cup of tea.' Laura rolled her eyes and it made Romany smile.

'Well, there's no danger of that at my house,' Romany replied. Her mum was never going to catch her with a boy again.

Laura looked momentarily horrified, but then gave her a sad half-grin. 'No,' she said. And then, 'At least Matt's got a car.'

'Have you ever tried that?' asked Romany. 'It's bloody uncomfortable. Anyway, that's not the point. The point is that Mum has abandoned me with all these misfits when all I want is her, and it's crap.' Romany could feel her throat starting to tighten and hot tears burned the corners of her eyes. She wiped them away savagely. There had been enough crying. She just wasn't going to do any more, not in front of other people, at least. Well, maybe a bit with Laura, but no one else. If she was going to be treated like the adult that she kept saying that she was, then she was going to have to stop behaving like a little girl.

Laura put her arms around her, pulling her chair back on to four legs. 'It's okay, hun. I know it's tough.' She whispered her words so that the boys sitting in the row behind them didn't hear.

It was tough. In fact, she doubted whether it got much tougher than losing your mum when you were still at school. And she hadn't even had that long to get her head around what was coming. When her mum had finally stopped trying to shake off whatever bug she'd thought she had with macrobiotic diets, obscure food supplements and reiki and actually gone to the doctor's, they had discovered that it was stage 4 ovarian cancer, terminal, and with little chance of any life-prolonging treatment being successful. She had been dead within two months.

To start with, Romany had blamed her mother for not seeking help earlier. How could you get so close to death and not even realise that you were ill? But the Macmillan nurses had explained that it was sometimes the way. Symptoms got missed or misdiagnosed. Even if her mother had been to the doctor, there was no guarantee that they would have picked it up any sooner. Ovarian cancer was called the silent killer, apparently. Or the whispering killer, at least, but in her mum's case it had whispered so very quietly that no one had heard it.

Then Romany had blamed the doctors for being incompetent, and then finally herself for not making the connection between her mother's rounded stomach and uncharacteristic lethargy and the deadly disease that was eating up her insides.

It was a process, apparently, grief. She had looked it up on Google, desperate to find some hope in the experiences of others. She reckoned that she was stuck somewhere in Stage Three, which was Anger, but some days, sometimes even some hours, she still fluctuated around Stage Two – Pain and Guilt. Of the two, Romany thought she preferred the anger. At least she could scream and throw stuff. The pain was unbearable.

And yet here she was, sitting in double chemistry and pretty much holding it together. Her form tutor, all sympathetic looks and tissues, had said that if she felt she wanted to take some time out then that would be perfectly fine. They would tell the exam board and allowances would be made. But what would Romany do if she didn't come to school? Sit in the house all day with Tiger? The idea was unthinkable.

No. The one good thing that she was determined would come out of this horrible situation was that she would get her A levels and go to Durham University to read biochemistry and make her mother proud of her. What else was there to do but carry on?

Mr Johnson strolled into the classroom and stood at the front, waiting for silence to descend. It took some time before everyone noticed that he was there.

'Good morning, year 13,' he said when the room was finally quiet. 'I trust we are all well and ready to get on with the biodegradable qualities of polymers. Get your homework out and we'll see what a dog's dinner you managed to make of it.'

And then there was no time to think about anything other than polymers, and that suited her just fine.

◆ ◆ ◆

After school, Laura had a job looking after a couple of primary school children, and so Romany was left to wander home alone. At least she knew now that Mum was gone, and there was no danger of things having got any worse whilst she was at school. She found herself dawdling, though, wandering home the long way, window-shopping in places that normally she wouldn't have given a second glance. Anything to avoid having to chat to Tiger. She felt bad about that. He was a nice enough bloke, but they had nothing to say to one another. What did he know about teenage girls? What did she know about middle-aged men, come to that? They seemed to have no point of connection other than her mum, and she was the one subject of conversation that they were both desperate to avoid. And so they hovered around each other in a strained kind of benign silence, neither having the raw materials nor the energy to begin a conversation other than to ask each other what they should eat. It was impossibly awkward, but there was nothing she could do to improve it. So, she spent as little time as she could at home, and when she was there, she hid herself away in her room to study or watch *CSI* on her laptop until it was time to go to bed.

It wouldn't be forever, she told herself. It was October already and the arrangement was that he would leave once her exams were finished in June. But when she counted down the weeks on her calendar it felt like an impossibly long time.

41

'Now, I don't want you to worry,' said Romany's form tutor. 'You still have plenty of time. The deadline isn't for months yet. But we do find that it helps students to focus on their coursework when their UCAS applications have been finished and sent off.'

Romany wanted to cry. Didn't she have enough to deal with? She knew what subject she wanted to study and where she wanted to go. Those decisions had been hard enough with everything else that had been going on. Wouldn't that do? Why did she now have to go through all the hassle of actually filling in forms? Surely it would be simpler for everyone if she sent Durham an email explaining that this was what she wanted, and they would just say okay? Then she could just get on with the job of trying to get the grades.

It didn't work like that, though. She had to fill in the form and write a personal statement to convince Durham that she was passionate about her subject and that they would be foolish to miss the opportunity of teaching her.

Unfortunately, this task was currently beyond her. She didn't have the bandwidth for it. It was sitting pretty in the 'too hard to achieve' box. She had tried to make a start. There was a new folder on her laptop that contained a document handily titled 'Personal Statement', but every time she opened it and stared at the white page and its little blinking cursor her mind went blank. What could she possibly say about herself? What did she have to offer somewhere as prestigious as Durham University? She had never even been to Durham, but somehow she knew that that was where she needed to be. In Durham, she wouldn't be the girl with the lost father and the dead mother. She would simply be Romany Osborne, biochemistry student, just like all the others.

Before her mum died, she had booked them on to the Open Day just like she was supposed to, but then her mum hadn't felt that well on the day and they had put it off, saying to one another that they would go to the one in September instead. They hadn't known then that there would barely be a September.

If Mum had been there, she would have helped her write something good for the form. Then again, if Mum had been here, she would have been able to do it by herself, because she would have been able get her thoughts to align themselves neatly in her head without everything becoming muddled and confused.

'It won't take too long once you start,' said her tutor, cutting across her thoughts. She was speaking in that gentle voice that everyone seemed to use to her these days, the one that made Romany want to scream at them to stop treating her like a victim. 'At least, you know where you want to go and which course, so that's half the battle.' She gave Romany a wan smile and Romany almost felt sorry for the woman. She doesn't know what to say either, she thought. She's probably been dreading this conversation for weeks, talked to her husband about it over a glass of wine in the evenings. 'I have this poor girl in my Year 13 tutor group. Her mum has just died. It's so tragic. Doesn't it break your heart?'

That's what Romany had become – a person who broke other people's hearts. But that was going to change. She had to get a grip and show them all that she didn't need their sympathy, that she was just the same person she had been before. And then maybe people would stop pussyfooting around her. It was her mum who had died, after all, and not her.

'And I'm here to help you,' her tutor continued. 'If we work together, then I'm sure we can get this done and off in no time at all.'

'Thank you,' replied Romany, looking up and meeting her tutor's eye for the first time in the conversation. 'But it's okay. I have someone who can help.'

◆ ◆ ◆

At lunchtime she texted Maggie. Maggie was the one her mum had left in charge of this kind of stuff, so it was time for her to step up. And anyway, she liked Maggie a whole lot more than she liked her tutor.

> *Hi Auntie Maggie. Can you help me with my UCAS form please? R x*

The text came straight back.

> *Of course. Are you still looking at biochemistry? I'll do some research and we can go through it together. This evening?*

Her mum was right. Maggie was possibly the most efficient person in the world.

> *Great. Come round after work.*

Maggie turned up at ten past six with a selection box from Hotel Chocolat and a huge smile. She gave Romany a quick hug – nothing too showy or tear-inducing – and handed her the chocolates.

'Sustenance,' she said.

They sat at the kitchen table with a pad of paper, a selection of coloured pens and their laptops fired up and ready to go.

'Right,' said Maggie. 'I've done some reading around, and it seems that this is all about the personal statement. You have to show the admissions tutors who you are, that you have the right qualities for university-level study and that you have a passion for the course you're applying for. It'll be a piece of cake!'

Romany nodded. It did sound easy when Maggie put it like that.

'And you can apply for courses at five universities,' Maggie said. 'So, biochemistry across the board?'

'Actually, I only want to go to Durham,' said Romany.

Maggie eyed her curiously.

'I've looked at all the other courses and the universities and that's the only one.'

'Okay,' replied Maggie slowly. 'That's a bold decision. But if you're certain that that's what you want then I can't see any reason why you can't do that. I'm not sure school will like it, though.'

Romany shrugged. She didn't really care what school thought.

'You're doing the right A levels so that's no problem. And your predicted grades are . . .'

'Three As,' said Romany. 'Or they were before . . .'

'Don't worry about that,' said Maggie. 'The main thing at this stage is that the university considers your application. We can worry about actually getting the grades later.'

They heard the front door opening and Romany saw Maggie start. Her hand went to check her hair and then to wipe any stray mascara from under her eye. Her mum had always said that these two fancied one another. Romany thought it was gross, old people flirting.

'Hi, Tiger,' Romany shouted brightly, pre-warning him that they had company.

Tiger sauntered in carrying two heavy-looking shopping bags.

'Oh, hi Mags,' he said when he saw her. He looked considerably less flustered than Maggie had done. 'I got everything on the list except for the capers. No capers to be had for love nor money.'

'Never mind,' replied Romany. 'Maggie and I are just working on my university application.'

Tiger nodded. 'Mags is the ideal woman for that job,' he said approvingly. 'Where are you thinking?'

'Durham,' said Romany.

'Ah,' he replied, nodding again.

God, he's useless, thought Romany. I bet he doesn't even know where Durham is.

'Beautiful city,' he said. 'The castle and cathedral are a UNESCO World Heritage Site, of course, and there are some amazing botanical gardens too. If you get the timing right, you can wander over Elvet Bridge when the sun is going down. The light there is just astounding. Top choice, Romey.'

Romany stared at him, open-mouthed.

'Well, you're a fount of knowledge,' said Maggie. She sounded impressed as well.

'How do you know all that stuff?' asked Romany. 'You sound like a travel guide.'

Tiger looked surprised to have been asked. 'Well, I've been, haven't I? It's a gorgeous place. Tiny but jam-packed full of medieval history. It's great.'

And then he started to unpack the shopping.

Maggie threw a glance at Romany, eyebrows raised, and they swapped an expression of pure incredulity.

'So,' Maggie continued, returning them to the matter in hand. 'Let's start with who you are . . .'

◆ ◆ ◆

By the end of the evening, they had produced a personal statement that read pretty well, and Romany was feeling much calmer about the whole process. Maggie's guidance had been clear and logical, taking her through what she needed to say in a way that made it flow with purpose and ended up at exactly the right place with a nice uplifting finale. She had the word count completely spot on, too. Romany would never have been able to do that on her own, and she had to admit that if Mum had been helping, they would probably have ended up arguing about what should go in and what be left out. Maggie had been the perfect person for the job.

'Thanks, Auntie Maggie,' she said as she selected a champagne truffle from the almost-empty box. 'That was really helpful.'

Maggie smiled. 'Glad to be of use,' she said. 'To be honest, it's nice to do something that makes me think for a change. I miss using my brain.'

'Do you not have to do that, then?' asked Romany. She wasn't sure that she entirely understood what Maggie meant. Surely, if you were clever like Maggie then you must use your brain all the time – you couldn't really avoid it.

Maggie wrinkled her nose. 'I'm a bit overqualified for the job I've got at the moment,' she said. 'I mean, it's a great business and the people are lovely. But I'm used to having a bit more responsibility.'

'So why stay?' Romany said.

Maggie plucked a chocolate baton from the box but didn't put it in her mouth. Instead, she tapped her lip with it thoughtfully.

'Well,' she began. 'I don't need to earn much money. There's only me and I'm cheap to run. And the job is easy and safe. Plus, it's great to go home in the evenings and just switch off . . .' She started to tail off.

'But it's boring?' suggested Romany.

Maggie nodded.

'And unfulfilling?'

Maggie nodded again.

'Maybe it's time to try something that's a bit more of a challenge?'

'I think maybe it is,' she said.

'But you're scared?'

Nod.

'Once bitten, twice shy?'

Nod.

Romany sat back in her chair and took a long, appraising look at Maggie. 'What would you say to me if it was the other way round?' she asked.

Maggie took a deep breath. 'I would tell you to pick yourself up, dust yourself off and get right back on the horse,' she said.

'Hmmm,' Romany said, letting her mouth twist into a wry smile. 'Would you now?'

She thought she saw Maggie blush.

42

Maggie was making dinner for her and Leon. It was going to be lasagne, made from scratch. There had been no time for meals with so many constituent parts when she had been working as a solicitor. Back then, she would have just made a quick pasta dish, a tomato sauce with a few veg chucked in for good measure, and eaten it without concentrating whilst she looked over emails or documents for the next day. Now, though, with the ragù already bubbling in the oven, she stirred the béchamel sauce carefully, making sure that it didn't thicken too quickly or stick to the bottom of the pan. It was nice to have the time to cook properly, therapeutic even. Ironically, however, now that she finally had the time to stir a sauce without doing anything else at the same time, she no longer felt the need for calm. She almost missed the grabbed meals eaten without thought because her mind was occupied with more interesting things.

Leon was sitting at the kitchen island, a glass of wine in front of him, flicking through the TV options for the evening on his iPad.

'There's a new four-parter starting on ITV that looks promising,' he said. 'Or we could just plough on with *House of Cards*.'

Maggie sighed internally.

'Shall we try the new thing?' she said. She had lost interest in *House of Cards* after season two, but she didn't want to disappoint Leon who still seemed to be enjoying it.

'If you like,' replied Leon. 'How did it go with Romany last night?'

'Oh, it was very productive. We got her personal statement whipped into shape. It was pretty much there in her head. She just needed some help getting her thoughts down on paper. She's a smart girl.'

Leon nodded. 'Good,' he said. 'Did she mention that list I sent her? A hundred books to read before you're twenty-one. I googled what to read and up it popped. There was some great stuff on it, although there were plenty I'd never heard of, too.'

'No,' replied Maggie. 'It didn't come up. And to be honest, Lee, I'm not sure that she needs things like that just at the moment, with her A levels just around the corner. She's under enough pressure as it is without feeling like she's supposed to read her way through a list of novels on top.'

'Yes. You're probably right,' he said. He looked dejected, resting his chin on his hand. 'Between you and me, I'm not quite sure what I'm supposed to be doing with this cultural guardian role. It's all right for you. It's obvious that she's going to need help with stuff like her UCAS form, but my brief is so vague. I wish Angie had given us a bit more direction.'

Maggie stopped stirring the sauce and took it off the heat. She poured herself a glass of wine and sat down next to Leon. 'I think what she really wanted was to make sure that Romany had some significant adults in her life. What you're responsible for isn't really the point.'

Leon looked surprised. 'Really? Then I'm not sure . . .'

'Why don't you try taking Romany out to something – the theatre or a film, something you'd both enjoy, and then you can have a chat whilst you're out.'

'What? Just her and me?' Leon asked doubtfully.

'Why not?'

He shrugged. 'I don't know really. It just seems a bit odd.'

'She's got no dad, the only men she knows are you and Tiger, and he's not going to sit in a theatre, is he? Why don't you see what's on at the cinema and make a couple of suggestions? She can only turn you down. But lists of books? I'm not sure that's the way forward.' She gave him an encouraging smile.

Maggie wanted to tell Leon about Tiger's astonishing knowledge of Durham. She wasn't sure why it had been so surprising, and yet it had been. And underlying that was the slightly uncomfortable feeling that she had underestimated him. She had always just taken him at face value and not looked any deeper. Thinking about it now, she supposed that there must be more to him, or his friendship with Angie wouldn't have survived for all those years. She didn't want to have this conversation with Leon, though. It didn't feel quite right. She needed to talk it through with Angie. God, she missed her.

Instead, she said, 'Actually, I wasn't the only one giving advice.'

'Oh?'

'No. Romany suggested that maybe I wasn't fulfilling my potential by working at the architects'.'

Leon raised an eyebrow. 'Well, I could have told you that,' he said.

'I know, I know. It was just, hearing it from her, a child.'

'She's eighteen, hardly a child.'

'No, but you know what I mean. It made me think, that's all.'

'And what conclusion did you reach?' he asked.

Maggie drew in a deep breath. 'Something needs to change,' she said.

43

'It's down here,' said Romany.

Leon was looking very unhappy, peering down the dark alley-way at the overflowing bins and stacks of beer crates.

'Are you sure?' he said. 'It doesn't look very promising.'

'Certain,' she replied. 'I've been here loads of times.

She led the way down the cobbled path, enjoying the unfamiliar feeling of being in charge, until they came to the peeling black door.

'It's up here,' she said.

Leon looked back over his shoulder as if he was being led into a trap of some sort, and Romany laughed at him.

'God, Leon. Don't you ever go out?'

'Not to strange pubs down dark alleys,' he said, but she was pleased to see that he was smiling.

The open mic night had been her idea. She had been a couple of times in the past and sat through the usual mixture of good, passable and downright dreadful acts. But there were always a few gems, shining like diamonds amongst the coal, that made it worthwhile. Tonight, though, Laura was going to sing and so Romany was mainly there to support her. A bunch of friends from school were going too, and usually she would have tagged along with them, but then she'd got a text from Leon.

Hi Romany, the text had begun. *I was wondering if you'd like to go to the cinema one night. I'm not sure what you're into but I'm happy to go with the flow.*

Bless him, she had thought. He was doing his best and it was definitely a step up from the list of worthy but decidedly unappealing classics that he'd sent her.

There wasn't much on at the cinema, though, and she'd have to choose a film carefully to avoid being inadvertently hijacked by anything emotional. The last thing she needed was to cry all over Leon. She wasn't sure the poor bloke could take it.

But then she had thought of the open mic night. It was perfect. It was culture; there was all sorts – poetry, folk guitar, singers and other musicians – and it was live, so that meant that there wouldn't be much time for conversation. He might even enjoy it! Leon didn't look like he got out that often and Maggie was hardly living life on the edge.

So, she had texted him back. *My friend is playing at an open mic night on Thursday. Do you fancy going with me?*

And he had said yes.

She led the way up the stairs and into the room at the top. It was a loft space that ran across the length of the pub downstairs with a bar at one end and a little stage at the other. The floor was just wooden boards and the walls and ceiling had been painted black, so that even though it was reasonably spacious, it felt intimate. The room was half-full already, and Romany selected a table not too close to the speakers and sat down.

'I'll have a bottle of Becks, please,' she said.

Leon's expression was sceptical. 'On a school night?' he asked.

She'd forgotten that he had two boys of his own and would be hot on that kind of thing. But this was her night.

She raised an eyebrow. 'And could you get a bag of salt and vinegar crisps as well. Tiger and I didn't quite get round to making dinner.'

Leon shook his head and tutted and she thought that he was about to comment on the precarious domestic arrangements at the flat, but he must have changed his mind and sauntered off to the bar instead, returning with two bottles and two bags of crisps.

'So,' he said when he'd sat down and she had torn one bag along its edges and opened it flat so they could share. 'How does this work?'

'Basically, you sign up the week before with what you want to do and on the night you get the mic and then it's up to you. They get a mixture of acts each month. There's a fair amount of crap poetry but the comedians are sometimes funny. And my friend Laura, that's who we're here to see, she's really good.'

'What does she do?' Leon asked.

'She sings and plays the guitar. She's fantastic. She does covers of Adele songs, Norah Jones, that kind of thing, but tonight she's going to try out one that she's written herself, so she's a bit more nervous.'

'I'm looking forward to hearing her,' said Leon, and Romany thought that he did actually look quite interested. As they chatted, his eyes kept flicking round the room, taking it all in. Maybe she had hit on something that they could do together, which would save her having to endure his other slightly painful suggestions.

There was a shout from across the room and Romany looked up to see a group of her school mates plus Laura, her guitar strung across her back. Romany had intended that they would sit separately so as not to inflict them on Leon and vice versa, but now they seemed to be coming towards her and before she knew it, they were all settling themselves down around them, borrowing chairs from other tables and getting drinks.

When they were all assembled, Romany did the introductions. Leon raised a hand in greeting and smiled widely. He didn't say much, but he followed their conversation attentively, nodding and laughing as appropriate. He seemed to be coming alive as the place filled up and the noise levels rose. She had always taken him for a bit of a loner, had wondered why her mum had been friends with him when they appeared to be polar opposites, but maybe this was it. Maybe Leon was a creature of the night? He was chatting easily to the others now whilst they waited for the acts to start. He was actually quite funny, she thought, with a dry, sharp sense of humour and, as they all warmed into the evening, Romany began to feel quite proud of him.

The first few acts were fairly standard – a comedian who only really had three good gags and a poet who seemed to want to rage against the machine quite a lot. Laura was down for the fifth slot and as it approached, she became quieter and quieter. Romany wanted to go and reassure her, but her chair was tucked into the wall and she couldn't easily get closer to her friend without make a fuss. Instead, she mouthed what she hoped were helpful comments. Laura nodded, but she was biting her lip and had gone a little pale.

Then she saw Leon lean in towards her and say something. He had turned his head away from Romany so that she couldn't lip read, but whatever it was, it made Laura smile. She sat up straighter and seemed to get some of her colour back. And then, when the MC announced her name, she looked at Leon again, as if he was a kind of mentor. Romany was curious and she wondered what Leon had said that had made the situation less nerve-racking. She would have to ask Laura later.

Laura took her guitar, stepped up to the little stage and perched herself on the stool in front of the microphone. Then, after a last-minute tuning check, she began. She picked out the opening melody confidently. It always surprised Romany how good she was.

She didn't go on about it and it wasn't a talent that you could see just by looking at her, so it was easy to forget, but now, as she began to sing, it was obvious that she had something. Her voice, with its distinctive style somewhere between Amy Winehouse and Dido, was tentative to start with but then began to gain in confidence as she realised that the room was with her. When she strummed the final chord, the audience burst into appreciative applause. Laura smiled bashfully and then came back to sit with them.

The girls all crowded around her with their fulsome praise, Romany amongst them, but she noticed that Laura only really wanted to know what Leon thought. He was nodding appreciatively and smiling widely.

'That was fantastic,' he said. 'I loved how you built the intensity as you went through, and your bridge was the perfect counter to the rest. Mesmerising, in fact. Really good. Well done.'

'Thanks,' said Laura, her eyes shining.

Romany was intrigued. What was going on? Where was the nerdy Leon that she had always known? Not here, that was for sure. This Leon was actually pretty cool. Her friends certainly seemed to think so as they each vied for his conversational attention. Then something sparkled at the back of Romany's memory. Hadn't her mother told her that Leon used to play an instrument when they were at uni, that he'd been quite good?

'Do you play, Leon?' she asked him.

The response was instantaneous and unmissable. He seemed to shrink a little in his chair and his shoulders hunched over.

'Not really,' he said into his lap. 'I used to play a bit of sax when I was your age, that's all.'

'Were you in a band?' asked Laura.

Leon shook his head. 'No, nothing like that. I just played for myself really.'

'You should do a slot here,' said one of the others.

'Yes!' said Romany. 'Yes, that's a great idea. We can sign you up for a slot for next month. What kind of stuff do you play?'

Leon bit his lip and folded his arms across his chest. 'Jazz, but I'm not sure . . .'

'Oh, go on,' urged Romany. 'There's barely anyone here anyway. It'll be cool.'

Leon was still looking as if he would rather be anywhere else. So then Romany deployed her killer point.

'You should do it for Mum,' she said.

44

'Did you get your uni application sent off?' Tiger asked Romany the following Saturday. Whilst they didn't see much of each other during the week, they had taken to coming together on a Saturday evening to watch whatever was on the television for a bit. It wasn't too much of a sacrifice. If Romany had plans for the night, they didn't generally kick off until a bit later, and Tiger seemed to appreciate the chance to chat. She was learning that he was good company, too.

'I once met this shaman in Bali,' he might start, or, 'When I was working in a shoe shop in Helsinki . . .'

She never knew what was true and what wasn't, but she assumed that most of his stories had either happened to him or to someone he had met. She could picture him, sitting round in hostels the world over, swapping tall tales to keep the other travellers entertained. He was good at it, a natural storyteller. She hadn't really thought that being able to tell an anecdote was such a skill until she heard Tiger weaving his. It didn't matter how the story ended, either, whether it was funny or tragic, or whether, like some modern-day fable, it came with a warning attached. The joy of Tiger's stories was in the journey. She had told him that he should write them down, but he just scoffed at the suggestion.

'Me?' he laughed. 'I can barely hold a pen.'

She thought he was joking – but she wasn't entirely sure.

'No, I've not sent it yet,' she replied. 'School said I couldn't put just Durham down. I need a Plan B apparently, so I've had to do a bit of research on other places. It took a bit of time.'

He nodded. 'Makes sense,' he said. 'Although I'm sure you won't need one – a Plan B, I mean. And Durham is still your top choice?'

'Yes, I think so,' she replied.

'Fancy a trip up there?' he asked. 'So you can get a feel for the place before you commit? We could get a train, if you like. Or we could hitch . . . ?'

'We'll get a train,' said Romany firmly. 'I'll dig into the money that Mum left for travel.'

They went the following weekend. Romany was a little apprehensive. Even though they had been living together for a month or so, they didn't see each other much. A whole day was a long time to spend together with no chance of escape. Still, she really should visit Durham before she finally sent her form off, in case she absolutely hated the place, and she wasn't that keen to make the trip on her own.

At the station, she bought them a steaming cup of coffee and a blueberry muffin each.

'Your mum would be turning in her grave,' Tiger teased her.

Romany had noticed that unlike everyone else, Tiger didn't avoid talking about her mum or flinch each time they said something that they thought might be insensitive. He just carried on as if her death was just another thing that had happened. To start with, she had found his bluntness inappropriate and had resented that he seemed to make no allowances for her feelings, but now it was refreshing.

'She would. Caffeine AND sugar at once. She didn't mind though, not really. Yes, we ate vegan at home and there was never sugar in the house, but if I came home with a packet of Haribos or had an egg sandwich at lunchtime she never made a fuss.'

'Why would you want an egg sandwich?' asked Tiger, pretending to push his fingers down his throat at the thought.

'You know what I mean. Mum had strong views about stuff, but they were her views. I was always free to have my own.'

Tiger nodded. 'Yeah, she was good like that, your mum. And how's this guardian thing working out for you? No complaints about yours truly, of course . . .' He huffed on his fingernails and polished them on his fleece.

'Well, now that I think I've got my head round what she was trying to do, it's not so bad,' she said. 'I am a bit young to be living on my own, I suppose, and there wasn't anyone else to take me in. Maggie's been great with this UCAS stuff and I'm sure she'll be able to help with other things. And Leon's sweet. I've bullied him into playing at this open mic thing in a couple of weeks. He didn't look best pleased, but he can always back out if he wants.'

'Is he playing his sax?' asked Tiger.

Romany nodded and Tiger whistled through his teeth.

'You're in for a treat then,' he said. 'I might even come with you.'

'Is he good?' asked Romany.

'Just you wait,' replied Tiger, knowingly. 'And what about that Hope woman? Have you heard from her?'

Romany shook her head. 'I'm not sure why Mum chose her,' she said. 'Maggie doesn't know either. She said that she'd only met her once before. You don't know her, do you?'

294

'No,' Tiger said. 'Seemed like an odd choice to me too, but I'm sure your mum knew what she was doing. She never did stuff by accident.'

Usually it annoyed Romany when people tried to tell her what her mum had been like, but somehow when Tiger did it she didn't mind. It was probably because whatever he said about her was generally spot on.

The train pulled into Durham and they got out, jostling along the platform with the other travellers. It was a cold grey day with rain clouds hanging threateningly overhead, but it didn't matter to them. They were on a mission. Tiger had planned a route for them through the city which he said would take in all the main elements, together with the university itself, plus a few corners to give her a feel for the 'real' city.

'Do you know all the places you've visited as well as you do this one?' Romany asked him as he marched confidently up North Bailey with her in tow.

'Pretty much,' he replied. 'I mean, there are one or two places where I wasn't exactly compos mentis, if you know what I mean . . .' He grinned at her. 'But I remember most of them.'

'I can barely find my way around York,' confessed Romany.

'I find that if something is important to you, it has a way of staying in your memory,' he said. 'I love travelling, seeing new places, meeting new people, so when I do it, it would be pretty stupid of me to just forget everything I'd seen as soon as I left.'

There was a pause in the conversation as they negotiated a group of tourists.

'So is it really bad,' Romany asked, 'being stuck with me?' She hadn't really thought about that before. She had been so busy resenting what had happened to her that she hadn't looked at the situation from anyone else's point of view.

Tiger didn't say anything for a moment. He's going to lie, she thought. He's going to tell me that it's all totally fine and that he doesn't mind in the least.

'Yes, it's bloody awful,' he said. 'Don't get me wrong,' he added. 'You're a nice kid and I'd have done just about anything for your mum. But this? Being stuck in one place for a whole year? I reckon it might actually kill me.'

Romany was horrified. 'I'm so sorry . . .' she began.

And then she saw his face. He was grinning at her and she thumped him gently in the ribs.

'You bastard!' she said, laughing. 'I thought you meant it then.'

Tiger's grin slipped a little. 'Well, I'm not entirely joking,' he said. 'It is hard, not being able to just take off whenever I want. But it's not forever and to be honest, I'm quite getting into the routine of it all. And there are advantages to being in one place. It's safe, for a start – I don't have to keep looking over my shoulder to see who's watching. And there's always food – well, if I've been to the shops, that is – and it's warm and dry. And you don't snore – or not that I can hear through the wall. So, no. It's not all bad. Right, less of this philosophical bollocks. Let's go and look at the cathedral. Oldest surviving vaulted ceiling of its size. Did you know that? Actually, I reckon that kind of thing is as much Leon's area as mine, but I bet he couldn't give you the guided tour.'

By the time the day was over, Romany had walked her legs to bleeding stumps and couldn't take another step, but she felt like she had a pretty good idea of what Durham was all about.

'So, still want to go to uni there?' asked Tiger as they sat in the train on their way home.

'Yeah, I reckon so,' Romany replied. 'Thanks, Tiger.'

'You're welcome. Glad to be of use.'

Something that might have been sadness flickered across his face, as if he wished he could be helpful more often. It made Romany wonder.

'Can I ask you something?' she began tentatively.

'Sure. Fire away.'

'Is it just you? I mean, have you got family somewhere or are you like me, with no one?'

'Is that how you feel?' he replied, answering her question with a question.

Romany pulled her lips together tight ready to stop her emotions from escaping, but then she realised that she wasn't going to cry.

'Yeah, a bit,' she said. 'I mean there's you and Auntie Maggie.' She could feel her cheeks warm at the babyish name. 'And Leon, of course. And I've got my friends. Laura is amazing and her mum's been great. But, basically, yes. It does feel like it's me on my own.'

'What about your dad?' asked Tiger. 'He's still around, some-where. We could try to track him down.'

Romany had thought about this. Since her adamant response to her mum's enquiry in Whitby that time, she had felt that she needed to continue to toe that line. But actually, given how things had changed, she wasn't quite as opposed to the idea as she had been at fifteen. That wasn't the same as actually wanting to find him, though. She shook her head.

'I don't think so,' she said. 'I mean, I've done all right without him so far. And maybe we're just not meant to meet?'

Tiger gave her a look that suggested he didn't agree, but he didn't challenge her view. 'You're young,' he said instead. 'There's plenty of time to decide.'

They fell silent then, each of them staring out of the window into the darkening sky for the rest of the journey. Romany didn't realise until later that Tiger had dodged her question.

45

'Hurry up, Leon! We'll be late.'

He was dragging his heels and Maggie knew precisely why. He just didn't want to go. He had been anxious about the open mic evening ever since Romany had bounced him into doing it, but he had said he would play, and he couldn't drop out now.

Maggie softened her tone. 'It'll be fine,' she said. 'You can do this standing on your head. All you have to do is play one piece, just show Romany that you're there for her. It'll mean so much to her, you stepping up like this.'

Leon refused to engage. Whatever it was that was going on in his head, he wasn't prepared to share it with her. He left the room without a word.

Maggie hadn't seen him vulnerable like this for a while. He had always worn his heart on his sleeve, but over the years, that side of him had become more deeply buried. It was just part of getting older, she assumed. You became more adept at keeping the softer parts of yourself hidden from view and, in time, sometimes maybe you even forgot they were there.

The prospect of playing at this open mic night, though, had definitely triggered something in him. Maggie wasn't sure what it was. Nerves, certainly, but it felt like there was something else beneath that, something that she couldn't quite put her finger on.

He reappeared at the door with his sax bag slung across his back. He looked very pale. Maybe it was too much? She should perhaps give him the chance to back out.

'I can tell her that you're ill, if you like,' Maggie said gently. 'We don't have to go.'

Leon shook his head. 'No,' he said. 'Let's do it.'

An hour later she was sitting in a dark room above a pub sipping a dubious white wine and feeling more than a little out of place. They were at least twenty years older than the rest of the clientele and quite a lot cleaner than many of them, too. There was a nice atmosphere, though, welcoming and warm, the air tinged with a crackle of excitement about what was to come.

'Do you know who else is performing?' Maggie asked, and then could have kicked herself for her choice of verb, but Leon just shook his head. She wanted to ask what had happened the last time he'd been here, but it was clear that she wasn't going to get any conversation out of him, so she took a sip of her drink and watched the door.

Romany arrived about fifteen minutes later, looking young and beautiful and surrounded by a gang of other young and beautiful girls. She had almost reached the age that Maggie had been when she met first Angie. Maggie had felt so grown up back then, but Romany still looked like a child to her. She must feel grown up though, just as Maggie had done, and of course, she had had far more to deal with so far than Maggie had experienced in the whole of her life.

Following behind them was Tiger, but Maggie's stomach stayed where it belonged at the sight of him. It had passed. It was gone. And she didn't miss it. It was time to fully appreciate what she had rather than hankering after make-believe. Spending time with Romany had taught her that.

Tiger raised an arm and came over and Romany and her friends dragged a spare table across so that they could all sit together.

'Hi, Auntie Maggie,' Romany said, leaning over and giving her a peck on her cheek. 'Hi, Leon. All set?'

Leon nodded. 'All set,' he replied, his voice flat and not revealing his jitters.

One of the girls broke away from the group and came to whisper something in his ear. He turned to look at her and for the first time that evening, smiled. This must be Laura, Maggie thought. Sweet. And whatever she'd said, it did seem to have made a difference, as he suddenly looked a little less tense. Then he lifted his untouched pint and drank the first half in one go.

On before Leon was a comic poet with a diatribe about Brexit and a folk singer whose tuning was a little bit off to Maggie's ear, although she was no expert. Then there was another poet and then it was Leon. Maggie gave him a supportive smile as he stood and made his way to the stage. Her insides were knotted so tightly that it was hard to get a lungful of air. She raised her eyebrows at the collected group as if to say, now just watch this, but under the table she was crossing her fingers. None of the girls knew how big a moment this was for Leon. Even Tiger might not really get it. But she did.

Leon arranged his instrument on its sling around his neck and pulled the mouthpiece in and out of his mouth a few times, moistening the reed. He was standing in a pool of light cast by one of the spotlights and his saxophone glinted as he lifted it, ready to begin. Maggie's mind skipped to the first time she had heard him play, in a corridor in their halls of residence. That had been the week she had first met Tiger, too. And Angie had been there. It felt like another lifetime.

As Leon played, the room stilled as the audience became completely caught in the spell of his music. Maggie let the tears trickle down her cheeks. She cried for her youth that was lost, for the dreams that had never quite come to fruition, for Leon's wasted talent, for missed opportunities with Tiger. But most of all she cried for Angie, her least likely and yet her closest friend. How she would have loved to have been here, egging Leon on just as she had always done. Of all of them, Angie had always been the one who had most believed in his talents, in him. In fact, Maggie couldn't think of anyone else who had tried to encourage Leon as much as Angie had, not even herself. God, she missed her so much that it was like a stabbing pain in her very core.

The performance was over before she realised, the crowd clapping and then on their feet, arms raised above heads. Sharp wolf whistles sounded around the enclosed space and there were cries of 'Encore'. Maggie hastily wiped the tears away from her eyes and then looked over at the stage. Leon was standing there in his pool of light and looking at his feet but then, as it became obvious that the applause wasn't stopping, he slowly lifted his head to look at his audience. And then he beamed, a wide, open-mouthed smile that lit up his entire face. He mouthed 'Thanks' and raised his saxophone in the air in a salute.

The crowd kept going, stamping their feet against the floorboards in a rhythmic tattoo and calling for more. Leon seemed uncertain what to do. Then a man standing behind the bar called out over the racket.

'Order, order! Let's have a bit of hush, shall we? Now, we don't normally allow encores, but shall we make an exception, just this once?'

The crowd roared and Leon looked over at Maggie questioningly.

Then Tiger stood up and shouted out over the cheers. 'Go on, Leon, mate. Show 'em what you can do!'

And so Leon played again. This time it was more upbeat and less soulful than the first piece, and it captured the mood of the audience perfectly. They listened, rapt, and then applauded vigorously once more, but this time Leon unhooked himself from the amplifier and pushed his way back to their table through the standing crowd. People were patting him on the shoulder and congratulating him as he passed them.

'There you go, Romey,' said Tiger. 'I told you you were in for a treat.'

Romany's eyes were wide and shining. 'Oh my God, Leon!' she said. 'Where did you learn to play like that?'

Leon shrugged. It was just the same as it had been thirty-odd years ago when Romany's mother had asked the question, Maggie thought: Leon self-effacing and his friends in awe. But this time there was a greater poignancy to the moment. Now, they were over halfway through their lives and Leon's talent was still mouldering away in a box, hidden from view.

'I don't really know,' Leon said. 'I just learned.'

'Did you play professionally?' asked Laura. 'Back in the day, I mean?'

Maggie flinched. They weren't that old! But then again, to these girls with their whole lives glittering ahead of them, perhaps they were.

Leon shook his head. 'No. It's always been just a hobby,' he said, putting the saxophone back in its case. 'Right,' he said decisively, indicating a change in subject. 'Who wants a drink before the next act?'

Leon wandered off to the bar, despite having bought the round before, and the rest of the group chattered on about how wonderful his playing had been. After a bit, Maggie realised that he had been gone a while and she looked over to see where he'd got to. He was still standing at the bar, chatting to the man who had allowed the encore. He looked lively and animated, his face bright and his hands gesticulating as he spoke. It was nice to see.

Eventually, he made his way back with the tray of drinks and settled himself at the table. The next act, a guitar player, was just getting the mic set up, no doubt feeling a little daunted by what she had to follow.

Leon handed the drinks round, still grinning like a Cheshire cat. 'The guy at the bar has offered me a gig,' he said.

'Nice one, mate,' said Tiger, slapping him on the back.

'What kind of gig?' asked Maggie.

'At a jazz club in Leeds. His mate runs it, apparently,' Leon said. He pulled a face that said he didn't know whether this was a good thing or not.

'Fantastic!' said Maggie, just to make sure that he did. 'What did you say?'

'I said yes!'

Maggie was delighted. She threw her arms around him and kissed him. When she looked up, Tiger was looking on, his expression wistful.

46

Durham had made Romany an offer. It had arrived when she was at school and had popped up, as casual as you like, when she refreshed her UCAS page at break. Romany saw it, did a double take and her heart paused for a second and then begin to pound. She screamed and then handed the phone to Laura.

'Does that say what I think it does?' she asked her.

Laura peered at the screen. 'Well, if you think it says that Durham have made you an offer of AAB then yes! It does! Well done, Romey!' Laura threw her arms around her and squeezed tightly, hugging all the breath out of her.

Romany just stood there, not quite able to believe it. It didn't matter what the other universities did now. She had her offer from Durham. All she had to do was get the grades. Just like that! This thought sent a wave of dread and panic crashing over her, but she told herself that actually having the offer changed nothing on that front. The grades were still within her capabilities. She just needed to keep going as she was doing and not take her eyes off the prize.

'And when I get in at Newcastle, I'll just be up the road,' grinned Laura, and Romany nodded.

That was all part of the plan. The gap between the two towns was big enough for them each to build new friendships, but small enough that Romany had a place to retreat to. They had discussed it at length. Romany wouldn't be coming home at weekends like most students did. When she left for university, Tiger would leave as well, released from his gilded cage to fly back into the world, leaving the flat standing empty. The thought of returning to an empty place, with all the memories that were woven into every plate or cushion, was more than she could contemplate. The holidays would be a different matter, but she would work that out when it happened. For now, knowing that Laura would be close by in Newcastle was enough.

'I can't believe how fast this year is going,' Laura said, as she scrolled down her phone for what she had missed whilst in class. 'Mocks coming up and then that'll be it – the actual exams. End of school! End of life as we know it!' Laura twisted her face into an expression of mock horror. 'Shit!'

Then the bell rang and they shuffled off to their next lessons. For now, life went on as it always had done. Romany had to agree with Laura about time racing by, though. It was already over three months since her mum had died. In many ways it felt like forever. Every morning, she woke with a list of things that she wanted to tell her mum in her head, and every night she went to bed with the dull pain of her absence sitting in her stomach like a stone.

But in other ways, time really was flying. How could it be nearly Christmas already? Decorations twinkled in every shop window and strings of lights festooned lamp posts and trees in all directions. They had even got a tree up at home. Romany hadn't been sure she had the heart for it, but when she got back one day and discovered that Tiger had bought one and decorated it himself, she was suddenly glad that he'd made the effort. Christmas wouldn't be Christmas without a tree. He'd even got a full set of new decorations. He told her he hadn't been sure where their old ones were, but Romany suspected that he hadn't wanted to stir up painful memories. And he'd been entirely right. This wasn't the year to have a tree decorated with all the old familiar things.

Romany hadn't realised that she had put Christmas in the 'too hard' box as well, and had avoided thinking about it until Tiger asked her what she wanted to do to celebrate.

'I haven't had a Christmas in the UK for . . .' His gaze went up to the ceiling as he tried to work it out. 'Well, I've no idea, but it's been a bloody long time.'

'I've never had a Christmas anywhere else,' said Romany. She could feel her throat closing up. Sometimes she fought hard to maintain control but sometimes she just let the tears come. This was one of those times. Christmas without her mum. She had no idea how she could even think about it, let alone get through it.

Tiger saw her tears and edged closer. Over the months, they had become more used to one another, the awkwardness of the first few weeks falling away little by little. Now, for the first time, he pulled her into a hug. It took Romany by surprise, but then she let herself lean into him, enjoying the warmth of another person's body against hers and the feeling of someone bigger than her enclosing her. Sometimes all she wanted was for someone else to take control so that she could be the child again. She cried into his shoulder, and he just held her until her sobs started to slow and then faded away.

'Tell me about Christmases with your mum,' he said. 'Come on, sit down.'

They moved across to the sofa and she sat cross-legged next to him.

'Well,' she began, 'Christmas Day was usually just me and Mum, but Maggie came sometimes too. We didn't do the whole turkey thing, obviously. There wasn't even a special meal that we always ate. We'd just make what we fancied. Last year we had curry takeaway, because Mum didn't want to cook. We did presents, though. Mum used to make me a stocking full of lots of little things. She must have collected them all year long. Sometimes there were things that I'd asked for and she'd said I didn't need, but then they'd turn up on Christmas Day. She was really thoughtful like that. We'd open one each per hour.'

Tiger pulled a face. 'I'm more of a "rip off all the paper in the first five minutes" man.'

'Yes. That's what I wanted to do when I was little, too . . .' Romany spotted the insult just too late, but she ignored it. 'But the older I got, the easier it was to take it slowly. And anyway, it was just the way we did things, so it seemed normal to me. Mum said it was so we could properly appreciate each gift and be grateful for it.'

'That sounds like your mum,' agreed Tiger.

'And then we'd play Scrabble and watch films and I'd eat chocolate. Mum might even eat some sometimes. And she bought beer! It was the only day of the year that she had it. She used to pretend that she didn't miss it, but she did really. I could just tell.'

'It sounds like the perfect Christmas,' said Tiger.

Romany nodded and the tears started to fall again.

'So, how about this year we do it differently,' suggested Tiger. 'Instead of staying here, let's go out for Christmas lunch. We can go wherever you like. You choose. And we can invite Maggie and Leon too, if you like. Make it a bit of a party.'

Romany's heart lifted a little. 'That would be great,' she said.

'We can start a whole new tradition,' continued Tiger. 'It might be the shortest run tradition in history,' he added. 'But still.'

She grinned at him. 'Thanks, Tiger,' she said.

He shook off her thanks as if it was nothing. 'How about you find a restaurant and I'll speak to Maggie and Leon,' he said.

'Okay,' she said. 'I've seen this place that looks really cool. I've always wanted to go. I'll see if they're going to be open on Christmas Day. I'll go and search it now.'

'Great,' said Tiger. 'That sounds like a plan then.'

Romany leaned across and surprised herself by planting a peck on his cheek. That was something she could never have imagined doing three months ago.

'Thanks, Tiger,' she said again, and he smiled back. His eyes were glistening, too.

47

Maggie looked at the sparkly Christmas tree earrings and wondered, yet again, whether she could get away with them. They weren't really her style, or even to her taste, but there was a kind of frivolous silliness about them that appealed to her. Other people wore festive jewellery and seemed to survive without looking like they were trying too hard. Maybe she could wear them in an ironic way, so that if anyone commented on how unlikely they were on her, she could toss her head and give them a sympathetic smile, as if they had completely missed the point. What if she just wore one, a nod to Christmas but showing that she hadn't totally bought into the commercial vibe?

Or could there be a possibility that she was overthinking the entire thing? She scooped the earrings up and dropped them back into the box. Maybe next year . . .

She had never eaten out on Christmas Day before, which was, of course, the point. It was touching that Tiger had been sensitive enough to realise that Romany would need something different this year. Touching, and quite surprising. Maggie had thought that out of Romany's guardians, she was the one with a monopoly on thoughtfulness, but in that, as in so many other things, she had been wrong.

It was sweet of him to invite her and Leon, too. There had been no suggestion that they should invite Hope, Romany's fourth and thus far absent other guardian. Maggie had wrangled with that. It felt wrong for them all to be going out together without even running it by her. She had managed to rationalise it by thinking that the fact that the three of them had been appointed 'guardians' was irrelevant to their decision to spend Christmas Day together. They were doing that because they were old friends, who were, quite rarely and possibly uniquely, all available on December 25 this year. Hope would no doubt have other things she would rather be doing, like spending the day with that boyfriend, if he was still on the scene. Maggie hadn't seen her since the reading of Angie's will and then the conversation hadn't strayed into the state of her love life, for obvious reasons.

So Maggie had stopped feeling bad and started looking forward to a Christmas lunch out. Romany had chosen the restaurant, a place that Maggie had taken clients to a couple of times, back when she had clients, but she didn't remember much about it other than that it had been perfectly acceptable. It possibly wasn't the kind of place she would have chosen for Christmas lunch but then again, wasn't that exactly the point? A change, something new and totally unconnected to anything that Angie had done – that was the driving force behind the whole day.

She heard a car pulling up in the driveway. Leon was here. He always wanted to be in Leeds on Christmas Day morning, so that he could pop round and see his boys. This tradition would come to an end soon, she imagined. Thomas was twenty-two and would surely want to be making his own Christmases soon enough, if only to get away from the all-controlling Becky, but for now Maggie didn't mind waking up alone on the big day and she rather enjoyed having the morning on her own, pottering about with 'Carols from

Kings' on the sound system and a glass of something bubbly in her hand.

She slipped her feet into her shoes and took a last glance at herself in the mirror – she looked fine, she concluded, and with no need for sparkly Christmas tree earrings.

◆ ◆ ◆

The restaurant was already busy, but there was a table for four right in the centre just sitting quietly and waiting for its occupants to arrive. It was stylishly dressed with white linen and sparkling glasses, but there were the obligatory crackers and party poppers at each place setting. You couldn't escape Christmas entirely, then, Maggie thought, throwing a glance at Romany to see if they troubled her, but she was smiling, sharing a joke with Tiger and didn't seem distressed. Maggie would be led by her as to whether they pulled them or dropped them discreetly to the floor.

They followed the waitress to their table and then, after a brief hesitation over seating arrangements, settled themselves down. Tiger immediately snatched up a cracker and offered one end to Romany. So much for his sensitivity, Maggie thought, but Romany seemed to accept it in the spirit that it had been offered, and soon everything that could be pulled had been and they were all sitting there in jaunty paper hats and squinting at terrible jokes.

'This is great,' said Romany, who somehow managed to look stylish in her yellow cracker crown. 'Thanks so much everyone.'

No doubt someone would have to mention Angie at some point in the proceedings, but not just yet, Maggie thought. Leon also appeared to be thinking that the moment needed to be delayed as he reached for the drinks menu.

'Shall we order some wine?' he asked, and they all jumped at the chance to focus on something other than the absence of Angie as a discussion on what type and how much ensued. After that there was much cooing over the menu, which gave a choice of several dishes for each course but with no turkey in sight.

Conversation began, opening with Romany's offer from Durham and the trip that she and Tiger had taken to look round, and then moving on to more random topics as the wine flowed. The meal was interspersed with various amuse-bouche and complimentary extras that they all passed judgement on, favourable or otherwise depending on taste. They were just finishing their main courses when a loud clapping started up behind them. Maggie turned to see that the chef and his team, all in glowing whites, had emerged from the kitchen to take applause. Maggie thought it a little pretentious, but perhaps it was a Christmas Day thing, which seemed fair enough when all the kitchen and waiting staff had sacrificed their own family Christmases to make their guests' days perfect.

Maggie turned in her seat so that she was facing the team, and then joined in the clapping. It seemed to be going on for an inordinate length of time, to her mind at least, and so she let her eye run along the line. It settled on the oldest, who was standing in the middle wearing a tall chef's hat and beaming. He was probably the main man, she thought. He looked familiar, but she couldn't place him.

The hubbub died down and the team headed back into the kitchen to prepare dessert. What was left of Maggie's meal had gone cold and so she put her knife and fork down, ready to wait for whatever was coming next. She was hardly going to go hungry, given the amount of food they had been served.

Then she felt a tap on her shoulder and turned round to see Hope standing there. Guilt flooded Maggie at once and she could feel heat roaring into her face. How had Hope found out? Was she, just like the bad fairy in *Sleeping Beauty*, going to make an embarrassing fuss about not having been invited to the party? It was, of course, unlikely, but Maggie couldn't help but feel terrible that they were so obviously all there without her.

But Hope was smiling broadly. She looked stunning in an elegantly cut black cocktail dress with sparkles cascading down the front like a diamanté waterfall.

'Hi everyone,' she said, quickly bestowing a dazzling smile on each of them that left Tiger barely able to close his mouth. Maggie's irritation began to fizz. Could he not show a bit more self-control? It was pathetic, it really was. She didn't look to see what effect Hope was having on Leon.

'Hi Romany,' Hope continued, 'and merry Christmas. Are you having a lovely time?'

'Hi,' said Romany. 'Merry Christmas to you too. Yes, we are, thanks. What are you doing here? Are you eating?' Romany looked around the room, trying to identify which group Hope was with.

'No such luck. I'm working,' replied Hope with a little shrug that made Maggie want to roll her eyes. 'This is my boyfriend Daniel's place. It's all hands to the pump today, so rather than sitting at home eating chocolate on my own, I thought I'd come in and help out.'

Maggie thought that it was highly unlikely that Hope ate chocolate, alone or otherwise. She probably did a full gym workout on Christmas Day. But that was why Maggie recognised the chef, she realised – from Hope's thirtieth party.

'And you're all here. How lovely. I suppose it must be hard, your first Christmas without your mum.'

Maggie's irritation rose still further. Did the woman have no sense? That was clearly going to be a difficult question, and one that didn't need asking.

But Romany seemed prepared. 'Yeah, it is hard, but Tiger suggested we did something totally different this year, and so here we are.'

'Good idea,' Hope replied, gracing Tiger with another of her beautiful smiles. Maggie smouldered, lips drawn in a tight line.

'And thanks for your card and present,' continued Romany. 'A spa day is a really lovely idea. I'd love to come. Maybe we could fix it for after my mocks are over. I'll need some serious me time then.'

'Whenever suits you is good for me,' said Hope. 'Just give me a ring and I'll arrange it.'

So, there had been some contact between Hope and Romany then, thought Maggie. She was both pleased and a little miffed at the same time, and wondered whether she might be a little bit jealous, which was, she knew, completely ridiculous.

'Listen,' said Hope. 'I have to go now, but we're nearly at the end of lunchtime service. Why don't you hang around for a few minutes after your coffee and we can have a quick drink and a catch-up? I'll drag Daniel out of the kitchen and you can meet him, although he probably won't be at his best!' She smiled again. She really was the most beautiful woman; Maggie did have to concede that.

'That would be lovely,' said Romany, speaking for them all. 'It'll be nice to say hello. We'll see you later.'

'Great,' said Hope. 'And now I'd better get back to the fray. I'll see you in a while.'

A long table along the back wall had broken into a rowdy and rather flat version of 'I Wish it Could be Christmas Every Day,' which was changing the ambience of the room somewhat, and she sashayed off to speak to them.

'Have you seen much of her, Romey?' asked Maggie. She knew she was being childish in hoping that Hope had been neglecting her duties. It was Romany that was important here, not her own petty dislikes.

'Not really,' replied Romany. 'Not nearly as much as I see of the rest of you, anyway.' Maggie tried not to feel smug. 'She messages me a bit, though, so we've had a few conversations. She's really nice but I think she's pretty busy. She sent me a voucher for Christmas for the two of us to go to a very posh spa over near Harrogate, which was kind of her.'

Maggie saw Tiger look down at his fingernails. He had obviously omitted to get Romany a gift, but she doubted Romany would have been expecting anything.

'Yes,' agreed Maggie. 'That was kind. Right then,' she added, wanting to change the subject away from perfect, beautiful Hope, 'who's for pudding?'

48

Coffee and delicious handmade chocolates had been served and most of the other guests had departed, leaving the four of them, an island in a sea of discarded napkins and half-filled glasses.

Romany was ready to go home. It had been a lovely idea, coming out, and she wasn't sure how she would have coped if they had tried to have a 'normal' Christmas at home, but now she was ready to slip into her pyjamas and watch whatever crap they were showing on the television. They couldn't leave yet, though, because of the invitation from Hope to stay for a drink, and so Romany resigned herself to another hour or so of her guardians.

She wasn't complaining. They'd been good fun, although they were all quite drunk now. Leon had been liberal with his ordering of wine, calling for fresh bottles almost before the previous one was drained, perhaps to make sure that things stayed jolly. Romany had drunk the first couple of glasses quickly, a kind of anaesthetic against the potential pain, but it had turned out to be a nice afternoon, light-hearted and not at all maudlin, and she had quickly decided that she didn't need an alcoholic crutch to get her through it.

Their conversation had meandered its way along familiar paths and ended up, as it inevitably did, with a trip down memory lane. The three of them didn't seem to be able to stay away from their mutual past, as if recounting at least one story was required to validate all subsequent meetings. It was sweet, really, and Romany hoped that when she got to university, she too would find a set of friends that she managed to stay close to for the rest of her life, like these three. Seeing them together, it was clear that they shared such an easy rapport born from familiarity. However, the thing she liked best was how they all cut each other slack for their failings, because they all had pretty huge failings.

Take Tiger, for example. It was obvious to Romany that he had been running from something for his entire adult life. She was beginning to get the impression that even he wasn't sure why he couldn't stop, but was it maybe that he was frightened of what might happen if he did? He would have to settle somewhere eventually, though. He was in his fifties now and he couldn't keep running forever.

Maggie, too, was frightened of something. Romany didn't really get it because from where she was standing Maggie always seemed to be completely in control, but at the same time she could see that there was always something holding her back, as if she'd got her coat stuck in a door and couldn't quite pull herself free. Romany wanted to tell her to just take the coat off and leave it behind, but it really wasn't her place and she liked Maggie – she didn't want to do anything to upset her.

And Leon. The world's most ordinary man with the world's most extraordinary talent. It was such a waste, having something like that and then just pretending that you didn't. What was that? Fear again? Who knew that being an adult could be so scary? But her mum hadn't been scared of the world, Romany thought. Her mum had never been scared of anything.

Hope was the real mystery, Romany thought as she watched her move from table to table clearing away the debris. She still had no idea why her mum had included her in the gang of four. She seemed nice enough. She was a bit frosty, but Romany imagined that if you looked like Hope then you probably needed to find ways to protect yourself from unwanted attention. But being beautiful wasn't enough of a reason to have landed her with the job of guiding Romany through this tricky year and beyond. There must be something else. If Romany knew anything about her mum, it was that she didn't do things by accident. No, there would have been a purpose in her mind. Romany just needed to work out what it was.

Romany's thoughts were interrupted then, because there was Hope, strolling across the restaurant towards them with a bottle of champagne in her hand. A waiter who Romany recognised from school followed behind with half a dozen sparkling flutes on a silver tray.

'Sorry I've been so long,' she said as she reached them. 'Things always take more time than you think, don't they? But I'm here now. Have you had a lovely time?'

'We have, thanks,' replied Romany, feeling that as the soberest amongst them the role of spokeswoman should fall to her. 'The food was great. You should tell your boyfriend from us.'

'You can tell him yourself,' she said. She turned and shouted back to the kitchen. 'Dan. Come and meet Romany and the others.'

Moments later the person who must be Dan emerged. His tall chef hat had gone now and there was a smear of sauce down the front of his whites, but his eyes were shining.

'Hi,' he said, pushing his damp hair away from his forehead. He scanned the group and then settled his gaze on her. Their eyes locked, but his look was so intense that it made Romany feel uncomfortable, as if she were being interrogated. It was weird, off somehow.

She held his stare, defiant, but then, when he still didn't look away, she dropped her eyes. Had she done something to inadvertently upset him? She couldn't think what. She had just said how much she had enjoyed his food, although she supposed he didn't know that yet. She'd heard that chefs were highly strung but not like this, surely. She wiped round her mouth with a tentative finger in case she had food on her face, but found nothing. She could still sense his eyes on her. What *was* it with that bloke?

'Romany was just passing her compliments on to the chef,' said Hope with a wink, and Romany looked at him again. He was still focusing on her, but now his expression was softer, the intensity gone. Maybe she had imagined it. Her mum was forever telling her that teenagers made everything about them when they really weren't.

Finally, Daniel smiled, and it changed everything about him, making him appear far more normal. He had lovely eyes, Romany thought, a deep rich brown colour, and a friendly face, when he wasn't staring.

'Did you really enjoy it?' he asked. 'That's amazing!' He sounded needy, as if her approval was actually important to him, which it obviously wasn't. 'What was your favourite part?' he added.

Romany didn't have to think. 'I loved that lemony taster thing,' she said, 'but I liked the triple chocolate tart best.'

'Ah yes,' replied Daniel. 'My own personal favourite too.'

'And the rest of you enjoyed it too?' he asked, finally turning his attention from her to the others.

There was a general murmuring of approval from around the group. Hope, who had been fiddling with the wire cage around the cork, opened the bottle in one smooth movement and poured a glass of the frothing champagne without spilling a drop. Romany was impressed. Whenever she'd seen people do it in films it always looked like a particularly messy business. Hope filled the glasses efficiently and Daniel passed them around.

Maggie seized the moment, raising her glass and slurring, 'To the chef!'

They all did likewise, and Daniel lowered his eyes modestly for a moment. Then he looked up and gave them a broad grin before settling his eyes on Romany again.

'What?!' she wanted to say. 'What is your problem?'

He raised the glass to his lips, took a sip and put it back down on the table.

'Right, must be getting back,' he said. 'Lovely to meet you all.'

He turned and headed back to the kitchen, leaving Romany confused. She had a quick look round to see if the others had noticed anything odd, but they seemed oblivious. Maybe she'd talk to Maggie about it later, at a soberer moment.

Maggie began to get to her feet. She was making heavy weather of it and grabbed on to the table to stop her falling back into her seat. 'This has been lovely,' she said, her words tripping into one another, 'but we should be going. Let you good people get back to your families on Christmas Day.'

'I'll get your coats,' said Hope, and sashayed away to find them.

Maggie was checking under the table to make sure she hadn't forgotten anything and Leon was looking at his phone, but Tiger was just sitting there staring at the spot where Daniel had just been standing.

'Come on, Tiger,' said Maggie. 'Time to go home.'

Tiger still didn't move, his face a picture of confusion.

'I know him,' he said.

'Know who?' asked Leon without looking up from his phone.

'That chef bloke, Daniel. I'm sure I've met him before.'

'Probably,' said Leon. 'You must have met half the population of the world on your travels.'

Leon set off towards where Hope was standing with a bundle of coats in her arms, but Tiger stayed where he was, his eyebrows knotted together as he tried to think.

'Tiger!' Maggie called. 'We need to leave.'

Tiger stood up and reluctantly moved towards the others, but Romany could hear him still muttering under his breath as he tried to work it out.

49

Maggie was in her usual place at the reception desk of Space Solutions. It was, as you might expect for a modern, forward-thinking architect's practice, a bright and airy space with trendy but uncomfortable furniture and a lot of bleached wood. In the corner of the space was a glass box, the board room, in which important meetings were conducted. Today it was full of exasperated-looking men. Jackets had been shed and sleeves rolled up, as if the discussions that were going on were complicated and arduous. There appeared to be some frayed tempers as well and her own boss, the senior partner (who was actually a good ten years younger than she was) was looking particularly frazzled.

As she watched, his junior assistant came out, closed the door behind him and rolled his eyes.

'It's horrible in there,' he said. 'Do you think you could rustle us up yet another round of coffee? Try to break the tension a bit.'

'Of course,' said Maggie, lifting her phone handset to ring the order through. 'What's the problem?'

She looked expectantly at the junior, but he just shrugged and said, 'Oh, you know, just business stuff.' He turned his back on her and headed back to the glass box. 'And if you could find us some biscuits too . . .' And then he was gone.

Maggie sucked in a deep breath through her nose, set her shoulders and then pressed the button to link her with the hospitality department.

'They would like more coffee and biscuits in the boardroom,' she said when the phone was answered. 'Yes. More! And you might want to bring a couple of extra trays to clear away the empties.'

Maggie heard the irritation at the other end of the line, where the coffee coordinating person clearly knew exactly how many cups there were to clear away, that being their job. She regretted that she seemed to rub people up the wrong way so regularly, but there was often a better way of doing a task than the way they were doing it. She should just bite her tongue and let them get on with it. Having ideas was above her pay grade.

The morning wore on, with Maggie answering the phone and dealing with visitors and emails as usual. She kept an eye on the meeting, but they didn't seem to be reaching any sort of consensus. She wondered yet again what the problem was, and found herself wishing that she was in there to help them sort it out. That had been her favourite part about being a lawyer – solving puzzles. The law itself was all very well; it was just there, and it either worked for you or against you, depending on what you were trying to achieve, and sometimes did both. Coming up with a solution to the problem was different, though. That took creative thinking, imagination and a knowledge of which risks you could take and which you absolutely shouldn't. Maggie had been good at that. Ironic really, considering how few risks she had taken in the rest of her life.

Around lunchtime, the glass box door opened and its occupants began to float out, rubbing necks and shoulders, replacing jackets over creased shirts. Eventually the only ones left were the senior partner Mark and the man who Maggie assumed was his client. They stood directly in front of her desk and continued their discussion as if she were invisible.

'It's a total cock-up, Mark,' the client said. 'And I can't believe that I'm in this deep and this problem is only just coming up now.'

Mark appeared to be exasperated but was doing his best to remain polite and positive – clearly a real struggle. 'The thing is, Tim, until we open the ground there's just no way of knowing what's under there. That's what contingency budgets are for.'

'The contingency budget is already shot to hell after all the issues about access to the site,' moaned Tim. 'At this rate, it'll all be spent, and we won't have even started the main build. And now this. An Anglo-Saxon burial site right under my beautiful new office block. Honestly, you couldn't make it up.'

Mark shook his head sympathetically. 'It is bad luck,' he said. 'We might have seen it before if . . .' But then he cut himself short.

Ah, thought Maggie. The client is one of those that wants all the bells and whistles but is only prepared to pay for the standard model.

'And I just don't have time to wait,' the client continued. 'Everything I have is sunk into this project. I need to get back on site and digging foundations pronto. Can't we just turn a blind eye to the bones? I mean, who's going to know?'

'I'll pretend I didn't hear that,' said Mark. 'We have to wait, go through the proper channels. But that can take months, I'm afraid. Forensic archaeology is a very specialised area and the expert I usually use in cases like this is booked up, sometimes for years in advance.'

'Oh, for God's sake,' hissed the client. 'It just isn't good enough. It's just one problem after another. I'm starting to regret using this firm in the first place and you can expect that I'll be looking for a discount on my bill for all the cock-ups.'

Maggie could see that Mark was really angry now and battling to control his temper.

'None of this is our fault, Tim,' he said calmly.

'Oh no? Well, whose fault is it? Because it sure as hell isn't mine.'

'Well, if you'd been prepared to spend a little more on . . .'

Maggie could stand it no longer.

'Excuse me,' she said.

Neither man took any notice.

'Excuse me,' she said a little louder. 'Have you tried Professor Vanessa Quinn? She's based at York St John's. She's quick and efficient and extremely good at coming up with solutions for this kind of problem.'

Both men turned to see who had spoken.

'I'm assuming that you uncovered a skeleton when you were digging the foundations,' Maggie continued. 'The contract should cover that kind of delay. It's got the standard warranties and indemnities, right? But if you get Professor Quinn in then you may find that you can sort the issue out and move on nice and quickly. She's not cheap, mind you, but considerably cheaper than laying off the entire site and potentially losing all your sub-contractors.'

The client was staring at her and then he shook his head. 'Who the hell are you? My fairy bloody godmother?'

The old confidence that had flowed through her a moment ago was now leaking out of Maggie as if she was a sieve, and she dropped her gaze.

'I'm sorry,' she muttered. 'I'm sure you have it all under control.'

'No,' said the client. 'We haven't. And what you just said is the most sensible, and practical, thing I've heard all morning.'

Maggie gave him a tight-lipped smile. 'I can make the call for you,' she offered, and then, when she saw Mark's face, added, 'or give you her number.'

'That'd be great,' said the client. 'Let's see if we can get her to start straight away. I'll pay what it costs.'

Maggie saw Mark's eyebrow rise.

'Good,' he said. 'I'll get my PA on it straight away.'

'Bugger your PA,' said the client. 'I'd go with your receptionist. What did you say your name was?' he added.

'Maggie Summers,' she said.

His eyes narrowed, as if the name meant something to him, but then he offered her his hand to shake and headed for the door.

'Get it sorted, Mark,' he called and then disappeared through the revolving door, leaving the two of them.

Maggie was aware of the awkwardness as keenly as if it had been sitting on her lap and stroking her hair.

'I hope I didn't overstep the mark,' she said. 'I just thought it might help.'

Mark was still staring at her. 'Maggie Summers,' he said. 'Why do I know that name?'

'I used to be at Brownlows,' she said. 'I was a partner in the commercial property department.'

'So, what the hell are you doing as my receptionist?' he asked.

Maggie shrugged. 'I just fancied a change.'

'I've just spent all morning arguing with that bunch of idiots about a whole range of crap and all the time I had you, just sitting there watching,' he said.

Maggie worried that he was about to explode at her, but he seemed to think it was funny.

'Do you know how much I pay our solicitor?' he asked.

'I could hazard a guess,' replied Maggie wryly.

'And you have been more help in five minutes than he has been all morning. All he's done is block my ideas and come up with reasons why we couldn't do things.'

'Then might I suggest you have the wrong solicitor,' Maggie replied.

'Yes! You might very well suggest that,' said Mark. 'Right. Well, if you can let me have that number, I'll get on to Professor . . . ?'

'Professor Quinn,' offered Maggie.

'Professor Quinn. Unless, of course, you fancied making the call for me. There's a lunch in it for you,' he added. 'And then we could talk about how someone like you has ended up working at my reception desk.'

Maggie had no intention of sharing her personal history with him, but she was happy to make the call. 'That's fine. Can I ring her now?' she asked, conscious that to do so would take her away from her reception duties.

'Please do,' said Mark with a sweep of his arm. 'And thank you, Maggie.'

He walked across to the lifts, shaking his head as if the whole experience had been slightly too surreal for him.

Maggie dug her mobile from her bag, retrieved Vanessa's number and made the call.

50

Later, when she had made her dinner and rung Leon to tell him about her minor triumph at work, Maggie settled down with her laptop and began to scroll through the jobs pages. It was something she hadn't done for a while. At the beginning, it had been too painful to even look at the details of job after job when her dream role had only just been snatched from her. Then, as the months and now years had gone by, she had gradually stopped looking. She was too long out of the game, she assumed. Things, people, the world in general had all moved on and, run fast as she might, she was never going to be able to catch up.

Today, though, when she had dipped her toe back in, in the most haphazard and impromptu manner, the water had felt surprisingly warm and welcoming. She had forgotten the pleasure she got from suggesting a solution that would help the client solve their problem. Today's had hardly been a legal question, just a case of knowing the right person for the job; but she knew of Vanessa Quinn because of her years of experience, and Vanessa had been happy to take her call because of the mutually appreciative relationship that she had built with her over the years when their paths had crossed more regularly.

It all served to remind Maggie of an important fact. Not only did she come alive when she was solving legal problems but also, and possibly more importantly, she was good at it. She should start looking for a job again in earnest, she thought. It wasn't too late. She didn't need a partnership position again – in fact she wasn't even sure she wanted one. She was happy to be a safe pair of hands in a decent commercial property department somewhere with a strong list of clients who liked and trusted her. That would be perfect.

As she scrolled down the legal recruitment sites, her mobile rang. She picked it up and looked at the screen. It was Tiger. A tiny frisson of excitement bubbled up on seeing his name, a sub-conscious response that it seemed would never leave her, and she answered the call. Tiger never rang. She wasn't even sure he had a working phone a lot of the time; it seemed to be generally turned off or out of charge. Something must be wrong. Her mind leapt to Romany.

'Tiger,' she said. 'Is everything okay?'

'Yeah, yeah,' he drawled. 'Why wouldn't it be?'

There was no point Maggie explaining, but she relaxed a little. 'So,' she said instead, 'what can I do for you?'

'Strange thing,' he said, 'but you remember when we went out on Christmas Day?'

Of course Maggie remembered, although she would have to admit that the tail end of the afternoon was a little bit hazy.

'Yes,' she said.

'That chef bloke, Hope's boyfriend.'

'Daniel?' supplied Maggie helpfully.

'Yeah. Except that's not it. That's why it's taken me so long to place him. Because he wasn't called Daniel then, when I met him.'

Maggie was lost. 'Tiger, you're not making much sense,' she said. 'Why don't you start at the beginning?'

'Right, yeah. So, I recognised that Daniel bloke, but I couldn't think where I'd met him. It's been driving me mad. I couldn't get it out of my head because something about it felt important, but I just couldn't place him. So, in the end I decided the only way I was going to remember was if I clapped eyes on him again. I reckoned that if I wasn't three sheets to the wind, I'd do a better job of recognising him. So, I went back to the restaurant today, hung around a bit outside to see if he appeared. And when he did, it finally came to me. I've worked out who he is, but he's changed his name. That's what threw me before. When I met him he didn't call himself Daniel. He was called Jax.'

There was a pause as Maggie's mind raced to join the dots.

'Jax, as in Angie's Jax?' she asked.

'The very same,' he replied.

'And so that means that this Daniel, now boyfriend of the divine Hope, is . . .'

'Bingo!' said Tiger. 'Give the woman a banana!'

'Shit!' said Maggie.

'Shit indeed,' replied Tiger. 'So, what should I do?'

Maggie's mind was making connections. She had never met Jax, but she had met Daniel before, at Hope's party. She searched her mind to remember how Angie had reacted to seeing him, but found nothing. Had they been introduced? She thought not. Slowly the pieces fell into place. Daniel had arrived late, and they had worked out who he was because Hope had told them he was on his way. And then not long after that they had left the party.

'Maggie?' came Tiger's voice down the line. 'Are you still there?'

'Sorry, yes. I'm just thinking it through,' she said.

'Do you think Ange knew?' Tiger asked.

'I think she must have done,' replied Maggie. 'We went to Hope's birthday party and he was there. She didn't say anything to me, but she must have recognised him. And that will be why . . .' All the shakers were falling into place now and the lock clicked open, leaving the answers like treasure, golden and twinkling in

Maggie's mind. 'That's why she chose Hope to be one of Romany's guardians.'

'The one looking after relationships,' interrupted Tiger, the triumph clear in his voice.

'The sly old minx,' replied Maggie with a wry smile.

'Exactly! But what do we do now? Now that we've worked it out?' asked Tiger. 'Do we tell Romey that we know where her dad is?'

And now Maggie remembered another day. A picnic in Whitby when Angie had insisted on having a rather forced conversation with Romany about her father. Had she done that in front of her so that she was aware of Romany's views on the subject? That seemed a little far-fetched, but now, in light of what they had just worked out, perhaps it had all been part of a plan, although she wasn't sure the timings worked exactly. She needed to think it all through more carefully. The point now was, what did Angie want her to do next? Romany had been very clear that she didn't want to know who her father was. Did Angie disagree? Was she expecting the four of them to step in and create an introduction?

'Maggie?'

'Sorry, I was thinking. I think we need to tread very carefully. Romany once told me that she wasn't interested in meeting her dad. I've got no reason to think that she's changed her mind. And right now, she's got enough on. It's only a few months until her exams. Do you think we should keep it under our hats, for now at least?'

Maggie could hear Tiger's disappointment through the silence on the other end of the phone. He must have been hoping that she'd suggest a big, drastic reveal.

'Maybe,' he replied reluctantly. 'Although I think she might be changing her mind on the dad thing.'

'But perhaps,' said Maggie, 'we could talk to Hope and Daniel and see what they think.'

Tiger sounded doubtful now. 'I don't know, Mags. Maybe we should just let nature take its course. As you say, the last thing Romey needs right now is another shock.'

But Maggie was thinking aloud. 'Daniel must have worked it out,' she said. 'Even if he didn't find his way to York to be close to them in the first place, he must have assumed that Angie and Romany might still be living here. And if Hope told him about her role as Angie's guardian then he would have made the connections. Another single mother called Angie with a daughter of the right age called Romany is way too much of a coincidence to be somebody else. And it's such an Angie thing to have done, involving Hope.' Maggie smiled to herself at the workings of Angie's mind. God, she'd have loved having them all running round in circles like this.

But then something else occurred to her and the smile slipped from her face. 'We have to tread carefully here, Tiger,' she said. 'What if Daniel hasn't told Hope who Romany is? That's not our news to share. And who knows what might happen if we do?'

51

Romany was on the final straight. The finishing line was almost in sight and all she had to do was keep galloping until she crossed it. She dropped her textbook and rolled back on her bed and stared up at the ceiling. That was possibly the worst metaphor she had ever used. It sounded like something the head of sixth form would come out with in one of her uplifting assemblies and Romany swore to herself that she would never let the image cross her mind again.

It did feel a lot like a race, though. This whole year had done. She had been running from one waymarker to the next, all the time getting closer to her goal, but without really having any time for anything else. Maybe that was no bad thing. If she stopped and thought for too long, she worried that she might go to pieces, and she simply didn't have the time. The most important thing now was to get through the exams – she could fall apart as much as she liked once they were over.

Elsewhere in the flat, she could hear Tiger pushing the vacuum cleaner around, the dull rumble a comfort of sorts, an indicator of a normal life continuing around her. When he had first started showing domestic tendencies, Romany had been astounded, and the first time she had spotted him with a duster and a tin of Mr Sheen in his hand she had laughed out loud.

'Oh my God,' she'd said through her snorts. 'Look at you!'

He had looked quite indignant. 'Well, there's no need for us to live like savages,' he said. 'And I reckoned it would take the pressure off you if I pulled my weight a bit more.'

She had stopped laughing then, seeing that he was serious. It was actually quite sweet.

'Thanks,' she'd said, feeling a little ashamed.

'That's okay. When I've done this, I thought I'd give the windows a bit of a going-over. They're looking a bit smeary when the sun shines on them.'

And so she had left him to it, grateful that he seemed happy to help out. Since then, the house had been transformed. He had gradually worked his way through every room, cleaning, polishing and replacing things as he went. Romany hadn't realised how grubby some of the soft furnishings had got until he washed the cushion covers and even threw a few things away, although he always checked an item for irreplaceable sentimental value before it went to the tip.

Their food had gone through a similar transformation. When Tiger had first moved in, they had existed on fresh but simple food that was heated and then served. Boiled vegetables, grilled meat or fish (Tiger was no vegetarian and neither, she discovered, was she), the odd veggie pasta dish; all perfectly nutritious but requiring no skill, just the application of time. Now, though, their menu had been entirely revamped. They even had home-made sauces as Tiger became increasingly confident in the kitchen. He had become a veritable domestic god.

So now, all that was required of her was to get the grades for Durham, and with so much support at home and school she really had no excuse.

Her mobile pinged and she flung an arm out and retrieved it from the bedside table. A few messages had all landed at once: three from Laura asking her how she was getting on with a past paper that they had been set, and one from Hope. Romany sat up and opened the Hope one.

Hi R. Shoot at Aysgarth Falls on Sat. Want to come? H x

Romany was used to Hope's abbreviated style of message and had got quite used to elucidating meaning from them. They were a contrast to Maggie's fully grammatical ones. She had to think about this one for a moment, however. She supposed that it was a fashion shoot and not the gun kind. Hope ran some kind of swimwear business. Romany wasn't sure entirely what kind, but she had been very impressed by the bikini that Hope had been wearing on their spa trip, and even more delighted when Hope had given her a bag of samples to keep. She had the nicest beachwear in the whole of York, although she had yet to wear any of it outside her bedroom.

Aysgarth Falls she had heard of but had never been to. It was a set of waterfalls not that far away. And Saturday? Well, what would she be doing but revising? She could probably give herself a day off and it would be great to go and watch how a fashion shoot worked.

She typed a reply. *Would love to. Thanks. R x*

◆ ◆ ◆

What did one wear to a fashion shoot? Romany and Laura agonised over it via FaceTime, Laura making suggestions from Romany's meagre wardrobe and Romany rejecting them as too boring, too out there, too try-hard, too safe and eventually just plain 'too'.

'Come on, Romes,' cajoled Laura. 'You have to wear something. And honestly? I doubt anyone will even notice. They'll be busy being shot, or whatever.'

'It's just that Hope's so gorgeous,' Romany complained. 'It was bad enough being at the spa with her.'

Laura rolled her eyes, exasperated. 'Then don't go,' she said. 'No one's making you.'

'No, but . . .'

'Precisely. So just choose something!'

In the end she had gone with a black and white dress with a sweetheart neckline and a ditsy floral print, and she borrowed Tiger's denim jacket on the absolute, solemn promise that she wouldn't let any of the supermodels steal it. He had been entirely straight-faced as he delivered this proviso and Romany had made an equally serious promise, her hand raised Boy Scout-style.

Hope picked her up at the agreed time, which was earlier than Romany had seen for months. The back seat of the car was filled to the roof with cardboard boxes.

'Stock,' Hope said. 'You can have a look through when we get there, if you like.'

Romany did like, hopeful of more freebies. She settled back into her seat, ready to enjoy herself. They set off, driving through the silent streets as the sun began to rise.

Hope peered up at the sky over the steering wheel. 'I hope the light stays right. I haven't got time to reshoot if we don't get what we need today.'

'Won't the models be a bit cold?' asked Romany, thinking of the last time she had dipped a toe in an English river.

'They're professionals,' said Hope dismissively. 'If they can't hack it then they just won't get booked next time.'

This was something that Romany had noticed before. There was a steeliness to Hope that was missing from her other guardians. She was uncompromising, focused, determined. She made Maggie look like a teddy bear. Romany liked it, though, and found it inspiring, and she tried not to be intimidated by her no-nonsense approach. Hope had told her that she'd created her business from nothing after her modelling career had slowed down, and worked hard at making it a success. Romany didn't know whether it was doing well or not, but she guessed that it probably was.

They rarely talked about her mum. Romany didn't mind; she wasn't short of people to have those conversations with if she needed one. But Romany still had no idea why Hope was one of her guardians and Hope wasn't the kind of person she felt she could ask. She was too prickly, and Romany worried that questioning her credentials might drive her away, and then she would never get to the bottom of the mystery.

They arrived at a car park that was already full of very tall women wandering about dressed in robes and those reflective crinkly blankets you saw on hospital dramas. A couple of them were already made up, striking geometrical shapes picked out on their eyes in bright metallic colours with very dark lips in unnatural blues and greys. It made them look even colder, Romany thought.

Hope shouted various questions and commands as she strode through the car park. Romany scampered after her feeling like a puppy, but happy just to be there and part of it. Who cared what her mother had in mind when Hope was as cool as this?

It wasn't far to the river. Romany had imagined tumbling cascades of water surrounded by a leafy glade, like something out of a shampoo commercial, but actually Aysgarth Falls appeared to be far more sedate. The water fell no more than a couple of feet, but it did fall three times in quick succession and the river was very wide and majestic. Romany, whilst initially disappointed, could see that the spot was dramatic in its own understated way.

The photographer was already in the water in a pair of waders and a heavy padded jacket. By contrast, the poor models were standing barefoot in the icy water, wearing only bikinis and striking their poses as directed. Not one of them seemed to be complaining, but just looking at them made Romany shiver.

Hope was busy and everyone else seemed to be very clear what their roles were, so Romany watched from the sidelines as shot after shot was set up and then captured. So much effort went into each image, and Romany thought she would never again be able to idly flick through a magazine without thinking about today.

Hope had mentioned that she had brought a flask of tea and that Romany was welcome to share, so, feeling chilly, she retrieved it from one of the many bags and was just pouring some into the plastic lid when she heard a voice behind her.

'You don't want to be drinking that muck,' it said. 'Tea from a plastic cup! Yuk!'

Romany turned and saw Hope's boyfriend, the chef guy.

'I can offer you a latte if you'd prefer,' he said. 'I love Hope dearly but she's crap at outside catering.'

He grinned, the skin around his eyes crinkling naturally as if it was totally used to smiling, but Romany could still remember how he had stared at her in the restaurant on Christmas Day and so was wary. He didn't seem weird today though, just smiley, but still, she didn't want to encourage him.

She raised the plastic teacup. 'I'm good with this, thanks,' she said.

'How's the shoot going?' he asked. 'There's no point me asking Hope. She won't speak to me when she's working.'

'Okay, I think, but the poor models must be freezing!'

Daniel nodded. 'Yeah. All in a day's work for them. You wouldn't catch me standing up to my knees in cold water though.'

'You prefer your hot kitchen, then?' Romany asked.

'I do these days,' he said. 'Although I've had my share of outdoor hardship in my time. I lived in a tree for six months once,' he added, pulling a face that anticipated her scepticism.

'Really?' said Romany, turning to look at him properly. 'My mum lived in a tree once too. She used to tell me how they moved from platform to platform without ever coming down, so they didn't get arrested. Sounded totally mad. And freezing.'

'Yeah, it was.'

His face had closed down and Romany wondered whether he'd been embellishing the truth, assuming that she would be impressed by his tale and not realising that she would have a tree story of her own. She felt a bit guilty for having stolen his thunder.

'So, how long have you had the restaurant?' she asked, to make amends. 'I think it's really cool, by the way. I've been in a couple more times since Christmas.'

His face lit up again. 'I've been in York for around fifteen years,' he said. 'I worked for other people for a while. Then I did event catering. That was hard work. And then I bought the restaurant with a friend, a couple of years ago. It's been a bit hairy at times, but things are going pretty well now. And how about you? Are you doing A levels? Hope said something about uni.'

Romany explained where she was and what she hoped to do next and he listened attentively. As they talked, they wandered closer to the shoot to watch what was going on. The photographer now had the models lying down in the breakers at the edge of the water. Romany had no idea how they kept smiling as the icy water lapped at their naked skin. A couple of them were looking quite blue. Daniel stuck at her side, and she was grateful because even though there wasn't much conversation, it made it look like she was there with a purpose rather than just being a hanger-on. Every so often he would give Hope a wave or a thumbs-up sign, and she would either ignore him or give him a half-smile in return, her lips pressed tightly together as if she didn't have time for the full smile.

By lunchtime it seemed to be all over. The models were back in their clothes and drinking steaming cups of hot chocolate, which Daniel distributed in small espresso-sized cardboard cups. Hope was peering at what they'd got on a screen set up a little

338

way away from the water and chatting through the shots with the photographer.

'They look pleased,' said Romany, nodding towards Hope who was smiling properly for the first time that morning. 'They must have got what they wanted.'

Daniel agreed. 'Looks that way. Hope usually gets what she wants,' he added, and winked at Romany.

She liked him, she thought. She liked his humour and his positivity. But mainly she liked how much he seemed to love Hope. It glowed around him. She could see no indication that Hope felt the same way, although she was so closed it would be hard to tell, but she assumed that she did. Romany liked what their relationship appeared to be: two people, independent and yet connected, each supporting the other whilst at the same time getting on with their own stuff. Maybe that was why her mum had given Hope the task of instructing her on relationships. She hoped so, because if ever she found herself in a relationship, she would like it to look a lot like this one.

Daniel was a totally different kettle of fish to private Hope, though. He seemed to wear his feelings on his sleeve where everyone could see them. From their conversation that morning there seemed to be no edge to him. He just said what he thought. It was refreshing. Romany was so used to people trying to hide what they felt from her, in case she might not be able to cope. Daniel just seemed to be natural and happy in his own skin. She liked it.

Time ticked on and Romany started to get a bit twitchy about the pile of revision that was waiting for her at home. She hadn't expected to be gone for the whole day. Daniel seemed to be the same. He kept looking at his watch and shuffling from foot to foot, but Hope was showing no sign of being finished. She was deep in conversation with someone on her phone whilst things wound up around her.

'I'm going to head back to York,' said Daniel. 'I like to support Hope wherever I can, but I've been gone long enough. I really need to get back to my kitchen. I can give you a lift if you like,' he added to Romany.

Romany didn't know what to do. The offer of a lift home was very welcome, but she didn't want Hope to think she was being rude or ungrateful.

Daniel seemed to read her mind. 'Don't worry about Hope,' he said. 'We can't interrupt her now, but I'll text her to tell her that I've taken you back. She'll be fine with it. In fact, she'll barely notice we've gone.'

He waved over at Hope, blew her a kiss and then pointed at Romany and flashed his thumb in the direction of the car. Hope nodded, smiled at Romany and then turned her back on them both to continue her phone conversation.

'There you go,' said Daniel. 'Sorted.'

Daniel's car was a black Audi. Smart, functional, dull. It wasn't that tidy inside, however, with empty coffee cups and the packaging of a couple of pre-packed sandwiches rolling around on the back seat.

'Sorry,' he said. 'Eating on the run. Occupational hazard. You'd think, working with food all day . . .'

He looked at her regretfully, but Romany just shrugged. She wasn't going to lose her shiz over a bit of rubbish.

As they drove back, he quizzed her in a little more detail about her plans for the next year, what she wanted to do when she graduated, and Romany was happy to tell him all. He seemed impressed, and it made her feel proud, as it often did, that she had got this all together despite what had happened to her mum.

They reached the turn-off for the house and Romany was about to give directions when he flicked on the indicators and turned anyway.

'You know where I live?' she asked.

He hesitated for a moment. 'Yes. Hope was going to get me to pick you up this morning but then the plans changed, and we ended up swapping over.'

He found a parking space not far from her house and slid the car neatly into it. Romany went to open the door and was about to say thank you when he spoke, his voice urgent as if he really needed to get the words out.

'Listen, Romany,' he said, his hand rubbing his chin. 'There's something that I should probably tell you.'

'Oh yes?' replied Romany, her hand resting on the door handle. 'What's that then?'

For the first time that morning he looked awkward, his easy confidence of earlier gone.

'It's just that, I knew your mum, back when . . . Well. I knew her.'

52

Romany's hand fell away from the door handle. She was all ears. Meeting someone new who had known her mum, particularly in the days before she had been around, was a rare treat.

'Did you?' she asked, curious. 'How come?'

'You know those trees I mentioned,' he said. 'Well, me and your mum, we were in the same trees.'

Romany eyes grew wide. 'Really! That's so cool! Mum always said it was one of her favourite times, being on that protest.'

Daniel nodded, his smile fond and distant. 'Yeah,' he said. 'It had its moments. It was tough, especially when it got cold. But we had a camaraderie thing going on. We were all in it together, with this one common purpose, to save the woods. We were so sure we'd win, that the government would see the sense in what we were saying. We were naïve, I guess, but we were bloody good at climbing trees.'

Romany bit her lip. 'Can I ask you a question?' she said.

'Of course.'

'What was Mum like back then?'

Romany loved talking about her mum. She hardly ever got the chance, because everyone assumed that she would want the complete opposite, and most people avoided the subject as if it might explode if they touched it. And here was someone who had known her before she'd even been born. Of course, she'd heard things from back then – Maggie and Tiger never shut up about the old days when they got together – but she knew all their stories as well as if she had been there herself. Daniel was offering a peep into a totally new area of her mum's life. It was too tantalising to miss.

Daniel flicked off his seatbelt and pushed his seat back so that he could stretch his legs. The mention of her mum brought a warmth to his smile. He had really liked her, back in the day, Romany could tell just from that expression.

'Your mum was like a force of nature,' he said. 'She just didn't care what others thought of her. She did what she thought was right. She was completely chaotic though. Was she like that later too?'

Romany thought of the mess the flat used to get into, the way her mum never had what she needed when she needed it, her refusal to ever make a plan and then her frustration when things didn't work out the way she wanted. She nodded.

'Yeah. Pretty chaotic,' she said with a smile.

'And she was loyal,' Daniel went on, his eyes focused on the bins further down the street. 'If you were on her team, she'd do whatever it took to make sure you were okay. Did she tell you about her own mum?'

'A bit,' said Romany.

Daniel nodded. 'Well, she had a pretty hard time growing up. I think that's why she never made plans. There just hadn't been any point when her life was so out of her own control. But I also think that was why if she found you and she liked you, then you could never quite shake her off. She stuck like glue and she would defend you against anyone. Like I say, loyal.'

Romany loved hearing this kind of thing and it fitted so neatly with her own understanding of her mum, so she knew he wasn't stringing her along.

'Did you two go out?' she asked, shyly.

Daniel, still staring resolutely out of the windscreen, nodded again.

'We did, actually,' he said, although Romany knew they must have done because of the way he was talking. She would guess that the two of them had been pretty close.

'That's cool,' she said. 'And how weird that you should be going out with one of Mum's friends now. That's a mad coincidence.'

Daniel turned his head and looked at her out of the tail of his eye.

'It is,' he said. 'But not in the way that you think.'

Romany was confused. 'How do you mean?' she asked.

'Well,' he began slowly, 'the coincidence isn't so much that I knew your mum. It's more that I was going out with someone that she met on a course.'

Romany didn't really follow, but it didn't matter. The main thing was that she had increased the number of people she could talk to about her mum.

'Actually,' Daniel continued, 'it is a coincidence that me and Hope are together, and that your mum met Hope, but the reason I moved to York in the first place was to be closer to your mum.'

He turned his head further still so that she could see his face.

'And you . . .' he added.

A hush fell. Now he stared straight into her eyes the way he had done in the restaurant on Christmas Day. Romany blinked and then blinked again. Daniel was obviously trying to make a point, but she wasn't following. Why would he want to be near her?

'Romany,' he began. He paused, rubbing his hand over his mouth, and took a deep breath.

But she was there.

She had got it.

She knew exactly what he was trying to tell her.

And suddenly there wasn't enough oxygen in the confined space. She threw the car door open, making a passer-by jump and then swear at her indignantly. She had to get away. She didn't know for certain what he was about to say but she didn't want to hear it. She ran from the car without closing the door and straight to the flat, fumbling for her key in her jacket pocket. She threw a look over her shoulder, but he wasn't following her. He was still sitting in exactly the same spot, as if frozen in time.

The key turned, the door swung open and Romany fell into the flat and slammed the door behind her.

53

Romany stood with her back against the door. Her breath was a ragged panting, and her heart was pounding so hard that it hurt. She squeezed her eyes shut while she tried to calm herself. A voice was speaking to her in her head and she knew it was her mum.

'Slow down, Romey,' she said. 'Focus on the breath. In through the nose. Out through the mouth.'

Romany tried to do what her mum had taught her, but it wasn't working. How could she make herself calm in the light of what she thought she'd just worked out? Was Daniel her dad? Was that what he had been about to tell her?

She tried to bring to mind all the things that her mum had ever told her about her dad, but there wasn't much, just that they had loved each other very much, but that it hadn't worked out. When Romany was younger and pressed for more details, her mum had just shaken her head and said that she would tell her everything she wanted to know when she was old enough. And then when she had been old enough, she hadn't wanted to know, had refused, in fact, to listen.

So now, she had nothing to go on, no way of verifying what she thought Daniel was trying to say. She tried to picture his face, to see if she had ever felt that there was anything familiar about it, but nothing came to mind. He was just Daniel, Hope's chef boyfriend, nice enough on the surface but with nothing to suggest that they shared DNA.

But he had known Mum. That she did believe. Her mum had told the tree stories over and over because Romany loved to hear them. She could accept that her mum and Daniel had been there in the tree-top camp together. She was even prepared to believe that they had gone out together back in the day. But this? It was too much to take in.

From upstairs she could hear Tiger calling down to her. 'Is that you, Romey? Have you had a good time?'

And then, when she didn't appear within the time he would have expected, his head appeared at the top of the stairs and he peered down at her.

'What are you doing down there?' he said, laughing at her. And then, 'Hey. What's up?'

Romany didn't speak because she didn't know how to start. She stayed where she was against the door with her eyes tightly shut like she'd done as a child when she wanted something to go away. She could hear Tiger making his way down the stairs towards her, but she was frozen to the spot.

'Come on, Romes,' he said as he got closer. 'What's this all about? Did something happen with Hope? Has she upset you?'

There wasn't much room in the porch area; Tiger stayed where he was on the second step, so that when Romany opened her eyes she had to look up at him. The space felt enclosed and intimate.

'Did you know my dad?' she whispered.

There was a pause, a heartbeat before Tiger replied.

'Ah,' he said.

What was that supposed to mean? She hadn't talked to the guardians about her dad for the same reasons that she'd refused to talk about him to her mum. But maybe they all knew, and it was just she who didn't. In fact, that would make sense. They'd all been friends since they were teenagers. They were bound to know.

Apart from Hope, of course. How Hope fitted in had always been unclear to Romany and, she suspected, to them all. But was this it? Maybe it wasn't Hope that her mum had wanted to be part of Romany's life, but Hope's boyfriend?

'What do you mean, "Ah"?' she asked. Her voice sounded harsh and she realised that she was building up to being angry.

'I met your dad once,' said Tiger. 'Before you were born.'

'And . . .'

Tiger made a face that said, what else do you want me to say? 'He seemed all right. A nice enough bloke. I mean, I literally met him once.'

'Is Daniel . . . Hope's Daniel,' she clarified, 'is he my dad?'

Tiger paused, ran his tongue over his teeth whilst he decided what to say.

'Yes. I think so.'

'You think so?!' said Romany, her voice suddenly louder and bordering on a shout.

Tiger ran a hand over his chin, apparently considering his next answer, and Romany felt a hot ball of fury building in her chest as she watched him decide what to tell her.

'Yes, then,' he said. 'He is. I thought I recognised him in the restaurant on Christmas Day, but I couldn't place him. He didn't seem to know me, and obviously he didn't say anything so . . . But I've thought about it since then and, yeah, I think he is.'

'And you were going to tell me when, exactly?'

He let out a sigh and looked at her forlornly. 'Oh come on, Romey. Don't shoot the messenger, mate? What was I supposed to do? I thought it was him, but I didn't know for sure. And you never seemed to want to know anything about him, so I just kept schtum.'

'And what about Maggie and Leon? Do they know too?' asked Romany accusingly.

Tiger shrugged. 'I mentioned it to Mags, yes. But she never met your dad. I only did by accident. So, we decided to wait and see how things played out. I mean, what with your exams and everything, it seemed like the right thing to do. Sorry if we screwed up.'

He looked genuinely upset and Romany felt her anger lift a little.

'What's happened, anyway?' he continued. 'Has Hope said something?'

'Not Hope,' Romany replied, her voice breaking as she tried to hold back her sobs. 'Daniel. He gave me a lift back and we got chatting and he said that he'd known Mum when they were young and then he said that he'd moved to York to be near her and me. And I just kind of put two and two together, and then I ran away.' Her words all ran into one another in her rush to tell the tale, and then emotion got the better of her and she began to cry.

Tiger put his arm around her and held her tightly. 'Oh Romes, don't. I can't stand to see you sad. But just so I'm clear. He didn't actually tell you he was your dad. In so many words, I mean?'

Romany shook her head into his shoulder, her voice muffled by his shirt. 'Well, no,' she agreed. 'Not in so many words. But it all fits, doesn't it?'

'Yeah,' replied Tiger. 'That's what I thought anyway.'

There was a pause whilst she tried to control her tears and Tiger continued to hold her. Then he said, 'Do you think you should talk to him? Get it all out in the open.'

Romany considered. Running off hadn't been the most mature response, she conceded, but she'd been taken off guard. It wasn't the kind of situation you had a plan for. But Tiger was right. It did need sorting out and now was as good a time as ever.

'Do you think he's still out there?' she asked.

349

'Only one way to find out,' he said. 'Let me go and see?'

Romany gave a single nod.

'And if he is, shall I bring him in?'

'Okay,' she said, a tiny tremor cracking the word in two.

She stepped aside so that Tiger could get past her and open the door. He flicked the latch and peered out into the street. Then he went as far as the gate, but in a couple of seconds he was back.

'I think he's gone,' he said.

54

It was a long time since Maggie had been nervous, properly gut-wrenchingly nervous, but she was now. It was only an interview, she told herself. She had been in hundreds before, although, to be fair, she had generally been the interviewer and not the interviewee. And it wasn't that important. Yes, this would be a great job to get, but there would be others. Now that she had started to look, positions that might suit her seemed to be popping up all over the place. What distinguished this one was that it would be the first. This was the benchmark by which she would measure everything that came next, all the things that were currently unknown. How would she perform under pressure? How would her career gap be taken? Was her legal knowledge still up to date? What would she be like as a team member rather than a team leader? Was Maggie Summers still relevant to the legal world at all?

She thought she had answers for some of these questions, but not all of them. She would only know where she stood after she had the first interview under her belt and was able to test their response to her. And that was about to be now.

Her phone buzzed and she snatched it up. It was a good luck text from Leon. That was sweet of him, she thought, but she was too anxious to reply just now. She turned her phone on to Do Not

Disturb and dropped it back into her bag. Then she stood up, took a deep breath and set off for the interview.

◆ ◆ ◆

Two hours later she was standing on the pavement outside the offices of what she hoped would be her new employer. It had gone well, she thought. She was fairly sure she had come across as measured and unflappable, with high levels of personal responsibility and integrity, a strong work ethic and a clear sense of team spirit. She had, in fact, just been herself. And they had liked her, she hoped at least. They seemed to respond well to her honesty when they asked her about why she had left Brownlows and what she had been doing since and, of course, her CV was impressive, her list of former clients and transactions substantial. They would let her know later, they had said. So now all she had to do was wait.

She had taken the day off from Space Solutions to accommodate the interview, so her time was her own. Having run through her options, she thought she might call on Romany and Tiger, see how they were coping. Romany's exams had begun, and so things were likely to be a little fraught. Maggie could still remember what it felt like. Of all the exams that she had sat over the years, her A levels had been the most stressful. She had truly believed that her entire life was on the line, that if she failed to get the grades to take the next step then everything would be ruined and her life would be over. How naïve and over-dramatic that felt now, but at the time she had been convinced it was right. There was even an A level stress nightmare that she still had when she was under extreme pressure, unchanged in its particulars since it had first haunted her thirty-five years ago. If only we could tell our younger selves what they should really be worrying about, she thought.

At Angie's place (when would she stop thinking of it in those terms?) she rang the doorbell and then waited, half-expecting that there would be no one in, but then she heard someone coming down the stairs towards her. The door opened and there stood Tiger. He was wearing an apron, a masculine-looking navy blue affair, but it was still, most definitely, an apron.

Maggie just laughed. 'Oh my God, Tiger, you are a picture of domesticity. What on earth are you doing?'

'I'm making chocolate profiteroles for Romey,' he replied with an air of defiance. 'They're her favourite and she's got another exam today, so I thought I'd make a batch for when she gets home. Are you coming in?'

'Only if you've got time,' Maggie replied, gesturing to his attire. 'I wouldn't want to interrupt.' And then she added, 'Chocolate profiteroles? My! I didn't know you had it in you.'

'I am a constant source of surprises!' he said, tucking his thumbs into the straps of his apron and looking like he might burst into song. 'Come on up and I'll stick the kettle on.'

Maggie followed him up the stairs. She let her eyes stray to his bum as he climbed. She told herself it was by force of habit.

The place was, as was usual these days, spotless with not a throw or cushion out of place, and even though he was clearly in the middle of baking, the kitchen was tidy, with everything he had already used piled neatly ready for washing up.

'So which paper was it today?' she asked, settling herself into one of the chairs to watch him work.

'Biology 1,' he said as he tipped coffee grounds into the coffee-maker.

'And how was she?' Maggie asked, thinking of her own nerves that morning.

He turned back to face her. 'She was okay. We seem to be through the panic stage and now she's remarkably calm. She's just getting on with it.'

'Good for her,' Maggie said. 'She's a wonder, that girl. Angie would be so proud of her.'

'Wouldn't she just,' agreed Tiger.

'And you should take some of the credit too,' she added. 'You've been brilliant.'

Tiger gave a modest little shrug, but Maggie thought she saw pride in his eyes. She had never seen him proud of something he'd done before. Was this actually a first?

'And the Daniel thing?' she asked. 'Where are we with that?'

It was a month since Tiger had rung to tell her what had happened on the day of the fashion shoot, but since then Romany must have decided that her A levels were more important than her long-lost father and had banished the subject from the agenda.

'Nothing,' said Tiger. 'It's like it never happened.'

'Have you heard from Hope?' she asked.

Tiger shook his head. 'I don't know if Romey has. She's being pretty tight-lipped about the whole thing.'

'Well, maybe when the exams are over . . .'

Tiger puffed his lips out. 'Yeah,' he said. 'There'll be a lot of changes after the exams are over.'

He made the coffee and passed her a cup, and then put on a pair of oven gloves and retrieved the golden choux puffs from the oven. Their smell filled the air and made Maggie's mouth water.

'So, I suppose you'll be heading off into the great blue yonder as soon as you get the green light,' Maggie said. 'You've done amazingly. We all know what a massive sacrifice it's been for you to stay here and look after Romany. I didn't think you could do it, to be honest. I bet you've spent the whole year planning where you're going to go when you can finally escape.'

He didn't look at her, she noticed, and focused instead on checking that each profiterole was properly cooked.

'Yeah, well,' he said. 'I've got a few ideas, but nothing concrete yet.'

She could sense his reluctance to talk about it. Perhaps he was actually going to miss Romany when he left. They had clearly become quite close over the year. But a deal was a deal, and he had very nearly fulfilled his side of the bargain.

'And it's Leon's gig soon, right?' he said, changing the subject deftly.

That was something else that wasn't being discussed. When it had first gone in the diary it had seemed so far in the future that it was hard to imagine that they would ever get there, but now, as inevitably happened, the date was almost upon them.

'How's he feeling about it?' Tiger asked. 'I bet he's in a right state!'

He grinned at her, and whilst she couldn't possibly have admitted that to anyone else, she nodded.

'God, yes. He's all over the place. If I had a pound for every time he's said he's going to ring and cancel I'd be a rich woman by now. But I've managed to talk him down. I think a part of him is actually looking forward to it.'

'He'll be remembering the reaction he got at that open mic night,' said Tiger. 'That's got to have some pull to it. It was like he was Springsteen or someone.'

Maggie laughed. 'Don't tell him that. But yes, I think you're right. It was the way that crowd cheered that's basically pushed him forward and made him brave.'

'Should have done it years ago,' said Tiger.

Maggie nodded. He was right. Leon could have been playing in public for all these years and been getting that reaction every time.

Tiger pulled up a chair and sat next to her. 'That's what Angie used to say,' he said. 'She was always going on about how he was wasting his talents.'

At the mention of Angie's name, Maggie felt her throat thicken, but she was all right. The pain of the loss was becoming manageable. That was something else that time could do.

She smiled fondly. 'Yes,' she agreed, 'she was. And she knew that when Leon finally did perform, he'd see what we all saw because of how the audience reacted. It's just a pity it's taken him three decades to get there.'

Tiger shot her a wry smile.

For a moment they sat, each in quiet contemplation. Maggie thought about Angie and the way she had continued to touch and guide their lives long after she had left them, impossible to forget.

Tiger broke the silence. 'I always regretted that you and me never . . . you know . . .' He made an inappropriate hand gesture to illustrate his point and Maggie rolled her eyes. 'Angie's predictions went a little awry there,' he added.

Maggie frowned. 'Did she predict that?' she asked. 'She never said anything to me!'

'Every time I turned up she used to go on about how I should ring you.'

'And yet somehow you never did.' Maggie laughed sardonically.

Tiger shrugged. 'Yeah. Sorry about that,' he said. 'I wish I had done, though.'

Maggie raised her eyes and found his and for a moment they shared a look heavy with meaning and regret.

'Yes,' she said. 'I wish you had done too.'

Tiger sighed. 'You're much better off with Leon,' he said. 'He's a far better bet than I ever was.'

Maggie nodded. 'Yep. That's true enough.'

A silence fell again as they each contemplated what might have been.

Then Tiger spoke again. 'She knew us all pretty well, didn't she? Ange, I mean.'

A single fat tear escaped and rolled down Maggie's cheek. She caught it with the tip of her finger.

'Yes,' she said. 'She really did.'

356

55

Her exams were over! Romany could hardly believe it. All that work and worry and sheer bloody shittiness of the year that had gone, and now it was finally behind her and a long hot summer lay ahead. It was going to be amazing, as long as she didn't let herself think about results day, hanging like a shadow over everything.

Still, if her mum had been here, she would have told her that there was absolutely nothing that could be done about it now, and so there was no point worrying about something she couldn't change. Romany decided, for once, to take her mum's advice. She was going to party! July was one long list of social engagements and if she was lucky, she might even get to go on holiday to Spain with Laura and some of the other girls. It was going to be great.

But there was one other black spot on her horizon.

Daniel.

Since the day of the photoshoot, she had pushed him and what he had said out of her mind. She had no room for it, no bandwidth to deal with any of its implications, but she knew that she couldn't just ignore him forever. They were going to have to talk and it was up to her to make the first move.

No time like the present.

She pulled her phone out of her back pocket and opened up messages. Then she stopped. She had only just finished her exams.

Surely she could give herself a couple of weeks off before she confronted what was waiting for her.

But she knew herself well. She needed to speak to him, get everything out in the open or she would fret about it and it would spoil her entire summer. Again, she could hear her mum in her head. 'Just do it, Romany. What's the worst that can happen?'

The worst that could happen was that she would end up with no dad. No change there then.

She didn't have Daniel's number, so she messaged Hope.

> *Hi. I need to talk to Daniel. Can you get him to get in touch please?*

Ten minutes later a message popped up.

> *Hi. It's Daniel. What works for you?*

◆ ◆ ◆

She suggested that they meet at a coffee shop in town. Neutral ground seemed best, so that either of them could get up and leave if the meeting didn't work out the way they hoped. Although what exactly she was hoping for Romany had no idea. She had always said that she wasn't interested in her father, that her mum could easily play the role of two parents for her.

But her mum wasn't there any more. The goalposts had shifted and Daniel was all the actual family she had. And on the surface at least, he seemed like quite a nice bloke. He wasn't a dick or anything, so that was a good start. Romany owed it to herself to at least get the story out of him, find out what it was that had split her parents up. There was no need to make any decisions about what might happen next. She could just take things slowly.

She ordered a gingerbread latte which arrived in a glass with a huge dollop of cream on the top. Daniel had a black americano. For a while neither of them spoke. He stirred a packet of sugar into his coffee and she stirred the cream into hers.

'So,' he said when they couldn't reasonably stir things any longer, 'who goes first?'

Romany decided that she did. This was about her, after all. She didn't want to appear weak and she definitely didn't want to cry, so she adopted a defensive tone and chose her words accordingly.

'Why did you abandon Mum?' she asked, using everything she had to look him straight in the eyes as she spoke.

Daniel looked hurt, and then breathed out heavily before replying. 'Harsh but fair, I suppose,' he said. 'Well, it wasn't what you'd call a conventional relationship in the first place. I was living down in Newbury and Angie came back to York after the protests because that's where her friends were. I'd come up every few months, whenever I could get a bit of cash together. It was great. It worked for us. Things never had a chance to get stale or boring.'

Romany imagined he was talking about their sex life, which she absolutely didn't want to think about.

'And then?' she asked.

'Well, then she got pregnant. It was a shock, Romany. I won't lie. Not that I'm blaming her in any way, but she stopped taking her pill without telling me. I wasn't ready for that. I mean, we weren't young – I was thirty-one, I think. Ange was a few years older. I think she thought it was now or never for her. But we'd never talked about the future or discussed having kids. So, I just wasn't expecting it. I mean, you,' he clarified awkwardly.

He picked up his coffee cup, took a sip, placed it back down. Romany watched him carefully, looking for anything that might be a clue as to how he really felt, but saw nothing.

'Angie'd had time to get her head round having a baby, but I got presented with it as a done deal. She was pregnant. She was having the baby. She made it obvious that there wasn't much room for what I thought and – and I'm not that proud of this – I was happy with that. I wasn't ready to be a father. The commitment scared the shit out of me. So, when your mum gave me the green light to take a back seat, I took her at her word and stayed away.'

He was being honest, at least. Romany could tell that. She could imagine her mum behaving like he'd said. When she made a decision there wasn't much that could be done to change her mind. And she had been fiercely independent, never looking for help from anyone. Ever. If Daniel was saying that her mum had pushed him away, then that could be what actually happened. Still, her mum hadn't been cold or unfeeling. He could have challenged her, if he'd wanted to.

'Did you see me at all?' she asked. This felt like an important question, but she wasn't at all sure she wanted to know the answer. If he had made no effort, then what did that say about him?

'Once,' he said. 'When you were tiny. I turned up at the flat unannounced. I should have warned her, but I didn't. She was good about it. She didn't kick me out or anything. She let me hold you. You were so perfect. So tiny. I barely dared hold you in case I squashed you or something. And she was so amazing with you. I couldn't believe that she just seemed to know exactly what you needed. She was a natural mum.'

'Well, she didn't really have much choice, did she? She was all I had in the world. She had to learn fast,' replied Romany angrily.

'Of course,' said Daniel, raising a placatory hand. 'I'm just saying that it looked like there was a bond between you from the very start. It was obvious that she adored you.'

'And you didn't.'

He dropped his shoulders and let out a sigh. 'Come on, Romany,' he said. 'Cut me some slack here, would you? It wasn't my finest hour, okay. I didn't try hard enough, and I should have done better. All I'm saying is that I had no concerns about you. I could see how much you were loved and cared for. I didn't just turn my back. You were safe. Angie didn't want me, not really. And so I went back to Newbury and got on with my life.'

He was trying, Romany could see that. He knew that he had made some bad choices and he was trying to paint himself in the best light possible, but he wasn't being defensive in any way.

'So how come you ended up in York?' she asked.

'We lost touch, Ange and me. The phone number I had for her was disconnected and I think you moved house. But I thought about you both, wondered how you were getting on.'

He met her gaze, and she could see in his face that he needed her to believe this.

'Then a job came up in York. I wasn't long out of catering college and there was nothing keeping me in Newbury, so I applied and then I moved up here.'

'But you didn't look us up?'

He shook his head. 'I didn't want to get in the way or spoil anything that Angie had going on with anyone else. But I looked out for you both when I was out, just in case I saw her or someone that might be you. I think I spotted you both on Parliament Street once, and I was going to say hello, but you looked so happy together, like a little unit. I lost my nerve.'

'And did you know about Hope and me?'

He nodded. 'That wasn't hard to work out. Angie and Romany is hardly a common combination of names. When Hope told me what Angie had asked her to do it was fairly obvious why.'

'And Hope?'

'She knows too. I told her. How could I not? We've just been waiting for the right moment to tell you.'

'But how did Mum know that you were in York?' Romany asked. She was trying to link all the pieces together, but this bit was missing.

'We think she saw me at Hope's thirtieth party, but we don't know for sure. That was the only thing we could think of that would connect all the dots.'

Romany sat and thought for a while as the café hummed around her. Her head was spinning with it all, but she could see that it did fit together.

'Tiger recognised you, at Christmas,' she said.

'Yeah, I thought he might have done. I've been waiting for it to come to a head since then. But I wanted you to be in charge, Romany. It had to come from you. It was only when it looked like Tiger wasn't going to say anything that I gave you a little nudge.'

Romany thought back to the journey home from the fashion shoot. It had been so subtle, his hint. She might easily have missed it.

'And there you have it,' he said. 'The whole sorry tale. I imagine you'll need some time now, to think it through, decide what you want to do. There's no pressure from me, Romany. I can be as involved in your life as you like. Or not at all, if that's what you choose.'

Romany scraped at the remains of the froth in the bottom of her glass with her spoon. She had no idea what she wanted to do, what her future might look like, whether he would be a part of it or not. But she liked him. He had been straight with her, she thought. Told her the truth. And that must count for something.

'Okay,' she said.

56

Romany hadn't told Tiger that she was going to meet Daniel. She hadn't wanted him to worry and she wasn't sure she needed the inevitable questioning that would follow. But as she let herself back into the flat, she wished that she had done. She needed someone to talk it all through with, but she couldn't be bothered with going back to the start, with what she had thought up until today. She just wanted to dive straight in with what had just happened without any preamble or explanation. But Tiger wasn't great with anything emotional. He would just crack some corny joke or other.

Maybe Maggie would be a better choice of listener. Romany had always found her easy to talk to in the past and she generally said something sensible, even if it wasn't what Romany wanted to hear. But Maggie was too close to her mum. She would judge Daniel for leaving them at the start and then staying away for all that time. And her anger at him for that action would skew her view. No, Maggie wasn't the right person. And anyway, she thought, her mum had left Maggie in charge of all things legal. This wasn't in her brief.

No, her mum had given Hope responsibility for relationships, a decision that had made no sense at the time but now seemed obvious. This was Hope's moment. But could she talk to Hope about Daniel? She didn't want to cause any problems between them. It wouldn't be fair. Then again, Daniel had said that Hope knew the whole story, and it wasn't as if he had ever been going out with Hope and her mum at the same time.

Romany picked up her phone and messaged her. The reply came almost instantly.

Yes. Meet for a walk on the walls? 6.30 Monk Bar?

Romany texted straight back agreeing to the arrangement.

It was lunchtime, so she had hours to kill until then. Tiger was in the bathroom repotting bedding plants for a window box. The flat had no outside space but he had fashioned a way of securing the boxes to the windowsills and was now using the bath to keep the compost under control whilst he planted red geraniums between some tiny blue flowers that Romany didn't know the name of. He knelt on the floor, bent over the bath as he worked.

'They look pretty,' she said as she stood in the doorway and watched him.

'Thanks,' he said without turning round. 'When I was in Aix-en-Provence picking lavender one year, I loved how all the houses had window boxes with geraniums in them. I know it's not quite the same here, but I thought they might look nice.'

'They're lovely,' she said. 'A treat for the neighbours though. We won't see much of them from in here.'

'No,' Tiger agreed. 'Maybe one day we could think about moving to somewhere with a little garden. I could grow some herbs, maybe a bit of salad.'

He didn't look at her as he spoke. This was the first time either of them had mentioned what might happen after she finished school. The whole focus of her mum's letter had been to keep her safe whilst she completed her A levels. She had done that now, and before too long she would be nineteen and hopefully going to Durham to study. What might happen after that hadn't been on her radar, but she had always known that Tiger would leave. It never occurred to her that he might be thinking about new places for them to live in together.

'Won't you want to get back on with your travelling?' she asked. 'I thought you had a plan. Guatemala, wasn't it?'

'I missed that one,' he said.

'But there'll be others, though. Surely,' Romany said.

Tiger shrugged. 'Travelling isn't the be all and end all,' he said. 'Sometimes it's nice to stay put for a bit. Put down some roots.'

He still wasn't looking at her, as if he didn't want to see her reaction. She wasn't at all sure how to respond. She had just assumed that he would leave her. Wasn't that what Laura going to Newcastle was all about, a safety net for her so that she wouldn't be entirely alone? Tiger would pick up his travels where he had left off and she would live in the flat on her own, with Maggie and Leon, and possibly now Daniel and Hope keeping an eye on her, ready to step in and help in case of disaster.

'What are you saying, Tiger?' she asked him.

'Nothing, really,' he said, full of bluff. 'Nothing.'

But he was. Romany could see it written all over his body language.

'Stop doing that a minute,' she said. 'Talk to me.'

Slowly he got to his feet, stretching and rubbing at the small of his back. He turned to face her. He looked anxious, nervous even. Romany didn't recognise it and wasn't sure she liked it. This wasn't who Tiger was. He was the joker in her pack, light-hearted and never taking anything too seriously, least of all himself. He stuffed his dirty hands into his jeans pockets and looked at his feet.

'Are you saying that you'd rather stay here than go back on the road?' she asked him.

'Well,' he began. 'It's kind of taken me by surprise, how much I've loved being here. It's cool, making a home. I started trying to make stuff nice for you, but then I really got into it.'

'You're really good at it,' said Romany. 'I mean, just look at this place. It's never looked so good. Mum would be amazed!'

Tiger gave a little laugh, more a huff than anything. 'Yeah, she wasn't that big on that kind of stuff, your mum. And I got to thinking that maybe I've had enough of not being based anywhere. Don't get me wrong. I still want to be out there. There's so much to see. But perhaps I'm ready to do it in smaller bites, more like a holiday than a way of life. God, listen to me. I sound so bloody middle-aged.'

He rolled his eyes, laughing at himself, but Romany thought she saw something else. He really wanted her to understand, to say that he could stay. This new plan was entirely dependent on her say-so.

She didn't hesitate. 'That would be fantastic!' she said. 'I'd love it!'

She opened her arms and threw them around his shoulders. She could feel him relax as she hugged him, as if he had been building up to this moment for a while and was deeply relieved that it was finally out in the open.

When they separated, he said, 'I don't mean that we have to move. That was just an idea. Obviously, this was your mum's place and it's full of all her memories.'

Romany nodded. He was right. It was. But the memories were in her head; in Tiger's, too. She didn't need a place to attach them to. In some ways, a fresh start as she went off to university might be perfect timing. It wasn't like leaving her mum behind, but more taking her with her into her new life.

'I reckon a place with a garden might be nice,' she said. 'As long as we're not too far out of town. I still want to be able to walk home from a night out.'

Tiger was grinning broadly. 'Well, maybe we can start looking over the summer,' he said. 'Get this place valued and see what we could afford. And I was thinking I could get a job. Maybe be a tour guide around the city. I reckon I'd be good at that.'

Romany nodded enthusiastically. 'You would,' she said. 'You'd be really good.'

She tossed his suggestion around in her head for a moment. A part of her was worried that things were changing too fast, that she needed to give herself time to process it all. But then she remembered that this was Tiger. He might have worked out how to use a vacuum cleaner, but he was no Maggie. They wouldn't be going anywhere fast.

'You know, you should have said what you were thinking before,' she said.

Tiger shrugged. 'I didn't really know that I was thinking it myself until recently,' he said. 'It was something Maggie said. I'm starting to wonder whether your mum didn't have all this planned out in advance.'

Romany thought about her conversation with Daniel earlier. She nodded. 'I'm beginning to think you might be right,' she said. 'Listen, Tiger, can I ask you something? Something personal?'

Tiger looked slightly uncomfortable, but he nodded.

'Tiger's a nickname, right?'

Another nod.

'So, what are you actually called?'

He looked at her, then up at the ceiling, then down at his feet and then finally back at her.

'You have to promise me that you will never call me it,' he said.

'Okay,' agreed Romany.

'And you absolutely, under pain of death, must not tell Maggie.'

Romany nodded.

He dropped his head and in a very quiet voice whispered, 'Derek.'

Romany bit her lip, but not before a snigger escaped.

57

Hope stood at the bottom of Monk Bar waiting for Romany. The shops were closing up, the streets full of people picking up last-minute things and tourists all determined to make the most of every moment of their day in historic York. The steps up to the ancient city wall were busy with a stream of visitors coming back down and the evening sun shone on the sandy-coloured stone of the medieval turret, making it glow.

Hope wasn't sure what Romany wanted to talk about, but she could guess, and she was prepared. She'd had time to get her head around it all. She had been confused that first day in the solicitor's. She'd had no idea why she had been invited, and knew none of the others apart from briefly meeting Maggie at her party. So, when the letter had been read out and she learned what Angie had asked of her, it made no sense.

She had gone home and told Daniel about the strangeness of Angie's request and he had gone very pale. She supposed later that he could have kept his mouth shut, waited to see how the situation would pan out, but he'd chosen not to. He had made her sit down next to him and then he'd told her everything, pausing only to make sure that she was all right as all the details emerged. And she had listened, horrified at first when she thought he might have been seeing both her and Angie at the same time, and then slightly more calmly when it seemed that he hadn't.

He had abandoned his child, though. That had taken some time to get her head around. If someone had asked her whether Daniel would be the kind of man to do that, she would have said emphatically no. And yet he had. He had run from his responsibilities.

Hope had remembered conversations that she and Angie had had in coffee breaks during their course, when Angie had confessed how hard she sometimes found it trying to be both parents to her daughter. She had never moaned about it, that wasn't her style, but she was running her business and looking after Romany on her own, and Hope had got the impression that it could be a struggle to hold it all together.

Daniel had been there all the time, and yet not there. Angie could have made him shoulder his responsibilities but she had chosen to press on alone. And from what Hope had seen, she had done an amazing job of it.

Hope wondered what Romany made of it all. When she had texted Daniel that morning asking how the meeting had gone he had simply replied, *Fine. Speak later*, which had told her nothing. She would just have to wait and see what Romany had to say.

She could see Romany coming down the street towards her, her auburn ponytail bouncing up and down as she walked. She didn't look as if she had the weight of the world on her shoulders, at least. When she got close enough to see her, she raised an arm in greeting.

'Hi,' Romany said, her smile broad, and Hope relaxed a little. Well, it seemed she wasn't angry.

'Shall we go up?' Hope asked, and they climbed the steep stone steps through the bar to the ancient wall above.

After the hustle and bustle of the streets below, it felt calmer and quieter on the wall. Hope looked across the city set out below them, a mixture of ancient and modern architecture with the Minster overseeing it all. It really was a beautiful place.

'So,' she said as they fell into step alongside each other, 'you spoke to Daniel.'

Romany nodded.

'And?'

'I want to be angry with him,' Romany said. 'He basically deserted us, so Mum had to cope on her own. But . . .'

'It's hard when he's so honest about it?' Hope suggested.

'Precisely. He's so up front about what he did wrong. He's not a bit defensive. He didn't even try to make any excuses, or anything.'

'No,' Hope agreed. 'The way he told me, he didn't want a baby and Angie understood that. Having you was her agenda, not his. She seemed to understand that that might mean she'd lose him. It was a choice she made, I assume. And I think Daniel would have been in touch eventually, if he'd known where to find you.'

Romany looked sceptical and Hope saw a flash of anger flare in her eyes, but she stayed calm.

'Well, he could have found us if he'd wanted. It's not hard to find people these days. He didn't want to, but that's okay. I think I understand where he was coming from.'

'He came to York, though,' said Hope. 'That was about you, I think.'

Romany nodded. 'He seems like a nice bloke to me,' she said. 'Is he?'

Hope wasn't sure what she expected her to say. They had been together for nearly ten years. It must be obvious that she thought that.

'Yes, he's a good man,' she said. 'He has a good heart.'

Romany shot a glance at her out of the corner of her eye. 'He's quite a lot older than you, isn't he?' she asked shyly.

'Fifteen years,' Hope said.

'Are you going to have any kids?' Romany asked with a grin. 'They'd be my half-brothers or sisters.' She sounded like the idea was growing on her, but Hope shook her head emphatically.

'Nope. Kids are not on the agenda.'

Romany shrugged. 'Oh well,' she said. 'No new family for me. Easy come, easy go, eh!'

'Sorry,' said Hope, but Romany was smiling. She didn't look bothered that there would be no siblings. 'So,' Hope continued. 'What are you thinking? About Daniel, I mean.'

'About whether I want him in my life?' Romany asked.

Hope nodded. She wasn't sure what she wanted the answer to be. She had liked their life the way it was, without a child in it, although Romany was hardly a child. Having her there added a layer of complexity to the relationship that hadn't been present before. That said, there had been a change in Daniel since September, when Angie's letter had first been read at the solicitor's. Even though it had taken a further nine months to finally get to speak to his daughter, just knowing that it would happen at some point in the future seemed to have given him an extra sense of purpose. If Romany took him into her life, then that would be another positive. Hope knew that Daniel felt bad about what he had done, even though Angie had accepted that he wouldn't be in their lives. Maybe, if Romany welcomed him back, that guilt would lift. He had missed the first eighteen years of her life but that didn't mean that he had to miss the rest.

Romany cocked her head to one side as she thought about the question.

'I think we should play it by ear,' she said.

58

The champagne cork popped, and Maggie laughed as the pale liquid squirted out of the bottle and all over Tiger's shirt.

'I told you not to shake it,' she said, but Tiger just laughed at her.

'You, Maggie Summers, are the most sensible person I ever met,' he said. 'Who opens champagne without shaking it first?'

'Well, somebody has to be sensible around here,' she said, but there was a lightness in her tone.

Tiger poured the champagne into six flutes and they each took one and raised them high. They all looked around at one another, no one quite sure who should make the toast, none of them wanting to claim seniority over the others.

It was Leon who took the lead. He never stopped surprising her these days.

'Congratulations, Romany,' he began, 'for smashing your A levels out of the park. Two A-stars and an A. It's bloody fantastic and Durham are very lucky to have someone as special as you coming to study.'

'Hear, hear,' they all chorused loudly.

'Yes,' added Maggie. 'To Romany.'

They all raised their glasses and drank to Romany, although she could barely stand still and was jumping from one foot to the other like a little girl, the champagne threatening to slop out of her glass and on to the neatly clipped grass.

Maggie had been unsure when Hope suggested that they have the celebratory drinks at her house. She had felt cheated and as if Hope, so newly in Romany's life, had overstepped the mark by offering, but now that she was here, Maggie could see that it was the perfect spot. With the garden elegantly manicured and the bifold doors open on to the huge white kitchen, it looked like a show house or something from a glossy magazine: the perfect place to make Romany feel special.

And Romany looked as though she felt special. And loved. She hadn't stopped smiling for a second and she kept looking around at them each in turn as if she couldn't quite believe that they were all there celebrating together.

'Thanks everyone,' she said now. 'But I couldn't have done it without you lot on my team.'

Smiles slipped a little then. It was hard not to think of Angie in that moment.

'Your mum would have been so very proud of you,' Maggie managed to say before her throat began to constrict. 'She loved you so much and all she ever wanted was for you to be happy.'

Romany started to cry, fat tears rolling down her pretty face.

'I've done her proud, haven't I?' she asked, looking round at them for confirmation.

'God, yes,' said Tiger. He reached over and swept Romany into his arms. She looked so small as she leant into him, her head resting on his chest. 'She'd be so proud of you, my darling girl. You have no idea.'

Romany peeled herself away from Tiger and wiped her tears with the flat of her hand.

'My turn for a speech,' she said. 'I want to say thank you. To you all. I admit that when we first read that letter, I thought it was the stupidest idea ever. I was so angry with Mum for dying and then for saddling me with you lot, especially you, Tiger.' She pulled a sheepish face, and he rolled his eyes. 'But now I can see that Mum knew exactly what she was doing. You've all been so great, helping me through this year. And it's lovely to have you in my life, Daniel.' She looked up at him shyly and he nodded. 'That wouldn't have happened if it hadn't been for Mum and her plan.'

She tipped her head to the sky and spoke to the heavens. 'Thanks, Mum,' she said, toasting the fluffy clouds.

Maggie wasn't sure she could keep her emotions in check for much longer. She blinked hard to stop the tears.

'And I know I'm not supposed to need my guardians any more,' Romany continued, 'but please don't abandon me just yet. I don't know anything about anything, not really. And I'll definitely need you all in the holidays, so please can you stick around for a bit longer?'

'Just you try shaking us off,' replied Tiger, smiling so fondly at her that Maggie wanted to rush over and hug him.

They drained their glasses and Daniel opened another bottle. Romany told them all about the college at Durham and what she knew about her halls of residence, and Maggie listened and watched as the excitement came off her in waves. She's just like we were, Maggie thought. So young and enthusiastic and ready to take on the world. If Angie had been here, then it would all have been so perfect. But then, she thought, if Angie had been here it was unlikely that they would all be standing here celebrating together.

Another wave of tears was about to crash over her and so, not wanting to dampen the mood, Maggie wandered away from the group to look at the garden. It was planted exclusively in shades of green and white, which complemented the slate grey of the hard landscaping, but a flash of red and iridescent blue caught her eye. It was a peacock butterfly fluttering from flower to flower, a tiny buzz of vibrant colour against the pale background. Maggie had never believed in anything even vaguely supernatural, but maybe she could make an exception, just this once.

ACKNOWLEDGMENTS

The trigger for this book was a conversation that I overheard. People really should be careful when they chat – you never know who might be listening! However, I hope that the book that emerged from that initial spark of interest would no longer be recognisable by the original storyteller.

When I began writing in January 2020 the world was still looking relatively normal. By the time the manuscript went to my editor, we had been locked in our homes due to the coronavirus pandemic for several months and life had become very different. Whilst I managed to visit York in the early part of the year, all other research had to be done from my desk using the power of the internet and my imagination, so please forgive any geographical errors that I might have made.

As ever, there are people to thank. My editor at Amazon Publishing, Victoria Pepe, is always wonderfully supportive of me and my ideas and this book has been no exception. Thank you, Victoria for always being in my corner. Thanks also to Sammia Hamer and Hannah Bond who worked with me on this one too. It was a pleasure. In addition, I owe a big thank you to Celine Kelly who never fails to improve my books through her skilful and good-humoured guidance. The wonderful team at Amazon Publishing is huge and I'm always reluctant to list names in case I miss anyone out by accident. Suffice to say they are all never less than positive and cheerful and it is a joy to work with them all.

Finally, to my family. The family unit, in all its many guises, is at the root of my books and I am blessed that my own is so very supportive of everything I try to do. Thank you to you all.

ABOUT THE AUTHOR

Bestselling author Imogen Clark writes contemporary book club fiction.

Her first three novels have all reached the number one spot in the UK Kindle store and her books have also been at the top of the charts in Australia and Germany. *Where the Story Starts* was shortlisted for Contemporary Romantic Novel of the Year, 2020, at the RNA Awards.

Imogen initially qualified as a lawyer, but after leaving her legal career behind to care for her four children, she returned to her first love – books. She went back to university to study English Literature whilst the children were at school, and then tried her hand at writing novels herself.

Her great love is travel and she is always planning her next adventure. She lives in Yorkshire with her husband and children.

If you'd like to get in touch then please visit her website at www.imogenclark.com, where you can sign up to her monthly newsletter. Imogen can also be found on Facebook, Twitter and Instagram.